A Novel

by

TS Beasley

Based on many true events of the West Family

A Work of Historical Fiction & Creative Non-fiction

The Winding Road

Dedicated to my grandparents
Oscar & Lillie Mae Woodcock West
who gave to me the best mother in the whole world!

Dedicated to my parents
who have always proven
their love for me...

Thanks to Robin T. Willis for the book cover design.
Robin's Web Pages:
www.facebook.com/pages/robinsartorg/236752599707
&
www.robinsart.org

Words can't express how much the West family
has meant to me in my life.
I was privileged to have known my
grandparents Oscar and Lillie Mae West.
They left a spirit of family and home in me that will last forever.

I love you Grandpa and Grandma!

I love you Mom and Dad!

Thanks Mama for all of your help in proofreading. I would not have been able to
complete this work without you...

Looking now into the past with an understanding eye,
Seeing what unfolds, what may live, what may die;
Tell me now…tell me all, what I need to understand,
Answer my numerous questions of the West home land!

Looking for an answer, an explanation for it all,
Crying out from the present…the distant past to recall!
Hoping to resolve the part that is not yet complete,
A portion of my inner person and my own two feet…

Be ye patient and be kind, read not too far ahead,
Live every moment of the lives of loved ones dead.
Go back in distant time and in time you will see,
The paths they have chosen…each manifest destiny!

Feel their pain and sorrow …all the tears they have shed,
Judge not their deeds lest ye be judged in their stead!
Bring them back to life and back to life they will be,
In the stories that are told…in the memories that we see.

———TS *Beasley*

Canst you see him there, in deep darkened mist,
The spirit of kinfolk gone by!
His eyes gazing out and calling to thee,
Canst you hear his solemn cry?

"Stop passerby! Sit by tis family old tree,
Whilst I talk of kinfolk past!"
Speaking to all who pass him there,
"Time turns and passeth fast!"

He knoweth much, and lendest what he must,
O be not afraid to ask!
Knowledge doth he part of long years ago,
Of parting stories his task!

Aged spirit tis he, by tis family ole tree,
Restin near...by Bay Gall creek,
I'll sit down and listen, and give ear to hear
What stories he doth speak!

His beard hangeth low, his hair tis all white,
How old tis he I thought?
And then with a smile he gazed toward the sky,
And as I learned he taught!

Many stories told he and shared with me there,
Of my kinfolk never known,
Of how they all lived and died in their time,
In shortest time I had grown!

I left him there tis spirit of kinfolk past,
Resting aged near Bay Gall creek,
Who will stop and listen, who will stop to hear
Of the past he doth so agedly speak?

—————*TS Beasley*

Near the ole log cabin not far from Bay Gall creek,
T'was then a long winding road,
Like a river turning strong against the tall twisted banks,
Directed by its weighted load!
Going here this earthen way…turning there yet once again,
Through the fields of cotton seed,
Downward towards the hidden West log cabin,
Where many untold stories didst breed!

————*TS Beasley*

Foreword

The author of this novel, Tony Beasley, asked me to read a manuscript of this book and to give him my "honest" opinion of it. *The Winding Road* is, in a word, excellent. In fact, Beverly, my wife – a serious reader who knows a good book when she reads it – says it "deserves a high ranking on any list of books, period!" I concur and say with conviction that this is a very good novel about real people of an area about which Beasley has taught me a great deal. Local history aside, this novel is simply good reading and provides fodder for much thought.

The author is a newcomer to the genre of historical fiction, but to read the stories he includes in a flowing and, at times, a gripping narrative is refreshing and rewarding. Here is a master storyteller who attunes his sensitive ear to the rhythm of the many conversations he has heard during his lifetime of forty-plus years. The purpose of Beasley's *The Winding Road* is to communicate the story of how the West family name came to be a part of the Bay Gall community in northeast Bulloch County. It is obvious that he knows genealogy and history, though his strongest suit is his portrayal of so-called "ordinary country folk." This is his territory – the very essence of Tony S. Beasley.

A successful historical novel is hard to pull off, because the characters must, first of all, be believable. In this case, the author must sustain his characters through his knowledge of how they talk, behave, and fit into their time slots, from the Civil War era through the Roaring Twenties and to the post-World War II era. The time period of *The Winding Road* consumes roughly eighty-five years of the nineteenth and twentieth centuries. Some readers will be especially interested in parts of the story that the author has researched and documented well from the *Bulloch Herald's* contemporaneous summaries of the Superior Court trials of two locally well-known brothers named Mark and Silas West. Readers can determine whether these incarcerated Wests are really the black sheep of the family.

The eldest son of John West, named Phillip Admiral West, was in his late teens and lived in fearful anticipation of his first trip away from his home in Georgetown, South Carolina. He would ride with the elder West's companion of many Civil War battles, the Confederate soldier from Statesboro, Georgia, named Thomas Hendrix. Once he begins the long trip by wagon to Georgia, Philip's fears subside, as he observes

Hendrix negotiate and, sometimes, fight his way through a series of adventures and near calamities. The trip through South Carolina, like Ulysses' postwar mythological travels, requires strength and courage as they deal with renegade Yankees and, later, with white Southerners, who act as though the war is not over.

These stories of danger, along with Phillip's growing respect for Thomas, are exciting and rewarding reading. Young Phillip's discussions with Thomas, likewise, are probing reflections about issues that many Southerners have yet to resolve, such as the Civil war and its causes. A conclusion both of them appear to reach is that the war was senseless and that Harriett Tubman had a noble idea when she encouraged slaves to "Follow the Drinking Gourd" and ride to freedom on the Underground Railroad. (Beasley treats us to the lyrics of this clever song.) Another topic they explore is whether Southerners had fought to defend the rights of rich landowners and planters to own slaves. Like most Johnny Rebs, Hendrix seems to have understood that he fought out of patriotism, out of love for his homeland that was under attack.

The technique of telling the story of his ancestor's past is this author's particular invention. Beasley obviously spent a great deal of his youth listening to stories and appropriating them in his imagination. Young Philip Admiral West and Thomas Hendrix became embedded in the interior life of the author of this novel. Perhaps he kept close to his heart these stories he heard from his elders. The author relives the memories of battles of Rebels versus Yankees through the interior monologues of Hendrix, especially as they encounter dangers on the way home to Bulloch County. Beasley's monologues are clearer than William Faulkner's "stream of consciousness" technique that has stumped many readers of his longer fiction, such as *The Sound and the Fury*. Young Philip sees firsthand what his father admired in Hendrix: He was a serene individual who was alert to his surroundings, including the little things in life that give pleasure and meaning. Yet Hendrix also was a realist who knew that danger sometimes lurked behind the facades of people.

On a bright afternoon in June, Beverly and I spent several hours visiting with Tony Beasley, his mother and his married sister who is his nearest neighbor. Barbara West Beasley, Tony's mother, told us that her son had designed this modern, new home that is situated at the end of a lane that is not far from the home place that Phillip and Annie Hendrix West built. This was where he had fallen in love with Thomas's pretty and talented daughter. About 140 years ago, this newly wed couple selected fine logs for a neat homestead that in 2016 partially stands in the Bay Gall region of northeastern Bulloch County. In the Beasley den we saw enlarged photographs that bear testimony to his family's past. There is a great photograph of Annie Hendrix West, and several images of subsequent generations of Wests. Among these is a framed photograph of Oscar West and his family that includes a cute little girl named Barbara West, the mother of the author.

The display is an affirmation of Beasley's commitment to the novel's storyline and more. His work is an imaginative reconstruction of what it was like to be alive between the 1860s and the 1940s. The story that grows out of the collection of images reveals the author's commitment to the truth about human beings, their frailties, and even their ultimate triumphs over obstacles that are all-too-human and real today.

We asked if it would be possible to review the graves of characters in the novel. "Sure," said the author, "I was hoping y'all would have time to swing by the grave yard at Oak Grove Church. It's just a few miles from here." We sealed the visit by following the car he drove northwest on the Old River Road for a few miles, and then we took another road that eventually led to the Oak Grove Missionary Baptist Church with a sign that includes these words: "Founded in 1856." This means that the church was among the early churches in Bulloch County. It is a neat and large rural church that has a well-maintained cemetery on a sandy ridge.

On this gentle hillside are the eternal resting places of so many whose names we now recognize from their roles in this most interesting novel. The experience late in this June afternoon was both sentimental and surreal for Beverly and me, especially, as we remembered the fascinating and rewarding journey of Phillip Admiral West, a young man who placed his future in the able hands of Thomas Hendrix. As I look back on this memorable afternoon at the Beasley home in the Bay Gall and at Oak Grove, I thank Tony S. Beasley whose able hands, keen mind, and kind heart gave us this unforgettable novel called *The Winding Road.*

Delma E. Presley
Statesboro, Georgia
October 15, 2016

Preface

The Winding Road is not only a work of fiction, but is intertwined with non-fictional creativity as well, "a literary genre which, broadly speaking, depicts real historical figures and actual events woven together with fictitious conversations and using the storytelling techniques of fiction." The time frame of the novel spans one hundred years, from 1865 to 1965, and moves quickly through several generations evolving around the West family that moved from Georgetown, South Carolina to Statesboro, Georgia. This book is not a typical novel or work of long prose flowing around a single or connected underlying plot. But rather, it is a book made up of many short-lived stories and short-lived plots spanning multiple generations. The goal and purpose of writing this multi-generational, one hundred year storyline, was to capture the lives and history of a family that had an influence on their surroundings and to preserve their place of significance.

The initial setting of *The Winding Road* is in Georgetown, South Carolina at the end of the Civil War. The characters' names used are the real names of the West family living near Black River in South Carolina and the Hendrix family living near the Ogeechee River in Georgia around the latter part of the 19th century; however, their actual ages are altered to fit the created storyline.

After John West returns home from Virginia, following the Civil War, the multi-generational chain of events begin to unfold with John's interest in his son's journey to Georgia with Thomas Hendrix. The origins of the relations between the Hendrix and West families as it relates to the opening of this book are purely conjectural. However, based on the service of John West and Thomas Hendrix in the Civil War in the same geographical area, along the coastline between Charleston and Georgetown, SC, it is highly probable the related conjectures of their original friendship are accurate.

Some of the events throughout the book are fictional, but some are factual. *The Winding Road* is a mixture, with created fictional events unfolding in light of actual non-fictional occurrences.

The preservation of family history is the driving mechanism for this non-traditional novel form in *The Winding Road*. I hope each reader finds a common strand of human emotions as they relate to struggle, tragedy, love, family and home…

——*TS Beasley*

Chapter One

The sky was blue, filled with white clouds floating like wind blown cotton from the fields below, and the coastal landscape stretched peacefully across the Carolina horizon with the sight of Spanish moss draped along the numerous live oaks, a setting of southern comfort for a soldier returning home from horrific scenes of painful conflict. John had just made it back to South Carolina, having suffered sickness and physical wounds while fighting for the old South in battles against the Union in the tragic struggle known as *The War Between the States.* Much had changed since he'd last been home, but in a calm and gentle way, by the subtle changes of time which often remind man of nature's unyielding work. Before he enlisted, his wife and children were all together living peacefully in Prince George Parish, Georgetown, South Carolina. His great-grandfather, Joseph West, had moved along Lynches Creek in colonial times from New Bern, North Carolina when he was barely old enough to ride a horse, having fought with the old *Swamp Fox,* Francis Marion, during the Revolutionary War. The names of John's children were William Capers, Phillip Admiral, John Willie, Charlotte, Sarah, and Louisa. His wife managed to take care of the family and the farm while he was away fighting in the war, a very difficult time period for a lot of Yankee and Confederate housewives to endure - the conflict taking most men away from their homes – women suffering hardships in the crop fields, putting their hands to the plow while trying to survive through the bitter winters and harsh elements without their husbands or sons. Margaret was busy washing clothes in the front yard with a washboard when she saw John walking up the long dirt road between the cotton fields to the old log cabin near Black River. It had been weeks since she'd last heard from him and the only letter she received concerning John spoke of his ill health at Jackson Hospital in Virginia, a place where many Confederate soldiers died from their mortal wounds. She didn't know if he would ever make it back home alive.

"John," she spoke softly to herself when she realized it was him.

She threw the shirt she'd been scrubbing and cleaning to the ground and made her way slowly toward her husband who was still dressed in his gray uniform and carrying a musket on his shoulder, his beard longer than usual and his face tired from the long journey. When John saw Margaret walking down the long road to meet him, he threw his musket to the ground, and not thinking of his wounded leg, ran to meet his darling wife he'd longed to see and hold once more, an image he'd pictured several times in his mind while traveling the distant miles alone. They embraced each other in joy as John picked Margaret up and turned her around in the air to get a good look at her, taking in all her beauty and charm, her eyes filled with elation over his return.

Sarah, the oldest daughter, was teaching the younger children grammar when she looked out the cabin window and saw her father and mother walking together through the front gate. She picked up little John in her arms and took the hand of Charlotte as she quickly ran out the cabin door to see her father who seemed to have aged into an old man in the few years he'd been gone. Louisa followed close behind.

"Daddy, you're home! You're home!" the kids all shouted, greeting their father.

"Hey, children, give your old man a great big hug."

John picked little John Willie up in his arms.

"Where's Phillip and Capers?"

"I think Phillip is plowing in the field with Yankee down in the bottomland, and Capers is at the river catching some fish for supper," Sarah told her father.

Yankee was an old mule that once belonged to a Union soldier, taken captive by Confederate Cavalry passing through, and given to John and his family in exchange for food and shelter. Phillip, a tall lanky figure, was almost eighteen now and had been the man of the house since their father enlisted in the war, working long hours in the dry dusty fields during the planting seasons. As John made his way down the hill behind the cabin, he saw Phillip wrestling with Yankee, trying to get the mule to turn the right way to plow a new field row. He was wearing overalls and had a Confederate hat on that his father had given him before enlisting in the war, a covering now of great sentimental value. Too busy fussing at the mule, Phillip didn't notice his father walking down the hill to meet him, the sweat pouring down his face as he threw the reins to the ground in frustration. By the time John made his way to the place where he was, he'd stopped with Yankee and sat down to rest in a nice shade from an old oak tree near the creek. Looking down at the water, he felt a hand rest on his shoulder - the image of his father's face reflecting off the water's surface in front of him.

"Dad, you're home!"

"Sure am, Son, those Yankees couldn't seem to put me in the ground, although they tried their best. What kept me alive was knowing you were all back here waiting for me, and remembering I'd promised, that no matter what, I would find my way home."

While Phillip and John were talking, Capers came walking up the river road through the woods with a string of fish hanging from his shoulders, barefoot, with his pants legs rolled up to his knees and a fishing pole in his hand, making his way from the wooded path into the open bottom field close to where John and Phillip were sitting.

"Capers!" his father shouted, "looks like you've caught enough fish to have a nice supper for us all tonight."

When Capers realized it was his father, he dropped his fishing pole and ran to his dad, his bare feet cutting hard into the earth, making his way across the field to the old oak tree.

"This fish is for you, Daddy, the biggest trout I've caught all year," said Capers, holding the fish up in front of him.

John and his two sons talked a while near the creek, catching up on all of the things that had happened at home since he'd been gone. He remembered all the fathers he had fought with, those who were mortally wounded on the battlefields, their last dying words, their last cries to see their loved ones one more time before the shades of death covered their eyes. It always ended with a sudden silence, a last whisper toward home, all the while grasping a family photo in their hand. It happened daily, too often, and it was hard to imagine a day in the future where he would find himself sitting with his sons. The sun was beginning to set on the humble West farm and all seemed to be normal again; even old Black River seemed to flow more quietly while John and his family sat down to eat supper at the table.

Margaret looked at John and asked him to say the blessing over the meal. He held his wife's hand and humbly prayed:

"O Lord, we thank you for the food we are about to receive, for young Capers and his nice catch of fish. I thank you for my darling wife Margaret, and the loving mother she is, looking after all of the children during the terrible war. And Lord, it sure is good to be home, amen."

"Daddy," asked little John Willie, "did you ever shoot a Yankee?"

"John Willie, you know better than to ask your father a question like that." Margaret didn't like to talk about the war. She was glad the whole ordeal had finally ended.

"No Margaret, it's ok. I'll tell John Willie a little story. Once, I was fighting at the battle of Cold Harbor. I remember it like it was yesterday: the crossroads…the old church…Turkey hill. The Yankees were marching near Richmond, Virginia under General Grant and we were fighting under General Lee. We had a long seven mile line of entrenchments built over swampy terrains, thick branches, and well-thought-out plans which seemed to be favored by God and man. I can still hear the screams of all those dying men, wounded soldiers lying underneath the darkened sky where the smoke from the guns filled the air and the cannon fire thundered death and destruction over the blood-stained battlefield. The shifting of soldiers, the movement of forces, both sides arranging and rearranging infantry through the night, marching until you had no strength left to fight, only to find yourself being commanded to fire, to engage, to fix the bayonet. I remember in particular a young Yankee soldier we'd taken prisoner near Bethesda Church, his clothes all muddy and his boots worn out, holding his side from a minor wound he'd suffered from a Confederate saber. He may have been the same age or younger than Phillip, but his spirit seemed to be somewhat aged from all the battle fatigue he'd suffered. The sun was going down when we took him into our camp, and the sound of enemy shots ceased for a short while until the next morning, giving us a little more time to dig in, to prepare, to pray, to speak our peace to the Creator for whatever we hadn't already pleaded with Him for…begged Him for. He looked like he was thirsty, so I walked up to him and gave him a drink of cool water, his lips dry, his body dehydrated from the summer like heat. I asked him what his name was. He looked at me as if I were someone he knew long ago in some distant past, and as I stared into his eyes, I thought about his father and his mother and wondered if they were home praying for the safe return of their son. I thought about my sons and felt as if I owed this young Yankee something…something that would bring him to his senses and feel welcome among the very ones he was fighting against. I put my hand on his shoulder which seemed unable to hold it up, his body slumping down from the small weight I'd placed on it - a clear sign of human exhaustion. I asked him to sit down by the tent where I was sheltered for the night, next to an open fire warming a pot of stew I'd fixed. He was being guarded by some of our soldiers while he sat down and ate some food, his hands shaking from hunger and fear as he picked his spoon up to eat. After his meal, he was to be taken directly to the place where the Yankee prisoners of war were being kept. When he realized he could trust me, he quietly asked me a question. He said something to me that haunts me to this very day. He asked me, 'Why are we fighting this war?' I thought about it for a moment. For the South, I'd believed it was for states' rights. For the North, it seemed they were trying to preserve the Union and stop slavery. But then I thought…why were we fighting this war? Why did it have to come down to cannons, artillery, rifles, knives, or muskets? Couldn't we have found some other way to resolve our problems between each other? Couldn't we have waited a little longer to understand each others view points? Did so many innocent lives have to be lost? I never did answer his question. That was the only thing he ever said to me, 'Why are we fighting this war?' So, Son, it doesn't matter if I have ever shot a Yankee or not. What matters the most is that we continue to ask ourselves, 'Why was there even a war at all?'"

After all the children retired to sleep, John and Margaret walked out onto the front porch and stood together in each other's arms, holding each other close in the cool night air. The moon was full and the sky was clear. The pretty oak trees with Spanish moss hanging from the branches seemed to be placed there by nature's kind hand, with a slight glow from the bright moonlight which filtered to the earth like a soft rain.

An owl, sitting on a tree limb nearby, looked down at John and Margaret while they spoke quietly to each other.

"John, I never thought I would ever get to see you again. It's so good to be able to hold you once more. Everything seems perfect now."

"The only thing that kept me going, Margaret, was thinking of you and the children. I want to make it up to you somehow for all the things you've had to go through since I've been gone."

Margaret tried not to reveal her worn-down spirit. Her one and only love had now returned, and this made all her past burdens seem so insignificant. She remembered the cold winter nights, and the long, sleepless hours of waking up after having had frightful nightmares of John getting killed in some horrible manner; she'd heard of the awful amputations from injury as well, and this kept her awake more than the dreams. She recalled the lonely walks down to the river in the early afternoon settings, praying and asking God to bring her husband home safe again. Then there was the falling star she'd seen one night over the cabin, and how it made her feel like everything was going to be all right, as if it were a sign from the heavens.

"I want this night to last forever." Margaret kissed John with a feeling of forgotten passion, releasing emotions she'd kept inside for so long.

John looked at Margaret in a moment of silence, then expressed his thoughts to her.

"Margaret, I know I've aged somewhat, but you look as young and beautiful tonight as you did the day we first got married. Do you remember the song you always sang to me when we used to sit on the front porch at night? I would love to hear you sing it again."

Margaret took John by the hand and sang softly to him while looking into his eyes, "Yonder is my gentleman, whose hands are marked with toil, once a day he brings me flowers, and plants them in the soil. I love my country gentleman, no matter what the toil, and cherish all the pretty flowers he planted in the soil…and cherish all the pretty flowers he planted in the soil."

****

A few weeks passed, and one morning, John got up well before daybreak, making sure the fields were tended to and the crops taken care of. He walked out onto the front porch - the door hinges squeaking louder through the morning quietness - and gazed out over the open field still sheltered by a light fog. Once again he felt the comforts of home, a place he thought he'd never get to see again after being wounded from Union cannon fire. He grabbed his wounded leg that often gave him trouble, but was thankful he still could walk, despite the increasing pain. The air seemed more clean and fresh than usual, and even old Yankee looked as if he were glad to see John coming to his stable. He had a lot of work to do before lunchtime and was expecting his good friend, Thomas Hendrix, to stop by on his way back home to Georgia, having received a letter from him a few days prior.

Thomas and John had gotten to know each other well while soldiers in the war. Thomas was assigned to guard the coast between Charleston and Georgetown, South Carolina, not far from where the West family lived, the same area John was assigned to protect – the many miles of oceanfront land in danger of attack from Union ships in the Atlantic. Thomas had a large family back home in Statesboro, Georgia, where they lived on a farm near a run called Bay Gall creek, not far from the Ogeechee River.

While John was plowing in the field with Yankee, he thought about how he and Thomas used to discuss old stories near the open fires, passing the time away while guarding the coastline…

The ocean waves were calm and the stars shone bright in the night sky. There was no sign of the enemy and many tents and campfires could be seen for miles along the coastline and inside of Confederate fortifications.

John asked Thomas, 'What do you think about the South?'
Thomas loved everything about the South and all that it stood for. He was a hard working farmer and loved his family.

'Well, John, I think of the South as a delicate kind woman that needs to be protected and looked after, knowing that there is something in her that gives you the strength to endure any kind of hardship.'

'I agree Thomas. I know the South is not perfect, and there are a lot of things that need to change, but no one should ever force her to change into something that she is not ready for. I can only pray that the God of heaven will protect us all from ruin and preserve the things that we all cherish and hold dear.'

In the distance you could hear a few soldiers singing. There was someone playing a guitar and another playing a harmonica.

"John! John!" Margaret called out to her husband. He'd been lost in thought when the voice of his wife calling his name brought him back from the coastline and from the campfires.

"John, I have a nice lunch fixed for us."

Margaret stood at the edge of the field like an angel with her hair gracefully blowing in the wind. As John looked at her, he couldn't help but think of all the sacrifices she'd made the past few years. He thought she deserved a lot more than what he was able to give her, yet she never seemed to complain or question her lot in life. She'd planned for a romantic picnic near a lovely spot on the bank of Black River, a place where she and John used to go when they first got married.

She spread a pretty handmade blanket down on the ground and placed the food she'd prepared on top of it: some tea, ham sandwiches, and peach cobbler for dessert – things she knew John loved. The scenery along the bank set a warm mood and a relaxing moment they both so desperately needed, sacred time alone for an emotional healing. The river's edge was lined with old cypress trees and its waters turned and flowed peacefully while the wind blew small ripples along its calm surface. They sat down on the blanket close to each other and enjoyed their meal together, time seeming to pause momentarily, allowing them to draw closer together as husband and wife. They talked about everything they could think of, and in a way, it was like another first date.

John held Margaret in his arms while they looked out across Black River.

"Margaret, what a wonderful treat! I've never tasted better cobbler this side the Mississippi."

"You sure you aren't exaggerating a little?"

John smiled at Margaret, then brushed her hair from the front of her eyes that had been placed there by a gentle breeze.

"Remember when we had our first child. We didn't know what raising a baby was about, but somehow our parental instincts took over, more yours than mine."

"You were wonderful. Little Phillip never cried when he was in your arms. What's troubling you, John?" Margaret knew her husband well enough to know when something was bothering him.

John wanted to share with her some concerns he had for their oldest son. "There is something weighing on me, Margaret. My health isn't as good as it once was, and my injuries from the war are starting to take their toll on me. It's made me think more about Phillip lately now that he is becoming of age. Here, there is no social life for him and he seems to be lonely. I was thinking about letting him visit Georgia with Thomas Hendrix. I don't want him to feel responsible about staying here on the farm due to my ill health."

"John, you are going to be fine. Everything is going to work out good for Phillip. I can see a lot of you in him. He is strong willed and full of ambition."

"That's what I'm concerned about. There's nothing here to satisfy that ambition. He has to discover what might be waiting for him beyond Black River."

"I would love for Phillip to fulfill all of his dreams here near us. But if you think it would be a good idea for him to visit Georgia, then I am all for it."

"I knew you would understand, Margaret. I know I don't tell you as often as I should, but I love you more and more each day."

****

Phillip and Capers were busy mending a broken fence near the barn.

"Phillip, do you ever think about finding a wife?"

"What kind of a question is that?"

"I was just asking. You don't have to get bent out of shape over it."

While Capers and Phillip were caught up in the subject of marriage, someone came riding up the road in a two horse wagon, the dust still flying in the air when the stranger came to a stop at the front gate.

"Hello, boys, is your daddy home?" the stranger spoke in a loud voice to Phillip and Capers who were still sitting on the fence. "My name is Thomas Hendrix. Your father John and I fought in the war together. I was on my way back home to Georgia and thought I'd stop by and see John."

Capers told the stranger that his parents were at the river, but he would be glad to go and get his father for him.

"There's no need for that young man, I'll just wait for him while I get my horses some water to drink. They've had a long journey and we still have a long ways to go. Their names are Lee and Stonewall. Say hello, Lee. Say hello, Stonewall."

The horses nodded their heads when Thomas spoke their names. Phillip and Capers directed Thomas and his horses to the watering hole, a creek not far from the cabin that eventually ran into the river.

While the horses were drinking water from the cool creek, Thomas looked out across the West farm and thought, *what a beautiful piece of land.* The creek was lined with numerous live oaks, their limbs twisting in terrific form, providing a safe haven for the fowls of the air. The cabin sat on a little hill that stood out from a good distance, well built, standing strong against the winter winds and passing storms, and the

Spanish moss hanging from the old oak trees gave the place a sense of history, to an aged time when no human steps crushed the fallen acorns or marked a common path. *No wonder John spoke often of his family and home.*

Close to where Lee and Stonewall were drinking water from the creek, a family of raccoons crossed a log in front of them - first the mother, then her little ones. A little farther away were some squirrels running and playing, climbing trees, chasing each other, unconcerned with any danger from their visiting guests. Thomas looked down into the water and saw a big catfish swimming around a stump, its fins slowly moving back and forth before darting out of sight. It was an entertaining moment, seeing all the wildlife come alive.

"Ok, Lee and Stonewall, you've drank your fill, now its time to walk you two back up to the barn and rest a while."

Little John Willie came running outside to meet the stranger as Thomas, Capers, and Phillip made their way back to the cabin.

"Who is this young fellow?" Thomas asked the boys.

"This is little John Willie," said Phillip, placing his hand on little John's shoulder.

"Why, you're the spitting image of your father. Let me shake your hand and see if you're as strong as he is."

Little John took Thomas by the hand and squeezed it as tight as he could. Thomas began to grunt and moan with pain, making little John think he was hurting his hand.

"Why, you sure are a strong boy; just as strong as your dad, if not stronger."

John Willie smiled and asked the stranger, "How do you know my dad?"

"Well boy, I don't know if time would allow me to tell you the whole story, but your dad and I did a lot of fighting together against those Yankees in the war."

Thomas had a clip-point Bowie knife he kept on his side, in a long leather sheath. Little John asked him if he could hold it. Thomas took the knife out of its holder and told little John he had to use the knife many times to defend himself with against robbers and thieves along the trail, but never on anyone that meant no harm to him.

"Never use any kind of a weapon on another human being unless it's to protect your own," said Thomas, letting little John hold the knife.

Little John's eyes grew big with amazement, captivated by its size as he grasped the handle with his hands, scared to move it one way or the other. When Thomas saw that he was satisfied with having held the knife, he gently took it from him before he cut himself with it.

While Thomas put the horses in the barn, John and Margaret came walking up the hill along the fence row running up to the cabin, a beautiful sunset providing a picturesque backdrop to end their romantic evening together. It was a common landscape across the South since the southern cause had surrendered, gray uniformed soldiers in the arms of loving wives whose sacrifice and tears had given them hope. Along the valley of Shenandoah, among the hills of Tennessee, near the ocean waves of coastal Carolina, walked the reunited hands of soldier and wife. Not all had made it back home safe from the war. Confederate President Jefferson Davis was still in chains in a cold dungeon in Virginia, the North not willing to let him go free quite yet, if at all. Would he be tried for treason and put to death? His fate and freedom rested in the hands of President Andrew Johnson and the courts. Many others feared trials of treason as well, officers and generals who had drawn their swords against the North. Many took the Oath of Allegiance, and some applied for special pardons granted by President Johnson, thus obtaining amnesty. It had been a long journey back home for John, and to be walking with his wife in the last rays of sunlight settled his spirit more than anything else.

Capers ran to his dad and told him that Thomas was in the barn. John walked up to the open door and saw his good friend brushing down Lee and Stonewall.

"Thomas! My old friend from Georgia!"

Thomas turned around with a smile on his face.

"John West! What a sight for sore eyes!"

John walked up to Thomas and gave him a strong southern handshake.

"Thomas, it sure is good to see you. When I heard you'd been taken prisoner by the Union army, I wondered if I'd ever see you again.

I thought about the days we used to spend together in Georgetown and Charleston. We sure had some good times."

"We sure did. Remember the time you and I were whistling Dixie walking down the streets of Charleston. I took my harmonica out and started playing when an old black man sitting close by started singing: *'Oh I wish I was in the land of cotton, Old times there are not forgotten, Cinnamon seed and sandy bottom, Look away, look away, look away Dixie land,'*" sang both Thomas and John while they walked from the barn to the cabin.

Thomas and John started laughing when they remembered what the old black man had said to them: *'Yes sir. That song was written by a Yankee himself. Sure is a shame he wasn't born in Georgia.'*

"I still can't believe it, Thomas, losing the war. I sure thought we had Grant and his boys on the run. Sherman sure turned the tide," expressed John, limping as he walked.

Thomas took his hat off before walking up the steps. "It's hard to understand, John. It's going to take some time for the dust to clear before the South can heal again. So how have you been getting along? I can see you have a limp in that right leg."

John motioned for Thomas to sit down and rest in one of the rocking chairs on the porch, knowing he was a little fatigued from his traveling. John sat in his favorite rocker.

It was on rare occasions that John smoked a pipe, and today was one of them. It was given to him by his grandfather, and it was during times of reminiscing that John took it out. "I'm a blessed man, Thomas. So many soldiers didn't make it back home to their wives and children. I know you can't wait to see yours. As far as my leg goes, well, courtesy of Yankee cannon fire. But it's just a small sacrifice compared to the ones that lost their lives."

Thomas dusted off his hat with his hands. He thought about all the ones he'd seen die in battle. "You're right, John. The blood sure ran deep. I guess Lee didn't have a choice in the end. The loss was just too great."

"There was a great loss of life, and the South suffered a great defeat. I'm glad there's one thing we still have to live for, and it's the most important thing of all, family. I still can't believe I'm back here in

Georgetown, near Black River, sleeping next to my beloved wife each night and hearing the voices of my children in the early morning hours."

Phillip paused.

"I know Georgia must be on your mind, Thomas."

"I can see it in my mind's eye, John. Home. It's the one thing that keeps me going."

Margaret was in the kitchen cooking a nice supper, the warm smell of a southern meal filling the air around the cabin, finding its way down near the creek where the wild animals favored its enticing scent. Sarah, Louisa, and Charlotte helped their mother fix chicken and dumplings. Margaret had the flour dough on the table flattening it out with a wooden roller, while the girls cut the dough in square pieces, except for Louisa, who decided on her own to cut some out in the shape of stars.

"Louisa!" exclaimed Sarah.

Margaret turned around to see what Sarah was fussing about.

"Louisa, now you stop that or I'll have you go to your room and sit for a while."

Louisa stopped. She knew her mother meant every word, and she didn't want to miss out on eating supper at the table. Margaret was a great cook, having learned from watching her mother fix meals when she was growing up, making some of the best chicken and dumplings in the country.

While Margaret was in the kitchen cooking, John remained on the front porch talking with Thomas about his journey back to Georgia.

"Thomas, I've been thinking a lot about my oldest son Phillip ever since I made it back from Virginia."

Phillip was standing near the barn feeding Lee and Stonewall some straw through the fence.

"He is of age now and has helped me out in more ways than a father could ever ask. While I was off at war, he stayed here the whole time and helped on the farm - fixing the fences, patching the barn, planting the crops. He's a good boy. Well, I was thinking that he might enjoy going to Georgia with you. He could help you out on your farm for a while until he could get on his own two feet. I know you mentioned you had a daughter named Annie Elizabeth that you would like to see get married. Maybe you could introduce Phillip to your daughter, and if he didn't like it there for some reason, he could always come back here to South Carolina."

"Well, John, I'd be honored to have Phillip ride along with me back home to Georgia. I need an extra hand anyway on the trip in case I run into any danger. There are a lot of rough roads between here and there, and if you don't mind him being put in harms way, then I'd be glad to have him tag along. You know I'll do all I can to make sure your son is kept safe. Why, he might turn out to be the one to keep me safe. And as far as Annie goes, well, who knows, they may come to like each other once they meet."

"I really appreciate you doing this for me Thomas, or should I say, for Phillip. You've been a real friend. If it wasn't for you, I don't think I could've kept my sanity during the war."

"John, suppers ready! Come inside and wash up!"

Margaret worked hard to prepare a nice supper for their guest. John Jr. came running in the house from the yard holding a cricket, which managed to escape from his hand when he walked into the kitchen. It found its way onto Charlotte's dress and she screamed to the top of her lungs.

"Mama, help me, get it off, get it off!"

The cricket jumped off her dress and landed on the kitchen floor. Sarah grabbed a broom from the corner of the room and tried to sweep the cricket outside, afraid to pick it up with her hands.

Little John screamed at Sarah. "Don't hurt my cricket!"

He tried to grab the broom from Sarah but slipped down and splashed into a washtub full of water sitting on the floor.

Everyone started laughing when Charlotte said, "Well, I guess little John is all washed up and ready for supper, Mama."

Chapter Two

The following day, John, Thomas, Phillip, and little John, took an afternoon walk to Mr. Hicks's country store about a mile or so away from the cabin, a two-storied mercantile built not long before the war. The isolated structure was centered near the crossroads, and a beautiful view of Black River gently attached itself to the scenic landscape with perfect symmetry. It was a social gathering place where old men sat and talked and young men listened, aged stories and tales floating around that date back as far as Columbus. Lately, the porch rockers were filled with deep feelings about the recent war, and the words they traded concerning the North weren't meant for innocent ears. Many of the old men had sons who'd fought for the Confederacy and never returned home, their names and existence buried beneath the sacred ground somewhere in some distant unmarked grave, leaving only a trail of resentment throughout the broken South.

Little John was barefoot and followed in the steps of his father's footprints, the sand feeling good to his feet as he slightly dug them into the earth trying to keep up.

Phillip walked next to his father along the oak-shaded road, and their conversation picked up where John and Thomas had left off the evening before.

"Son, what do you think about visiting Georgia with Thomas? He's leaving tomorrow, and really needs someone to travel with him along the backcountry. Who knows, you might like it when you get to the Hendrix farm. You could stay a while if you wanted to. Don't worry about your mother or me. We'll get along just fine."

Somehow Phillip felt like it was the right thing to do. He'd been working his fingers to the bones trying to farm and take care of the family while his dad was away. He had no social life here, and being lonely for companionship, he often thought about what it would be like if he could get away somewhere and start a family of his own. There weren't many girls around his part of the country in which to find a wife - not that he'd planned on getting married any time soon – so he agreed with his dad to make the trip to Georgia.

John's leg seemed to bother him more the longer they walked, and in some small symbolic way, his limp portrayed a single fragment of what remained of the injured South. It would be a slow healing process for the defeated states, and the scars would last forever. Lincoln, two days following Appomattox, sought to cover the widespread wounds by looking past secession and the long bitter war, declaring in his first public speech since Lee's surrender and his last before Ford's theater: "I believe it is not only possible, but in fact, easier to do this, without deciding, or even considering, whether these States have ever been out of the Union, than with it. Finding themselves safely at home, it would be utterly immaterial whether they had ever been abroad. Let us all join in doing the acts necessary to restoring the proper practical relations between these States and the Union." These were the reconstruction years, but to many in the South, their land would be fraught with carpetbaggers and scalawags, tempered with forced federal overreach into state constitutions. Lincoln would not live to see the workings of reconstruction within the southern states; it would be handed to Andrew Johnson after his tragic death. John was grateful for Lincoln's words of reconciliation and for President Johnson's compassion for the South, and he sought to find a place of resolve in his own heart for the North.

It was a beautiful walk along the Spanish moss road, where overhanging tree limbs stretched gracefully across the path on both sides, the shadow of the oaks blending softly into the white soft sand. The warm quiet breeze whispered gently across the fields into the dense-shaded woods, and the lightly brushed leaves left a peaceful sound.

They arrived at the country store thirsty for a drink from old man Hicks's artisan water. The well was in front of the store near the road facing Black River, and it stayed running over an enclosed cemented basin. Little John's father picked him up and held his lips to the faucet. Thomas seemed to enjoy the well as much as little John, placing his hat underneath the water, then back on his head. The water ran down his face and chest, cooling himself off from the burning heat but wetting his clothes in the process.

Mr. Hicks came walking out of the store and saw John West standing near the well. "Hello, John, who do you have with you today?"

"Good morning, Mr. Hicks, this is Thomas Hendrix. He's from Statesboro, Georgia. He's just passing through. He'll be leaving tomorrow to go back home."

"Another one of Lee's men...It's an honor, Thomas," smiled Mr. Hicks, extending his hand.

After quenching their thirst, Mr. Hicks walked them inside.

The first thing Thomas noticed when they entered the store was a large framed picture of General Lee hanging on the wall behind the counter. So many things came to his mind. He thought of all that Lee represented for the South: devotion, sacrifice, honor, bravery, and so much more. It was as if the picture had captured the spirit of all the war had tried to destroy, the strength and virtue of southern gentility. He thought of the mournful landscape that had changed the South beyond recognition, and how much work it would take to overcome its pile of ashes. Seeing Lee's picture on the wall reminded him it was possible.

Mr. Hicks noticed Thomas staring at the photo.

"It is one of his best. Taken by Vannerson I believe in '63."

"He is one general I deeply respected," said Thomas, his voice filled with emotion.

"It was an honor to serve with him," said John.

President Jefferson Davis was attending church services at St Pauls in Richmond, Virginia when Lee's message to the Confederate President had been delivered: "I think it is absolutely necessary that we should abandon our position tonight." Lee had made all attempts to hold his position until nightfall at Petersburg, but Union forces were too overwhelming. Richmond would soon be abandoned and the city left in turmoil and flames. When General Lee surrendered the Army of Northern Virginia to Grant a few days later at the McLean family home, his expressions were clothed with monumental sadness, the weight of surrender too heavy. He felt he had led his army under God's providence and to the best of his ability, and he fought to the last. His men had given their all to serve under his command, and he felt their grief as well as his own.

After sharing their feelings about the war, John walked around the store looking over the shelves: "Mr. Hicks, Thomas is going to need a few things to take along for the trip. He'll be coming by in the morning to pick up some supplies. If you don't mind, can you put the cost of whatever he needs on my bill, and I'll pay you come harvest time?"

"You don't have to do that, John. I've got some money here. I can pay for what I need."

"No, Thomas, I want to help out. After all, Phillip is going to be traveling with you, and he's my son. It's the least I can do."

Mr. Hicks placed a piece of paper down on the counter.

"That will be fine, John. Mr. Hendrix, just write down here on this paper what you'll need and I'll make sure I have it all packed up and ready to go for you in the morning."

"Much obliged, Mr. Hicks."

"Glad to be of assistance, Thomas."

They walked out onto the storefront porch and sat down a while, talking, sitting on rockers made of old hickory. The open view toward the river reminded John of the battle of Petersburg along the Appomattox…

He could see the Union enemy near the river, and the peaceful fog lifting toward the dawn's first ray of light seemed like a great contradiction to John. How can something so innocent be mixed with the blood of cruelest war? He thought. The central junction of the railroads crossed in Petersburg, the main supply lines to the Confederate capital of Richmond, and Grant wanted to crush the South by taking control of it. Anchored down behind the Dimmock Line, John waited like the rest of the men, for the enemy to attack, to rush in like a storm of fury and take whatever punishment their artillery could inflict on them. The air seemed thick and humid, and he felt his hands holding tight to his Springfield…tighter than usual. Why am I so tense? He realized his fear wasn't so much of what was in front of him as what lay behind him… home. He wasn't afraid of dying. But he didn't want to leave his wife a widow and his children fatherless, and this scared him more than the enemy approaching. He knew at that moment, like some great epiphany, he had to make it back to Georgetown no matter how difficult the conflict.

The marsh, the open fields, Appomattox River, all came flooding back into his mind, and the sound of the cannons echoing out from the South's defended positions against the Yankees filled his thoughts with past memories of war.

"It's funny how time puts things into perspective. It seems like an old dream. Yet, the sounds of the guns are as fresh to my senses as the early morning dew. I don't know if I'll ever get past the battlefields."

"You fought hard, John, and did what you had to do like the rest of us. And if I know you well enough, and I'm sure I do, you'll pick your musket up and move on like you always have."

"I reckon so, Thomas."

John looked over at Phillip, sitting on the edge of the porch hanging onto every word, trying to grasp the imagery of war. "Son, you sure you want to go to Georgia?"

Phillip acknowledged his father, and for the first time, noticed how much he'd changed since "*the great conflict*," the open sunlight revealing the aged lines on his face. His heart softened and he didn't know what to say, his words lost to the sudden realization of elapsed time. He wanted to walk up to his father and tell him how much he loved him, how much he appreciated his sacrifice, not only as a soldier, but in all paternal matters as well. He wanted to let him know that he couldn't be more proud to be his son and that his decision to go to Georgia wasn't based on any dissatisfaction of living on the farm.

"Remember the last thing you said to us the day you left to join the war?" asked Phillip.

John thought about it for a moment…then remembered: *"Even though I'll be miles away, my heart will always remain here, with my family."*

About that time, Sam Johnston came riding by in his horse-drawn buggy. He was one of the wealthiest landowners in the territory, with a spread of over several hundred acres, consisting mostly of rice and some cotton fields, and he had his own gin and a large barn to store all of his cotton in. His plantation workers consisted mainly of former slaves, and everyone wondered at what would become of his fortune after the war.

He yelled out to everyone as he rode by, "There's a fierce storm coming this way like Sherman's troops marching through Georgia. Better get things anchored down!"

He kept right on going without looking back, popping a whip on his horse like some say he'd done with his slaves. And although he was a church going man, few people respected him due to his hard and rough spirit.

The noise of thunder sounded in the distance.

As they walked back from the store to the cabin, the storm appeared over the horizon and dark clouds rolling in from the west brought whirling winds and lightning, a bolt striking an old tree overshadowing the road. A strong rain poured down from the darkened sky, and they found themselves looking for shelter before the storm engulfed them. Phillip picked little John up by his collar and carried him along, running to the barn where they watched the pouring rain flood the ground around them, forming streams that washed down the hill toward the bottomland. It'd been a long time since it'd rained this heavy, but the fields needed the water to soften the land, which until now, had been dry and unbearable.

After the rains diminished, John noticed a large cloud of smoke rising above the tree line near Johnston's plantation. *Something must be on fire* he thought. He and Thomas jumped on their horses and galloped over toward the burning haze. As they approached Johnston's place, they could see that the huge barn he'd used to store all of his cotton in was on fire, lightning having struck the wooden-shingled roof, causing the shakes to go up in flames. There were a lot of workers carrying water buckets back and forth, from the well to the barn, but the fire appeared to be out of control. John and Thomas dismounted and assisted the servants in pumping water from the well, but in a little while, the barn and his stored harvest were nothing more than smoldering ashes.

Sam just sat on the front porch of his plantation home, dazed and stone-like, looking disheveled: "It's all gone," he kept saying. "We've lost the war. I've lost my wealth. Nothing will ever be the same again."

****

The sun had long gone down, and John and Margaret were preparing for bed when they heard some dogs barking outside in the distance. John pushed back the curtain at the window and looked out beyond the cotton fields, then back toward the barn, where Thomas was soundly sleeping on a cot in the loft. He noticed the cloud-to-cloud lightning in the night sky, but nothing else more than a few raindrops hitting against the pane. Margaret walked outside onto the front porch and saw some torch lights scattered along the road a good piece from the cabin. She called for John, who rushed to put his boots on, grabbing his Springfield 1861 from behind the door.

"What is it, Margaret?"

"Look." Margaret pointed toward the torch lights at the edge of the cotton field. John could feel a gentle mist from the open air hitting his face, and he wondered who could be carrying torches at such a frantic pace. And the dogs, what were they chasing? Were they looking for someone?

He yelled out in the dark: "Who's out there? What do you want?" He could hear a baby crying.

A black man hollered out. "E me, John. Asa fom maussuh Johnston plantesshun."

Margaret yelled back. "Asa. What on earth are you doing out here so late? Is Pearl with you?"

"Yaas ma'am. Uh yuh. E Pearl." The dialect was unique to the coastal plantations, but Margaret understood it.

"Well come on up here, Pearl. You needn't be afraid of us."

"Uh know dat. Bot maussuh Johnston swellup b'kause we leabe e faa'm. E bin drink tummuch an ent bin 'ese'f, wus'den'ebbuh. We freedmun, bot e don' t'ink dat way. E hab some dog attuhr'us an uh know e gwine whip us ef e ebbuh git e han on we, fsutt'n."

The dogs were getting closer.

"Now Pearl, if you don't get on up here, you'll get caught for sure. We'll hide you all in the cellar."

There was silence. Then Pearl, holding her baby, Asa, and a few other freed slaves from the plantation, came walking out of the branch toward the cabin. John could tell they had been running and hiding all day, their clothes all wet from the passing rains. The dogs were almost at the top of the hill, and the men from Johnston's plantation followed close behind.

"Hurry Pearl. Over here." Margaret led them down into the cellar, situated between the barn and the cabin. "Now y'all be real quiet. And don't let that baby do any crying."

Margaret hurried back up the steps and closed the cellar doors. The men from the plantation were nearing the top of the hill as Margaret stood next to John in the front yard. The dogs came closer and closer, sniffing and barking, running back and forth before coming to a stop near the cabin. The men holding the torches came walking up to where John and Margaret were standing, some carrying guns.

"Sorry for all the noise ma'am. How do you do, John?" asked one of the men.

"What seems to be the reason for all of this?" questioned John.

"We're looking for some slaves of ours. They ran away this morning. Now, John, we know they're here. Their tracks lead right up to your cabin. We're just doing what we've been told to do and nobody's going to get hurt if they come on back. Mr. Johnston's done promised. But if they don't, then they'll have to be punished."

"Now Earl, you know them slaves have been set free. Lincoln signed the document; and if my memory serves me well, the North won the war. They can now come and go as they please."

"I hate to do this, John, but if you don't step out of the way, we'll have to take them by force. Search the property." The baby in the cellar began crying. Margaret held her head down, knowing the men had heard it. Two of them aimed their guns at John, and another proceeded toward the cellar.

"Hold it right there. Don't take another step." A voice came from the barn loft window. It was Thomas, and he had his Whitworth rifle pointed directly at Earl. "If anyone moves any closer to that cellar, I'll send them straight to the pearly gates, and you'll be the first one I shoot."

"I believe he'll do just that," said Phillip, holding his gun out the cabin window.

Earl told the men to get back, and then looked over at John: "Fine. Have it your way. Come on men. There's no sense in anyone getting shot over this."

As soon as the men and dogs were gone, Margaret opened up the cellar door and motioned for Pearl: "Come on out Pearl. It's safe now, they're all gone."

"Uh fsutt'n t'engky, ma'am," said Asa. "Uh t'ink Pearl sick. Dem rain done got to'um."

As Pearl stepped out of the cellar, Margaret noticed she had a terrible fever. "Why Pearl, you're sweating to death. You're running a high temperature."

She handed Margaret her baby and fainted to the ground. "John, go get some water. Asa, pick Pearl up and carry her inside the house. Hurry, Asa."

Asa put his wife down near the fireplace. Margaret took a washcloth and dipped it in a bucket of water, placing it on her forehead. She took a blanket and put it over Pearl's body to try and dry her clothes with. Pearl kept murmuring, "Don' leh nutt'n' happ'n tuh me baby. Me po' baby. Don' leh nutt'n' hu't me baby. Ten' tuh de baby." Then she became quiet and still. Her fever had gotten too high, and Pearl had no more breath left in her. It was too late, she was gone.

"I'm sorry, Asa. I don't know what to say. If there's anything I can do, please let me know," said Margaret.

Asa held his head down and cried. He took the baby in his arms and walked outside where the others were waiting. He looked around at John and Margaret who were now standing on the edge of the front porch: "Uh t'ink uh cya'um an pit'um een de grabeyaa'd ob de fambly." Pearl's ancestors were buried near the river, and Asa left toward the place where he would bury his wife.

****

The morning sunlight beamed across the West log cabin on the hill and the blue sky framed the Carolina morning with its cheerful color. Some puffy white clouds floated in the sky like Spanish ships on a deep ocean voyage, as if looking for more land to discover or people to conquer, and the winds carried them along to their place of rest. The previous day's rain refreshed the parched landscape and filled the creeks and the streams below, while the birds sang beautifully in the trees, flying from branch to branch, full of life and optimism. Black River flowed stronger than ever and the time seemed to be perfect for saying goodbye.

The storm from last night had been forgotten, but the memory of Pearl dying in front of the fireplace was still fresh on Margaret's mind as she awoke to the sound of the early morning birds singing in the crepe myrtle tree near her open bedroom window.

She eased out of bed to get dressed.

"John, it's time to wake up." Margaret didn't like to disturb her husband while he was sleeping so well, but their son would be leaving today.

John opened his eyes and smiled at his darling wife. "Good morning beautiful. I hope I didn't oversleep."

"No. You didn't." Margaret was sitting at the dresser in front of the mirror brushing her hair. John could see that she was crying.

"What's wrong, Margaret?"

"He's leaving us today. I'm trying my best to keep a smile on my face, but inside, it hurts. Once he leaves, we may not get to see him for a long time. He's never been gone from home for more than a day or two his whole life..."

"Come here, Margaret, and let me tell you something."

Margaret walked over and sat down on the bed next to John.

"What is it?" She rested her head on his chest.

"I love you more than anything else in the world. Phillip is a young man now, and you've given him something that will carry him throughout the rest of his life...a mother's love. Letting go isn't easy, and sometimes it's the hardest thing to do. It'll be hard at first, but we have each other, and Phillip will be in good hands...everything's going to be all right."

"You are a wonderful man, John West. You know just how to cheer me up." Margaret kissed John on his forehead before leaving the room to have a goodbye talk with her son.

Phillip had taken a morning walk down to the bottomland and sat underneath the old oak tree near the creek, a place he'd go to in times of indecision to think things through. He looked forward to getting away for a while, but didn't want to leave his parents or siblings behind, his only source of earthly strength and comfort. He loved them all dearly and knew that he wouldn't get to see them for a while once he left Carolina and crossed the Georgia line. He was closer to his mother than he was to his father. During the war they had grown even closer and he knew she'd be sad over him leaving. But somehow, he still had peace over his decision, and as hard as it was to leave, he'd made up his mind to find his place among men. He thought to himself, *how will they ever make it without me?* The only other man around the house, besides his father, was Capers. Sarah was grown, but she couldn't handle the toil and labor of the fields and help her mother take care of the children. As he wrestled in deep thought, his mother walked up and sat down next to him.

"Phillip." His mother's voice sounded like a calm ocean wave to him.

He looked over at her, his eyes teary from thoughts of leaving home.

"Mama, I'm going to miss you all very much. I really don't want to leave, but somehow I feel like something is waiting for me in Georgia."

"Son, don't feel bad about leaving. If it was up to me, I'd have you stay here forever, but I love you and want to see you happy. Now it would hurt me more if you didn't go. You'll always have a place here and you can come back whenever you would like to. I'm excited for you, Son, and know that whatever you do will be the right thing. Now let's go up to the cabin and get your things ready."

His mother's words gave him the strength he needed to say goodbye and leave the only place he'd ever known – the cabin on the hill…the bottomland…Black River - all the familiar things of life that gave him a sense of belonging.

Thomas had everything ready and loaded up with the supplies from Mr. Hicks's store, each item packed neatly in the covered wagon: water containers, food supplies, ammunition, and a few cooking utensils.

Phillip walked into the living room after returning from the creek, his mother's endearing words still fresh on his mind. John stood near the fireplace mantle, his right leg being supported by his cane, and his countenance reminded Phillip of the day that his father had left for the war years ago…a sad going away look. John leaned his cane against the rocker close by and picked up a little wooden box he'd kept beside the old clock. He opened up the lid and took some money out he'd been saving.

"Son, I want you to have this and use it whenever you need to."

"Daddy, I can't…"

Phillip gently interrupted.

"I have enough to get us by. Consider it payment for all you've done on the farm."

"Thanks, Dad," said Phillip, hugging his father, trying to hold back the tears.

Phillip glanced over at the fireplace mantle, and at that moment, as if suspended in time, he reflected on the many times he and his father had spent together during his childhood…

The time was late spring and the winter rains which filled the swampy creeks had completely dried up near the river. It was Phillip's first real turkey hunt, a day he'd been anticipating for weeks since his father had promised to take him near Trap Lake, where the big gobbler had been strutting and roosting. His father had named the wild tom, Beauregard, and his beard nearly touched the ground he strutted on. For weeks, his father tried his best to teach Phillip how to make a turkey call with his mouth, for it was the way his father taught him, and he didn't like to use any kind of manmade callers.

"Try it again, Son," his father would say, "but this time try not to make it too loud, but more soft and natural."

After much practice, Phillip sounded just like a real gobbler and was very proud of his new found skill.

"Dad, can I do the calling when we get to Trap Lake? I know I can get old Beauregard to come strutting off that island."

Trap Lake was a creek that formed one side of the island and the river flowed around the rest of it, where the turkey loved to roost in the old oak trees, especially in the one overlooking the lake, where a sandbar joined the shallow creek bottom to the mainland.

"Ok, Son, you can do the calling and I'll do the shooting," smiled John, as they sat around the table eating supper. After discussing and planning the next day's hunt, John hugged his son goodnight, "Now it's time for you to get some sleep. The morning hours will come soon and we'll need to get up early to reach our spot before daybreak."

That night, Phillip dreamed of sitting in the palmettos, the green fans he called them, calling to the old gobbler, and making him walk out to the sandbar - the perfect place for his dad to have an open shot.

The morning hours came early and they didn't use any lights from the lanterns as they walked through the woods into the swamp. John didn't want to alarm the tom and he knew the lights would spook the turkey from his roosting place.

"Be real quiet, Son. Any noise we make must be small. See the large green palmettos near the banks edge. That is where we'll sit for the hunt."

"Daddy," whispered Phillip, "will you tell me when I need to make the call?"

"Sure, Son. Now be still and wait for the light to come through the trees."

Just as the morning fog lifted above the flowing water, John whispered to Phillip, "Now, Son."

Phillip didn't hear the gobbler, but John had heard him through the palmettos and knew the tom had landed on the ground from the old oak tree. He didn't realize how nervous he would be until he heard his father's words to give the call, to make the sound he'd practiced over and over for weeks, but never in any real situation, only in the open air where there was never any danger of spooking a real gobbler.

Phillip swallowed hard and then made the call.

Beauregard heard the sound and walked out onto the sandbar, cautious of his surroundings, but curious at the call he'd heard from the palmettos. John lifted his gun slowly when the gobbler turned his face away from them and toward the river.

"Steady," he whispered in a low voice to himself.

Phillip made another gobbling call and the turkey stood tall on the sandbar, moving closer and closer to the shallow water toward the mainland. John held the gun steady and fired the shot. When the smoke cleared, they looked out through the trees and saw the gobbler fly away, disappearing into the swamp.

Phillip held his head low as if he were to blame for the turkey getting away.

"It's not your fault, Son. You called the gobbler to the spot where we needed him to be, but I aimed too much to the left and hit the thick vines hanging from the trees near the creek's edge."

Phillip would always remember hearing the words of his father: "It's not your fault, Son." It became an integral part of his memory, his dad's response to adversity, teaching him to never blame others for one's own misfortune. His father had always been that way, had always held a kind nature. He'd never known John to point his finger at another human being when suffering from some setback, as if they were the cause of his hardships. Past thoughts flooded into his mind as he and his father walked outside to the wagon - heartfelt reflections that served to remind him of the love his family had for him and for each other.

Everyone gathered to tell him goodbye.

"Son, I'm very proud of you. I know you'll have a great time with Thomas and he'll take good care of you on the trip. Remember everything I've taught you and put it to good use. Maybe me, your mother, and the kids can come down to Georgia and visit sometime."

Phillip hugged them all goodbye. John, Margaret, Sarah, Capers, Charlotte, Louise, and little John, all stood at the gate and watched Thomas and Phillip ride down the road until they were completely out of sight.

John put his arms around Margaret who had tears streaming down her face.

"Phillip will be fine, Margaret."

"I know...I'm just going to miss having him here with us. He'll always be in my heart each and everyday."

****

The journey to Georgia wouldn't be an easy one. The trip would stretch across some two hundred miles of country roads, crossing rivers and passing through areas where there was no protection against thieves or robbers. The route they'd planned on taking would first lead them through Charleston, and then, after traveling a good ways, cross the Savannah River into Georgia, near Savannah. From there, they'd continue on until they would go over the Great Ogeechee into Bulloch County, and finally, to the Hendrix farm.

It was Saturday morning when the two of them left from Georgetown. They rode down the road from the West log cabin through the wide open cotton field, then under the overhanging oaks that led past the Hicks Store, and finally southward from Winyah and the rice fields toward the historic town of Charleston. Phillip looked back and said his silent goodbyes to the only place he'd ever called home.

As they neared Johnston's plantation, several black families were walking from the main entrance into the open road. Thomas slowed the wagon down.

"What's the purpose of this great exodus? Is everything ok?" asked Thomas.

A young black lady cried out, "E maussuh Johnston. E done gone an kill 'ese'f."

The former slaves were now free to leave without fear of being hunted.

Thomas remembered the look on Sam Johnston's face the day before while sitting on the front porch of his plantation home. He wasn't surprised to hear of his self-inflicted end, knowing Sam's life was wrapped up in all his lost possessions. So many of the South's aristocrats would never regain their riches, never experience the ease of life from other men's servitude as they had before. To many Confederate soldiers, the struggle wasn't about preserving the rich lifestyle of wealthy plantation owners or owning slaves to work plantations, but about preserving their rights as they knew them to be, about protecting their lands and homesteads, no matter how indigent they might be. Their loyalty had nothing to do with defending the belief of the superiority of the white race. Their common link to the Confederacy rested in citizenship and duty, not in any particular political doctrine or dogma. There were those in politics, both North and South, who had felt the colored race was inferior, but this was mainly expressed within government; it existed among a certain segment of society as well, within all states, under the flags of both nations. There were citizens who wanted to abolish slavery and provide for their emancipation. However, the greatest sentiments *within politics* before the war toward freeing the slaves rested within the Union, and seemed to be mostly absent within the Confederacy. There were abolitionists in the North, and pro-slavery fire-eaters in the South, but not all held to these two positions. It was true, before the war, the nation was half free, half slave, as far as state constitutions existed. Free states rested in the North, and slave states in the South. This was not always the case. Before the Revolutionary war, all thirteen American colonies allowed slavery. The transition from slave to free occurred gradually, and at one time, New York homes had owned just as many slaves as Charleston, SC. The Union did not declare war on the South because they practiced slavery. The institution of slavery was protected by the United States constitution itself, the very constitution of the Union, the supreme law of the land, and it would have been illegal to declare war on slave states due to slavery. Lincoln knew this. His declaration of war on the Confederacy was initiated solely on the basis of a land dispute over Fort Sumter. To many southerners, the North's invasion of the Fort meant a direct invasion against the Confederacy and all its states, no matter the political rhetoric of the day regarding slavery. Secession involved slavery. The legality of the war, in direct contrast to secession, had nothing to do with slavery. Fort Sumter commander, Major Robert Anderson, was pro-slavery and past slave owner himself. Knowing this, Lincoln and the Union still wanted him there, and supported his defense of the fort. South Carolina was, in essence, firing on a fort where a pro-slavery commander was in charge, and this, at its very core, reveals the Civil War was not pro-slavery against anti-slavery. After his loss of the fort and return to the North, Major Anderson was deemed a national hero by the Union, and an approximate 100,000 northerners came together in Manhattan's Union Square Park to honor the man, albeit pro-slavery, who defended the fort and defied the South. For the North, the war was to force the Confederacy back into the Union, under the pretense of claiming a fort in Charleston harbor that was clearly in southern territory. For the South, it was to defend its homeland, Fort Sumter, from attack by Northern invasion. It was clear by Lincoln's own words, that freeing the slaves was not his mission, but preserving the Union. In his letter to Horace Greeley in 1862, Lincoln wrote…

"I would save the Union. I would save it the shortest way under the Constitution. The sooner the national security can be restored, the nearer the Union will be the Union as it was. If there be those who would not save the Union, unless they could at the same time save slavery, I do not agree with them. If there be those who would not save the Union unless they could at the same time destroy slavery, I do not agree with them. My paramount object in this struggle is to save the Union, and is not either to save or to destroy slavery. If I could save the Union without freeing any slave I would do it, and if I could save it by freeing all the slaves I would do it; and if I could save it by freeing some and leaving others alone I would also do that."

Even before the war, during his presidential inaugural address, March 4th, 1861, Lincoln declared his approval of protecting slavery in the states by openly endorsing the Corwin Amendment.

Lincoln said…

"I understand a proposed amendment to the Constitution, which amendment, however, I have not seen, has passed Congress, to the effect that the Federal Government shall never interfere with the domestic institutions of the States, including that of persons held to service…holding such a provision to now be implied constitutional law, I have no objection to its being made express and irrevocable."

Lincoln clearly detested slavery, but he never intended to stop it where it existed. If the South had not seceded, and the war had never occurred, slavery would have remained in all the states under his administration, and would have long been reinforced under the Corwin Amendment. It is without question, that Lincoln's declaration of war against the South had been over territory, not slavery.

To Thomas, it was good seeing the former slaves of Johnston no longer under the yoke of bondage, and he knew their freedom meant the freedom of all races of people.

After passing the plantation workers, Thomas told Phillip to keep an eye on their surroundings for anything out of the ordinary; for the post war years were full of turmoil and unrest in a great majority of the South. There were bandits and robbers who didn't care whether you claimed to have been a Yankee or a Confederate; they were willing to steal from anyone, especially from vulnerable travelers along the isolated roads. There was great disquiet and disorder in many areas of the country, and Union soldiers and federal troops dotted the southern landscape to keep the peace and provide safety in areas where reconstruction demanded their presence.

"Thomas, I know I'll eventually get to see the Hendrix farm, but can you tell me a little bit about what it's like before we get there?"

Thomas told Phillip to grab the reins and lead the horses while he pulled his knife from his side. He began carving on a small piece of wood he'd broken off from an over-hanging tree limb in the road.

"Well, Phillip, to me, it's one of the most peaceful places on earth to live. The lands mostly flat with good soil for farming. The Georgia pines are tall and blanket the earth every year with their fallen straw and the springtime brings wild blooming dogwoods to life, along with sweet smelling wisteria, which provides a charming fragrance in the air. There are plenty of honey bees that make some of the sweetest honey you could ever put in a jar, more than you and I could ever eat. There's a nice creek that flows through the north end of the farm, full of water during the winter months, but shallow during the spring. Just a couple miles away from the cabin is a nice river to fish in, called the Ogeechee, with sandbars during the summer time stretching out across the river, nearly touching the opposite bank where the cool shallow water is clear enough to swim in, the sandy river bottom touching your feet. We have some of the best neighbors a man could ever ask for, willing to help each other out in the toughest of times, and I've never seen them turn away a stranger in need. I know you'll like the farm, with its country-life living, but you may not like the work, where the labor in the fields, like picking cotton row after row for countless hours, seems like an endless eternity. There's a lot of hard work and sweat that goes into keeping up a large place. But your daddy told me how you kept up the West farm while he was away, so I don't think you'll have any problems adjusting to the work load in Statesboro."

The first river past the Sampit that Thomas and Phillip had to cross was the Santee. There was a ferry crossing that would give them easy access across the water.

"There's a nice tavern on the south side of the crossing where we can get something to drink."

"My first drink of ale," said Phillip, taking his hat off, wiping the sweat from his forehead. "I guess I'm becoming a man now."

"Not ale, but tea. If they have any," laughed Thomas.

The sun's rays were beaming down heavy on them without any clouds in the sky to block the heat, and the humidity was high in the Carolina air – a typical hot summer's day in the south.

After Thomas and Phillip crossed the Santee on the ferry, they walked over to the tavern.

Thomas unhitched Lee and Stonewall, leading them to a nearby watering trough. "Now you didn't think I was going to get something to drink without letting you two have your fill, did you?" Thomas whispered to Lee and Stonewall.

There were many travelers hanging around the tavern, a popular coastal water haven that provided room and board for many travelers passing through. A large branched tree near the building formed a nice shadowed shelter from the sun's sweltering heat, lowering the temperature twenty degrees cooler in the shade. Some of the people there were fishermen boating up and down the river, while others were local farmers taking a break from the burning heat.

When Thomas and Phillip walked inside, a nice lady, the tavern proprietor, asked them if they wanted something to drink.

"We would like some sweet tea if you have it?"

"Well, this isn't the eighteenth century," she said with a smile, "but I happen to have some of the best stored away. Some of our locals have chosen a much stronger drink to satisfy their thirst. Needless to say, they're not standing on their feet anymore. By the way, my name is Kate."

"Hey, Kate. My name is Thomas and this is Phillip. I'm from Georgia and he's from Georgetown."

While Thomas and Phillip sat down at a table and waited for their drinks, they noticed a young lady walking up to a piano in the corner of the room. She sat down and started playing a somewhat sad piece as her fingers moved gracefully across the keys. She had a beautiful voice and Phillip was somewhat attracted to her. When the proprietor brought them their tea, she noticed Phillip's interest in the young lady.

"She's a special girl isn't she?" inquired Kate to Phillip.

"She sure is. What's her name?"

"Juliet."

"Well my name is Romeo," said Phillip laughing.

Thomas knew Phillip was young and very interested in the ladies, but he hoped Phillip would find interest in his daughter Annie. He also knew it would be Phillip's choice of who he liked or married and no one else's.

"She was fourteen years old when her father was killed at the beginning of the Civil War. Her mother died giving her birth. She had no one to look after her when her mother's sister moved to Tennessee, so I took her in as one of my own. I paid for her to have professional piano and voice lessons. She really didn't need any voice lessons though. She already had a beautiful voice. So, I thought it would be a good idea for her to get some experience here in the tavern. She just started a few weeks ago," said Kate.

The more she played the more Phillip became drawn to her. When she finished, she walked over to Kate, still standing next to Thomas and Phillip's table.

Kate introduced Juliet.

"Phillip is from Georgetown, not far up the road from here," said Kate, smiling at Juliet.

"Really...What brings you this way, Phillip?"

"I'm going to Georgia with Thomas. He's got a farm there and I plan on staying with him a while."

"Georgia. I like Georgia," said Juliet.

"Say, why don't you two go walk down by the river while I get Thomas some more tea?"

"Kate," said Juliet, as if it were inappropriate for her to suggest such an idea.

"It's ok with me, Juliet, if it's ok with you," replied Phillip, hoping she would agree.

"Yes, I would like that very much."

Phillip and Juliet walked down by the Santee River. There were great egrets walking on the sandbars and in the shallow waters of a nearby stream. The tall cypress trees along the river banks filled the place with majestic beauty and charm.

"So, how long do you plan on staying in Georgia, Phillip?"

"I really don't know. It was kind of a sudden decision. I haven't had much time to think about it. I don't mean to change the subject, but you really are a talented young lady. I guess you've heard a lot of guys tell you that before."

"A few times, but most guys are afraid to walk up and talk to me. They think because I am this beautiful girl with this beautiful voice that I wouldn't be interested in talking with them, at least that's what Kate says. But I'm not like that. I don't see myself as being beautiful. I'm just a country girl looking for happiness and fulfillment like everyone else."

"I'm sorry to hear about your father, Juliet. I know you must've been devastated."

"Well, my father never really cared for me much. When my mother died giving me birth, he sort of locked everyone out of his life. I was mainly raised by his sisters. He stayed drunk most of the time that I can remember."

"I'm sorry to hear that. So do you plan on staying here with Kate for a while?"

"I don't know. Kate is a great woman. If it wasn't for her I don't know where I'd be. I owe her a lot for paying for my music lessons and taking care of me. I don't want to break her heart by leaving her, but someday I want to see the world."

Thomas walked out of the tavern and hitched up Lee and Stonewall, feeling revived after drinking the tavern's tea. He jumped into the wagon, ready to go, and hollered out to Phillip who was still standing by the river, his full attention focused on Juliet. Phillip told her it was nice talking with her, and hopefully, if he ever came back through, he would like to pick up their conversation where they left off. Juliet smiled and said she would love to see him again.

As Thomas and Phillip rode away, Juliet stood by the river's edge waving goodbye.

"Well, Romeo, how did it go with Juliet?" said Thomas laughing.

"It went great. But something tells me I'll never see her again."

"Why do you say that?"

"I really can't explain it. She was a very beautiful girl, but she seemed like she wasn't at peace with herself. I don't want to judge her or anything, but I don't think she'll ever stay in one place very long."

Phillip thought it best to get Juliet out of his mind.

Thomas and Phillip crossed a couple more rivers before they reached the outskirts of Charleston. When they neared the historic city, Thomas asked Phillip to take a different route into town. There was a high bluff on the ocean front that he wanted to see, a place he had discovered when he stood guard there during the war. The sun started going down and it formed a beautiful sunset in the sky which seemed to glow like hot coals burning red from a recent fire. While they rode along the coast, the ocean waves pounced against the shore and a salty mist filled the air, the tide turning inland.

"What a beautiful sight," said Phillip.

The road led through some old oak trees standing out in mystical manner against the backdrop of the Atlantic Ocean, and floating seabirds soared above the waves with their wings being guided by swirling winds.

Phillip stopped the horses to give them a rest, sensing they were fatigued from the long-galloped miles. Both of them sat in the wagon listening to the seabirds and feeling the warm wind brushing against their faces. Thomas took out his harmonica and played the song "Lorena," a mournful Civil War ballad, while thinking of his wife Elizabeth.

"*The years creep slowly by, Lorena, snow is on the grass again, the sun's low down the sky Lorena, the frost gleams where the flowers have been.* I played that song for my wife the evening I left to join the Confederacy. I can't wait to hold her in my arms again," said Thomas, putting the battle worn harmonica back in his shirt pocket.

"I wish I had that kind of companionship with a woman."

"You will, Phillip. You just have to be patient and wait for the right one. It's the greatest feeling in the world being in love with the one that's in love with you."

It was a peaceful moment before what was to be a rough night in Charleston.

"Now you can give me back the reins, Phillip…I'll take over from here. I know a good place where we can spend the night and rest up for tomorrow."

Darkness had fallen when they entered the limits of the southern town. Thomas looked forward to seeing some of his old friends there, but it had been a while and he didn't know if any of them were still around. The streets were filled with horses, wagons, and people as they rode through the middle of the city, stopping in front of an old building called the *Charlestown Inn*. Thomas told Phillip to hop off the wagon and go inside to ask for a room while he put the horses in the stable that belonged to the Inn.

Phillip walked inside and asked for a room.

The front desk attendant asked him, "How many rooms do you need and for how long?"

"There will be two of us and it's just for one night. If you have a room available that has two beds that would be great."

"What are your names and where are you from?"

"My name is Phillip West and I'm from Georgetown. The man I'm traveling with is from Statesboro, Georgia."

"Statesboro," said the attendant with a sense of familiarity. "That's where I was born and raised. It's a small town, but the people there are some of the friendliest folks you'll ever cross paths with. They'll take the shirt off their own backs if they thought you needed it. Yes sir, I ought to know, I lived there for over sixty years. What's the man's name you're traveling with, son?"

"Thomas Hendrix."

"Thomas Hendrix. The same Thomas Hendrix that fought for the Confederate States of America and taken prisoner by the Union forces?"

"Yes sir."

"Well I'll be. What a nice surprise. Thomas Hendrix and I lived no more than two miles from each other. I'll have to give you two the finest beds the Charlestown Inn has to offer. There'll be no cost. It's on me for the night."

Thomas walked into the Inn: "Well if it ain't old Charlie Dixon."

"Thomas Hendrix, what a nice surprise. I just knew you had died in that Yankee prison camp in Maryland."

"There were times when I felt like I had, Charlie, but the good Lord knew I was too stubborn to die. It sure is good to see an old friend from back home. All right Phillip, lets go on over to Harper's Ferry Kitchen and get us a nice meal to eat."

When they walked out the front door, Thomas noticed two men standing near the horse stable belonging to the Charlestown Inn.

"Phillip, don't look now, but there's two men standing in the alley near the stable. I think they're going to try and steal our things out of the wagon tonight. I don't believe they'll be too stupid to try this early, so we'll go ahead and feed our bellies a nice warm southern meal."

"But, Thomas, don't you think…"

"No, Phillip, I've traveled long enough to know how these thieves work. We'll be ready for them later."

Thomas was not afraid of anyone. He could pull his knife out and use it on a man before they knew what hit them. He was also good with a pistol but preferred to use his knife in most circumstances where justice called for it.

While walking to Harper's Ferry Kitchen they noticed a ball of some sort at a nearby Charleston mansion. There was outdoor music being played, and men and women were on the lawn dancing with their chosen partners to the sound of the violins. Thomas and Phillip stood there for a few minutes being entertained by what they were seeing. Phillip had never seen a ball before and to him it seemed like a fairy tale, men with suits on and women wearing pretty beautiful dresses dancing in perfect harmony.

The lantern lights from the Charleston mansion reflected against their faces as they watched in the distant darkness.

"Thomas, do you think any of those men or women ever picked cotton or plowed with a mule in the field?"

"Oh, I don't know, Phillip, I'm sure there's a few in the crowd that have picked a cotton boll or two. Most of them probably own plantations and have field workers that do most of the work. But now, without the right to own slaves, I'm sure a lot of them will have to get their hands a little dirty. Now lets get on over to Harper's Ferry Kitchen and get our hands a little dirty eating a warm cooked meal."

They walked into the restaurant and were surprised by all of the varied people there, different characters of men and women from all parts of society: the rich and elite, the Yankee and Confederate, the poor and uneducated, all eating and socializing together. It was a strange mixture of people that had one thing in common, a desire to eat some of the best food the city of Charleston had to offer. Thomas and Phillip found themselves sitting at a table next to two Yankee soldiers, fully dressed in their blue military uniforms, wanting everyone to know which side of the war they were on. The soldiers looked at Thomas and his frontier-like rugged appearance as if he were a man on the run.

Thomas sensed their eagerness for conflict.

"Phillip, just keep your eyes on the menu and let's order us a nice cooked meal. We've got plenty enough trouble waiting on us tonight back at the Inn."

Just as he spoke those words, one of the Yankee soldiers asked them, "Where are you two from?"

Thomas told Phillip to let him do all the talking. "We're from Georgia. Where are you two from?"

"Are you trying to be smart mister? We know where we're from and it's none of your rebel business."

"How do you know that I'm a rebel?"

"By the way you talk," laughed one of the soldiers.

"Well, I take that as a compliment," smiled Thomas.

The other Yankee soldier got up and started over to their table toward Phillip, looking to start a fight. But Thomas quickly stood up, pulled his knife out and held it to the soldier's throat before the blue coat could get a word out.

"Now, boys, we don't want any trouble tonight. The war is over and we're just here like everyone else trying to fill our hunger. Now I suggest you two get yourselves out of here before I make the decision for you."

The two soldiers knew Thomas meant every word and slowly walked out of the restaurant.

"Sorry, Phillip, I didn't want you to see that side of me, but I had no other choice."

"No, that was great, Thomas! I mean, the way you stood up to those two soldiers and pulled your knife out on that blue coat before he could blink his eyes. After seeing you do that, I don't think we'll have any trouble handling those two men near the stable tonight."

A waitress walked up to their table.

"What can I get you two fine gentlemen to eat?" She had a strong southern accent in which was quite charming. She kept eyeing Phillip as if she were interested in him.

Thomas noticed the attraction and whispered in Phillip's ear, "Don't even consider her, boy, we don't plan on staying here long and she ain't the type your daddy wanted me to hook you up with."

Thomas looked up at the waitress smiling and said, "We'll have the Harper's Ferry special and a pitcher of tea."

"Will that be all?" The waitress looked at Phillip trying to catch his eye. Thomas looked at Phillip, then at the waitress, and said with a tone of certainty, "That'll be all."

Phillip was a charming young man. He was tall and good looking and the ladies seemed to be attracted to him. After the waitress brought them their food, Thomas pulled his hat off and sat it in the chair next to him.

"It's time to say the blessing. If there's one thing I've learned in all my travels is to always give thanks."

Thomas and Phillip bowed their heads as Thomas prayed.

"Lord, thank you for the food we are about to receive. I sure don't want to take any of it for granted. I remember those days of hunger during the terrible war when we had little to eat. Bless the Yankee and the Confederate and may we learn to sit down and eat together at the same table. Amen."

Thomas looked around at all the people sitting at the scattered tables. "This town sure has changed a lot since I've last been here. Nothing ever slows down for progress very long and it sure does draw all sorts of characters."

"Daddy always said that nothing ever stays the same or lasts forever, just love for family."

"Well, your daddy sure told you the truth. You know, the whole time I was with him, all he talked about was his family; while kneeling down in them muddy trenches, while marching in all those soaking rains, while sitting around all those open campfires, not knowing if we would make it through another day, his family was all he ever talked about. He always had that far away look in his eye, like he was somewhere else, but he wasn't. It's the only thing that kept him going...his family."

"I don't want to fail my father, Thomas. I don't know the purpose of my going to Georgia yet, but whatever it is, I want to make him proud."

"He's already proud of you, Phillip. Just remember where you come from and always hold to your roots."

Thomas heard gun fire outside and quickly put his hand to his pistol. "Just war reflexes..." said Thomas. "Skills that kept me alive on the battlefield while others around me got killed. Your father sure was fast with a gun too."

"I sure would like to learn how to shoot a pistol."

"It's not that hard, Phillip. It's like anything else, practice makes perfect. When it comes to defending yourself, just remember to never hesitate, and always trust your instincts. Here, hold it in your hands." Thomas gave Phillip his pistol. "First lesson, be comfortable holding it until it becomes as much of a part of you as your own hand."

Phillip kept playing with the pistol, first placing it on the table, then picking it back up again, some of the blue coats sitting close by looking a little nervous. Thomas and Phillip laughed at each other, humored with their facial expressions.

After finishing their meal, they left the restaurant to go back to their room for the night, walking past the Charleston mansion where the ball was still going on.

Near the Inn, Thomas noticed the two men still standing near the stable in the alley, but pretended not to see them. He told Phillip to go ahead to his room and he would be up in a little while. Phillip knew Thomas had a plan and was very capable of handling the matter himself. But still, he wanted to see what was about to unfold, and *who knows*, he thought, *Thomas may end up needing my help*. He went upstairs and pretended as if he went in his room, but instead, opened the window in the upstairs hallway and quietly made his way out onto the roof. He slowly walked around to the front side and looked over the edge to see if he could see the two men or Thomas. By this time, the men had made their way from the alley to the front of the stable. One of them went inside while the other remained near the door, kneeling down behind a large barrel to keep lookout.

When Thomas walked out of the Inn into the street, he looked around but didn't see the men, so proceeded to walk into the stable barn. The man behind the barrel was about to grab him from behind, but Phillip quickly jumped from the roof onto his back, knocking him out cold. Thomas looked around and saw Phillip standing there and one of the men lying flat on the ground, unconscious.

"Well, Phillip, I guess you might be of some help after all. I should have known you were a natural born fighter being the son of John West."

As they walked near the barn entrance, Thomas held his knife in his hand, gripping the handle tight, while Phillip walked close behind, trying not to get in the way. They opened the door very quietly and looked inside. The air was dark and full of shadows. The light from a burning lantern on the street suddenly rushed through the barn when the thief opened a large door leading to the back. The man climbed into Thomas's wagon and started putting things into a cloth bag.

Thomas walked up behind him and said, "Is there anything I can help you with, mister?"

The man turned around and jumped out of the wagon onto Thomas, pulling him down by his shoulders and causing him to fall backward against the hard dirt. They rolled and tussled on the ground, knocking over wooden boxes filled with liquor bottles, stirring up dust. The horses in the stalls neighed wildly as they wrestled for control of Thomas's knife that had fallen from his hand into a bed of straw. One of them hollered out in pain from being stabbed.

Phillip ran to Thomas and rolled his body off the other man.

"That was a close one, Phillip. He almost got the upper hand on me with my own knife."

The other man was lying there in pain, losing a lot of blood. They picked him up and carried him to the town doctor and explained to him what had happened. The doctor immediately sent his assistant to get the sheriff while he proceeded to stitch up the man's wound.

An unwelcome weight of troubling scenes had unfolded in the short amount of time they'd been in Charleston: the Yankee soldiers in the restaurant, the two thieves in the horse stable. *What else could happen in one night,* Thomas thought.

"I believe we each have a nice soft bed waiting for us, Phillip. Let's get some shut eye and we'll leave early in the morning."

"I won't argue with you there, Thomas. I'm just about worn out. But if you don't mind, I'd like to walk down to the marsh alone and sit on the pier for a few minutes. I'll be up in a little while."

Thomas turned toward the marshland and felt a warm breeze brush against his face. "You did good today, son. Your father would be proud."

Thomas dusted his clothes off and walked into the Inn while Phillip walked down to the pier, the stars shining bright in the night sky above the coastal town. He could hear the music from the ball at the nearby mansion still playing in the distance.

He sat there alone, thinking, talking to his parents who were miles away, looking up at the stars and watching the full moon edge its way above the horizon along the creek's waters...

'Hey, Mama. Hey, Daddy. I just wanted to tell you goodnight. I already miss you both very much. Charleston sure is a pretty town. I wish you could see it all lit up. I know its shining bright over Black River, but the moon sure is pretty from where I'm sitting. I'm kind of homesick, and a part of me wants to turn around and go back home. But I know you wouldn't want me to give up now. We've had a long day today, and things could've turned out bad for us. I know it's your prayers keeping me safe, along with Thomas's fighting abilities. He really knows a lot about the land and I'm learning a lot from him. Well, I guess it's time for me to call it a night, so I'll talk to you later. Goodnight, Mama. Goodnight, Daddy.'

Phillip walked back to the Inn...

After Thomas turned the lantern light off, he and Phillip fell fast asleep. The last sound of the violins from the ball fell silent, and it wasn't long before the streets of Charleston became quiet too as the night grew late and beckoned each soul to their place of rest.

Chapter Three

Thomas and Phillip slept later than they'd planned. The sun was well above the tree line when they hitched the wagon to Lee and Stonewall and thanked Charlie Dixon for his generosity in letting them stay the night at the Inn. It was Sunday, and there were men and women dressed in their best walking to the tall, thin framed church - standing out like a lighthouse – in the middle of town, where an old man stood ringing a church bell that echoed throughout the whole city, sounding far into the countryside into the homes of the blacksmith and the banker, of the sharecropper and the landowner, beckoning them all to the place of equal status among men. Families attending the services were greeted by the town minister standing near the front entrance of the church that faced the center of town.

Thomas hollered for Lee and Stonewall to move forward.

They slowly rode by the steepled building on their way out of Charleston. By this time, the church service had begun and Thomas and Phillip could hear the congregation singing...

Rock of Ages, cleft for me, let me hide myself in Thee. Let the water and the blood, from Thy riven side which flowed, be of sin the double cure, save me from its guilt and power.'

"Listen to that, Thomas. Isn't that some of the prettiest singing your ears have ever heard?"

"Sure is, Phillip, the Lord's songs are full of grace and truth. I guess about now my darling wife and children are at Oak Grove singing some of them old time hymns."

"Oak Grove?"

"Yep, Oak Grove. It's a country church in the Bay Gall."

"The Bay Gall?" Phillip had never heard of such names.

"That's right, the Bay Gall. They named the area after a creek that runs through it. When folks back home ask where I live, I just tell them in the Bay Gall. Then they know exactly where I live."

After they passed the church, they could still hear the people singing in the distance...

While I draw this fleeting breath, when I close mine eyes in death, when I soar to worlds unknown, see Thee on Thy judgment throne. Rocky of Ages, cleft for me, let me hide myself in Thee.'

Before they left the town limits, Thomas wanted to take Phillip to a place near the water known as the Point. Here, there were numerous antebellum homes aligned along the shore – known as the Charleston Peninsula – a place of important history during the *War of Southern Independence* where the first shots were fired against the Union-held-fort in the distance.

Thomas stopped Lee and Stonewall in a cool shade, and took his hat off after pulling the brake lever back and locking the wheels in place. He stepped down from the wagon and whispered a few words to himself in what seemed to be a short prayer - a moment of remembrance for the unknown dead scattered all along the countryside, both Yankee and Confederate, buried beneath the earth without a name to honor them by. *Bull Run...Shiloh...the Wilderness...Antietam,* he remembered, *so many lives lost in the destructive labyrinth of lost kinship.* Phillip noticed the tears swelling up in Thomas's eyes as he looked out across the water to the fort called Sumter – the sacred chosen place of civil discord.

Thomas walked over to the water's edge and knelt down, the lines of age showing on his face, his shoulders weary from the many marched miles of war. His eyes scanned across the landscape above the surfaced water, as if he saw something or someone in the distance - his face stern and full of battle, reminiscing on the long days past.

Phillip stepped down from the wagon and walked over to where Thomas knelt near the water.

"Thomas, are you ok?"

Thomas put his hands in the water and splashed a little on his face and neck.

"I'm just taking in the view and storing it away forever in my memory. I'll probably never make it back this way again in my lifetime. You're looking at the place and the fort where it all began, the dividing of soul and spirit, the line drawn in the sands of time by kinsmen apart, like Cain and Abel, brother against brother in bitter rival, hammering the nail in the coffin meant for enemies alone but used for closest of kin. Abraham Lincoln forced South Carolina to make a decision to fire upon Fort Sumter after they'd seceded from the Union, thus prompting a war that would send many American sons home dead, never to see their loved ones again."

"Was it Abraham Lincoln's fault, Thomas?"

"I wouldn't say so, Phillip. The fault was in all Americans not seeing the division of our Country over a long period of time. We let ourselves grow further and further apart until our differences became our vices. War is a cruel taskmaster and should never be fought between one's own countrymen. We Americans, of all civilized people, should never have let our differences start a war between us, but rather, we should've looked within ourselves to determine if the things we believed in were moral and just. Slavery was not a just institution, but neither was a War Between the States which killed so many of our greatest sons. War, Phillip, in and of itself, is not evil, but the reasons for it will either justify or condemn it. America must defend, at all costs, her freedom, but not at the expense of killing her own children when there is no just cause for it. Where was life in this? Where was liberty for all in this? Where was the pursuit of happiness in this? It wasn't in slavery or in a War Between the States. I blame both sides for it. I condemn the North for forcing the war upon us and I blame the South for their unwillingness to give up an immoral institution like slavery that would cause such a division between us."

It seemed Abraham Lincoln had betrayed his own rule of conscience and ethics in declaring war on the South. When Lincoln was in the United States Congress, serving as a Whig, he had protested the Mexican-American War, which lasted from 1846 to 1848. His reasons for protest against the Mexican-American War should have led him to be against declaring war on the Confederacy. Why? Because both were over a controversial land dispute. The siege of Fort Texas prompted the Mexican-American War just as the firing on Fort Sumter sparked a war between Union and Confederate. The Mexican government claimed the land that Fort Texas was built on belonged to Mexico. Contrary, the United States declared that the land north of the Rio Grande belonged to them since the treaties of Velasco. In 1844, US President James Polk made a proposition to purchase the disputed lands from Mexico just as Confederate President Jefferson Davis made a proposition to purchase the disputed land of Fort Sumter from the United States. Just as Mexico refused the US, the US refused the Confederacy. The United States proceeded to build a fort on the north bank of the Rio Grande, the disputed land, just as South Carolina continued to claim Fort Sumter, the disputed land of the Confederacy since secession. Mexico fired on the US fort, killing the United States commander in charge. This sparked the United States President to declare war against Mexico for firing on a federal fort. Abraham Lincoln protested this war, even though a US fort had been fired upon…even though a US fort commander had been killed…even though the US President supported the war. The reason why Lincoln protested the war was because the land in question was "in dispute." If Lincoln had stayed true to his own political past actions, standing up against a war over controversial land disputes, he would have never declared war against the Confederacy. The firing on Fort Sumter was less cause for war than the firing on Fort Texas. No one was killed at Fort Sumter. Only a Confederate horse died. A US commander was killed at Fort Texas. Fort Sumter had clearly belonged to South Carolina at one time, and conditionally sold to the US on the basis that the US wouldn't violate South Carolina laws. Both causes of conflict were over a controversial land dispute. Lincoln's mendacity in declaring war against the South for firing on a US federal fort seemed to contradict his own moral principles that had led him to protest the Mexican-American War. Why did he go against his own ethical code by declaring war against the South? Was it because he didn't want to appear weak in the eyes of his northern colleagues, especially among the Republican Party? Instead of following those same principles that had led him to protest the Mexican-American War, he seemed to have changed his own political code of ethics, going against his own moral conscience in declaring war against the Confederacy. How could Lincoln show great pity to a foreign nation like Mexico, and little regard toward his own brethren and countrymen, the South? If he was blind to his own contradictions in his actions, it came at a heavy cost that would forever stain American soil with blood and loss immeasurable.

On the other side, and just as genuine, many Northerners put the blame on the South and its leader, Jefferson Davis, for leading the country into war, for supporting slavery and its expansion into western territories, and for their unwillingness to remain in the Union. To them, Lincoln was a hero and great leader, a true patriot of the American cause, and Davis, a man guilty of treason. When Sherman's troops were leaving Atlanta on their march to the sea, Sherman looked back toward Atlanta at the black smoke rising high in the air, and he heard some band strike up *John Brown's Body*. He listened with delight as his men sang the song. John Brown was an abolitionist leader who had been hanged for leading a raid at Harper's Ferry, having seized the federal armory and arsenal. This was the same John Brown who previously had five people in Kansas hacked to death with broadswords in front of their families simply for being pro-slavery. For the Union soldiers of Sherman to be singing a song in honor of the murderous John Brown, whose lyrics of *John Brown's Body* praised Brown as being a soldier of the Lord, but spoke of hanging Jefferson Davis to a tree, seemed like a great contradiction. Jefferson Davis believed, as many did up to this time period, that states had a right to peacefully secede. And that this right was based upon the fact that within the United States Constitution the sovereignty of each state of the Union had been maintained and preserved. This peaceful secession seemingly gave the South the right to defend their own coastline and rightfully regain possession of the fort in Charleston harbor that was believed to have been in their territory. Yet, to many in the North, Jefferson Davis was a traitor, the states were in rebellion, and firing upon Fort Sumter was looked upon as an attack against the Union.

It was an emotional moment for Thomas. He loved the South, but he loved America as a whole. Leaving South Carolina was another step for him in getting farther away from his war memories…farther away from the bloody-rivalry now ended. He loved Carolina, but he needed to get back home to Georgia in order to find himself again.

Their next destination was Savannah. They had a long day ahead of them, but were well rested and ready for the trip. After crossing the Ashley, Edisto, and Ashepoo rivers, Thomas and Phillip headed for the Combahee. When they neared the Combahee Ferry crossing, Phillip was amazed at all of the destroyed plantation homes and barns along the road, the burnt-wooden structures that once stood tall and majestic, now brought low by the fires of bitter resentment for slavery. Thomas slowed the horses down so Phillip could take in the devastation the Union forces had brought to the area not long before.

"Thomas, do you know what happened here? Why is there so much destruction in this place?"

"There was a raid against the Confederates positioned here a few years ago from Union forces led by Col. James Montgomery in command of the 2nd South Carolina Infantry. A black lady named Harriet Tubman assisted James in the attack and provided him vital information about the area. Tubman's main purpose was to help rescue black slaves from the region's plantation owners."

"Did they succeed? I mean, did they free any of the slaves or did most of them get killed?"

"I heard they'd freed around eight hundred."

"It sounds like Harriet Tubman is a hero to her own people."

"Well, Phillip, in a way she's a hero to all races of people. I know I fought for the South and pledged my allegiance to the Confederate States of America, but I know when something is immoral like slavery." Thomas paused for a moment. "Miss Tubman did a noble thing here, helping her own people. These burnt ashes had nothing to do with her. Her struggle was one of deliverance, not destruction."

"I've never talked about the issue of slavery with anyone before, not even with my own family. I guess I was afraid of what people might say to me if I told them how I really felt, but I think slavery was an immoral institution like you do. All mankind should be free from being in any kind of bondage against their will, so long as they abide by the moral laws of their own home land."

Thomas rode up to one of the plantation homes that was heavily burnt, stopping the wagon near what used to be the front entrance, where only the door framing and half the front wall now stood, the rest flattened to the foundation.

"Sure is a shame to see all these southern structures burnt to the ground. These large homes were as much a part of the land as the fields and creeks running through it." Thomas could only imagine how magnificent the house once stood amidst the large oaks along the Combahee bluff.

As they walked around the property, they noticed an earthen grave in the back yard, the carved, marked wood showing it to have been the burial place of a small slave boy, named Jacob. They wondered at what illness or misfortune could've fallen on such a young soul. Near the well, a line of water buckets were scattered along the narrow pathway that led toward the house, each covered with twisting vines and weeds, the decaying remains of a *last effort* to weaken a fire that would destroy a way of life. The only thing not covered in ashes was the wood framing posts supporting a large dinner bell – suspended in mid air – attached to a top post. Phillip walked up and pulled an iron handle with a hammer-end that struck the inside of the bell, causing it to ring out along the forsaken landscape where once black slaves worked in the dry dusty fields from sunup to sundown…

Ding…Ding… Ding…Ding

The ringing of the bell brought back past memories of the old plantations, and Thomas could hear the voices of the slaves singing in the fields as they labored in the scorching hot sun…

"When the Sun comes back and the first quail calls, follow the Drinking Gourd,
For the old man is waiting for to carry you to freedom, if you follow the Drinking
Gourd.
The riverbank makes a very good road. The dead trees will show you the way.
Left foot, peg foot, traveling on, follow the Drinking Gourd"

When the last, long sound of the bell ended, a pistol shot echoed through the woods not far from where the river flowed.

Thomas and Phillip climbed in the wagon and hurried down the road through the marshland to the river's edge where the ferry crossed the blackwater. There was a small group of white-soldiered men gathered near the crossing with their horses, waiting for the ferry to work its way back across from the other side. Thomas stopped the wagon and watched the men from a short distance to see what they were up to. The men discussed how they planned on throwing the black man that worked the ferry into the river, but not before beating him with a whip.

There was a white man that operated the ferry too, but he was fast asleep on deck with a whiskey jug sitting next to him.

The men were carrying pistols, and one held a whip, eager to release their hatred on the colored race; by the sound of their voices, Thomas and Phillip could tell they intended on carrying out their evil deed. There had been a lot of hatred for blacks since they were emancipated, even to the extent of some whites murdering them.

When the ferry docked on their side of the river, the black man asked for ferriage from the white men, his voice somewhat afraid and timid, as if still shackled in some small way to his enslaved past. One of the white men walked up to the black man and grabbed his arm: "The only ferriage you're going to get out of us is the tail end of a whip."

"Uh don' wan no trubble mistuh. Uh dis' doin' whuh Uh git pay fuh."

The black man was from the islands.

"Is that a fact? Hear that, boys? 'I'm just doin' what I get paid for.' Well, you shouldn't get paid to do anything. Only humans get paid to work."

About that time, two of the men grabbed the black man and held him up to one of the posts on the ferry, tying both his hands, while another tore his shirt from off his back. The man with the whip positioned himself a few feet away, grasping the handle tight as he prepared to unleash his unbounded hatred. The black man begged them not to beat him, but they only laughed as the cord of the whip struck hard against his back, drawing blood marks on the surface of his skin.

Thomas looked at Phillip to let him know he'd seen enough. He slowly eased his knife out of its pouch with one hand and slipped Phillip a pistol with the other, stepping closer to the ferry and to the men.

The black man hollered out in pain. This woke the passed out operator up, almost causing him to fall off the ferry into the water, his liquor bottle falling in instead. When the operator realized what was going on, he took his pistol out and pointed it at the man with the whip. Then the other men pointed their pistols at the operator. This gave Thomas the time he needed to make his move. Close to where he was standing, there was a long wooden paddle leaning next to a tree trunk near the dock. He picked it up and swung it across the backs of three of the men, causing them to go flying into the water. When the others turned around to see what had happened, Phillip hit one over the head with the butt end of his pistol, knocking him out cold. The white operator held his gun on the other two left standing while Phillip pointed his pistol toward the men in the river. After each man was accounted for, Thomas warned them never to cross this way again, and if it wasn't for a good natured upbringing, he would've drowned them all in the Combahee, but let them go instead. He then reached up and untied the black man's hands from the post, the blood still running down his back over past scars from old slave whippings.

"T'engky, Mistuh. Uh owe oonuh me pay."

"You've paid enough already in one lifetime," said Thomas. "If you did owe me anything, you've already paid me back in giving me the privilege of hitting those men over their backs with this nice wooden paddle."

It was the first time Phillip had ever seen a black man get whipped, and it was something he never wanted to see again as long as he lived. It had never been *common practice* in the South for slaves to be whipped by their white owners, although, depending on their masters, cruel and unusual punishment did exist here and there throughout the states. To see any slave treated with such unjust whippings could never be justified in any decent human beings reasoning. It had never been an accepted practice by those whose southern roots respected all slaves, even if considered property by the federal government. Thomas was one of those southerners, and the black man couldn't thank him enough for what he'd done.

After crossing the Combahee, they wheeled their wagon steadily toward the Georgia line. The sun was scorching hot to the summer sand and storm clouds brewed wildly in the distance, overshadowing the horizon in front of them. The overcast clouds quickly approached and a few stray drops touched Thomas's dusty beard. The wind began blowing and turning with force, bending the tree tops back and forth, almost snapping them into. *No hiding in the back of the wagon for this one*, he thought.

"We're going to have to find a place to weather the storm. The rain is no more than a few fields away. There's an old abandoned barn not far off the road up ahead. Here, Phillip, hold my hat."

He hurried Lee and Stonewall as fast as he could and managed to get to the barn just as the storm hit, the axel in the rear of the wagon being somewhat damaged in the rush. The rain fell heavy and the wind beat hard against the old structure, as if it might fall on them, causing it to lean one way more than the other. Some of the roof came apart and blew away with the twisting winds.

Knowing the lightning might frighten Lee and Stonewall, they tied them to a board attached to the outside corner wall.

After a few minutes, the winds subsided but the rains continued.

"What a beautiful rain, Phillip. I think it might settle in for a while. We'll just sit down right here until it's over. No need in getting any wetter than we have to. We can't afford to get any kind of sickness."

They gathered some loose boards that had fallen from the roof and from the rafters to build a nice warm fire. The air had become chilly cold and they needed to dry their damp clothes from the rain. The light smoke from the burning wood filtered its way through the openings in the barn, rising slowly through the damaged roof into the misty air.

They sat around the small kindled fire talking.

"Thomas, why do you suppose those Yankee soldiers at *Harper's Ferry Kitchen* in Charleston hated the South so much?"

"There could be many reasons, Phillip. There was a lot of hatred that existed before the war, and after it was all said and done, it only grew stronger. Neither side really came out a winner. I can still see all of those dead bodies on the ground lying on top of each other...Yankees on top of Confederates, Confederates on top of Yankees, each one shot by the other in hopes of gaining the higher ground. After all those dead soldiers were buried and the bodily injured returned home, an awful bitterness followed; and it will last for a long time. I guess one good thing that came out of all this was the slaves were set free."

"Do you think the South can make it without slaves?"

Thomas stared into the fire with a look in his eyes that seemed to burn more than the crackling wood, the ashes of human thought rushing through his mind and igniting a red lit passion.

"Nothing can ever destroy our way of life, Phillip. Once it gets into a man's soul, it's there forever...the South. The kind-spirited mother sitting in her rocking chair, the large family Bible resting on the fireplace mantle, the smell of the fresh turned crops in the harvest fields, the toil and sweat framed inside every humble cabin...all exist without the labor of slaves. The ending of slavery in the South will only make us stronger."

"How can that be?" asked Phillip, warming his hands near the fire.

"Slavery and freedom are two vastly different forces of nature and can never co-exist. The one must overcome the other. Getting rid of slavery is like getting rid of some awful disease and the end result makes the body stronger. And so it is with the South. A country that holds to freedom for all races of people will only make those people stronger."

Phillip began to understand the inner struggle that Thomas, and his father, had faced during the war. He could see it in the eyes of Thomas, hear it in his voice, an underlying regret that the South had practiced an institution he had always abhorred. Yet he knew his father and Thomas had to fight for their states...for their country. He knew they were loyal and brave soldiers, and that the institution of slavery did not define who the South was as a whole.

Suddenly, they heard the sound of horses coming from what seemed to be all directions.

Phillip looked out a back wall window and motioned to Thomas: "Yankee soldiers approaching…"

A company of them rode up to the front of the barn from along the muddy path, their sabers clanging with noise as they quickly dismounted.

One of them yelled out to the others, "get those two horses tied to the barn…we'll need them for the journey."

Thomas was not about to let them take Lee and Stonewall. He opened the barn door and with caution walked over to the men in blue uniforms, each soldier well suited and carrying a gun. Phillip came out behind him with his hand by his pistol, ready to fight if necessary.

"How are you men doing?" Thomas paused, could see the suspicion in their eyes. "What brings you soldiers this way?"

"We're on a mission for the Union army. I'm sorry to have to inform you two but we're going to have to take your horses," said one of the high ranking soldiers.

"Now hold on there. How do you expect us to move our wagon on down the trail? Besides, the war is over, and you don't have the right to take our horses."

The captain of the men walked up to Thomas with his finger next to his trigger, "I do apologize for the inconvenience sir, but some things have to be sacrificed for the Union. You'll just have to figure out a way and do the best you can."

There were too many of them to contend with, and no matter how much Thomas wanted to, it was impossible to stop them. He'd seen these kinds before…blue bellies, marked with no regard for decency or respect for another man's property. It wasn't the fact that they were Yankees that made them seem so vile, because he'd seen the same in Confederates. He'd seen the damage that spirit had brought on both sides, from men who chose to ignore the proper path and forsake the common boundaries of civility. He watched as the soldiers plunged through the wagon and took whatever they could get their hands on, leaving only a meager supply. After untying Lee and Stonewall, they rode off through the woods toward Savannah in the damp thick fog, the mud from the horses' hooves kicking high behind them.

He felt helpless. But he'd think things through. He always did.

As the rains subsided, he stared quietly out the window, one hand running through his hair and the other holding tight to his hat, his thoughts lost somewhere in the fading horizon...

For a moment, he was back in Virginia, standing near the banks of the Potomac. He'd went on dispatch and was riding alone to deliver a message, only to be blocked by a company of Yankees passing along the main road. The rains were coming down, and only the thick foliage from the trees blocked the downpour and kept him from getting pneumonia. He would wait for them to camp along the river for the night, and by morning, he would be miles away in safer territory...

Thomas felt his senses come alive, and like that rainy night in Virginia, this would be no different.

"Get ready, Phillip, we're about to rescue Lee and Stonewall from those Yankees."

"Do you really think we'll be able to get your horses back? They have a company of men with rifles and ammunition. Anyway, how are we supposed to catch up with them?"

"I know where they're headed and they'll camp for the night before they cross the Savannah."

"How are we going to get there? We don't have any horses, remember?"

"Actually, I know where we might be able to borrow a couple of steeds. I have a lot of friends along this trail. Just about a mile or so down the road is where old man Wilson Burch lives. I fought with his son during the war and he'll let us use his horses without question. Let's get going."

Wilson was glad to let Thomas and Phillip borrow two of his best horses, especially since using them involved catching up with Yankee soldiers and getting back what was taken from them. They made a mad rush to the Savannah, to the place where the soldiers would be for the night. When they arrived at the river, the Yankees were there just like Thomas had said, some putting their tents up, others sitting around open fires that seemed to light up the whole encampment like scattered lanterns. They stayed in the woods watching the Yankees from a safe distance, waiting for them to settle down…the rains still lightly falling.

"Once we take Lee and Stonewall, we'll head back to the barn and get our wagon, then circle back around to old man Wilson Burch's place to hide for a day or so. I'd expect them to come after us when they find the horses are gone, but they won't know to look for us there," whispered Thomas.

"Supposing we don't make it out alive…supposing those Yankees get wind of us and don't stop shooting until there's nothing left of us."

Thomas thought about John and his promise to look after Phillip.

"Supposing we get Lee and Stonewall back and those Yankees never see hide nor hair of us," whispered Thomas, "that's what I'm supposing."

It was around midnight before the Yanks fell asleep, and the campfires - slowly smothered from the misty rain - burned down to a light smoke. Thomas whispered to Phillip, "Find Lee and Stonewall and I'll keep watch over the soldiers…"

Phillip didn't have any light to see with other than what remained of the weakening fires, and through the darkness a light fog from the misty river hovered low, making it more difficult to see. He crawled through the mud and the wet dirt, careful not to make any noise that might alarm the Yanks; Thomas watched from the distant tree line. He finally spotted Lee and Stonewall not far from the river's edge away from the other horses, somewhat calm in demeanor despite their recent capture. He made his way slowly to where they were and untied them, leading them past the soldiers' tents into the woods nearby.

One of the soldiers woke up, and having heard a noise, walked out of his tent to look around. He saw Phillip edging his way into the woods with Lee and Stonewall, after which, he took his pistol out to fire into the air. But Thomas took the butt end of his knife and knocked the soldier over the head with it before he could pull the trigger.

Thomas rushed to the woods.

"Quickly, Phillip, they'll be looking for us as soon as they find out we've taken the horses."

They took off toward the old abandoned barn to get their wagon and then circled back around to Wilson Burch's place.

When the Yankee soldier came to, he woke the others up and informed them that the men they'd taken the horses from earlier had stolen them away.

They quickly mounted their horses.

"Any man that manages to take these rebel men captive will be promoted and given a week's wages!" exclaimed their Yankee captain. "We'll show them what happens to rebels who steal from the Union army."

The soldiers made their way back to the abandoned barn, but by then, Thomas and Phillip had managed to get the wagon and hide it near Wilson's place.

The Yankees encircled the area and managed to stumble onto the Burch farm, their lanterns lit up like the dawning of a new day. Mr. Burch could see the lights spread out in every direction, appearing and disappearing through the trees from the main road.

Thomas and Phillip had climbed up in the rafters of the barn, while the horses and the wagon were hidden in an old shelter down below Burch's field.

The soldiers knocked on Wilson's door.

He took his time before coming to the front. "How may I help you gentlemen?"

"We're trying to find two men who stole two of our horses tonight. Have you happened to see anyone pass this way?"

"I sure haven't, captain. If anyone passed by my place, I would know it. I wish I could help you soldiers but I can't."

"Well, do you mind if we look around?"

"I sure don't. Feel free to look anywhere you would like." But Wilson hoped they wouldn't.

The Yankee soldiers walked up to the barn where Thomas and Phillip were hiding, their musket rifles pointed in front of them, ready to fire at any sudden movement. After searching the stalls and the hay stacks, one soldier looked up toward the rafters, his lantern light fading in and out, creating a dark shadow that helped conceal Thomas and Phillip from his view. Phillip held his breath, careful not to make a sound. He knew they'd be caught, no way to hide if they kept searching, and his journey with Thomas would come to an abrupt end. He thought about his mother and father and wondered how word would get back to them. Would it be the old man? Surely he'd be the one to take his bullet-ridden body back to Black River. *But Wilson didn't even know where his parents lived.* The sweat poured from his face to the dirt floor below. He knew Thomas wouldn't surrender and it would be a fight to the end. Then suddenly, the captain gave orders for the soldiers to mount up, that there was no need in wasting any more energy looking for the rebels. *Time is of the essence,* he said, *and we have to get to our destination.*

Phillip wondered at their retreat. *Why would they give up?* It didn't matter now. He was glad they were out of danger and he'd live to see another day. He and Thomas climbed down from the rafters once the soldiers' horses fell silent along the darkened road.

Thomas grinned with a sigh of relief.

"Well, looks like we've outsmarted those Yanks again, Phillip. Or should I say, Lee and Stonewall did…"

They laughed and gave the rebel yell.

By this time, Mr. Burch had made his way to the barn, his fragile body marked with an unfolding age. He didn't have much to keep him going other than a few farm animals he fed each day, and one could readily sense his days were coming to an end.

"Mr. Burch, we sure do appreciate everything you've done for us," said Thomas.

"Well…to tell you the truth, I haven't had this much excitement in I don't know when. I feel more alive than I have in a long time, and I have you two to thank," laughed Wilson. "Y'all are welcome to stay here as long as you want."

That night they slept in Wilson's barn.

The katydids could be heard in the warm night air as Thomas and Phillip rested on their straw beds, still awake and talking about the ending of another long day. The stars shone bright in the cloudless sky now touched dimly by a crescent moon and the Spanish moss hanging from the aged trees mourned with the surrounding land. It was the sadness of Mr. Wilson that brought a depression to the place. They could see him through the barn door sitting on the front porch in his rocking chair, the glare of the moon reflecting off his straggly white beard as he rocked back and forth, his eyes gazing out into the dark as if to a time and place far distant yet so near.

"He looks as if he's a lonely old man," said Phillip. "He doesn't have a family?"

"It's a sad story. His son was killed early in the war. When they brought his body back home in a wagon, his mother couldn't handle the loss of their only child and slowly grieved herself to death. They're both buried a good ways from the house, underneath the old oak tree. That's what he's looking at…their graves."

"I can't imagine the sorrow he must be feeling…"

"It's tragic…when everything you've worked for your whole life is suddenly taken away. He'll probably take his last breath sitting in that old rockin' chair…staring into the past…"

They watched Mr. Burch rock back and forth until they both fell asleep.

It was late the next evening when they left the Burch place, hoping by then the federal soldiers would be gone. Mr. Burch waved goodbye to them as they started down the road toward Savannah.

"It won't be long now, Phillip, and we'll be in Georgia. Have you ever been to Savannah?"

"I don't reckon I have. I've always wanted to visit there, but never had the chance."

"Well, you're going to now. We're going to pass through Savannah on our way to Statesboro. One of my wagon wheels is damaged and I know a good wheelwright there who can fix it up like new."

As they approached the Savannah River, Thomas told Phillip the story of Tomochichi.

"It was near the bluffs along the Savannah where an Indian named Tomochichi once lived. He was instrumental in helping General Oglethorpe settle Savannah and make peace with other Indian tribes."

"What ever happened to him?"

"Well, he died of a good old age and was buried in the city not far from the river. Yes sir, Indians used to roam all along this whole territory. Now, they're all gone. I reckon the times had to change and make room for the settlers."

"Seems like we owe a lot to Tomochichi for having done so much..."

"Time and eternity will forever reward his memory. They will not forget his hands of friendship reaching out toward an unsettled people. The works of man sometimes goes unnoticed in the annals of history, but you can trace them down in every phase of society: on city sidewalks, in town squares, engraved in words on chiseled stone."

Soon they arrived near the place where they were to cross the Savannah, and the Yankee soldiers they met the day before were no where in sight.

The river was large, and on one side was South Carolina, and on the other, Georgia, and there were boats going up and down it all the time, cargo and passenger ships alike, traveling along its wide waters. The ferry crossing they came to was a few miles up river from the city of Savannah, in a quiet place once known in colonial times as Joseph's Town.

The tenant of the boat welcomed all the passengers.

"Ladies and gentlemen, all aboard! It's time to cross the old Savannah. You best be getting on the ferry now if you plan on reaching Georgia clay, cause I won't be coming back across today!"

There were a few others besides Thomas and Phillip who were crossing the Savannah into Georgia, all boarding the ferry with their possessions. It was a well built ferry and capable of carrying a good many people at one time. The tenant released the vessel from the dock and Phillip was now on his way, floating smoothly beneath the open sky, away from the old life and into the new. From this day forth, both sides of the river would hold a special place in his heart.

One of the passengers was a well dressed lady, standing next to a young, rich looking man in a suit and tie. The man struck up a conversation with Thomas and Phillip. "Hello gentlemen. With whom may I say I have the pleasure of speaking with?"

"My name is Thomas Hendrix and this is Phillip West."

"Hello, Thomas. Hello, Phillip. My name is Pierre de Leon."

"Don't you mean Ponce de Leon," said Thomas laughing.

"Oh no," said the man, "Pierre de Leon. I am on my way to Savannah to inherit a fortune my great uncle left me in his will. And this is my fiancée, Guinevere."

"You sure your name isn't King Arthur." Thomas seemed to be entertained by this odd couple.

"Oh no," said the man, "Pierre De Leon. I was born in Spain. My father came over on a passenger ship from Europe in hopes of finding a better life in America. He started out as a tax collector in Boston. After the war ended, my mother's brother wrote a letter to her. The letter stated that he was in ill health in Savannah and needed us to come right away. My mother and father both caught a terrible fever and died in Richmond on the way here. I sent a letter to my uncle in Savannah letting him know where I was and that his sister had died. Just when I was about to put my stakes down in Richmond, I received a letter from Savannah addressed to one Pierre De Leon. It was a letter from the Executor of the Estate of my uncle. It seems as if after my uncle had died, I was the only heir left in the family. I inherited his entire fortune."

Guinevere was a beautiful lady but seemed to be a woman of high maintenance.

"She is from Charleston," smiled Pierre. "We met there while I was passing through to Savannah. Didn't we dear?"

She nodded and smiled to confirm. She didn't seem all that excited to be with him, and a sort of shallow façade covered her facial expressions that made her less desirable to honest men. Her interest seemed to be more in Pierre's inheritance than in his charm. Thomas had met many like her while traveling through the southern towns, gold diggers he called them, not the kind that dug into the mountains or in the streams but in the pockets of rich young suitors. He kind of felt sorry for Pierre.

"Sure is a beautiful day to be crossing the river," said Thomas, looking out across the water into the clear blue sky.

When they approached the Georgia side, the tenant of the ferry maneuvered the boat in line with the dock. "Ladies and gentlemen, get ready to step off the ferry and onto rich Georgia soil."

Just as the ferry approached the dock, something floating underneath the water jarred the ferry, and the young lady, Guinevere, lost her balance and fell overboard. Without thinking, Pierre jumped in after her, swimming frantically toward his newly found fiancée. But her body quickly disappeared underneath the flowing river and her last call for help faded beneath the surfaced water. The young lady had been pulled under by a swift underlying current, and just as quickly as she'd come into this world, she'd now left it. Thomas threw a rope over the edge of the boat toward Pierre and yelled for him to grab hold of it. Barely able to keep his head above the water himself, going under, then up again, he was finally able to secure a tight grip. Once safely onboard, the sudden shock of losing Guinevere forced him back into the water, but Thomas grabbed his arm and pulled him back in, reassuring him it was too late. The Spaniard leaned on the side-railing weeping, shivering wet, unable to be consoled. He no longer held an air of superiority, but was terribly humbled by the tragic drowning of his fiancée. Only time would heal such a nightmare occurrence.

Once on land, Thomas and Phillip said their last goodbyes to the Spaniard, still lost in his grief holding to the side railing, unable to reconcile himself with the loss of Guinevere.

After they hitched Lee and Stonewall to the wagon, they rode toward Savannah along the old Augusta road, sometimes near the river's edge, the scenery bringing back former memories to Thomas. It was beautiful land along the old Augusta, where the warm breeze gently blew the Spanish moss hanging softly from the coastal trees. There was so much history along this stretch, a place where magnificent plantations were established along the banks of the river. Thomas stopped the wagon at the entrance of *Mulberry Grove* and thought how quiet it was.

No wagons or buggies going in and out. No recent tracks in the sand to mark the turning of wheels. He led Lee and Stonewall down the road that led to the large plantation house that rested on a high bluff by the river, gracefully overlooking the rice fields along the great marsh land. Live oaks lined the road on both sides as they rode along, and a cast of shadows from the twisting limbs quietly touched the sands beneath. As they neared the plantation, the image at Mulberry reminded Thomas of Sherman's *March to the Sea*, a vengeful path marked with smoke and ash and debris. The Union general had spared no plantation homes along the river, burning them to the ground, without the slightest regard for their rich southern heritage, and the beautiful landscape that once belonged to the Grove had gained no sympathy. The antebellum home that once reflected the morning sun beaming across the Savannah had been burnt to its foundation, and the silence of the land could be heard by the flowing of the water in the river. The history at Mulberry dated back to 1733, to the time of General Oglethorpe and his plan to use Joseph's Town as an outpost for the city of Savannah. The Trustees of Georgia also wanted to use the Grove as a place to plant mulberry trees and produce silk. After the Revolutionary War, it became the living quarters of General Nathaniel Greene, and near the turn of the century, Eli Whitney's cotton gin was invented on its fertile soil. But now, it seemed a ghostly and forsaken place. The river beyond the bluff had not changed its course, but Sherman had forever silenced the Grove. Thomas turned the wagon near the edge of the Savannah and stopped to view the abandoned rice fields being softly touched by the passing winds. It was here, in 1791, where President George Washington stopped his boat to visit the widow Catharine Greene on his way to Savannah during his southern tour. *Sacred ground,* he thought, despite its history of slavery and indentured servitude. The plantation's past was not unlike the rest of America, in that the continent as a whole had been built, in some part, from such labor, directly or indirectly. Sherman neglected to remember this, and his burnings of southern homes was nothing more than individual dissimulation.

He felt a small part of himself come alive again, a natural human element that had been silenced by the blood and brutality of the last few years. It was as if the dust and debris that had covered his soul during the war had been suddenly swept clean by a refreshing southern wind and he could breathe normal again. A tear trickled down his cheek and across his beard as he thought of home being not so far away. *Home...it won't be long. All the lonely nights sleeping under the stars wondering if the sun would ever rise...all the cold winter mornings waking up to the sounds of war, separated from loved ones, will soon be a thing of the past.* He wondered if she'd be in the shadows somewhere waiting for him...his loyal and precious wife. Maybe he'd find her sitting quietly on the front porch where they used to sit every evening, or standing beautifully alone underneath the oak tree with her hair fixed like an array of spring flowers awakened by the morning sun? He could hear the laughter of his children all around as if they were playing near the river's edge, but the sound of a steamboat passing in front of Mulberry Grove reminded him he wasn't home yet. He watched until the boat passed out of view from the plantation bluff.

On their entry into Savannah, Phillip was astonished at all the people, and the city layout fascinated him. There were merchants and seamen, farmers and city folk, a town full of activity and life, without any signs of ever being captured by Sherman's army. Beautiful live oaks lined the streets downtown, marked with numerous squares, one in which, Tomochichi, the Indian leader of the Yamacraw, was buried. Despite the fires that had taken two-thirds of its homes in the early part of the century, there still existed great architectural structures. There were stone foundations and walls along the river and a cobble road built with ballast taken from ships harbored along the wharves and warehouses.

Much history had been preserved in Savannah, its beauty marveled at like a painting or work of art by Michelangelo. Its splendor was recognized by Union General Sherman when he spared burning it in 1864. He wrote to President Lincoln on December 22nd, "I beg to present you as a Christmas gift the city of Savannah with 150 heavy guns and plenty of ammunition and also 25,000 bales of cotton." Notwithstanding the fires and storms and wars, the city had kept much of its history intact and vibrant.

They rode down by the riverfront and asked a passerby if they knew of an Inn where they could spend the night. The stranger pointed them toward *The Pirates' House*.

"*The Pirates' House?* What kind of a name is that? Thomas, I don't know if it's such a good idea to go to a place where pirates might be."

Thomas laughed.

"No need to worry, Phillip. There are no pirates around here anymore."

They made their way near the waterfront and found the wheelwright shop just past *the market district*, facing the ships and sails moving along the river. The wheelwright was a former Confederate soldier that had made and repaired wheels for the South during the Civil War, and he knew Thomas well.

"Why, if it isn't Jim Banks…the wheelwright of all wheelwrights," said Thomas, parking his wagon near the front of the shop. Jim looked around and smiled.

"Thomas Hendrix. What on earth brings you this way?"

"A rear axel. I didn't think I'd make it this far and I know I won't make it any farther without your help."

"Well let me take a look and see how bad it's damaged."

Jim walked over to the rear wagon wheel and knelt down.

"I would say it definitely needs working on, Thomas. I can have you fixed up and ready to go by tomorrow."

"Thanks, Jim. We planned on spending the night in Savannah anyway. We're about to head over to the Pirates' House and see if any rooms are available."

Jim had his own livery stable next to his blacksmith shop, so Thomas left the horses with him for the night as well.

As they walked along the waterfront, Phillip couldn't help but wonder in amazement at all the ships in the river: steamships, brigs, barks, schooners, and many other sailing vessels.

It was here in the Savannah harbor, on May 22nd 1819, where the SS Savannah set sail for Liverpool, the voyage lasting some 27 days. It would be the first steamship to cross the Atlantic. Earlier that same month, US President James Monroe had visited the port city and took an excursion to Tybee Island on the SS.

"Thomas, have you ever been on a sailing ship before?"

"I can't say that I have, Phillip."

"I haven't either, but I've always wanted to get on one. They seem to represent a sense of freedom and adventure, a departure from all that ties a man down, sailing into the deep blue ocean along lands uninhabited, filled with huts, dark caves, and tropical scenery that make you forget everything that's bad in the world. What do you think about going on one of those scheduled tours?"

"Well, I guess we have a little time to spare."

They walked over to one of the bark ship's captains and asked him if there was a ship that gave short tours. The captain pointed them to a schooner vessel. The schooner was a lot smaller than the other ships but was faster and easier to maneuver in the water. They walked over to the tour boat, where a sign near the walkway plank read:

"Come aboard and hear tales of fishermen, traders, pirates, men of war and privateers! See the attendant for tour times and costs. Be sure to make friends with the Captain to avoid having to walk the plank!"

They paid for their tickets and walked across the plank onto the schooner. There was a good crowd of people boarding, all eager and waiting to sail the waters of the Atlantic. The tour would last a few hours, but would leave them enough time to get their rooms for the night.

It was a dramatic boat ride for the both of them. Phillip's eyes filled with wonder as the schooner made its way out to sea, hearing stories of pirates and privateers. Still young and impressionable, he could feel the characters come alive in front of him as the captain took great liberty in describing the old sea tales handed down from generation to generation. The salty water in the air, the bow of the ship cutting through the waves, and the wind pushing against the sails made the boat ride memorable.

"Have you ever seen anything like it?" asked Phillip, standing straight and tall with his hair twisting in the breeze, fighting the wind blowing across the deck.

"I've seen a picture or two of boats sailing in the open waters, but being on one expresses more to me than a thousand paintings of all the ships in the sea."

They seemed to forget about the purpose of their journey. It was good for Thomas to get his mind off the war that had taken him captive behind the gates of a Union prison camp, the memory of it still fresh in his thoughts, imprisoning him behind the bars that had separated him from family and home. His spirit seemed to heal even more as the vessel sailed the Atlantic Ocean and took him farther away from the landscape that had caused him such emotional injury and fatigue. Out there, in the deepening sea, there seemed to be no dividing line between North and South, just the salty air and the open waters that welcomed anyone who wished to sail her turning tides.

After the boat ride, they walked over to the Pirates' House where they were cordially welcomed by the attendant.

"Welcome to the Pirates' House, mates. Me name is Silver Hairs and I'll be seeing to your stay."

The man was very old and dressed in seamen's clothing.

"We're just here for one night and we don't need anything fancy," said Thomas.

"No problem, captain. I'll see to your things and take them to the shipmaster's quarters." The attendant had a wooden leg and walked with a cane. He gave the impression that he was an old pirate. "I'll be fixing you two ye breakfast in the morning before ye sail the seven seas."

"Seven seas?" asked Phillip.

"Oh, I'm sorry, me lad, I have me ole flashbacks now and again. Before ye go your own way me lad." The man appeared to be almost a hundred years old.

Silver hairs took a key out of his side pocket and opened up the door to their room upstairs.

"Here ye go me lads. If ye need anything at all, I'll be down below looking at some old treasure maps through the night."

Thomas and Phillip were anxious to climb into their beds and get some rest for the night, for the days journey had made them unusually tired and the old man wanted to talk until the oil burned low, telling mystical stories of ocean pirates whose spirits still roamed the hallways.

Once they made it to their room, they wasted no time in pulling back the covers.

"Goodnight, Thomas."

"Goodnight, Phillip."

Just when Thomas was about to fall asleep, Phillip began talking out loud, more to himself than to Thomas.

"I can't get that woman out of my head."

Thomas groaned from being awakened. He leaned up in his bed and looked at Phillip half asleep. "What woman are you talking about? I don't remember you talking to any woman this evening. Besides, there's not a woman we've met on this trip worth losing any sleep over."

"Guinevere. She was there one minute with her whole life in front of her and then gone the next. That's the first time I've ever seen anyone get killed."

"I understand, Phillip. I saw a lot of people die in the war. You never really get used to it. The first one you see die is always the worst. You have to realize that life is short and we have to live everyday as if it were our last."

"I just can't get her out of my mind. The whole incident seemed so purposeless," said Phillip, as if he were searching for an answer to his own hidden questions concerning life.

"There's nothing on earth purposeless. We're all God's creatures and we are put here for a reason. When it's our time to go, then it's our time to go," said Thomas, trying to assure Phillip the best he could. He had been through this before in the war and had to overcome the emptiness that life sometimes brought whenever he saw the death of someone he knew.

"I believe that too, Thomas," said Phillip, "I guess I just needed to hear someone remind me that everything has a purpose, even when someone dies."

After Thomas fell asleep, Phillip stayed awake for sometime, hearing the small thumping sound of Silver Hair's wooden leg going back and forth on the wide plank flooring downstairs. There was something about the old man that drew his curiosity, and the remark about treasure maps caused Phillip to ease out of bed and go see what the aged seaman was up to. He walked quietly down the squeaky stairs, and once below, he saw Silver Hairs studying something sitting on a table in the middle of the parlor. The old man had his back to Phillip, and without turning around, he said, "A young seaman in the making. Hmmm…so ye have an interest in the treasure maps, do ye? Well, don't just stand there…"

Phillip was amazed that the old man had even seen him. As he entered, he noticed the parlor was decorated more like a masked ship belonging to the sea than it did for land, and a large spyglass mounted on a tripod faced an open window that looked out over the river.

"I was just curious about the…"

"Hidden treasure?"

The old man turned from the table and walked over to the spyglass. He put his eye to the scope and gave a few sighs. "Yes, the hidden treasure. Well…I've been searching for it me whole life. It would take a month's end to tell ye the endless stories, but I can see the pirate's interest seated in your eyes."

"Is there really hidden treasure out there?"

"Come here and look in the scope and tell me what ye see."
Phillip walked over to the spyglass and looked through the lens.

"What am I supposed to be looking for?" inquired Phillip.

"Anything that catches your eye…"

"I can see a masted ship leaving the port."

"How many hold the sails?"

"Just one."

"And the sails, are they square or triangular?"

"Triangular."

"Are they set along the keel or perpendicular to the center?"

Phillip looked puzzled. "What is a keel?"

"Sorry me lad. I forget ye are no seaman. The keel is the beam that runs through the middle of a ship from the bow to the stern. The spine me lad…the strength of the hull."

"If I'm correct in saying, it appears the sails run along the keel"

"Arrrr, sounds like a quick *sloop* to me. The kind that Blackbeard himself favored in the open seas."

"I've heard of Blackbeard."

"I'm sure ye have me lad. But not many know of the tragic death he met...his head severed from his body; and with it, a secret knowledge of where his hidden treasure was buried. I've been studying these maps for years in search of it. But now I'm an old man, and I doubt I will ever find it."

Phillip walked over to the table where the maps were spread out. Sillver Hairs had dates and lands and names of ships and battles involving Blackbeard marked all over, trying to connect the missing pieces.

"I am so close I can smell it," murmured Silver Hairs. "And it is for hidden treasure ye seek after yourself me lad."

"What do you mean?"

"The right lady to spend your life with. It is what every young man searches for...more valuable than anything Blackbeard ever buried beneath the deep coastal sands. Falling in love is the greatest treasure of all, and one day you'll find it me lad."

The old man didn't say anything much after that, he just kept looking at the maps, lost somewhere in deep thought between land and sea.

The next morning, after eating breakfast Silver Hairs had prepared for them, Thomas and Phillip walked over to the wheelwright shop near River Street. When they got there, Jim Banks had the wagon wheel fixed like new. Thomas gladly paid Jim for his services, hitched up Lee and Stonewall, and left Savannah for Statesboro.

Chapter Four

The day began like any other on the Hendrix farm, with the normal, day to day operations being carried out by a scheduled set of chores that kept things in a natural order, like an electromagnetic pendulum. The boys, Elbridge, Andrew, Thomas, George, David, and William, had responsibilities of their own feeding the livestock, chopping the wood, tending to the crops, while the girls, Laura, Annie, and Mary Jane, helped with the sewing, cooking, and washing of clothes. Elizabeth, the wife of Thomas Hendrix, was incessantly finding ways to keep her children busy and out of trouble, something she found quite challenging at times without a father figure around to help keep the young ones in line. Her strong-willed and determined spirit never failed to see beyond the current war to a day when the struggle would be over and Thomas would be home again. A deep felt longing for her husband's return clung to the chambers of her heart with every breath she took, and in the evenings, before the sun went down, she'd keep her eyes on the fading horizon in hopes of seeing the man she'd given her life to come walking out of the darkening shadows.

She was a woman of inexorable resolve despite all the hardships and difficulties that had swept across the South the last few years. Her unwavering hands held the tie that binds and provided her family with an unfailing sense of security. After she'd received the letter that Thomas had been released from the Union prison camp in Maryland and expected to return to Statesboro any day, her countenance glowed with increasing anticipation.

She asked the children to get dressed after hitching the horse to the wagon: "Today, we're going to visit your Uncle Enoch and Aunt Emeline Beasley. We have to tell them the goods news that your father Thomas is coming home from the war."

The sound of her own words seemed like a distant reality to her, as if it were a passing dream. *Thomas coming home*, she thought, *is it really true?* She'd seen so many southern widows dressed in mournful black and passed by too many familiar homes filled with ashes of death that she found it difficult to accept the reality of her own husband's return. She kept whispering the words in the letter over and over to herself…*Thomas has been released from the Yankees…Thomas will be home any day*, until she convinced herself it wasn't just a passing dream. Tears trickled down her softened face as she rode along the country road, years of worry and fatigue finally released with every quiet breath she took.

Enoch and Emeline lived just across the creek from the Hendrix farm in an area known as Beasley Town, where the Bay Gall waters emptied into the Ogeechee just north of where the old road ran. They had several children of their own: Enoch Jr., Wash, Steven, Joe, Van, John, Mary Jane, Laura, and Adeline. The Beasleys owned a sizable amount of land along the river, a place of swampy terrain, vast lowlands, creeks, green palmettos, swamp chestnut oaks, and aged cypress.

When Elizabeth arrived at her sister's house, Emeline was sitting on the front porch making a dress on a *Howe* lockstitch for her daughter, Mary Jane, while Enoch experimented with a self-scouring *John Deere* moldboard being pulled by his mule named Caliber…a strong wind forming a dust bowl behind him that swept across the open field.

Some of Enoch's sons were busy digging for *Eisenia fetida*, the red wigglers, out behind the barn, and others were making fishing poles out of dried bamboo canes straightened by the weight of the brick. Enoch had promised to take them fishing after finishing the fields, a tradition he kept every year during the planting season.

The girls were busy picking flowers along the edges of the field to give to their mother, placing them in a tall thin-glass vase, neatly arranging the various colored blooms.

Now go find your cousins smiled Elizabeth as she stepped down off the wagon. She loved her children deeply, and the thought of them having their father back filled her heart with joy.

"What a nice surprise, Elizabeth," said Emeline, putting the fabric to the side.

"Emeline, I've got great news to tell you."

"I know. You've finally saved up enough money to buy that new dress you've been wanting?"

"I wish. Thomas is coming home!"

"I can't believe it. When are you expecting him?"

"Any day. I received a letter a few days ago telling of his release. It still doesn't seem real though. It's been such a trying time raising the children and tending to the farm all alone. But now, all of that's about to change."

"Oh, Elizabeth, I'm so excited for you. I know you've been through a lot and have kept a good spirit through it all. It will be like old times again. You and Thomas, me and Enoch, all together again. Say, why don't we prepare for a nice big gathering, a sort of welcome home celebration for his return? We can have an open dinner at Nevils Creek Church."

"Why, that sounds wonderful, Emeline. I'll start the planning and we'll have a *welcome home* celebration Thomas won't ever forget."

As soon as Enoch finished working in the field, he put the *plowshare* under the shelter, and the deep furrowed rows he was able to cut into the soil convinced him of the *John Deere's* worth.

He walked over to the porch where Elizabeth and Emeline were sitting, talking up a storm like they hadn't seen each other in years. "Hey, Elizabeth, what's all the conversation about?"

"It's Thomas, he's coming home!"

"That's great news. Emeline and I were just talking last night about how much we hoped for his safe return."

"Emeline came up with a wonderful idea of having Thomas a welcome home celebration dinner at Nevils Creek Church."

"I think that would be an honorable thing to do. I'll help spread the word around the community. I'm sure he'll find a lot of family and friends showing up to welcome him home," said Enoch, dusting off his overalls as he called out for the boys to grab their fishing poles.

Enoch Jr. ran to get his container filled with worms he'd dug up earlier in the day, only to find that his brother, Wash, had emptied them all on the ground. Wash was mad at Enoch Jr. for having broken his tan cane-pole, although by accident, and emptying his brother's tin can seemed like the vengeful thing to do.

"Daddy!" cried Enoch Jr. to his father. "Wash emptied my can of wigglers."

"Don't worry, Son, I've got plenty enough and to spare. We'll settle this dispute later," said his father, staring at Wash with a stern look of sure-to-come discipline. "Now let's get to the river before the fish stop biting."

Enoch, his sons, and the Hendrix boys, all walked together down to the river along the old road, passing through the narrow gate by the old tobacco barn, standing tall and narrow in the open pasture, then past the *Langstroth* bee hives set wide in uniform rows at the end of the field. Just before entering the piney woods, they stopped at the catalpa trees to gather some worms.

"Watch out for the coachwhip boys."

Enoch smiled when they bunched up close together.

"Daddy," said Van, "tell us the story of the old man who fought the fast snake."

Enoch stood still near a running creek that passed over the old road.

"Well…it happened a long time ago, when the coachwhips were more aggressive and numerous, crawling all along these mystic bottoms. A few of the old snakes still lurk in the hanging vines and shady trees. One day, an old man went fishing down to the river in hopes of catching a ray-finned catfish for supper. As he walked along a twisting creek, he stumbled across one of the fastest coachwhips he'd ever seen. The snake was in no mood for strangers, and he proceeded to chase the old man through the flat-woods, his head almost reaching above the palmettos as he followed hard after him. Knowing he was unable to out run the snake with his worn-out knees, he turned and faced the *coach*, using his long cane pole to hold it at bay. The line attached to the end got caught around the snake's tail just as the *coachwhip* tried to lash him with it. The aged man was finally relieved he'd hoodwinked the old whip. No one knows exactly what happened to the snake, but many say he still lurks in these woods with the fishing line still wrapped around his tail."

The boys enjoyed hearing the *tall tale*, and they kept their eyes wide open as they walked along the river road.

When they got to the river, Enoch walked the boys close to the sunken trees and low hanging limbs stretching out along the river banks and creek entries before paddling his boat out to the bends and eddies - first upstream, then back down. The Ogeechee waters were low and the redbreast sunfish and bluegill in the deep holes loved to go after the hooked mole crickets, nightcrawlers, and worms. Before the sun lowered, they'd managed to catch numerous stump knockers, warmouth, and redeye. They cleaned them underneath the long shelter Enoch had built near the river's edge the previous spring.

Returning from the river, Enoch walked next to his son Wash, who kept his head down, knowing his father was about to give him a talking to.

"Daddy, I'm sorry for what I did to Enoch Jr., but he broke my favorite *cane* pole."

"Son, when I was a young boy, around about your age, my father gave me the whipping of my life for fighting with another boy at school. He'd stolen my lunch and I confronted him about it, which turned out to be the wrong thing to do. I was upset and didn't think good of him for doing such a thing. I later learned that his father had abandoned *him and his mother* and left them without any means of support. The boy was hungry and hadn't eaten anything for days when he decided to steal my lunch. When my dad told me of what the boy had been going through and that revenge was never the answer to settle such disputes, I felt sorry for him instead of anger. I learned the lesson of my life: many times what we think deserves revenge may only need understanding."

"Thanks, Daddy, for telling me that story. I feel bad about what I've done and I'll apologize to Enoch Jr."

"You're welcome, Son. I'll make you another fishing pole just like the one you had before."

Wash smiled and ran to Enoch Jr. to make things right. It made their father proud when he saw them talking again.

Elizabeth stayed and ate supper with her sister and family, the kitchen table covered with stew and corn dodgers and fried fish, a tasty southern meal seen quite often in the country homes aligned along the river.

The sun began to set when the Hendrix family made it back home from the Beasleys. Elizabeth was putting the horse in the stall when she heard the dogs barking. She looked out of the barn window and saw a covered wagon coming up the road in the fading twilight, the distant sound of a harmonica echoing out across the green grassed fields. She could hear someone singing a familiar song...

'The years creep slowly by, Lorena, Snow is on the grass again, the sun's low down in the sky Lorena, The frost gleams where the flowers have been.'

It was the song Thomas sang to her before galloping off toward the crimson lines of the *Blue* and *Gray*, where soldiers gathered like the uniformed dried kermes of the Mediterranean. She hurried to the front gate and stood near the garden of blossomed Madonna white lilies whose scented flowers framed the sultry air with a perfumed fragrance descended years ago from the Balkans. She wished she'd had time to put a more suitable dress on, something that would match the beauty of the lilies that surrounded her. She looked down at her hands and noticed how rough they'd become, unlike the smooth skin she'd nurtured before the war. Until now, she hadn't thought much about it: her nails, her hair, her dress, her perfume. *After all, city women weren't the only ones who nurtured their femininity.* The conflict had taken all of that away from her - her desire for beauty - and she'd accepted it. But now, hearing his voice echoing out across the open field swept away the last few years of relentless labor like a soaking rain. She suddenly felt like a lady again. She'd been invariably lost in being a mother and father, but now, she could return to being a wife. Thomas was home.

She ran to meet him.

Thomas stopped Lee and Stonewall near a grove of cedars when he saw the shadowed form of his wife approaching like a wind blown silhouette across the pale horizon. He quickly stepped off the wagon toward Elizabeth, her face lit up with such cradled passion as she hurried up the rising hill toward him. Thomas had been accustomed the last few years to seeing Yankees running up ridges at similar paces with only deadly projectiles whizzing past his head. But now, those tragic images were being replaced by the warm flowing tears running down his wife's face. No screams of death and destruction approaching…no defenses necessary. He could now let go of the coldness and open up to the love that now tenderly embraced him.

"Elizabeth, my precious wife, it's so good to hold you. I've never felt anything warmer in my whole life."

"Thomas…I've been waiting for this day for so long," said Elizabeth, kissing him multiple times on his face and lips.

After Thomas wiped the tears from his wife's eyes, Elizabeth noticed Phillip sitting in the wagon.

"Why, who do we have here, Thomas?" Elizabeth asked as she straightened her hair and dress.

"This is Phillip West from Georgetown, South Carolina. His father John West and I became best friends during the war. His dad thought it would be a good idea for him to visit Georgia and stay with us a while."

"How do you do, Phillip?"

"I'm kind of tired, ma'am. We've had quite a long trip, but I sure am glad to be here. I'm looking forward to spending some time with you fine folks. You're married to a good gentleman ma'am and I can't thank Thomas enough for letting me come along. And you're just as beautiful as Thomas said you were, ma'am."

"Thank you, Phillip, for the compliment. But you don't have to lie on behalf of Thomas."

"Oh no, ma'am, you're all that he talked about on the whole trip."

"Is that a fact? Well, Thomas, I guess that means you'll get a nice warm cooked supper tonight."

Phillip drove the wagon up to the Hendrix's front yard near the barn, while Thomas and Elizabeth walked hand in hand along the narrow road, whispering in each other's ear and laughing at whatever they were talking about. When they walked through the front gate, the children were standing on the front porch all bunched up together like a brood of chickens, anxious to see their daddy who'd been gone for so long.

When Phillip stepped down off the wagon, the first thing that caught his eye was Annie, the oldest of the Hendrix girls. Her wonderful smile, her beautiful hair and deep-felt eyes, and her *southern hello* made him fall instantly in love with her. He'd heard people talk about it before, love at first sight, but never really put much stock into it, if there ever was such a thing. His throat was still dry from the dust, and his response to Annie was somewhat hoarse. "How do you do?"

"Fine, thank you," smiled Annie. She felt the same attraction toward Phillip, his tall form and handsome physique, and her heart almost beat out of her chest. She hoped he hadn't noticed.

Thomas saw the connection between the two and gently smiled, knowing it was his and John West's intention from the beginning to have them meet, and possibly come together in marriage if fate would have it.

"Well, children, lets all go inside and catch up on what's been going on around here."

"Daddy, we just got home from Uncle Enoch and Aunt Emeline's house. We ate supper with them this evening," said Elbridge, holding a tiny fishing pole in his hand that one of the Beasley boys had made for him.

"Well, glad to hear that, Son. That means there'll be more food for Phillip and me tonight."

Thomas walked into the house and looked around at all the things he'd missed so much. There was his wife's rocking chair, sitting near the living room window, the framing still as sturdy and strong as the day he'd made it. He put his hands on one of the arms and rocked the chair back and forth, the tears gently streaming down his face. He'd pictured Elizabeth sitting there during the past few years knitting something with her hands or rocking one of the children to sleep. The gun-rack holding the musket his father had given him still hung over the fireplace. He walked over and took it off the rack, rubbing his hands across the barrel, remembering the times his dad used to take him hunting. His dad would always say…

"Remember, Son, never point a gun toward another person when you're out hunting, even if it's not loaded. Every good hunter is first a safe hunter."

After he put the gun back on the rack, he walked into Elizabeth's and his bedroom, and past memories flooded his thoughts and awakened feelings he believed were lost forever on the dark battlefields, buried beneath the earth somewhere like many of the soldiers whose lives had been taken by war's misfortunate fate. *Everything is the same as it was before,* he thought, rubbing his hands across the bed quilt his mother had made for Elizabeth and him as a wedding gift. He wanted to touch something familiar, something common to his senses, something that would bring his emotions back from the harsh realities of war, pieces of the past convincing him he was home for good and the conflict was finally over. Elizabeth put her arms around him as if to awaken him out of a deep sleep.

Thomas and Phillip sat down at the kitchen table to eat a warm cooked meal Elizabeth quickly put together, the children sitting around and asking their father questions about what he'd been through the last few years. Thomas didn't feel like much conversation, being fatigued from the past few days of travel, and his attempt at trying to stay up late fell short when his eyelids grew heavy, unable to keep them open for any length of time. Elizabeth noticed her husband's weakening frame and sent all the children to bed, saying a little prayer with each of them before kissing them all goodnight.

Phillip slept on a cot near the stone fireplace. As he drifted off to sleep, his last thoughts rested on the banks of Black River.

The following day, Thomas took Phillip around the community to see all the neighbors: the Beasleys, the Finchs, the Daughtrys, the Mixons, the Mallards, and the Hendrixs. There was something about the Bay

Gall that made Phillip feel at peace with himself, like he was supposed to have been here his whole life. He couldn't help but think of his mother and father miles away in Carolina, already missing them deeply, trying to imagine what they were doing without him.

Elizabeth had asked Thomas to pick up a few items from Finch's store near Bay Gall creek, not far from the Hendrix farm. It was large and offered just about anything the folks in the community needed. On the way there, Thomas stopped by to see one of his sisters, Delina Jo Daughtry. Delina Jo had married Francis "Frank" Marion Daughtry, who owned a lot of farmland in the area. After he left Delina's house and picked up the items from Finch's store, he took Phillip to see his other sister, Sarah Ann Rigdon. Sarah had married Mitchell Rigdon and they lived on the north side of Statesboro about ten miles from where Thomas lived. Mitchell's father, Daniel Rigdon, had built a Grist Mill on the creek and purchased several hundred acres of land around it. Just before the Civil War, Sarah's husband Mitchell died when he accidentally fell from his horse, and Thomas felt sorry for his sister having to raise her children without a husband. She lived in a nice house on a hill that overlooked a body of water called *Mill Creek*.

When they passed through the expanded gate that led up the hill to Sarah's house, Phillip was in awe of the beautiful cedar trees that were aligned along the entry path like wooden statues of nature's crowning jewels. The trees were filled with Spanish moss hanging from the lower branches that nearly touched the ground and brushed the land that sloped downward towards the lake on the north side. The Rigdon home was two stories high and its location at the top of the hill stood out like a lighthouse on a peaceful shore, beckoning all safely into its harbor and place of quiet rest. There were many tall, well-built shake roof barns, smokehouses, elongated stables, and the whole premise was framed by a chestnut split-rail fence. When they rode up to the front of the house, a former slave girl named Patience took them around to the back yard where Sarah was sitting down at a table drinking lemonade with her children.

"Well if isn't my favorite brother Thomas!" exclaimed Sarah.

"It's been a long time, Sarah. It sure is good to see you. I guess I should introduce you to Phillip West. He's from Georgetown, South Carolina."

"Hello, Phillip. How did you meet up with my kind brother?"

"He and my father knew each other in the war. I came to stay with him for a little while."

"The War Between the States was a terrible tragedy. Sherman came through here and tried to take everything. I was afraid his soldiers were going to burn the house down," said Sarah, keeping the gnats from her face using a hand-held fan. "One of them loathsome Yankee bluecoats took a burning log from the fireplace and turned it across the floor threatening to set the whole place on fire."

"They came here?" asked Thomas.

"Oh yes. They took everything they could find. All my poor hogs and chickens. They killed some of the cows that managed not to disappear into the woods."

"What about your horses?"

"They didn't get my horses. I hid them down near the Mill house on a little island in the woods. If it wasn't for some small skirmish on the west side of town, they would've burned the whole place down I'm sure. They took out fast when they heard the gun shots in the distance and I couldn't have been more thankful for our Confederate troops for defending Statesboro as much as they could. Why don't you two sit down for a while? There's so much we need to catch up on, Thomas."

"I would love to, Sarah, but I just wanted to let you know I was back from the war and I wanted you to meet Phillip as well."

Sarah knew about the celebration Elizabeth was planning for Thomas and she did her best to keep it a secret.

"Well then, if you two have to go, at least take a sip of some good homemade lemonade. It's kind of hot out today. It'll help quench the thirst."

Patience brought the lemonade out and sat it on the table, pouring each of them a glass. She had been a house slave in the Rigdon home before the war, and since her emancipation, decided to remain a house servant to Sarah. To Sarah, she was more than a house servant, she had become family. If it wasn't for Patience, she knew she would have never survived the harsh elements the war years brought to the Rigdon place. With most men in the county gone off to fight, Sarah was left as the lone adult to oversee the farm, except for Patience, who helped tend to the fields, along with Sarah's two oldest daughters, Anne and Elizabeth, aged 8 and 10. By the end of the war, she had almost lost her will to live. Raising the family as a widow during such harsh conditions had broken her spirit, but Patience was there to lighten the load in such a dark time. After the war, she had lost most of her wealth, but not due to a shortage of labor. Sarah had sold her cattle, ninety head, to her brother-in-law not long before the war's end. He had paid her with a sack full of Confederate money, which after the war had become worthless. It was during this time that her mother, Elizabeth Beasley Hendrix, who lived near the Ogeechee River, road ten miles on horseback from the Lockhart district to visit her daughter. Her mother tried to console her, but in the end, Patience was the one who helped Sarah find her way back on her feet, looking after the children, and doing most of the housework and fieldwork.

Sarah looked at Thomas, and in a quick glimpse, his features reminded her of their brother David who had died from disease during the first year of the war. He had enlisted on June 10, 1861, Company I, 9th Georgia Infantry, and died just three months later in Richmond, Virginia.

"Have you been by David's house yet? I still can't believe he's gone. Buried up in Hollywood Cemetery in Virginia from what they tell me."

Thomas thought of his brother David. He had tried to block it out of his mind. Before they both rode off to war, he and David had declared they would look after one another. But now he was dead. He had not mentioned it to Phillip, the tragic death of David, keeping silent about it the whole trip. He found it easy to talk about the battles and the death and destruction he had seen. But to think of his brother being dead and buried far away from home, he chose to block it out of his mind. His sister had unlocked a part of his emotions that had long been ignored. How could he not think about it now? He was home. The last place he had seen his brother alive. He remembered his brother's house on the hill near Bay Gall creek...the big hickory tree in the front yard…the wave of terraces in the fields… and David with his back to the sun riding off to fight against the Union army. He had left behind eight children to be looked after by his wife Elizabeth Mincey, the oldest child being fourteen years old.

"I haven't been by there yet. How are Elizabeth and the children?" asked Thomas, holding his lemonade glass.

"They have survived this God forsaken war. But Sherman's troops did as much damage to her property as they did to mine. They took all the livestock, and if it wasn't for those sweet potatoes, they wouldn't have had anything to eat through the winter months. They took her long gun used for hunting and beat it against a tree, bending the barrel. And for what good? Leaving them without a way to shoot any wild game for food. They make my hair stand up on my neck. The awful thought of them Yankees."

After drinking their last sip, Sarah walked Thomas back to the wagon.

"Sarah, I know you miss Mitchell a lot and no one can ever take his place, but if you ever need anything, you know where to find me."

"Thanks, Thomas. Just knowing you care means a lot to me. Patience was a big help during the war. She did most of the work for me day and night, along with my oldest girls."

Thomas thanked the former slave for helping his sister on the farm, then told Sarah goodbye as he climbed into the wagon.

"It sure was nice meeting you, ma'am."

"Likewise, Phillip."

Sarah waved goodbye as they rode away in the horse-drawn wagon.

"There's one more place I want you to see, Phillip."

"Where's that?"

"Oak Grove. I know I talked a lot about Oak Grove on the trip home from Carolina. The Hendrix farm is along the river road, a few miles from the church, and I would like you to meet my parents."

"Your parents are still living? I thought that maybe since you haven't mentioned them they'd passed away."

"No. They're still alive. My father's name is James David and my mother's name is Elizabeth. She was a Beasley before she married my father."

"How old are they?"

"My father is a little over seventy years and my mother just turned sixty. They taught me from a very young age what to expect out of life. If there's anything worth learning from me, it came from them."

"You have a good family, Thomas. Everyone seems to be kind and considerate. I sure am glad you and my daddy became friends."

While Thomas and Phillip were away visiting, Elizabeth and Emeline were busy planning for the *welcome home celebration* the next day at Nevils Creek Church. They went around in a wagon inviting all of the people in the community to the welcome home celebration, being careful not to be seen by Thomas and Phillip, asking their neighbors to keep it a secret. One place in particular that Elizabeth wanted to pay a special visit to was the James Young plantation, currently the home of the widow Laura Young. A dark cloud presently overshadowed that large southern dwelling near Nevils Creek since Laura's husband Thomas was mortally wounded in one of the last battles between the States. Thomas's father, James Young, died just before the war, and his mother, Lavinia Jones Young, had left to go stay with her brother, Thomas Jones, on his Greenwood Plantation down in the *Red Hills Region* of southern Georgia. Before the war, the Young plantation along the old Louisville road sheltered nearly a hundred slaves, and the vast fields surrounding the antebellum home abundantly flourished with Sea Island cotton. The passing of James and the death of Thomas transformed the plantation into a dark shadow, and the once lighted halls filled with laughter and life were now mournful with unlit candles and a haunting silence. Centered between Beasley Town and Nevils Creek, the Young plantation's fertile soil crossed over the narrow flowing creek beyond the rising bluff where the broken-boarded church stood irregular atop the hill like a wounded soldier leaning against a pale horizon. Elizabeth hoped to cheer Laura's spirits, and she knew a special invitation to the social gathering would be a first step toward getting her out of that lonely house. The large magnolia tree near the front porch seemed to be the only thing filled with life around the plantation, such a stark contrast to before the war when James Young Sr. kept the southern estate thriving with various guests. Laura Williams had been taken in as a child by the Youngs after the death of her father, Washington Williams, a partner with James in an adventure known as *The Ogeechee Navigation Company*. During the start of the war, Laura had moved to Atlanta, and it was there that Thomas Jones Young sought her hand in marriage. The war had left her a grieving widow, although still quite young in years, and the unexpected knock at the front door was the last thing she wanted to hear. She looked over at the clock next to her bed and couldn't believe the time. The curtains had been fully closed and she had buried herself underneath the cover, the light from the outside world unable to awaken her senses to a new day. She wondered why her maidservant hadn't answered the knock, and then she suddenly remembered…*everyone was gone.* She'd decided against going to the door until she heard Elizabeth's voice faintly calling her name from the outside. Laura thought well of Elizabeth Hendrix, and considered her a true friend, always cheerful no matter the setting or atmosphere. She quickly put on her morning wrapper made of paisley challis, straightening her hair as she passed by a wall mirror in the hallway leading to the front door. Laura welcomed her friend inside.

"What a nice surprise, Elizabeth. Won't you come in?"

"I'd love to Laura, but I have others with me. We are kind of on a mission. We're having a welcome home celebration for my husband Thomas tomorrow at Nevil's Creek church and I wanted to personally invite you to come."

A few tears fell down Laura's face. "I'm sorry for getting so emotional, Elizabeth. Just hearing the name Thomas, I guess. You know our husbands shared the same name. I would love to attend, but I just don't know if I'm up to any form of socializing."

"I know, Laura. I'm so sorry for your loss. This war has caused a lot of grief for so many, and those Yankee shells have made many widows of our southern women. But you must be strong, Laura. You are still young and have so much to offer."

Laura looked out over Elizabeth's shoulder at the other women in the wagon, all bright-eyed and bushy-tailed. She wanted to join them, to feel laughter and life again, but she'd been chained to her misery and mourning since her husband's death that it didn't seem possible for her to ever escape the dark corridors of her home.

"I'll think about it, Elizabeth. Thank you so much for coming to see me. It really means a lot. I'm feeling kind of light headed at the moment and must go lie back down, but I will consider your invitation."

"If you need anything, Laura, you know where to find me."

Laura smiled, acknowledging Elizabeth's concerns, then slowly shut the door behind her, quietly disappearing into the dark hallway.

Elizabeth left the Young plantation for Nevils Creek church with a heavy heart, hoping she'd said the right words to somehow convince her grieving friend to attend the celebration. Once at the church, the ladies put up all sorts of beautiful decorations. Nevils Creek was the oldest standing Primitive Baptist Church in Georgia, and when Sherman came through the area on his march to the sea, some of his soldiers used the church pews and pulpit for firewood.

****

The sound of the rooster crowing in the early morning hours sounded like sweet music to Thomas, and the ordinary scenes of waking up on the farm reached out through the foggy mist toward a common strand that made him feel at rest: the sheltered barns, the livestock fields, the push-handled plows and the patches of rich growing sugarcane. He'd only been back home for one day and was still overcome with emotion, slowly regaining a sense of normalcy around his wife and children whose presence provided him the perfect ingredient for a complete recovery.

Phillip had spent the night in a little log cabin situated near a running creek along the north side of the Hendrix farm. It would be his temporary living place. He'd been up long before day break sitting on the raised porch drinking his morning coffee, watching the sun light clear away the misty fog.

"Do you have any fresh coffee left?" asked Thomas, walking up to the side of the porch where Phillip was sitting.

"Good morning, Thomas. Nothing like a good cup of boiled beans before the day brews," smiled Phillip, holding his cup high in the air as if to toast the morning dew.

"Sounds like a good way to start the day."

Phillip and Thomas sat on the front porch talking, enjoying their coffee while discussing the trivial things of life.

"Thomas, did you fall in love the first time you saw Elizabeth?"

"That's not an easy question to answer, Phillip. It depends on what you mean by love. Sometimes love begins in the slowest way and in the simplest form. It starts mostly on the outside, in what a man sees, and gently works its way to the inside, on what a man feels. Do you know what I'm trying to say?"

"I reckon so. But I've never been in love before, so I really can't say for sure."

"You'll know it when it happens. It'll make you put your hat on backwards."

Phillip smiled as he made sure his hat was on the right way.

"Say, how would you like to try your hand at catching some red-finned pike?" asked Thomas.

"Coffee and fishing…this is the life," said Phillip.

In the meantime, all of the Hendrix relatives, neighbors, and friends gathered at Nevils Creek Church for the welcome home celebration. Thomas was not a general in the war, but to his family he was as much of a soldier as one - a true hero and Confederate soldier that stood up for states' rights and for the great state of Georgia. The dirt road that led to Nevils Creek Church was filled with horses and wagons of people making their way to the wooden structure now marred by Union hands. Several former Confederate soldiers reunited for the event, dressed in full military uniform, anxious to welcome home one of their own. There were boys standing down by the creek, talking, skipping rocks across the water's surface while the girls congregated near the church steps smiling and giggling. The adults conversed near a long table of food that stretched out from one side of the church building to the other, a rich display of some of the greatest southern cooking a man could put his lips to. It was a day of jubilation for the people in the Bay Gall, and although the South as a whole had nothing to celebrate, each Confederate soldier that returned home was considered a reunion worth gathering for.

Thomas and Phillip returned to the Hendrix house from fishing only to find everyone gone. *Unusual*, Thomas thought, as he looked in every room, only to find a small note on the kitchen table.

He read it with strained suspense:

Thomas, please come to Nevils Creek church. Your Loving Wife.

"Is that all it says?" asked Phillip.

"Yeah, that's it. Maybe they're holding some sort of community meeting and need my assistance or something. We'd better go over there and see what's going on, but first, I have to change my clothes."

While Thomas was getting ready, Phillip walked over to the fireplace and looked at the pictures on the mantle, in particular, at a framed portrait of Annie. He took it down to get a better look, his eyes brightening up as he noticed how pretty she was. *What if she's the one for me? Look at those beautiful brown eyes. And the way her hair falls...she's prettier than anything I've ever seen.*

Thomas walked into the living room and saw Phillip holding Annie's picture, but pretended like he didn't notice.

Phillip, embarrassed that Thomas might've seen him, quickly placed it back on the mantle.

"Well, Phillip, let's head on over to the church and see what this letter is all about. There's no need in taking a wagon. We'll just saddle up. You take Stonewall, and I'll take Lee."

They slowly galloped to the church across the branch, and as they trotted over the bridge at Bay Gall creek, a watchman hiding up in a slender-leaved willow tree signaled to the band that Thomas was approaching.

They struck up "Bonnie Blue Flag."

We are a band of brothers, native to the soil, Fighting for the property, we gained by honest toil. And when our rights were threatened, The cry rose near and far, Hurrah for the Bonnie Blue Flag that bears a single star! Hurrah! Hurrah! For Southern rights, Hurrah! Hurrah for the Bonnie Blue Flag that bears a single star!

The former Confederate soldiers stood at attention as Thomas and Phillip galloped in front of the rustic aged church, and a line of gun fire echoed out like peals of thunder when their muskets targeted the clear blue sky. Thomas, sitting on Lee, was surprised by the ebullient gathering, and scenes from the battled past came alive when he saw a wounded soldier waving the Bonnie Blue through the gun powdered air. He held his hand up and saluted what so many from the North never could understand, that so many beyond the Potomac never could forgive. Thomas's mind drifted back to the last time he saw the *River of the Army* as it joined the Chesapeake bay, his eyes peering restlessly through the misty fog hovering around Lookout Point, the Union prison of war camp. His journey there began at Trevilian Station, the bloodiest and largest all-cavalry battle of the war, mounted with Company B of *The Seventh Georgia Cavalry* under Col. Gilbert J. Wright's Brigade. The day began on the Fredericksburg Road, on June the 11th, 1864, near Trevilian Station, with two of Hampton's brigades, Butler's and Wright's, advancing toward the crossroads at Clayton's Store. Maj. Gen. Philip Sheridan commanded the Cavalry Corps of the Union Army of the Potomoc, while Maj. Gen. Wade Hampton commanded the Cavalry Corps of the Confederate Army of Northern Virginia. The opposing Union forces on the Fredericksburg Stage Road leading to the station from Clayton's Store were two of Torbet's brigades under Merritt and Devin. But it wasn't Merritt's or Devin's men that shot Thomas's horse out from under him near Netherland Tavern, but the powder from the *Seventh of Michigan* under Brig. Gen. George A. Custer's command…

'It's ok ole boy, don't you worry about me,' Thomas whispered to Lightfoot, his horse. 'You did a good job today. Now just close your eyes and rest before them Yankees come upon us.'

He'd hoped for Custer's capture and his own freedom after the Union General found himself completely surrounded by Hampton and Fitzhugh Lee along the Gordonsville Road, but Sheridan came to his defense and Thomas's journey to Lookout Point as a prisoner of war had begun. Just a few nights before Thomas's capture, he and John

West were at Cold Harbor together; John fought with Hagood's Brigade in Hoke's Division. Thomas had ridden with *Lightfoot* over to John's camp sometime after midnight on June 9th to let him know about Lee's plan for the Cavalry to leave Cold Harbor. He found John sitting by a small campfire outside his tent close to Gaines's Mill drinking coffee, the stars of Hercules shining bright in the northern hemisphere over the battlefield of trenched warfare. It would be the last time he would see his friend from Carolina until the South's surrender, the Union prison camp confining him to Maryland's peninsula soil for the remainder of the war. The Bay and the River at Lookout Point were now part of a dismal past that Thomas wanted to forget.

After dismounting, Thomas walked over to his wife standing underneath the shade of a large white oak.

"Elizabeth, I guess this is what the letter was all about?" smiled Thomas.

"That's right, Thomas, we wanted to give you a hero's welcome and let you know how much we love and appreciate you."

Thomas gave Elizabeth a kiss and began to socialize with everyone present, receiving words of gratitude and thanks for his sacrifice.

"Thomas, we are very proud of your service to the South."

"Thank you, Uncle David."

"Phillip, this is my Uncle David Beasley, Ordinary of the Court of Bulloch County. His son George Ross served with Company E, 5th GA Cavalry. Uncle David, this is Phillip West from Georgetown, South Carolina. His father John West and I crossed a lot of territory together fighting those Yankees."

"It's an honor to meet you, sir."

"It's a privilege meeting you too, Phillip."

Thomas's Uncle David was married to Catherine Rigdon, the sister of Mitchell Rigdon, husband of Sarah Hendrix, Thomas's sister.

"Thomas, I'm having a gathering tomorrow at my plantation home for the men of our county who fought for the Confederacy. I would like you and Phillip to attend."

"We would be honored to, Uncle."

After Sherman's troops came through Statesboro and burned down the courthouse, the inferior court met at the plantation home of David Beasley. During the war, he'd ordered for all the court documents to be taken from the courthouse before Sherman's troops destroyed them, thus preserving all the important records of Bulloch County.

Elizabeth was surprised to see Laura Young, the widow to Thomas Young, attend. She'd worn a black dress, and at first stood alone near her buggy until being introduced to JG Blitch and a few other businessmen in the area that had done business with her deceased father-in-law, James Young. Laura smiled at Elizabeth as if to let her know that she was all right.

Phillip stayed close to Thomas, until he saw Annie sitting alone on the steps of the country church. He walked over to where she was and asked her, "Do you mind if I sit down?"

"No. Not at all…"

Annie was quiet and shy, not really knowing how to carry on a conversation with a guy she was very much interested in; she'd never had a beau before, but there was something in Phillip that made her feel like she was floating in the clouds.

"Sure is a nice welcome home celebration for Thomas. I wish we would've had something like this for my father. It must've been a lonely time for your dad in that *Union Prison Camp*."

"I'm sure it was. I tried to ask him about Lookout Point last night, but he didn't want to talk about it. Did your father make it through the war ok?" Annie finally found the courage to ask a question of her own.

"He was injured a few times and hospitalized in Virginia. His health isn't what it used to be, but he's home and that's all that matters."

"I reckon so. Why did you come here, Phillip? I mean, you're a long ways from home and in a strange new place. I'm sure it took a lot of courage to make the decision to leave Carolina and come to Georgia."

"I guess so, Annie. I don't know exactly the reason why I'm here just yet. I somehow feel like it's the right place for me to be at this time in my life. The hardest part about it all was leaving my parents behind. It's like leaving the most important part of you somewhere else."

"What are your parents like?"

"They mean the world to me, Annie. Ever since I can remember, they've always shown me unconditional love. When I was a child, my mother would sit me on her knee and sing to me in the prettiest tones. I could tell then that she loved me very much. My father always took up time with me and made sure I learned how to be a man by standing on my own two feet. I want to make them proud of the choices I make in life. They deserve the best I have to give to myself and to those around me."

"That is so sweet, Phillip. I don't know that much about you yet, but I can tell that you are a very sincere person."

****

The evening sky displayed a deep glowing sunset in the western horizon as the men who fought for the South galloped up the long entrance way toward the Beasley Plantation. David had prepared for a large gathering for the men of Bulloch County who'd worn the gray uniforms and given their lives for the Confederacy. It was to be a time of healing and restoration for the county, *and what better way*, David thought, *than to bring the men together for a renewal of kinship, a bond of peace, and a reminder of what made the country strong.* The population of the county had numbered 3000 souls at the start of the war, and out of the 750 men accounted for, 600 of them fought in the struggle for succession. The county had paid a heavy toll for those who'd served and died in the war, and David Beasley wanted to honor them all, not only the dead, but those who'd returned home to their families.

When the former soldiers arrived, they were seated in rows of chairs positioned in front of the tall portico porch facing the open fields, with overhanging limbs from live oaks stretching out like natural ceilings between the sky and the ground where they sat. Thomas Hendrix, dressed in full military uniform, and Phillip West, the honored guest, sat in front with the Ordinary's family.

David stood alone, tall and erect, on a podium positioned in front of the steps. He recognized everyone present and read out loud all of the different family names represented who'd served as Confederate soldiers, his facial expressions sincere and his voice filled with a kindred respect that only a common ancestor among them could feel. After reading all of the names, he stood quiet for a short moment, and then with a sense of solemn remembrance, spoke earnestly of the not so distant past…

"I remember the year 1864 very well, for it wasn't long ago when I took the oath of office as the new Ordinary of Court of Bulloch County. It, my sworn oath, was to the Confederate States of America, not to the sacred Union, or to the United States. Then, during those battle torn years, we lived and breathed in a time of secession, and our individual steps were marked by a common path for states' rights. What one person could have known, or what one man could have foreseen the endless struggles or raging discourses that would follow? Those tragic events were manifested and displayed in the midst of our own ancestral soil, from the common land owners' estates in Georgia to the poor sharecroppers' abodes in Tennessee, from the rich plantation grounds along Carolina's coastal waters to the rich fertile lands of Virginia's born Valley. The war raged and the wounded and disjoined years crawled painfully for the North and the South, both feeling the deadening blows of horrific battles, bloody skirmishes, and unending conflicts. Today, we are joined not in part but in whole, not by shackles that bind slaves together, an unjust and cruel hold, but by a more gifted and binding strand, by freedom's born right. We are each and everyone birthed and adopted citizens of a land whose resolve is to unite under a sewn and sacred flag that represents restoration of principles destroyed and freedom in a union untainted, not only for our numerous states, but for our several races. We now, this day, all joined states united, salute *Old Glory*. And if we salute it, as our forefathers gone before, let us also serve it, not only with internal honesty but with eternal integrity."

When David ended his speech, all of the men present stood up and applauded his charge for restoration and saluted him for his solemn words for both sides to forgive each other. After the cheering subsided, the Ordinary walked over to an old black man, a former slave, standing in the background leaning against a covered wagon, and led him carefully to the podium near the portico porch in front of the soldiers. The old man's face bore the emotional scars from numerous years of servitude, but now, being free, he could come and go as he pleased.

"I would like everyone to meet Otis. He's been a slave his whole life, here, among us, in Bulloch County. After being so long a time in slavery, but now, no longer in servitude, I thought it would be a good idea for him to tell us what it feels like to be free."

Otis spoke good English, having learned it from an early age.

The crowd grew very quiet and you could hear a pin drop as Otis stood on the podium…

"Good evenin'. My name is Otis and I'm an old man. I've seen lots of good and bad days in my life. But I never dreamed of the day I would be free. My mama used to sing them old songs in the fields pickin' cotton about bein' free, but we didn't know what bein' free would feel like. I don't hate no white man for what I went through, 'cause God won't let no one in the pearly gates that's got hate in him. I thank God that I'm free. If I could say what it feels like, I have to say it's probably like a bird flyin' in the sky, floatin' in the winds and goin' and comin' as he pleases, free from the cage that held him in his whole life. I can now fly and rest my tired weary bones, and I feel like a real human being. I like to end by singin' a song I used to hear my mama sing in the cotton fields."

Thomas Hendrix joined in with the harmonica while Otis sang the old spiritual song:

> *'I looked over Jordan and what did I see, Coming forth to carry me home,*
> *A band of angels coming after me, Coming forth to carry me home…*
> *Swing Low Sweet Chariot, Coming forth to carry home,*
> *Swing Low Sweet Chariot, Coming forth to carry me home.*
> *Coming forth to carry me home…'*

Tears streamed down the old man's face, and the soldiers sat in silence, many in admiration for the former slave, realizing for the first time what it meant to be free, not by the words in which he described it, but by the way in which he spoke of it, and sang of it, with such deep emotional feelings from having been enslaved his whole life.

****

After returning from the Beasley plantation, Phillip felt unusually tired. The journey to Georgia and the last two days' events had finally caught up to him. He sat quietly in a chair resting his feet on an ottoman, and for the first time since his arrival from Carolina, began to think of home. He'd talked about Black River with those he'd been introduced to, just to make conversation, but now, sitting alone, his thoughts turned inward, and he began to brood over the possibility that he'd made a mistake in coming here. The only thing that kept his mind on staying was Annie. It had only been a couple of days and yet she'd made a lasting impression on him, her inner beauty radiating like streams of sunlight piercing through thin white clouds in the southern sky. *I should give it a little while longer*, he thought. *Then, if she doesn't show any interest, I'll leave for Carolina.*

He wished he was back home, for the night at least, just to see his mother and father; he'd been so busy that he hadn't taken the time to wire a telegraph, letting them know he was all right.

****

John and Margaret couldn't sleep.

"I hope Phillip and Thomas are safe, John. Shouldn't they have made it by now?" expressed Margaret.

"Don't worry, Margaret. We'll hear from Phillip soon. I'm sure he's trying to get settled in."

"You know how I am with the children. Always a little over concerned I guess."

"I'd be worried if you weren't worried," smiled John. "I love you for being you. You are a wonderful wife and mother."

****

Phillip rode to Rocky Ford the following day to send a telegraph to his parents…

Dear Mom and Dad,
Thomas and I made it safely to the Hendrix farm. I like the people here,
and it seems to be a great place to live. I'll keep in touch as much as possible. I love
you both very much and already miss you.
P.S. I wish you could meet Annie. She is a good girl and one that I am very much
interested in!'

Phillip's parents wrote back:

'We are glad to hear you've arrived safely, Son. You are always in our thoughts and
prayers. If you need anything don't be afraid to ask us. We will always be here for
you and you have our eternal blessings.
Love you, Son. Mom and Dad.'

Phillip and his parents corresponded through letters over the next few months. In each letter that Phillip wrote to his parents, they could sense their son was falling more and more in love with Annie. Annie had attempted to keep her feelings reserved somewhat for a time, afraid that Phillip wouldn't remain in Georgia. But she'd finally opened up as the days and months passed; and once, after thinking Phillip was leaving to go back home, she let him know how much she wanted him to stay. It was then that their relationship flourished into something more meaningful…into something more permanent.

Chapter Five

The winter winds had come to South Georgia, and a new season of frost covered the fields like a bed of resting snow. Annie adored the cold months as much as the spring, in particular, the warmth of the fireplaces that came to life in the smoke-chimneyed homes. She would be the first to gather the fatwood from the pines that had long fallen, leaving a stump of rich lighter as priceless as gold to a starting fire. However, the one thing she wasn't prepared for *this winter* was falling deeper in love. Lately, she'd spent much of her time in front of the mirror looking for new ways to wear her hair, and the sweet smell of floral perfumes had now become an essential part of her plush skin. She had a few copies of *Godey's Lady's Book* lying on her dresser - the famed published "Queen of Monthlies" from Philadelphia. The volumes had somehow managed to filter their way across the Potomac, over the Appalachians, past Southern blockades, and finally, into the hands of fashionable women subscribers of the South. Annie hadn't subscribed herself, but she'd had cousins that did. All of this, of course - the perfumes, the hair, the reading of Godey's - was motivated by her new found desire to be as attractive and as culturally refined as possible in front of Phillip; although Phillip himself was not a refined man. He was a youthful representative agrarian, not a socialite. Tall and handsome, his good manners exceeded most aristocratic gentlemen who sported their gentility like Mount Everest rising from some rigid terrain of trampled earth beneath.

It was also during this time that Annie had been given a new Steinway piano from one of her generous uncles that had taken an interest in her musical talent. The handmade piano from Park Avenue and 53rd street in New York had traveled a long ways from the famed Steinway factory in the northern city to the South. The Steinweg piece provided for a unique blend, an unusual work seldom seen in rural countryside homes. Annie was naturally gifted. She'd become fluent with various musical styles through the years, but never really played any romantic pieces until now. She spent her evenings near the fireplace in front of her Steinway playing musical compositions filled with complex passion and romance, and it was more than just infatuation with Phillip - she was sure of - that motivated her; it was an inner love, characterized by a deep felt longing to know more about the man from Black River and what their deepening relationship meant to each other.

****

Thomas and Elizabeth and the rest of the children were away for the weekend, but Annie stayed behind for the purpose of spending some time alone with Phillip, asking him over for dinner. They hadn't had much time to themselves, and she wanted to make sure the setting was perfect before he arrived: a warm fire, candles, and her favorite songbook opened to the page of a song she planned on playing for him after dinner. She had the curtains pulled back with the view of the snow falling outside, and a framed picture she and Phillip had taken together in the late summer was placed in the open on top of the Steinway. She didn't know why she was so nervous, but she knew her basic instincts would take over once Phillip arrived and everything would somehow fall into place. She looked out the window and saw Phillip walking in the distance up the narrow pathway leading from the cabin to the house, his tall form calmly overshadowed by darkened winter clouds and the falling of snow. She suddenly felt warm inside, not from the warmth of the fire she'd made earlier, but from the realization that she'd now fallen deeply in love.

Annie opened the door as Phillip walked up the steps onto the porch.

"Hello, Annie."

"Phillip," smiled Annie. "Come on in. Let me take your coat while you warm yourself by the fire." Phillip noticed the new perfume Annie was wearing.

The cool air that had rushed in from the outside could still be felt after Annie closed the door and placed Phillip's coat on the wood-standing rack her father had made before the war. She turned and walked over to the fireplace to put on some more oak.

"Here, let me do that for you, smiled Phillip," his eyes looking into hers as she handed him the split wood. "New perfume?"

"I wondered if you would notice," smiled Annie.

Phillip placed the wood on top of the burning coals.

Annie felt her heart racing.

"I have to go check on the pie baking in the oven. You sit down and make yourself feel at home and I'll be right back."

Phillip waited in the living room, sitting near the fire.

It was the first time they had ever been alone together and it made him think about their relationship in a way that he'd never thought about before. There was always someone around to help keep them company, to help carry on the conversation. But now, it was just the two of them. The quiet setting brought all of his feelings to the surface, and he suddenly realized how much his love for Annie had grown. The crackling fire sounded peaceful to him, and at that moment, he was more sure of himself than he'd ever been before.

He got up from his chair and walked over to the Steinway facing the double window, looking at the framed photo that Annie had placed on top of the piano. They'd taken the picture on a rainy day, and he remembered how close Annie had come to getting her dress spotted by a splattered mud puddle from a passing wagon. They both laughed at the near disaster, and after they took the photo, he remembered the photographer commenting on how well they looked together.

"So what do you think?"

Phillip turned around. Annie had walked back in from the kitchen and was relighting a candle on the table that had went out. She looked at Phillip and waited for his response, pushing a part of her hair back that had fallen in front of her eyes.

"I think you look beautiful," smiled Phillip.

"I wasn't talking about me," smiled Annie. "I was asking about the picture."

"The picture? Oh, yes, the picture. I think it turned out very well. I was just remembering how close you came to ruining your dress that day," laughed Phillip.

"Thanks for shielding me," laughed Annie.

The snow fell gently against the window panes as Phillip and Annie ate a candlelight dinner. Afterwards, they sat and talked by the fire. They didn't sit close at first - both still trying to find their way into each other's arms – but when Annie got a little chilly, Phillip sat next to her on the floor, placing a light throw blanket around her shoulders. It was all innocent: the gentle holding of hands, her head resting on his shoulders, whisperings of 'I love you' between them. It was the first time they'd spoken those words to each other. They sat with their backs against the front of the couch, looking into the burning coals.

"You know, there was a time when I had dreams of moving away to a big city somewhere up north, like New York."

"Really? I can't imagine someone like you moving to a large town. You're too used to the country life like me."

"That's what I admire about you. You have a genuine ability to see right through me. I'm so glad we found each other. When I think of how close I came to changing my mind about coming…"

"But you didn't," interjected Annie. "You came here to Georgia like you were supposed to. Now it's my responsibility to keep you here."

"Well, you're doing a pretty good job of it."

Phillip noticed an attractiveness about Annie he hadn't recognized before, and the perfume she was wearing was only a part of it.
She'd always been pretty, he thought, but tonight was somehow different. She carried a sense of maturity that attracted him as much as her beauty and he felt relaxed and complete in her arms.

"You think so?"

"I know so," smiled Phillip, his eyes fixed on hers. "I don't think I'm ever going to see Carolina again."

Annie felt warm inside. This was the conversation she'd been waiting for – an assurance that Phillip had more than just a passing infatuation with her. She'd been worried that he'd keep his feelings at a safe distance, with thoughts of going back home always at the forefront.

For sometime, they sat quietly, Annie's head resting on Phillip's shoulder as she watched the fire slowly burn down to bright red coals.

"I'm glad we've had this time together. There's no other place that I'd rather be right now than in your arms."

"I can think of one other place that I'd rather be…"

Annie looked at Phillip with concerned curiosity. "Oh…and where is that?"

"In your arms," smiled Phillip.

"If you'd said anything else I would've sent you back to the cabin," laughed Annie.

With all the romantic talk, Annie almost forgot about the song.

"I have something I want to play for you on the piano, Phillip. Do you want to hear it?"

"I'd love to."

"It's a piece I just learned."

Phillip helped Annie from the floor and walked with her over to the Steinway, resting one hand on the piano framing after setting the lid open. As she played, Phillip stood enchanted, looking out the double window at the lightly falling snow. He could see Annie's reflection on the large panes, her hands moving gracefully across the ivory keys. Every now and then, a flake would blur her image on the cold surfaced glass, and then, slowly melt away.

The rest of the evening would prove even more enchanting, and the stars that had been hidden by the thick wintry clouds brightly appeared again as Phillip made his way back to the cabin through the misty night air. At first, his clothes were warm from having stood in front of Annie's fireplace, but by the time he made it back across the winter coated field, he was shivering cold. Once inside, he quickly lit a candle next to his bed, then put a few logs into the potbelly stove, the room slowly warming to a comfortable temperature as he took the framed photo of him and Annie out of his coat pocket and placed it on the small nightstand next to his bed; Annie had wanted him to have it as a reminder of their special evening together. He looked at the picture until the candle burned low, his head resting lightly on his pillow, and after a few glances, his eyes gently closed into a restful night's sleep.

Chapter Six

*I*t was the time of Spring, when the flora and fauna come to life, like the prepossessing blooms of albas and the aesthetic allurements of gallica, like the hovering of buff-bellied hummingbirds and the floating of monarch butterflies. It was on one of those early springtime mornings that Annie awoke to the warblings of a horned lark outside her window near the open pasture, and brushing back the thin white curtains she could see the early dawn's reddish glow just over the cabin where Phillip was staying. Watching the lark take its flight, she whispered the words of Wordsworth softly under her breath, a quote she once learned in her reading somewhere but never forgot...*Up with me! Up with me into the clouds! For thy song, Lark, is strong; Up with me, up with me into the clouds! Singing, singing, with clouds and sky about thee ringing, Lift me, guide me till I find that spot which seems so to thy mind!* Annie had fallen deeply in love, and her feet were as light as the lark's in the early morning sky. She rushed to get dressed to meet Phillip for an afternoon picnic, putting on her engagement ring before anything else; it had been a year long courtship, and Phillip had finally proposed to her. At the picnic, the two discussed where they'd like the wedding to take place, and after several possibilities, Annie expressed how much she wanted to get married at her Aunt Sarah Rigdon's place overlooking Mill Creek: "I think Aunt

Sarah's house would be a great spot to have an outdoor wedding, Phillip." She'd always admired the scenery there.

"What a wonderful idea, Annie! The moment I first laid eyes on that place I was captivated by its beauty."

"Then it's settled. Let's go tell everyone!"

They informed Thomas and Elizabeth of their wedding plans. Both were very excited to hear of the news and congratulated them on their future union together. "Phillip, I know your mother and father will be as happy as we are," said Thomas smiling, embracing Phillip as his soon to be son-in-law.

Phillip wrote home to his parents…

'Dear Mom and Dad,

I've asked Annie to marry me and she said yes! We have already set a wedding date and would love for you all to come down and attend. I will help make arrangements for you for a place to stay once you get here. The date has been set for May the 11th. It is only a few weeks away, so please make preparations. Love you all, your son, Phillip.'

Phillip's father wasn't in good health, and his bad leg still gave him trouble, but he didn't want to disappoint his son at such an important time in his life. He and Margaret talked it over and wrote back to Phillip:

'Congratulations, Son! We are so happy for you! We are looking forward to coming down to the wedding and spending some time with you and Annie. We love you very much and we'll see you in a few weeks.'

Annie's mother, Elizabeth, Thomas's sister, Sarah, and Annie's Aunt Emeline, all worked hard preparing for the wedding, making sure everything was in place and in order. A week before the big day, the West family arrived from Carolina in a little place called Rocky Ford, located across the river just a few miles from the Hendrix farm; Phillip and Annie met them at the depot to pick them up.

John West stepped down off the train with a walking cane in his hand, his hair now filled with strands of gray, and his frame much weaker than when Phillip had last seen him. John turned around and took the hand of his wife Margaret, helping her down the steps onto the platform below, being careful not to let her fall down. Seeing his family again, after so many months, caused tears to trickle down Phillip's face. His thoughts raced back to Georgetown, back to Black River, back to the log cabin where he lived with his family on the countryside hill. He knew those days were forever gone: mornings sitting around the table eating breakfast with his siblings, evenings sitting on the porch with his family until the sun went down. The reality of it all set in as he stood there looking at his parents he'd missed so much. He walked over to his mother and father, giving them a long warm embrace.

He then introduced them to Annie.

"Daddy…Mama, this is Annie Elizabeth Hendrix, my bride-to-be."

"Nice to meet you, Annie," said Margaret. "You're more beautiful than Phillip described you to be."

"Thank you, Mrs. West. It's an honor to finally meet you."

"Annie, words can't express how much this means to Margaret and I. We can look at Phillip and tell you've already made a change in his life."

"I hope for the better, Mr. West."

"Absolutely."

After Phillip introduced Annie to all of his siblings, they loaded into the wagon and rode to the Hendrix place. On the way there, Annie discussed with the West family about their wedding plans and where they would be living once they got married.

"Let's go show them the log cabin where we'll be staying, Annie."

"Your parents are probably tired by now, Phillip. I'm sure they would like to get some rest."

"No. We're fine. We would love to see the cabin."

The road leading to the small log cabin was narrow and winding, twisting and turning like a long meandering river. The cabin had been fixed up and remodeled the last few weeks, and Phillip and Annie were proud of their future home. There was a separate building in the back used for the kitchen, just a few feet away from the back porch, furnished with a wood-burning stove on one end for cooking and a long wooden table in the center, with long wooden benches on either side. The setting was pioneer-like, with all the elements of a southern homestead: chopped wood stacked on the back porch - no board flooring, only bare ground - used for the woodstove, iron cooking pots hung on nails outside near the kitchen door, broom-sage tied up in bunches - used for sweeping the cabin floor - leaned against a corner on the front porch, and a shallow well, just a few feet away, supplied them with clean drinking water.

"It's lovely, Annie," said Margaret, stepping down off the wagon. "It feels like a home already; like it has a warm, kind soul."

"We still have some work to do, Mama," said Phillip, "but at least we have something to work with."

"Son, I couldn't be more proud of you," said John.

Phillip's siblings walked from room to room looking the place over. They all noticed the piano in the corner of the living room.

"Annie, do you play the piano?" asked Margaret.

"I play a few notes."

"Let's play them our favorite song, Annie."

Phillip and Annie walked over to the piano while the rest of the family sat down to listen.

Annie played a beautiful tune that seemed to calm everyone's spirits – a much needed relaxing moment for them after the long trip from Carolina.

Phillip stood by Annie's side at the piano while they sang a song together:

"The river flows beyond the hills, through the mountains, and down the fall, to the place where my true love awaits, I can hear my true love call.
The winter snows have come and gone, and the years have passed us by, and still my love is lovely still, and our growing love will never die."

Tears filled the eyes of Phillip's mother; she knew her son had found true happiness, and she couldn't have been more at peace with his choice of Annie.

After they left the log cabin, Phillip took them to see Thomas and Elizabeth near Oak Grove. It was a peaceful countryside ride as the wagon wheels turned slowly along the tree-shadowed dirt road, and a light breeze blew softly against the southern pines standing tall beneath the clear blue sky.

Thomas was sitting on the front porch resting his eyes when he looked up and saw Lee and Stonewall pulling the old wagon up the hill, the noise of singing and laughter waking him up.

"Looks like y'all are having a good old fashioned time," said Thomas after Phillip parked the wagon in front of the house. "Get on down and stay a while. Hello, John…Margaret."

"I think we will, Thomas," said John, grabbing his walking cane.

"Good to see you, Thomas," smiled Margaret.

John and Thomas sat in the living room reminiscing on the battles they'd fought in during the war; and to hear them talk, you'd think they were right there in the midst of the smoke and powder, marching up some hill.

"Well John, looks like my daughter and your son fell for our plan after all, didn't they?"

"Sure does. I never dreamed it would happen this fast, but looking at them two, you can see where they were born for each other."

Margaret and Elizabeth sat on the front porch getting to know each other better, going over the fine details of the upcoming wedding. It was a good time of fellowship for everyone.

****

The week passed quickly and the evening before the wedding day finally arrived. The Hendrix and West families gathered together on the grounds of the Rigdon home place for the wedding rehearsal. There was a string of lantern lights fixed around the back yard and long tables were spread out underneath for the guests to eat on and fellowship around in the late evening hours. Many neighbors and friends were invited to attend.

As guests arrived, young, well-dressed men were assigned to walk them around to the dining area to their assigned tables for the night's rehearsal dinner.

After the sun fell below the western horizon and the darkness gently crowded in around them, family and guests gave toasts beneath the string of lights to the soon-to-be newly weds. The moonlight reflecting from off the lake's water at the bottom of the hill, almost candlelit like, provided an appropriate romantic setting for the occasion.

"I would like to propose a toast to my niece and to her future husband," said Sarah Hendrix Rigdon. "The War Between the States has brought us all a lot of strain and struggle. I think this wedding serves to remind us that we have so much to look forward to in life despite the past few years of death and destruction. It is good to see such a beautiful young couple come together in holy matrimony and brighten up our hopes and dreams for a better tomorrow."

Everyone cheered the words of Sarah and many others followed with similar toasts of gratitude and encouragement for Phillip and Annie.

John West stood up, supporting himself with his walking cane while trying to keep his composure as he gave a father's toast: "During the War between the States, Annie's father, Thomas Hendrix, became my closest friend. Thomas talked a lot about his family in Georgia. After hearing him say so many wonderful things about Statesboro, I wanted my son to come and visit here," said John, holding Margaret's hand. "I'm not going to lie and say that we haven't sat around the fireplace many nights wishing Phillip was back home with us, or that his mother hasn't walked in his room each night hoping to find him there. During this time of separation, we have witnessed our oldest son become a man. Thomas was kind enough to let Phillip ride with him to Georgia and stay on his farm. He and I talked a little about Phillip and Annie, and the possibility of them getting together. We didn't know if they would come to like each other or not, but it all worked out for the two of them to fall naturally in love. Phillip, your mother and I just want to say we are very proud to have you as our son. Annie, we welcome you into the West family as one of our own. I want to propose a toast to

Thomas and Elizabeth for being so kind and generous to the West family."

Thomas got up from his table and walked over to John, giving him a soldier's embrace. They had been through a lot together in the war, and now to see their son and daughter come together as husband and wife was more than they could ever ask for. It was a very emotional moment for everyone.

Phillip stood to give a toast: "To Annie, my one and only true love. When I left South Carolina to come to Georgia with your father, I had no idea what this part of the country would be like, how long I'd stay, or if I would even like it here. I didn't want to leave the only family and home I'd ever known, but my father, along with the support of my mother, wanted to give me an opportunity to see if I could find happiness here. I decided to take the trip, and that decision, I firmly believe, was the right choice for me. I can honestly say, Annie, that no matter where I am, as long as I'm with you, I will find true happiness."

Annie fought back the tears as Phillip reached for her hand, the backdrop of the moonlit-lake at the bottom of the hill glowing around them. While they stood underneath the string of lights, their faces expressed to the crowd what it truly meant to find the right person to spend forever with. They could see that Phillip and Annie were madly in love with each other and ready to spend the rest of their lives together.

After all the people left, Phillip and Annie walked over to the edge of the dock on the side of the hill overlooking Mill Creek, the water sparkling from the splintered moonlight reflecting off the water's surface underneath the starry sky.

"Well, Annie, tomorrow's the big day."

"I know. It doesn't seem real. I can't believe my dreams of marrying *the only man for me* are about to come true."

"I feel the same way, Annie. When I first looked into those beautiful brown eyes of yours, I knew you were the one."

"I really enjoyed meeting your parents, Phillip. You have your mother's heart. She is so sweet."

"I'm glad you like her. She adores you too."

"I love you, Phillip West."

"I love you, Annie Hendrix."

Phillip held Annie in his arms underneath the starry sky, their passion and love for each other bringing them to this place in time, to this point in their lives where they would commit themselves to each other…forever.

The night had made for many wonderful memories and the Rigdon home was the perfect place for it all to unfold. The following day, Phillip and Annie became husband and wife, and after their wedding reception, they left to go on a short honeymoon.

The Wests said their goodbyes to the Hendrix family, thanking them for their hospitality and for all the accommodations they'd made for them during their stay.

****

The following week, Sarah Rigdon rode out to her brother's farm in the Bay Gall where he was busy building a new barn large enough to put all of his mules and horses in, having several stalls, and enough sheltered space to store his farming equipment under. Elizabeth had invited Sarah out to eat lunch with them, and *a visit to the country would do me good*, she thought, being lonely for companionship. She needed to talk to Thomas anyway about fixing the Mill House, the water wheel being damaged due to a lack of maintenance during the war, having no men help around.

"Sarah, we're glad you could make it," smiled Elizabeth, greeting her at the front gate. Sarah brought along her children, who always loved to visit their Uncle Thomas in the country.

"Hey, Elizabeth. I cooked a hot apple pie for dessert," said Sarah, handing it to Elizabeth to take inside.

"Mmm…it smells delicious!" said Elizabeth.

Thomas was high up on the barn working on the rafters when Sarah arrived, putting the last nail in the center piece before climbing down the ladder to meet her. It was time for lunch anyway and he was tired from the early morning labor, getting up long before daybreak to work on the barn - using the light from the lantern to see with.

Sarah and Elizabeth walked over to where Thomas was pumping water from the well.

"Hey, sister. What do you think about the barn?" asked Thomas, splashing water on his chest and neck.

"It looks great! You've always had a great hand at building things. Which reminds me, can you come to the house tomorrow to work on the broken wheel at the Mill? Harvest time is not far off and it would be great to see the water moving the wheel again."

"I don't see why I couldn't break away a little."

"Thank you, Thomas. You don't know how much it means to me."

Everyone walked inside and sat down at the dinner table to eat the wonderful meal Elizabeth had prepared.

"So tell me, Elizabeth, how have the young newly weds been getting along?" asked Sarah.

"We've only seen them once since they've been married. Phillip and Annie have been busy at the log cabin getting settled in. Yesterday, Phillip came over to help Thomas on the barn. "

"Phillip is a wonderful young man. He reminds me of you, Thomas. He seems to know what he wants out of life," said Sarah, sipping on a glass of tea.

"Once he sets his mind to doing something, he accomplishes it," said Thomas. "We're proud to have him as our son-in-law. He's a hard worker and we know he'll treat our daughter with respect."

Suddenly, they heard the sound of many horses riding up outside. Thomas left the dinner table and rushed out the front door to find a *posse of men* gathered in the yard.

"What seems to be the problem, sheriff?"

"We're looking for an escaped prisoner. He's armed and dangerous. You all need to be very careful until we can hunt him down and put him back behind bars. I would advise you folks to stay put until you hear otherwise."

The posse rode off in a storm of fury towards Statesboro. Thomas walked back inside with a look of concern on his face.

"What's wrong, Thomas?" asked Elizabeth.

"Sarah, I'm afraid you and the kids are going to have to stay the night with us. That was a posse looking for an escaped prisoner. You don't need to get on the road by yourself with the kids and put you or them in harms way."

The next morning, Thomas got up to go work on the broken water wheel at Rigdon's Mill.

"Thomas, you're not going to town now while they're still hunting down the escaped prisoner, are you?"

"It'll be all right, Elizabeth. He's probably long gone by now. I'll be back before dark."

Thomas kissed his wife on the cheek goodbye and told her that he loved her. Elizabeth was still somewhat worried for her husband's safety. Before he walked outside, he thought to himself, *I better get the old musket down from above the fireplace.* He knew the prisoner could possibly still be in the area and wanted to have something to defend himself with in case they crossed paths. He hitched Lee and Stonewall up after loading some necessary tools into the wagon he thought he needed in order to fix the water wheel.

After arriving at the Mill, he saw no sign of the posse or of the escaped convict.

The creek had been kind of low but started to rise a little due to some heavy rain the past few days, bringing a nice flow of water through the old cypress trees into the open basin.

****

Back on the Hendrix farm…

"Sarah, I sure hope Thomas will be all right."

"Me too. The sheriff said no one should go out unless we heard something different. But Thomas is a grown man and he knows how to take care of himself. There's no need to worry, Elizabeth."

"I guess you're right. Let's not think about any bad things today. Thomas said he would send Phillip and Annie over to spend the day with us. I'll feel a lot better when Phillip gets here."

****

At the Mill House, Thomas worked hard at fixing the water wheel, the sweat pouring down his face as he labored alone, only his horses were there to keep him company. Earlier, he'd unhitched Lee and Stonewall, letting them walk down by the creek to get a drink of cool water. He finally found the broken piece that had kept the wheel from turning, and thought, *this will take a while to fix without someone to help me hold the part in place.* He walked over to the wagon to get the tool he needed, his lower back hurting from having leaned over in one spot for so long, but his resolve to get the wheel moving again kept him going. The old musket he'd carried with him was sitting on top of the box he needed to get into, and when he reached over to move it out of the way, it caught hold of something and discharged, the load striking him in his stomach. The pain went through his body like a streak of lightning, and when he put his hand to his side, he could feel the blood soaking through his shirt. He looked around for someone to call out to, for someone to help, but no one was in sight. He was bleeding profusely. He tried to walk around to the front of the wagon, but became faint and lightheaded, stumbling back and forth. He called out to Lee and Stonewall and they walked over to where he was. He fell to the ground, unable to regain his balance or find the strength to stand on his feet again, and looking up into the blue sky, he thought about Elizabeth and his children, *how will they ever make it without me?*

"Well, Lee…Stonewall, looks like this is the end for me my faithful friends. We sure had a lot of good times together and traveled a lot of rough miles, didn't we?" whispered Thomas, holding his side in extreme pain.

Lee and Stonewall knew something was wrong. Thomas sat on the ground, alone, bleeding from his stomach, his back resting hard against the wagon wheel.

"Don't worry about me, boys. Just be sure to look after Elizabeth and the children, and be good to Phillip too. We sure had a good journey with him from Carolina, didn't we?"

Lee and Stonewall stood there helpless, nudging on him, not knowing what to do.

Thomas's voice got weaker and weaker as he mumbled his last words:

"Our father, which art in heaven, hallowed be thy name, thy kingdom come, thy will be done, on earth as it is in heaven. Give us this day…our daily bread, and lead us… not into temptation…but deliver us…"

In just a little while Thomas was dead.

****

It was getting late and Elizabeth began to worry about her husband; he'd been gone all day and she had a bad feeling something was terribly wrong. Phillip and Annie were about to go back to their cabin but didn't feel good about leaving Elizabeth, Sarah, and the kids behind. Just when they were getting into their wagon, a team of riders came galloping up the road.

"Who could that be this time of the day?" questioned Elizabeth.

Behind the horse riders, she saw two men driving Thomas's wagon. The closer they got, the more she looked for her husband, but didn't see him anywhere.

The riders were the posse that had visited them the day before. A man stopped the wagon a good distance from the house, and the sheriff dismounted from his horse and walked over to Elizabeth, who was standing near the front gate feeling something terrible had happened.

"Elizabeth, I don't know how to say this. Sarah, you might want to stand next to her before I tell her what I have to say. Something bad has happened to Thomas. We found him at Mill Creek this evening lying beside his wagon near the Ridgon Mill house. Somehow he took a load of shot to his stomach from what we believe to have been his own musket."

"Where is he? Thomas! Thomas!" cried Elizabeth.

"Elizabeth, he didn't make it. He's in back of the wagon," informed the sheriff.

"No, Thomas! Thomas!" Elizabeth screamed in disbelief.

Sarah held onto her. Annie tried to console her mother as much as she could without becoming too emotional herself. All three of them were crying and sobbing heavily. Phillip walked over to the wagon to take a look at Thomas, his body lying underneath a white sheet they'd placed on top of him. He could see the blood soaking through and noticed his stomach had taken a bad hit. Standing there, almost numb, he looked at Thomas's cold, lifeless form, and couldn't believe that the man he so highly esteemed and counted as his closest friend, and most recently, as his father-in-law, was now dead.

"What do you think happened, sheriff?" asked Phillip.

"It appears to have been an accident. We found Thomas's musket in back of the wagon. From the size of the wound, it looks like the gun may have gone off while Thomas was standing close by."

Elizabeth didn't want to go anywhere near the wagon, her body trembling and shivering in shock. Sarah held her close, trying to console her, but felt helpless and didn't know what to do or say, for no amount of words could take away the emotional pain her sister-in-law was now feeling. She'd gone through the same thing with her husband Mitchell a few years earlier and knew what it felt like to lose a husband to some tragic accident. The sheriff told Phillip he would need to take the body back to town for the night to examine it more closely and make sure no foul play was involved. After the posse rode off with the body of Thomas, Phillip sought to comfort his mother-in-law and wife Annie, knowing they needed him now more than ever. Sarah and the children spent the night with Elizabeth to help look after the kids and provide the emotional support she desperately needed.

The next day, Phillip sent a telegram to his father in Georgetown, South Carolina…

'Dear Father,
I don't know how else to tell you other than Thomas Hendrix is dead. He had a fatal accident with his musket and took a bad shot to his stomach. The funeral services will be held two days from today. I can understand if you can't make it, but I would love to see you come. I really need to see you and mother and I think it would be good for Elizabeth and Annie to have you around for a few days.'

Margaret read John the telegram. He held his head down in disbelief, unable to come to grips with the fact that Thomas was now dead. *How can this be*, he thought, *I just saw him at the wedding*, and to hear that his friend was no longer living on this earth was hard for him to digest. He walked out of the cabin and down to the creek to sit for a while; it was a place he'd always go to whenever he needed to clear his mind, whenever he needed to find the answers to things that often perplexed him, like the tragedies of life that made him ask God, "Why?" He sat for a long time underneath the old oak tree reflecting back, his leg somewhat numb, lightly tapping his cane against a stump as his mind paused in deep thought, recalling the time he and Thomas first crossed paths, never knowing how much of a role Thomas would play in his life and in his son's life.

While John and Margaret planned for their trip to Georgia, they asked Sarah, their oldest daughter, to stay behind and look after the other children. John had seen many of his friends killed during the war, but none as close to him as Thomas Hendrix, and to have to watch them lower his body into the ground was going to be one of the hardest things he'd have to prepare for.

Phillip's father wrote back…

'I'm saddened to hear of the death of Thomas. Your mother and I will make it to the funeral service. Our deepest sympathies are with the Hendrix family. Please let them know we are thinking of them and we'll be glad to help out anyway we can.'

Phillip took care of the preparations for the funeral, and made sure everything was attended to so that no burden fell on Thomas's family, especially on his wife. Elizabeth wanted Thomas to be buried at Oak Grove, since the church was located on his land. Thomas's parents, James David and Elizabeth, looked to Phillip for strength during this time, and in many ways, he was a godsend to the Hendrix family.

James David and Phillip walked over to the cemetery from Thomas's house to pick out a burial plot.

"I can remember when Thomas was just a little boy. He used to climb that old oak tree over there," remembered James David.

Phillip looked over to where Thomas's father was pointing to and noticed the old oak tree had died and fallen down, as if to represent the life of the boy who'd played on its limbs, grew to a man, and now, like the oak, had died. He looked at James David whose eyes seemed to be fixed on the past and on memories of his son, to a time and place far away from where he was now standing, detached in memory from his present surroundings. Phillip didn't talk much, just quietly listened to James David capture stories of the past with such recollections that brought tears to his eyes.

"This is where Thomas will be buried," pointed James David.

Phillip marked the spot. To him it would now be considered hallow ground, for Thomas had taught him many things about life - about things that mattered most. He thought about the lady who'd drowned in the water when crossing the Savannah River and what Thomas had told him that night concerning her death...

"There's nothing on earth purposeless. We're all God's creatures and we are put here for a reason. When it's our time to go, then it's our time to go."

Those words helped Phillip make it through Thomas's death and he used them to comfort the rest of the family as well. After he and James left the cemetery, he visited some of Thomas's old soldier friends from the war, and expressed to them how he wanted his father-in-law to have a soldier's burial. It wasn't long ago when they'd fired the guns for Thomas's return home celebration at Nevils Creek, and now, they would be firing them for his funeral service at Oak Grove.

John and Margaret West made it safely to Statesboro the evening before the funeral. Phillip met them at the train station took them to the Hendrix home where many of the family relatives and loved ones were gathered, some sitting on the front porch and others standing in the yard. It was an emotional moment for John when he arrived, feeling a spirit of mourning all around, an old time wake they called it, and it made him feel as if the cold hand of death were present. Phillip helped his parents down and walked them inside the house to the living room where the body of Thomas lay in a casket. The line was long and everyone waited patiently to pay their last respects to the man they'd all come to admire, one born and raised among them. The sunlight beamed bright, shining through the open windows where a soft breeze lightly blew the thin, white curtains back and forth, almost like angel's wings flapping quietly in the wind. John shared his condolences with Thomas's wife and parents as he entered the room, not saying much, mostly expressing his grief through handshakes and tears. He didn't know how he would react seeing Thomas in the casket, usually full of energy and life, but now lifeless and still. Many wept when John walked up to the casket and took his hat off, placing it over his heart while he spoke to his friend, in the natural way he and Thomas used to talk to each other around the open campfires at night. He had a lot he wanted to tell him, but knew many of the relatives and friends were waiting behind to express their final farewell. He wanted to thank Thomas for being such a good friend, for looking after Phillip on the journey from Carolina, for blessing his son with such a wonderful wife. There was so much he wanted to say, so much to reminisce on, but the time had come to say goodbye. After paying his last respects, he leaned over the casket and placed one of Thomas's harmonicas next to his side. Thomas had played many spiritual tunes with it during the war and had given it to John as a gift.

He quietly whispered…

'I want you to have this harmonica back, Thomas. Play it for the angels in heaven. I know they will be touched by your soulful playing as much as we poor creatures did here on earth.'

It didn't seem right, John thought, for his friend's life to end this way, this quick, in this manner. He walked out onto the veranda and dusted off his hat, taking in a deep breath as he looked out across the southern landscape that Thomas had farmed and cherished his whole life. Phillip walked with his father over to the barn that Thomas had been working on before he'd died; *his last unfinished work*, John thought, as he rubbed his hands across the framing of a stall. They walked over to Lee and Stonewall who'd traveled hundreds of miles with Thomas pulling the old wagon up hills and across creeks along the southern Atlantic coast, their last long journey ending here, in the Bay Gall, their final resting place. It was a sad ending that brought them all together, but John knew Thomas had prepared himself his whole life for the unexpected, and this comforted him.

The next day the funeral service was held and Thomas's body was taken to Oak Grove Church in a wagon pulled by Lee and Stonewall. Two soldiers galloped on horses in front of the procession, a wagon train of friends and loved ones taking part in Thomas's final farewell. When they arrived at the church, Thomas's body was taken out of the wagon by some of his fellow soldiers who were dressed in full Confederate uniform. As they carried his body into the church, a soldier played one of Thomas's favorite songs on the harmonica, *Amazing Grace*, a melody that filled the atmosphere and set the mood for the funeral service. The immediate family members entered the church doors first and were seated in the front pews, while everyone else followed close behind, the small church quickly filling to capacity. Many friends and neighbors stood near the front and side doors, others congregated in the churchyard, and the rest gathered near open windows to hear the funeral sermon.

The minister stood behind the pulpit and spoke a few words to the great crowd of people:

'Today we are sad and tearful. One of our greatest community leaders and sons of the Confederacy has passed from this life into the next. We are all gathered here to pay our last respects to Thomas B. Hendrix. It is evident by the amount of people here that he touched many of your lives. Thomas was in many ways, a father to us all, to the young and to the old. He fought in the War Between the States. He often said that he didn't fight to procure slavery, but to defend the soil that many of the slaves labored on. Many of his fellow soldiers are here with us today. To you and to Thomas, we honor your service and sacrifice.

I wrestled with what words I would say to you today, especially to the Hendrix family. I know there is nothing I can say that will bring Thomas back to life. Even if I could, I don't think that is what he would want. He wouldn't mind us mourning over his loss, I am sure, for he mourned the death of many of his loved ones gone before. He wouldn't mind us reminiscing on the past and on cherished memories we have of him. He often spoke of the past in passing conversations. What he would mind is any of us getting bitter over his sudden death. He wouldn't want us questioning God as to why He let this terrible tragedy occur. The Scriptures say we now look through a glass darkly, but then face to face and we shall know even as we are known. Life is filled with mysteries. There are so many things that happen in life we don't understand and that keep us in a state of wondering. Wondering about things that could have been or things that never happened. We have to keep our faith in the One that can not be seen with the human eye. We must trust in the Creator of all mankind to lead us all home safely in whatever manner he so chooses. Let the death of Thomas bring us all closer together and not further apart. Let the life that he lived remind us of our duty to God, to each other, and to ourselves. Let us remind ourselves daily of the uncertainty of life. I am sure Thomas Hendrix never thought the morning he left his house it would be his last day on earth. When he kissed his wife goodbye and told her that he loved her, I'm sure his wife never expected that would be the last time she would hear him speak those words. The Scriptures teach us not to boast ourselves of tomorrow, for we know not what a day may bring. We shouldn't take for granted the people we love and hold dear to our hearts. Tell them you love them more often. It may be the last opportunity you have to let them know how much they mean to you.

To his parents, his wife, and his children, we all mourn with you today. We lift you up in our prayers and thoughts. We, like the Heavenly Father, seek to spiritually hold your hand and lead you on into greener pastures. May the Lord bless you, keep you, and reunite you with Thomas when the trumpet of the Lord shall sound.'

After the minister finished speaking, the men took the body of Thomas out to the cemetery, only a short walking distance from the church, where the crowd gathered around to watch them lower his body into the earth. Three cannons were lined up outside the cemetery, and three men, dressed in full Confederate uniform, fired each cannon once in honor of his military service to the old South…

Boom……….Boom……….Boom!

The smoke from the cannons rose high in the air.

Elizabeth and her children walked up to the casket and placed roses on top, and when they lowered his body into the ground, John West and the other soldiers saluted him one last time. Phillip looked over at Thomas's children, and thought, *it sure is sad seeing them hold such lonely expressions on their faces, as if their only hope in life had faded away.*

It was now up to him to keep the Hendrix family strong and moving forward, a responsibility he regarded with deepest respect.

****

It wasn't long before Phillip and Annie started having children of their own, the first-born named John W West, after Phillip's father; then Thomas, Annie Elizabeth, Silas, Phillip Jr., Paul, and Mark were born. The Wests lived peacefully together near Bay Gall creek, along the winding road that led to the little log cabin they'd remodeled years before when Phillip had come from the Carolinas in hopes of finding a new life, which forever changed when he fell in love with Annie. He sometimes sat down by the creek wondering what his life would've been like had he not decided to come to Georgia. *Would I have ever found true love?* He thought. *Would I have ever learned how to deal with life's tragedies like I did traveling with Thomas? Would I have ever met the people or seen this part of the country that has become so much a part of me and has defined who I am as a person?* These questions often perplexed him, but he knew he'd traveled the path meant for him. The only regret he had was leaving his parents behind and not being there when they grew old and passed away.

He worked hard the following years…plowing in the fields, planting crops, and tending to the livestock, but he wanted to find a different line of work to do other than farming…*something in the city*. One day, after putting the mule in the barn, he felt the time had come to put the plow down for good; his body felt tired and worn as he walked over to the basin of water sitting on the back porch. That evening he shared with his wife his thoughts of turning the farming over to John, their oldest son.

Annie stood near the open door watching the sun go down when she felt Phillip wrap his arms around her - his soft and gentle embrace making her feel special and warm inside.

"Phillip, isn't it beautiful? Such a rich-colored sunset."

"It sure is, Annie. But not as beautiful as you."

"Oh really?"

"Oh really," said Phillip, brushing her hair back...kissing her on her neck.

"So what has put you in such a happy mood?"

"Well, I've been thinking about making a change and I've finally come to grips with it."

"And what is that?"

"I've decided to turn the farming over to John. He's old enough now and is able to handle the work load. I came across a sales job ad in the paper the other day looking for someone to sell farming equipment. I know just about everything on the market and how it all works, and it looks like it pays a pretty good salary too."

"So what's the downside?"

"I'll have to do a lot of traveling."

"If you're ok with it, I am too. Of course I'll miss you while you're gone, but you deserve a job like that and John will carry out his new responsibilities well here on the farm. I'm very proud of you, Phillip."

"Why do you say that?" smiled Phillip.

"Because of the man you are, of the man you've become. You've worked hard your whole life for everyone else and never taken time for yourself. You deserve to do what makes you happy."

Phillip would leave home during the week and return on the weekends. He gave Annie a little black book to keep, and he asked her to put the names of the children in it that had disobeyed or misbehaved in any manner. When he got back home on the weekends, he would look in the black book and properly discipline any of the children that had their names in it. This helped to keep the children in order and made life a little easier for Annie to handle while Phillip was away. He would always bring home a bag of groceries when he returned.

Tragedy struck the West family twice during those early years. Young Phillip Jr. died of a fever. He was only a few months old. Then Paul died when he was ten from a similar illness. They were both buried at Oak Grove Baptist Church where Annie attended services regularly. The death of her young sons, Phillip and Paul, hurt her deeply, but she had all of the other children to worry about and didn't have much time for grieving.

She would say a prayer over their graves whenever she would visit them…

"O Lord, I miss little Phillip and Paul. They were so kind and gentle. They were like angels to me. I know you had a reason for taking them while they were still young. Lord please protect the rest of my children and let them live to be strong and healthy."

Phillip knew Annie was feeling sad over the death of their two sons. He wanted to find a way to cheer her up, so he made a special trip to Statesboro and bought her a beautiful dress, hoop skirt and all, just like the ones he saw the ladies wearing in Charleston at the *'Outdoor Ball.'* He also purchased an expensive frock suit, top hat, and new pair of shoes for himself. He'd planned for a nice romantic evening in the old barn near the cabin, decorating the inside with candles and fragrant flowers. For dinner, he'd placed a small wooden table near the open window where white thin-flowing curtains were hung - the branched limbs of an old oak tree in open view. He'd swept the barn floor clean so he and Annie could have a good place to dance, just like the rich plantation owners danced at the open ball in Charleston. He'd hired a musician from Rocky Ford to stand in the barn loft to play the violin and Annie's sisters prepared a rich, southern dinner for two.

When Phillip arrived back at the cabin, Annie was in the garden picking some fresh ripe tomatoes.

"Annie, I've got a present for you."

"Phillip, you shouldn't have."

"Come inside and open it."

Annie walked inside with a big smile on her face, for it had been a while since she'd received any kind of a present. When she unwrapped the present, she could hardly believe her eyes. She held the dress up and pranced around the room with it against her body.

"Oh, Phillip, it's lovely! I haven't worn a dress with a hoop skirt since our wedding! What did I do to deserve such a gift?"

"Annie, you deserve a lot more than a dress. But don't feel too spoiled. I got myself something new to wear too."

Phillip took out his suit and spread it over the chair. Annie didn't know what to think. Why was Phillip buying a suit? Why did he buy her a dress?

"Annie, I need you to get dressed for a special occasion tonight. I'll be dressing up too…and don't ask any questions," smiled Phillip. "You'll find out soon enough."

Annie walked to the bedroom to try on her new dress, her face beaming with delight and interest over the mysterious evening.

After putting it on, she walked into the living room, and Phillip's eyes were instantly captivated - her hair wonderfully fixed and her dress fitting perfectly. He thought she looked like a princess. Annie looked at Phillip in his new suit and tie, and thought he looked like a prince.

"Ok, Annie, follow me."

"Where on earth are we going?"

"I want to take you to a ball."

"A ball? I've never been to a ball in my life. Besides, no one goes to balls in our part of the country."

"Well, we'll be the first," said Phillip, holding her hand while leading her to the barn.

When he opened the double pine doors, Annie looked around in awe, *lovely beyond anything I've ever seen* she thought. Phillip nodded to his friend to start playing the violin, choosing a lovely Italian song he'd heard somewhere along his travels. Phillip bowed and motioned for Annie to enter the romantic setting he'd worked so hard to prepare, her eyes watery with tears, bowing in response to his. She slowly walked inside, taking in the beauty of the burning candles carefully placed all around the barn.

The violin set the mood. Phillip took Annie by the hand and asked her for a dance.

"Shall we, my lady?" motioned Phillip with his hands.

"I'd be honored to," replied Annie.

Together they laughed and danced like the men and women did in Charleston, only to Phillip it meant a lot more. There they were, Phillip West from Georgetown, and Annie Hendrix from Statesboro, dancing in each other's arms as though time and eternity had stopped to watch and admire them, providing a special place for sorrow's wounds to subside. Every turn they made dancing around the barn made Annie's burdens feel lighter and lighter, her thoughts and emotions centered on the one she'd given her heart and life to. To her, this moment was an emotional healing she so desperately needed, never realizing until now how much it meant for her and Phillip to have time alone, just the two of them. He made her feel like she was the only person in the world and it made her feel wanted.

"Annie, I just want you to know that I love you more than anything else in the world. You know that, don't you?"

Annie was silent, her head quietly resting on Phillip's shoulder while they danced. He could tell she was crying, and that was a good thing - all of her bottled up emotions coming to surface. He understood the moment. It was what he'd wanted, the reason for the occasion - to allow her to let go. He held her gently, dancing back and forth until there were no more tears.

Chapter Seven

*F*rom Bay Gall creek, the iron track in Rocky Ford measured a couple miles away, and the people in the deepest regions of the swamp were used to hearing the rumble of the train through the dense woods of uncut virgin pines along the Ogeechee. It was a time of great progress in the Lockhart district, especially across the river in Rocky Ford, where a sash and door factory was newly established. The company also made pre-cut houses, and to accommodate the employees and associates, a hotel and thirty houses were built in the fast growing town. On the Bulloch County side of the river, not far from the West log cabin, the E.E. Foy Manufacturing Company built a large mill where they sawed and planed lumber. Foy also built a large railroad trestle across the river near *The Rocks*, and obtained a small train engine to haul the mill's products across the trestle to the Central of Georgia station for market. He'd recently purchased a smaller mill from George R. Heard, who not long before had built the first bridge across the Ogeechee in order to move his lumber to Rocky Ford. Mr. Heard was a distinguished businessman, and he kept busy selling lots for businesses and residents in the little town that had remained quiet for so long.

For the people of the Bay Gall, the times were quickly changing, but many welcomed it as a *positive change*, since it brought new jobs to the area and provided a new means of transportation – a train engine! On weekends, the lumber tram would pick up anyone along the track from Old Portal to Rocky Ford that wanted to go to Tybee Island for a weekend excursion. The coastal island provided a newly built hotel, *The Hotel Tybee*, with all the modern luxuries for its guests, and the sandy beach and quiet shoreline made it the ideal place to get away and relax.

A few weeks earlier, Phillip had read a description of Tybee by *BH Richardson* in a tribute concerning *The South's Long Branch* that made him want to take Annie on a weekend excursion there.

Listen to this Annie, said Phillip: "a magnificent seaside resort, attractions for strangers, recreation for all, a summer resort with allurements for winter tourists, 12 ½ miles from Savannah, and 18 miles to the extreme southern end, historical incidents, reminiscences, fortifications, picturesque scenery, pure water, perfect drainage, ample hotel accommodations, a railroad from the Forest City, the Seaport of the Empire State of the South, to the Sea, a gigantic enterprise conceived and successfully accomplished by Captain D. G. Purse, a prominent capitalist and citizen of Savannah." Purse, owner of the greater part of Tybee, had newly constructed a railroad - *The Savannah and Tybee* - that reduced the time of travel from the mainland to the island from two hours to thirty minutes. Before, tourists and travelers had to take a two-hour steamboat ride to the north shore, but now, thanks to the insight and ingenuity of one man, access to the island was shortened considerably. The Foy track, the Central of Georgia, the Savannah and Tybee R.R., were three connections that now made Tybee a not-so-distant and welcome destination for the people of the Bay Gall, some 100 miles away.

****

The Foy track was less than a mile from the West place, and on one sun-kissed summer day, Phillip and Annie boarded the train to meet with the Central across the river destined for the coastal island near Savannah. It would be Annie's first trip to the beach, and having only seen pictures of ocean shores in various magazines, she could only imagine what the gentle sea breezes would feel like brushing softly against her face. Her skin had been made tan each year from spending time in her vegetable garden and in the fields, but never from the suns rays touching her face walking along some sandy beach. Her whole marriage had mainly consisted of the quiet setting around Bay Gall creek and the log cabin. Leaving for a weekend excursion to the ocean seemed foreign to her, but with a little persuasion from Phillip, she'd finally given in to the idea.

The Central of Georgia made its way from Rocky Ford to the Savannah waterfront near *Yamacraw Bluff*, the track passing by large cotton warehouses along the cobblestone road leading to the Tybee Island Depot on the eastern side of town; Hutchison Island could be seen from the passenger carts as the train moved alongside the river and several seagoing vessels in the Savannah overshadowed the Central. After connecting to the Tybee Railroad, the track worked its way back toward the Savannah near Fort Jackson, crossing to McQueen's Island over Wilmington River, then along the southern channel all the way to the northern shore of Tybee Island after passing over the trestle at Lazaretto Creek.

It was a beautiful ride between Savannah and Tybee, and Annie took in the scenery with every breath she took as the smokeless train made its way through the marshland. The coastal cedars, cabbage palms, and yaupon hollies etched the lowlands, and the brown pelicans and flying osprey painted the coastal air with their presence. The salty marsh winds blew gently across the Central and warmly touched the faces of the passengers.

After passing by Long Island, Fort Pulaski could be seen on the eastern end of Cockspur, its brick walls badly damaged by Union cannon shells in 1862. Looking out toward the Fort, Phillip thought of his father, John, and of Annie's father, Thomas, and how the war had forever changed their lives and the landscape of the South. It had been that way since they'd both passed away…every *Civil War* structure bringing back past memories of his father and father-in-law. A quiet sadness would always ensue, but he'd learned how to hide it from Annie. After all, that was the reason for the trip, to cheer Annie up and forget about the sadness of the past, if not for a little while.

As they neared the northern shore, the top of Tybee Lighthouse could be seen in the distance, and Annie's first view of the ocean left her speechless. "We'll have to visit the Lighthouse," mentioned Annie in passing. Her attention quickly shifted from the sea to the shore when Hotel Tybee came into view, anchored in the sands on the southern end like some magnificent ship. "Look Phillip, Hotel Tybee. Isn't it wonderful? I've never seen anything like it!" Thousands had flocked to Tybee Island since the railroad was built, and the need to build a grand hotel was born in the mind of Herman Myers and other investors in Savannah who created the Tybee Hotel Company. Hotel Tybee was constructed on the South shore overlooking the Atlantic Ocean.

The Savannah Morning News had reported the following about the Hotel: "It has 120 guest rooms and thirty rooms for other purposes. The main building is 250 feet in length, and has a frontage on the beach of 205 feet. It has all the modern improvements of electric bells, speaking tubes, gas and water, bath rooms, stand pipes, and hydrants for fire protection. The guests' rooms have, in addition to the usual doors, slat doors, so that the rooms can be private and at the same time have ample ventilation. Passages are left between the rooms so as to let the breeze pass through the rooms from whichever direction it may flow. In every respect the hotel is a model for a seaside resort, and the architects deserve credit for their successful effort in planning a building so admirably adapted for the purpose for which it is intended. The dining room is large, airy, and handsome. It is 126 feet by 46 feet which is 10 feet wider and 15 feet longer than that of the DeSoto Hotel in Savannah. Immediately adjoining it, and separated by double doors, is the carving room, and adjoining that is the kitchen and other rooms belonging to the culinary department. A bar and billiard room is also provided."

One feature that stood out above the rest was a large observatory on top of the Hotel that overlooked the island. Also, artesian waterworks decorated the premise and an outdoor pavilion was added for meetings and dancing.

The train came to a stop at the depot in front of Hotel Tybee on Fifteenth Street and Strand.

"I can't believe we're finally here. Our dream vacation," remarked Annie. "It's more than I'd anticipated. The beautiful train ride through the salt marshes…the view of the ocean…the wonderful hotel!"

"I'm glad you are enjoying the trip, Annie. It's good to see you smile again."

That is what Phillip lived for, to see Annie smile. He wanted more moments like the one they had had in the barn a few weeks earlier, moments where Annie could free herself from the hurt and heartache of losing her children. She would always feel their absence, but getting away for a little while would help in the healing process. She'd always had a strong spirit, and growing up during the Civil War positioned her to expect tragedies and death, but not the loss of her children. Her wounds were beginning to heal a little at a time, and every now and then, Phillip would catch a glimpse of the youthful smile he'd fallen in love with. And today was one of those times.

The sound of the ocean waves hitting the shore made for a peaceful setting, and the island breeze sweeping across the depot followed them inside Hotel Tybee. After a bellboy assisted them to their room, Phillip and Annie paused to take in the ocean scenery from the open window, a clear view of the sand dunes and sea oats between the waves and the walkway below.

"Oh Phillip, look at that view!"

There were several people walking the beach, and a band was playing music at the pavilion.

"Do you recognize the tune, Annie? I don't think I've ever heard it before. Makes me feel like dancing."

Annie wasn't quite ready to feel the island spirit. Outwardly, she beamed like the sun's rays along the ocean shore. But inwardly, she still hadn't left Bay Gall Creek. One part of her wanted to dance and feel the sand beneath her feet, wanted to rent a bathing suit and run toward the ocean waves and feel the Atlantic waters wash away the sadness that had followed her aboard the Central. The other part kept her at bay. It seemed that in every boy's face she saw, it was young Paul's. Or if she passed a mother holding a baby, it was young Phillip. She stepped away from the window, hoping Phillip hadn't noticed the tear running down her cheek. She quickly brushed it away with her hand. She thought of their reason for coming and found a way to dance to the sound of the music, and for a moment, felt the light of the sun beneath her feet.

The rest of the day would be spent relaxing on the sandy beach and touching the ocean waves, ending with a candlelit dinner in the hotel dining area as the sun went down. Afterward, they walked up to the large observatory overlooking the island. The stars shone clearly over the Atlantic and the summer solstice brought a champagne colored harvest moon low in the sky.

"It's so lovely up here," smiled Annie.

"You can see the whole Island," said Phillip.

"The moon is so beautiful. I feel like I can reach out and touch it."

Annie extended her arm out and pointed her finger toward the moon. "There. I told you I could touch it," smiled Annie.

"You have always had that ability," smiled Phillip, "touching the moon. I recognized it the first time I saw you."

Phillip held Annie in his arms.

"Thank you, Phillip."

Phillip knew what she meant by thanking him. There was no explanation needed, no questions asked. He could see it in her eyes, a growing light he hadn't see in a long time. It wasn't anything he'd done. He had only allowed her to be herself without any lines drawn in the sand. There was no need for words, just a silent conversation that brought healing for the both of them.

They could see everything in front of them being touched by the bright moonlight. To the right of the hotel were the rental cottages. Straight ahead was the dancing pavilion. To the left was the picnic pavilion with multiple covered picnic tables in front of it. To the left of the picnic pavilion was the beach bathhouse.

The ocean waves pounced against the shoreline as Phillip pointed toward the Tybee Lighthouse: "Look Annie, the Lighthouse on the northern shore."

The burning kerosene inside the Second Order Fresnel lens identified Tybee Roads, the inlet to the Savannah River, and mirrored its prism light for miles out to sea for passing ships.

"Looks like a blinking star from here," said Annie. "Let's walk the shore tomorrow to the Lighthouse."

"Wonderful idea…," said Phillip, holding Annie in his arms, looking out toward the blinking light.

The wind blew softly in the warm night air, and the ocean waves hitting the shore seemed louder in the dark. They didn't want the night to end. There would be few times like this, and they held on to each other in the late night hours until the stars disappeared behind the clouds.

The next morning found the coastal skies filled with a steady rain. It was late in the evening before they left Hotel Tybee to walk the ocean shore toward the Lighthouse, the thunder and lightning keeping them inside most of the day. Not many people were out on the beach due to the storms rolling through, but the pause in bad weather lured a few souls from the hotel. Phillip and Annie collected seashells as they walked along the shore toward the northern end of Tybee. A few seagulls dotted the coastal sky, and they noticed the air had become somewhat cooler. As they neared the Lighthouse, a chain of dark clouds from the Atlantic reached the land with a blast of strong winds and torrential rains, and they rushed to the Lighthouse keeper's home in order to find relief from the storm. The keeper's home was a lovely two-story structure overlooking Tybee Roads. They could see in the distance Hilton Head and Dafuskie Islands across the tidal inlet. Annie's sister, Laura Jane, had indirect ties with Dafuskie. She'd married William Mongin, whose French Huguenot family had settled on the nearby island in 1812.

The Lighthouse keeper was in the kitchen when he heard a knock at the door. He looked out the living room window and saw Phillip and Annie standing on the front porch, soaking wet. He kindly welcomed them inside and started a warm fire in the fireplace. After leaving them alone for a short while in the living room, he returned with two cups of hot coffee.

"Thank you. That is very kind of you," said Annie.

"I hope we are not intruding," said Phillip, taking a sip of coffee.

"No. Not at all," said the keeper, sitting down in a cushioned chair.

He wore a hat of dark indigo-blue wool with a black leather visor, the US Lighthouse Service insignia embroidered on the front.

The wind howled outside and the rain beat against the windowpanes.

The keeper took out a wooden pipe from his coat pocket, then lit it with a match.

"I haven't had any company in a long time. It's good to have unexpected visitors," said the keeper, the smoke rising from the burning tobacco in his pipe. "So how did you two end up on this side of the island on a day like this?"

"This is our first time on Tybee and we wanted to see the Lighthouse before we left in the morning," said Phillip. "We thought the worst of the weather had passed."

"Ah," said the keeper. "I've been caught off guard myself by many a coastal storms. Sometimes as if the sea would swallow me up," his eyes focused on a family portrait hanging above the fireplace.

"Who are they?" asked Annie. "The family in the picture…"

The keeper's eyes filled with a watery mist. "That was taken when we first moved here. My wife and I with our children before the fever came. It was last winter…"

The quietness of the house revealed the man was all alone.

"It took them all away from me, the fever, a storm as fierce as any the sea has ever brought to shore."

Annie could feel the pain and loneliness in his voice. She thought about her two sons she'd lost to sickness, and how blessed she was to still have her husband and other children with her. All the pain she'd been feeling over her loss seemed so small compared to the keeper's deep sorrow, his whole family taken so suddenly from him.

"She loved to play the piano…" he said.

Annie saw a piano in the corner of the room. She hadn't played any since her two sons had passed away. But now, she felt the need to in light of someone else's grief and loss. She walked over to the piano.

"Do you mind?" asked Annie.

"No. Not at all. I'd love to hear you play something," said the keeper.

He sat quietly in his chair looking up at the portrait above the fireplace as Annie played, the tears streaming down his face. He imagined his wife and children were with him again along the northern shore, the sound of the music bringing back past memories of his family that seemed to bring them back to life. The rest of the evening would be spent around the piano and the portrait and the keeper sharing stories of the past.

The storm outside had finally subsided, and in a way, the Lighthouse keeper felt his grief subside as well. It was a meaningful visit no one had expected, and it helped heal the wounds of Phillip and Annie as much as it did the keeper.

The next morning, Phillip and Annie left Tybee with a renewed strength, and Hotel Tybee and the Lighthouse would always hold a special place in their hearts.

Chapter Eight

Winter season had arrived in South Georgia and the air was chilly cold. It was Sunday, and Phillip, Annie, and the children loaded up in the wagon and rode to church together, dressed as warm as they could be. It was good to see them all sitting together on the middle pew at Oak Grove – the same pew Annie's parents used to sit on.

"Daddy," whispered Thomas, "I plan on going to South Carolina tomorrow to visit Sarah for the week. We've been seeing each other for a while now and I wanted to get your permission to marry her."

"We won't talk about it now, Son. Lets wait for the service to be over with and we'll discuss it on the way home."

Sarah West was a distant relative of Thomas, coming from different West lines, and they'd fallen in love with each other, wanting to spend the rest of their lives together.

As soon as the minister finished the closing prayer, Thomas hurried to the wagon anxious to start the ride home, worried about how his father was going to respond to his request.

"Well, Daddy, you said you would talk about it with me after church," reminded Thomas, gripping the reins to the horses in his hands.

"Son, you know I want the best for you and want to see you happy. If you and Sarah love each other, then that is all that matters. She's a good girl, and your mother and I gladly approve."

"Thank you, Daddy! Thank you, Mama!"

"You're welcome, Son, now slow the wagon down a little."

"Oh...sorry, Daddy, I guess I got too excited."

When the Wests arrived back home, Thomas jumped off the wagon and rushed inside to prepare for his trip to South Carolina. He didn't want to waste any time in asking Sarah to marry him, especially now that he had gotten his parent's approval. That night, everyone sat in the living room around the piano singing Christmas songs. It was Christmas time and the spirit of old Saint Nicholas was in the air, making everyone feel jolly and in good spirits.

Mark was only twelve years old and was more excited about getting wrapped presents than the rest of the children.

"Daddy, I want a redbone coon dog for Christmas," said Mark.

"Why do you want a redbone, Son?"

"'Cause I want to hunt them coons down near the creek and make me a coonskin hat to wear."

"Well Mark, we'll have to wait and see what old Saint Nick brings us."

Mark lay on the floor in front of the fireplace thinking about what he would name the redbone if he were to get one for Christmas.

Meanwhile, Phillip and Thomas sat nearby keeping warm, discussing Thomas's visit to Carolina.

"I remember when I made the trip from Carolina to Georgia many years ago, Son."

"What made you come to Georgia, Daddy?"

"It was my father's idea. He wanted to see if I could find happiness here. His health was failing and he didn't think I would be content in taking over the farm in Georgetown."

"You don't talk about Granddaddy much. Why?"

"It's too painful, Son. Sometimes I blame myself for not being there when he died. Whenever I start talking about him, I think too much about the past. I start missing him and Mama. Tell me, Son, are you sure Sarah is the one for you?"

"I've thought about it a lot, Daddy. The more I think about her not being in my life, the more I realize she's the one."

"I know what you mean. I remember when I first saw your mother. She stood there in the front yard like she was waiting for me the whole time. As soon as our eyes met, I was hooked forever. Even now, when I look into her eyes, I get that old time feeling."

"I hope she says yes."

"Just hope for the best and everything will work out fine. If she says no or if she needs more time to think about it, don't get discouraged. Sometimes a woman likes to think about things before they give an answer. Then again, she might be over her thinking and just waiting for you to ask her."

"Tony!" exclaimed Mark, interrupting his father's conversation with Thomas.

"What? Who is Tony?" asked Phillip.

"Tony will be the name of my redbone coon dog, Daddy."

"Well, if you get one, Mark, I couldn't think of a better name. Tony sounds perfect for a coon dog," said his father, putting another piece of wood on the fire.

Phillip continued his conversation with Thomas.

"Tell me, Thomas, where do you plan on getting married? Here, or in South Carolina?"

"I'm going to ask Sarah to marry me here in Statesboro, sometime after the New Year, if she agrees to it. I want to settle down and raise a family close to you and Mama."

"I'm glad to hear that, Son. I was afraid you might want to move to Carolina."

The next day, Phillip and Annie took Thomas to the train station in Rocky Ford, giving him their full blessings and making sure he had everything he needed.

"Thomas, don't forget to send word that you made it safe. We'll be praying everything works out well for you."

"Thanks, Mama. I love you."

"I love you too, Son."

"Son, I just want you to know that I'm proud of you. Give your old man a great big hug."

"Thanks, Daddy. I'll be home soon."

The air was freezing cold and the horses were anxious to get out of the winter wind. Thomas boarded the Central of Georgia and sat down in his seat, looking out the fogged up window waving goodbye to his mother and father as the train pulled away.

****

In Georgetown, South Carolina, Eva and Dodie West were finishing up on making a dress for their sister Sarah. They knew Thomas was coming and wanted her to have something pretty to wear at his arrival.

"Tell me, Eva, do you think Thomas and Sarah will ever get married?"

"I don't know for sure, Dodie, but I've never seen two people look at each other the way those two do. Sarah talks about him all the time and kisses his picture every night before going to bed."

William, Theodosia, Sarah, and young Herbert arrived home from the store; they'd needed some lamp oil and didn't want to give out now that Thomas was coming to stay the week. Before they walked into the house, Eva and Dodie quickly took the dress and hid it away in Sarah's bedroom closet. They didn't want her to see it just yet.

"Hello, Daddy."

"Why, Eva, what's the reason for the special visit? Did William Henry come with you?"

"No, Daddy. I came alone. I wanted to spend some time with you and Mama."

William West was a distant relative of Phillip; he was a teenage boy when Phillip had left for Georgia.

"It will be good to see Thomas. He reminds me of his father a lot when Phillip was young. He was tall and handsome back then, and quite a lady's man," said William.

"Daddy, what time are we supposed to meet him at the train station?"

"He should be arriving around five o'clock this afternoon. It won't be long. So if you plan on meeting him at the station, you best be getting prettied up."

When Sarah turned around to go to her bedroom, Eva and Dodie walked into the living room holding up the dress they'd made for her.

"Oh my…it's beautiful. Where on earth did you get it?"

"We made it for you, Sarah. We want you to look your best when Thomas steps down off that train."

"It's lovely. I can't wait to try it on."

Sarah hugged Eva and Dodie. She was somewhat surprised they'd made her such a pretty dress, and they helped her get ready to meet Thomas. When she walked outside to get into the wagon, everyone was amazed at how beautiful she was.

"Sarah, you look outstanding!" exclaimed her mother.

"Thank you, Mama. I hope Thomas likes the way I look."

"I'm sure he will. If he doesn't, I know a lot of young men in Georgetown that will jump at the first opportunity you give them."

William, Theodosia, and Sarah slowly made their way to the train station. It was colder in Carolina than it was in Georgia, and Sarah kept a scarf around her neck and a thin blanket on her lap to keep warm with in the cool air. Thomas had asked Sarah to prepare to dine with him the evening of his arrival at an historic antebellum mansion in the historic part of Georgetown on a place overlooking Sampit River. The mansion had been turned into a restaurant and social gathering place.

Georgetown reminded Thomas of Savannah and Charleston. He loved the live oak trees that lined the streets and the rich history that surrounded the coastal town.

When he stepped down off the train and saw Sarah standing there in her new dress, his heart almost jumped out of his chest.

"Sarah, you look wonderful."

"Thank you, Thomas. You don't look so bad yourself."

"Hello, Mr. West. Good afternoon, Mrs. West," said Thomas.

William and Thomas walked to the wagon together while Sarah and Mrs. West stayed near the station talking.

"Mr. West, I want to ask your permission for Sarah's hand tonight at dinner."

"Thomas, you've had my approval since the day you two started courting. I wish you the best and hope you two have a long life together. You and Sarah can stay out as late as you want. I've arranged for a carriage to bring you both to the house whenever you're ready."

"Thanks, Mr. West. I promise I'll take good care of your daughter."

William and Theodosia left the train station waving goodbye.

Thomas looked at Sarah and gave her a warm kiss.

"What was that for?"

"For being so beautiful."

He took Sarah by the arm and walked with her from the station to the riverfront mansion.

"It sure is cold out, isn't it?"

"That just gives me an excuse to hold you closer," smiled Thomas.

They approached the doorkeeper in front of the restaurant.

"I believe we have a table reserved for two," Thomas informed the attendant.

The doorkeeper asked for their names while looking down at the reservation list to see if a table had been reserved.

"Yes. I see your names now: Thomas and Sarah West. I presume you are husband and wife."

"Not exactly, we just happen to share the same last name," said Thomas laughing.

"Oh, excuse me, sir. You looked like a charming young couple and I'd only assumed since you had the same last name. Nevertheless, follow me," said the attendant, somewhat embarrassed by his mistaken assumption.

The attendant took them to the second floor and sat them down at a table near a large window that overlooked Sampit River, *a relaxing scene for such a special occasion*, Thomas thought. The sun was beginning to set and there were boats coming in from Winyah Bay, a picturesque scene of coastal life with seagulls sitting on river walk poles positioned along the dock. The table was set with lit candles and fine china. A waiter walked up to their table and gave them their menus, then sat a bottle of wine down and told them it was on the house. He opened the bottle and poured a little wine in a tiny glass he kept in his shirt pocket. He told them it was a house tradition to taste it before the guests to make sure it was of good quality. Something told Thomas and Sarah it was more of his own tradition. He took two or three taste tests before approving, enjoying each swallow more than the other.

"I will give you two a few minutes to decide what you want," the waiter said, then walked away looking a little tipsy.

"Sarah, I know we hardly ever celebrate, but tonight, let's consider this moment a special time for us."

"What do you mean?"

"Well, tonight just seems like a special occasion. You, in your beautiful dress. Me, in my suit and tie. How often do we get to dine in such a luxurious mansion?"

"I guess you're right."

"I propose a toast."

"What kind of a toast?"

Thomas stood up and walked over to Sarah's chair, kneeling down on one knee beside her before sitting his glass down on the table.

"Thomas, what on earth are you doing?"

He took out a ring from his coat pocket and held it out for Sarah to see. Her eyes began to swell up, and being overcome with emotion, couldn't hold back the tears. She couldn't believe Thomas was about to propose to her, something she'd hoped for, patiently waited for, for so long. She used the napkin she'd held in her hands to dry her tears with.

"Sarah, I want to spend the rest of my life with you. I want us to raise a family and grow old together. I want to kiss you good morning and good night every day for the rest of our lives, until we take our last breath. Sarah West, will you marry me?"

Sarah tried to hold back the tears but was unable to. She held out her hand for Thomas to put the ring on her finger.

"I would be glad to marry you, Thomas. I've been dreaming this day would come for a while, and now it has. I can't think of another man that I would rather spend the rest of my life with."

He gently put the ring on her finger, her hands softly shaking, a reaction more of immediate joy than complete surprise. They kissed as the last rays of sunlight beamed in through the un-glassed window, and a light wind blowing in from the outside gently swept against their faces.

After dinner, they walked by the old clock tower, then along the harbor walk holding hands, their conversation filled with detailed wedding plans: invitations, bridesmaid choices, the wedding dress, etc. It was chilly cold outside and Thomas held Sarah close to his side, making her feel warmer than ever. She looked down at her ring to make sure she hadn't imagined the whole proposal, reassuring herself that Thomas had really asked her to marry him. There were other couples walking along the marina, but none as happy as they were. A light snow began to fall, slowly blanketing the tree tops and buildings around them, forming a winter backdrop lovely enough to put on a postcard that Phillip mailed home to his parents, with the good news written on the back: "She said yes!" They walked from the harbor to the front of the mansion where a group of community kids were singing Christmas carols.   They joined in the singing while waiting for the carriage to pick them up and take them home: *"O little town of Bethleham, how still we see the lie, above thy deep and dreamless sleep, the silent stars go by. Yet in thy dark streets shineth, the everlasting light, the hopes and fears of all the years are met in thee tonight..."*

It was the ending of a romantic night. Thomas stayed the week in Georgetown and had the time of his life before returning home to Georgia.

His parents congratulated him on the good news as soon as he stepped off the train.

"Welcome home, Son! We're so happy for you. Tell us everything that happened. Have you set a wedding date?"

"Yes, Mama. We're going to get married here in Bulloch County on January the 8th."

"Well then, we don't have much time before your wedding day comes. We'll have to prepare for the wonderful occasion," said Annie.

Christmas was just a few days away.

****

Phillip and the boys left the warmth and comfort of the cabin to cut down a cedar tree for Christmas that Silas had hand-picked himself, a tree he'd marked a few seasons ago, only waiting for it to grow a little taller.

As they walked through the woods to look for the chosen cedar, each going his own way, Silas yelled to his father, "Over here, Daddy! I've found the tree!"

Wow, Silas thought, *it sure has grown a lot these last few years*. Phillip and Mark walked up behind him, surprised as much as Silas was on how fast it had shot up, its height almost doubling since they'd last seen it.

"Well, Son. It's your tree. Here's the axe."

Silas almost felt sorry for the cedar, but knew its proper place was in the living room with the Star of David on top. When they arrived back home, the boys rushed inside to the living room to clear a spot for the tree in front of the window. Annie walked in from the kitchen and saw the beautiful cedar.

"What a lovely tree! Silas, you've brought home the prettiest cedar in all the Bay Gall. We'll decorate it with the ornaments Lizzie and I made for last year's tree. Lizzie, go get that box sitting on top of the shelf in my bedroom closet."

"Mama, can I be the one to put the Star of David on top?"

"Of course, Silas. It's your tree," smiled Annie.

When Christmas Eve arrived, everyone sat around in front of the fireplace, including some West relatives that visited every year, and listened to Phillip as he told Christmas stories: Old Saint Nick's Wagon, The Snowman's Cotton Sack, and The North Pole Mule.

The fire made crackling sounds while Phillip painted images in their minds of the snowman picking cotton in the fields during the early winter months to take to the cotton gin, then to the weaver's house to make clothes for all the little orphaned children of the town:

"One winter night, while picking cotton in the Bay Gall from the gleanings left over from harvest, the snowman almost melted from a sudden warm front passing through. He had a large sack full of cotton on his back, but couldn't carry it all, for his strength became weak when he began to melt," imagined Phillip, his eyes staring into the kindled fire.

"Did he make it to the weaver's home in time?" asked Mark.

"Yes. But he couldn't have made it without the help of a farmer who had an ice house…" Phillip paused, and then continued, the children hanging on to every word.

When Phillip finished telling the story, Annie let the children take turns reading a portion of the Bible about the birth of Jesus and the three wise men. Afterwards, she sat down at the piano and played Christmas songs while everyone gathered around and joined in with holiday singing:

'Silent night, holy night, all is calm, all is bright / Round yon Virgin mother and child / Holy Infant so tender and mild / Sleep in heavenly peace, sleep in heavenly peace.'

A light snow falling outside made for a special white Christmas.

Early the next morning, Mark woke up and found a redbone puppy lying next to him in bed. He picked it up and held it in his arms.

"Tony. That's your name, puppy. I'll call you, Tony," said Mark, rubbing the dogs head. The puppy licked Mark on the cheek and wagged his tail at his new owner.

****

Not many days after Christmas, Thomas married Sarah West from South Carolina on January 8th, 1911; a cold winter wedding but a warm and memorable ceremony. The dress Sarah wore was beautifully southern, and her sister, Dodie, came down from Georgetown to be her bridesmaid. The union between the two Wests formed an indelible bond, and only heaven knows the full purpose and plan behind the struggles that would follow.

They moved into a pine built house not far from the West log cabin, close to where Phillip and Annie lived - along the winding road.

****

Mark and Silas were busy raising the redbone puppy Mark had gotten for Christmas, training it to hunt coons all along Bay Gall creek. But after many hunting trips, Mark hadn't trapped a coon to make his coonskin hat with.

One dark night, Tony was hot on the trail of a big coon.

"Go get'em, Tony!" hollered Mark, as he and Silas followed close behind, running as fast as they could.

Tony had chased the coon clear across the creek; it had managed to find its way up a tall tree. It was unusually dark, but Silas held a lantern up in front of them, giving them enough light to see where they were going.

"Hold the lantern up, Silas!"

"Right there, Mark, on that long tree limb. He sure does look like he's mad about being run up that tree."

Tony barked and barked at the coon, which seemed to be more afraid of the dog than he was of Silas or Mark. Mark took a shot, but missed, taking a large chunk of wood out of the tree limb instead. The coon climbed onto another tree that had fallen across the limb it was on, in a desperate attempt to get away, fully aware of the consequences of being trapped. When the coon came running down the trunk of the fallen tree, Mark tried to reload his shotgun in time to shoot it, but accidentally dropped the shell onto the ground. Silas hollered for Mark to hurry up. The coon was almost right on top of them when Mark finally got the shell into the gun and pulled the trigger, barely able to see in front of him. When Silas held the lantern up, the coon was lying dead on the ground just a few feet from Mark's feet, a sight that brought cheers to the two West boys. Mark had shot his first coon and could now make his first coonskin hat. Soon Tony became the best coon dog in the county. Well, at least to Mark and Silas he was the best they'd ever seen, helping them tree many more coons along Bay Gall Creek. It wouldn't be long before Tony would be put to the test in the 10th Annual Bay Gall Coon Hunting Contest. The Bay Gall hunting club was sponsoring the event to determine who had the best coon dog in the county; there was a sense of pride and honor in knowing that your dog was the premier coon dog. There were a lot of coon hunters in the county and every owner swore up and down their dog was the best. The place and location had been set in an undisclosed location. It was finally revealed that the contest would be along the Ogeechee River swamp in a portion of land where never a coon dog had made its mark, near Beasley Town.

Posters were put up everywhere around the county on public buildings, with big letters in red which read:

We've got the fastest and the meanest coon trapped in a cage and ready to be let loose! Looking for the best coon dog in the county to tree it!

The Bay Gall hunting club had trapped a coon in a cage that had been reaping havoc on many neighbors' sweet corn; a coon that had managed to evade all the coon dogs that had attempted to track him down. Now they would release it back into the wild to see if any dog could run it up a tree. The coon was to be given a large lead time before the coon dogs could be let loose on his trail. It would be tagged with a red tag on his ear to let the hunting club know the dog had tracked and treed the correct coon.

Mark and Silas were eager for the event. They'd taken down one of the posters from a public building and put it up on the wall in their room, looking at it every night while lying in bed and dreaming of the day when Tony would have a chance to prove himself. They'd trained him hard, running him back and forth through the swampy hollows near Bay Gall Creek, his bark bellowing out in the darkness on many moonlit nights while chasing coons out of obscure hiding places.

One night, when the moon was full and bright, the light shone through Mark and Silas's bedroom window onto the poster they'd put up on the wall. They both lay awake in their beds staring at it.

"Silas, I want you to be the one to run with Tony during the contest."

"I couldn't. Tony is your dog and you deserve to be the one running with him."

"I've seen Tony. He responds better to you than he does to me. I would only hurt his chances. He needs every bit of edge he can get over the other dogs. I don't know exactly why, but he has taken a special liking to you and that's how I want it to be."

"Ok, Mark. You know I'll do my best to see that Tony is the one to tree the coon. I would consider it an honor."

"Thanks, Silas. I knew I could count on you."

The contest was only a few days away and the tension had been mounting for weeks.

****

Phillip had placed a large stack of wood near the fireplace and was reading the newspaper near the oil lamp when Silas and Mark walked in from the outside. As the sun went down, the cool night air dropped the temperature well below freezing, but the burning wood helped to generate a nice warm atmosphere for the family to sit around and socialize.

"Pa, do you think Tony stands a chance?"

"Well, Son, you and Silas have put a lot of time into training that dog and I don't think there's a coon anywhere in the whole United States that he couldn't tree. I've seen you boys run with Tony and tree some of the meanest coons, probably twice as mean and smart as the one he'll be chasing next week in Beasley Town."

Tony was lying down close to the fire, wagging his tail back and forth, barking in agreement with Phillip.

Annie walked in from the kitchen to where Mark and Silas were sitting and kissed them goodnight: "It's time to go to bed, sons. Tomorrow will be a busy day and Tony needs his rest too."

"Ok, Mama. Goodnight. Goodnight, Daddy."

"Goodnight, sons."

****

The early morning sunlight beamed across the West farm as Mark and Silas got ready to go with their father to cut some firewood for the winter months. They'd burned more wood than usual and the pile was getting low - barely enough to last them through the week. While riding down the road in the wagon, they could hear some dogs barking loud in the distance, echoing out through the woods in front of them.

"I wonder who those coon dogs belong to that are running this time of the morning. They couldn't be chasing coons, unless they're training for the contest," said Mark, standing up in back of the wagon behind his father.

"I don't know, Son. But something tells me we're about to find out."

When they made it to Bay Gall creek, they saw a few wagons and people they'd never seen before standing near the wooden bridge. There was a place just off the road, bordering the creek, where a small open field was hidden from view by a small tree line around the edge, protecting the inside from the winter winds. When they got closer, they recognized Mr. Roy Daughtry, Johnny Mallard, and some Finch boys standing near the wagons. Mr. Finch had a coon dog named Spotter that could see a coon running in the darkest of night and in the tallest of trees. Johnny Mallard's family had been raising coon dogs for years and could probably train a house cat to hunt down a coon. Johnny had his favorite dog named Nose that he was going to enter into the contest. He was called Nose because of his great sense of smell, and even though he was getting up in age, he could still sniff out a coon a mile away. Then there was the talk of the town about a coon dog from the southern part of the county named, Swimmer, owned by Trevor Bone. Swimmer could swim a body of water backwards faster than most dogs could forward. His skill would play a huge advantage in the swamp lands of the Ogeechee where many creeks flowed through the palmetto lowlands, making it harder to track down a fleeing coon. Roy Daughtry was an avid coon hunter in the community and was appointed to be in charge of the Bay Gall Coon Hunting Contest. He was going to let his son Billy run his dog named, Fighter. Fighter could wrestle any coon down to the ground into humble submission and had many scars on his face to prove it, in particular, a missing eye.

Phillip stopped the wagon and conversed with the crowd gathered at the bridge.

"What seems to be all the commotion?"

Roy Daughtry knew Phillip well.

"Hello, Phillip. Some of the men entering the contest wanted to get a little practice in. We set a coon loose in the branch over there and let the dogs chase it. Some of the owners wanted to see what their dog could do against some of the others running next week. Nothing like a little sneak preview."

"Pa, can I go get Tony and let him run with them?" asked Mark.

"No, Son. Let him rest up this week. He'll be ready next Friday night."

"See you later, Roy."

"Take care, Mr. West."

Mark was disappointed that his father had told him no. He wanted to show them all that Tony could tree the coon before the other dogs could. However, he knew the contest would give him the chance to officially prove that his dog was the best.

On the way back home, Phillip took the boys by the Bay Gall hunting club to pick up their entry form, including all the rules and regulations. The rules called for one official being with each owner and dog during the duration of the hunt. The officials would be chosen at random for each entry into the contest by the hunting club members. Each official would carry a pistol. The pistol would be used by the official to fire two shots into the air whenever a dog had treed the tagged coon. The contest would last no longer than two hours.

Silas read a portion of the rules out loud to Philip and Mark:

'A designated official will carry a pocket watch with him to mark the time. If no dog has treed the tagged coon at the end of the two hours, a designated official will fire three shots into the air to let the contestants know that the match is over and no dog had treed the tagged coon. No contestant will be allowed to interfere with the progress of another owner or his dog during the course of the run. The coon being chased can not be shot or killed, only treed by the dog. If a dog corners the coon on the ground and tries to kill it, it is up to the owner to call his dog off. The dog must run the coon up a tree and keep it there long enough for the owner and the official to witness it. In the event where two or more dogs make it to the tree where the coon has climbed, the tie breaker will go to the owner who first puts a red collar around the neck of his dog. The red collar represents the dog and his owner drawing first blood by treeing and spotting the coon as being marked with the red tag. This displays the ability of the dog and its owner to work together. As soon as the official sees the dog with the red collar on and the tagged coon in the tree, then he will fire his pistol into the air twice to let the other contestants know that a dog has treed the tagged coon. No contestant will be allowed to shoot the coon. No guns are allowed by the contestants in the contest. The goal is to see which dog can track and tree the coon before the others. The officials will carry a lantern, as well as the owners of the dogs. Thus, two lanterns will be present for each dog running the coon. No official can assist the owner in identifying the tagged coon before he collars his dog. It is up to the owner to identify the treed coon with his own lantern. If an owner collars his dog in haste, mistaking a treed coon for the tagged coon, then that owner and his dog are disqualified from the match. He is to take his dog back to the Hunting Club. The event will begin at 9 o'clock at night. Regardless of the weather, the event will not be canceled for any reason. Any failure by the owner or his dog to appear at the starting line on time will result in disqualification. Any contestant found to break any of the rules listed will automatically be disqualified. Each coon dog will be allowed to sniff the caged coon once before the contest.

****

The week passed slowly for the West boys. Tony was the center point of every conversation and he seemed to enjoy the attention, having never been pampered so much.

The day of the contest finally arrived, and hundreds of people gathered to witness the event, their wagons stretched out across the open field with their mules and horses still attached. There were lanterns and torches placed all around the starting point, giving the large crowd the needed light to see with under the starless sky. The Hunting Club had set up a large tent for visitors to sit under, and there were many tables placed around for all the people to eat on. Earlier in the day, there was a band that played to keep the people entertained and numerous tickets were sold for prize drawings. A dance was also held, with fiddle playing and banjo picking filling the crowded atmosphere with old time music. After the sun went down, the crowd made a huge bonfire to stay warm with in the night air.

The horn blew five minutes before 9 o'clock for the owners and their dogs to position themselves at the starting point. An old man took the caged coon and walked to the edge of the woods to let it loose, waving a small red flag in the air to let them know he'd set it free. Silas looked over at Swimmer, Nose, Fighter, Spotter and the other coon dogs that were lined up next to Tony, all appearing to be anxious and ready to hunt down the tagged coon and win the prize for their owner.

"Ok, Tony, don't be in such a rush. We'll have plenty enough time to hunt down the coon. Now is your chance to prove to everyone that you're the best coon dog in the county," whispered Silas in Tony's ear.

Roy Daughtry walked up to the starting line with a pistol in his hand.

"Contestants and fans, now for the event we have all been waiting for. We have the meanest, smartest, and fastest coon in the country, caged, being let loose into the wild swamp of the Great Ogeechee as I speak. We have the finest coon dogs in the county, all lined up and ready for the hunt. We thank the Beasleys for letting us use this fine piece of land for the 10th annual Bay Gall Coon Hunting Contest. This event has been sponsored by many of the finest gentlemen of our community and county."

Roy looked at the contestants and loudly spoke, "Contestants, remember the rules, and may the best coon dog win!"

He then fired the pistol into the air, the smoke of the shot disappearing in the darkness as the dogs, owners, and designated officials took off running toward the woods where the coon had been let loose. The coon knew the area well and had traveled the Ogeechee swamp numerous times, being comfortable with its surroundings in the jungle like terrain. But the dogs had never run the area before and were facing a challenging chase against the clever animal that had a good head start in front of them.

The air was chilly cold and it was completely dark due to storm clouds hovering in the sky, blocking the light of the moon and stars, making it more difficult for the dogs and their owners to see in front of them. The creeks had filled with water and the coon's plan was to head for the river in hopes of losing the blood thirsty dogs. The first dog that made it into the woods was Swimmer, and the last one was Tony; but this didn't worry Silas any, for he knew it wasn't a race to the woods, but a contest of who could tree the coon first. He held his lantern tight, running as fast as he could, stumbling a few times over the leaf filled holes and hidden surfaced roots. At times, Tony would slow down to a snails pace, sniffing and barking, then speed up again, running swiftly through the woods, jumping over logs and stumps in his pathway. Silas knew he had to stay as close to Tony as possible in case another dog and owner made it to the coon before they did. He kept pushing Tony to stay on the coon's trail, making sounds that only he and his dog could understand. Back at the starting line, many people could hear the dogs barking and bellowing in the distance. They could see the lantern lights flickering in the woods, then vanishing out of sight again, as the dogs made their way deeper and deeper into the swamp and farther away from the warmth of the bonfire.

Tony and Nose stayed close together for the first part of the chase, the one being cautious and the other being slow. Nose was getting old, but he could smell the coon's scent in the air where the other dogs had to sniff for it on the ground. The coon managed to make it to the first creek in a line of many creeks to the river, swimming across the water in hopes of losing the skilled hunters, his determination stronger than ever to escape through the great Ogeechee swamp. The other dogs had a hard time picking up the coon's scent, running back and forth through the palmettos, but Nose sensed the coon had crossed the cold water, barking and bellowing out to his master, yet unwilling to jump into the freezing water himself. Swimmer made it to where Nose was standing and leaped into the creek, hot on the coons trail, leaving Nose standing behind with the others. Tony tried to walk across a fallen tree over the water in an attempt to stay dry, but managed to fall in just as he neared the other side. Fighter fell a good distance back.

The raccoon turned around and saw Swimmer right on his heels and decided that his best chance of escape was to fight the approaching dog. Swimmer growled and snarled at the coon, his hair standing straight up on his back, still wet from crossing the creek. The two turned and twisted, fighting hard to get the upper hand on each other, attacking, then retreating, waiting for the open strike. The coon lashed out his sharp claws against Swimmer, bringing deep cuts to his ribs, his side bleeding profusely before his owner was able to call him off. It was now over for Swimmer, he was hurt too bad to continue in the chase.

The coon was now anxious more than ever to get away, picking up his pace through the swampy terrain, his natural instincts of escape increasing the more he felt threatened. Nose and Tony ran side by side tracking the coon, the trail going back and forth, leading them through large cypress knees, entangling them in long twisting vines, taking them farther and farther away from the starting line and closer and closer to the deep running river. The coon decided to take refuge in an old hollow stump, hoping the dogs wouldn't see him there, a perfect hiding spot for most animals in trouble. But Nose managed to sniff his way to the old hollow stump, and the coon lashed out at him when he got too close; however, Nose wasn't up for a fight, especially after witnessing what happened to Swimmer. He kept his distance. When the coon saw Tony about to jump into the stump with him, he jumped out and took off toward a nearby creek. Fighter saw Nose and Tony chasing the tagged coon and joined in the fray. When the coon made it to the water, Fighter jumped in after him. The coon swam across the lake and left Fighter swimming in his own tracks. By the time Fighter made it to the other side, the coon had managed to disappear into the palmettos. Tony, Nose, and Fighter were now bunched up together, step for step. But Fighter took a sudden turn and followed some tracks that led him away from the others. He came to the trunk of a swamp chestnut oak and bellowed loud and long at a coon high up in the tree, convinced he'd treed the tagged coon. His owner held his lantern high, searching through the shadowy branches with little light reaching the top, then placed the red collar on Fighter.

"We've got him. We've got him!" exclaimed Fighter's owner. "Fighter has treed the coon!"

Silas heard Fighter's owner yelling in the distance. He thought to himself, *It can't be…why would Tony and Nose keep tracking toward the river at a fast pace unless they were tracking the wrong coon?* The official, running with Fighter and his owner, held his lantern in the air. Silas was waiting for the official to fire the pistol, but he never did. He knew then that Fighter had treed the wrong coon and was disqualified from the contest. In all the commotion, Spotter had joined in the hunt from out of the darkness, running close behind Nose and Tony, still on the coon's tracks. The coon had one more creek to cross before making it to the Ogeechee. It was a wide lake and deeper than the rest, being closer to the river than the others. When the coon made it to the water, instead of swimming all the way across, he turned in its deepest part and swam up creek. Tony, Nose, and Spotter all jumped into the water after him. Spotter started losing his strength and began to go under, too weak to keep his head above the water, completely exhausted from the chase. He swam back to the south side of the creek and fell out of the hunt. The coon turned and swam to the other side of the creek toward the wide river, with only Nose and Tony left to track him. Silas and the others crossed the lake in boats positioned at the creek's edge. It was too deep and wide to wade through. They had to leave the chase momentarily to get to the boats and paddle across the water, which put them in a crucial position in being separated from their dogs. While paddling across the creek, Silas could hear Tony bellowing in the distance. He also heard Nose. He knew they'd treed the tagged coon, but time was running out with only ten minutes left before the two hour contest was over.

Silas made his way to Tony as fast as he could: "Hold on, Tony! I'm coming! I'm on the way!"

Nose's owner was running as fast as he could to get to his dog. The people back at the starting line were now anxious at the time, and Mark looked at his watch and began to worry.

Then, they heard the shots…

The clock was about to strike 11 and everyone just knew the third shot would be fired, thus ending the contest. The clock struck 11, but no third shot was heard. The crowd rushed to the starting point and anxiously waited to see which dog would emerge from the woods with the red collar on. The bonfire had dwindled down to nothing and the lantern lights dimly flickered in the darkness when everyone saw a dog come running out of the woods. Mark and the rest of the family looked anxiously at the dog running toward them, but couldn't make out which one it was. Then he let out a bellow that Mark would recognize anywhere; it was Tony, and he was wearing the red collar. Silas came running out of the woods behind him and the crowd cheered with applause. Roy Daughtry ended the event by announcing to the crowd that Tony was now officially the 'Best Coon Dog in the County'.

****

A few winters passed since the Coon Hunting Contest, and John, Annie's oldest son, had moved away to the neighboring county of Emmanuel. He married a lovely girl named Rachel Greenway and worked in the timber trade. Lizzie, Annie's only daughter, married Walter Neely. Silas and Mark stayed home with their parents and farmed the land, while Thomas and Sarah lived down the road just a little, not far from the cabin.

One day, while Annie was in the garden, Mark and Silas came running out of the cabin yelling.

"What's wrong Silas?" asked Annie.

"It's Daddy. He's not breathing."

This can't be happening, she thought. Phillip had just come home from work and was quietly resting in bed, tired from a long week of traveling. Young Mark had walked up to his daddy's bed and asked him if he wanted to go coon hunting, but his father didn't respond. He'd had a major heart attack while sleeping, lying face up when they found him, looking up at the ceiling as if toward heaven. Annie called for the doctor to come, but it was too late, Phillip had slipped away without any warnings…without any goodbyes. Annie broke down in tears.

****

Two nights later…

"Mama, are you ok?" asked Silas.

"Yes, Son. Where are the rest of the children? Did John make it in ok? Is Lizzie here?"

"They're all here, Mama. John and Rachel got in this evening from Summertown, and Lizzie is here too."

Annie had a terrible fever. She'd stayed strong for so long, and now, two days after her husband's passing, her physical constitution began to suffer. For hours she she'd sat up at Phillip's wake without getting any rest, and her health began to weaken as the hours progressed.

"Here, Mama. Take a sip of water."

Annie leaned up in her bed, her daughter supporting her as she took a small drink from the cup Lizzie had placed to her lips. All through the night she kept talking out loud, her mind burning with heat, not knowing what she was saying. Things like: "Your father will be home any minute now. He'll need his rest after working so many hours. I need to prepare him a nice supper before he gets home." Lizzie kept a cool washcloth on her mother's forehead during the night trying to keep her temperature down, and when the morning light broke through the darkness over the horizon, so did her fever.

****

The following day, the funeral service was held at Oak Grove. The minister knew Annie and how gentle of a woman she was, and he expressed to her and to her family how sad he was over their sudden loss.

As the family and neighbors gathered around the grave for burial, the minister said a few kind words...

"Today we bury a good man and a kind father. He came to us from the Carolinas and brought with him a sense of adventure and wonder. He wasn't afraid to put his hands to the plow and earn an honest living for his family. The word of God says that death will be the last enemy to be destroyed. And what an enemy he is! This formidable foe the scriptures call death - snatching souls from this life in the cruelest of ways. Phillip Admiral West is no longer with us, but his memory will always remain here, among us, in the midst of his family and friends. There was a purpose and plan for why he came down from Carolina to spend a little time with us here in the Bay Gall. And it would do us all good to remember that there is a reason for everything under the sun, no matter how sad or tragic. Phillip loved to talk about his adventurous trip with Thomas Hendrix many years ago from Georgetown, South Carolina to Statesboro, and the many lessons of life he'd learned along the way. After Thomas had died, Phillip often spoke of his friendship with him and how much he'd missed him. And now, Phillip has left us, and we will miss him the same as he did with Thomas. Let us talk often of his memory and of the things he taught us, of the things we learned. He left behind a precious wife and several children. I know Phillip West is looking down from Heaven with Thomas Hendrix, asking God to help lead us and guide us on our pilgrim journey through life."

The minister bowed his head to say a final prayer…

"O Lord, bless Phillip's dear wife Annie and her children. May you keep them in your loving care and let us always remember Phillip Admiral West. Amen."

Annie and her children left the church in the wagon together, the horses galloping at a slow pace while they reminisced on the past and on memories of Phillip. It was a lonely ride for Annie not having her husband by her side, a place he'd served so well, for so long, an exemplary partner and subservient spouse for almost thirty years. When Thomas stopped the horses near the cabin, Annie got off gently, looking tired and frail, her eyes fixed on a time and place belonging somewhere to the past, somewhere long ago and far away from the lonely present. Her children tried to console her, but they knew she needed more time to herself, more time to think and come to grips with the loss of her closest friend and confidant, the one she'd looked to for guidance and strength in the most difficult of times. She walked along the winding road alone, reminiscing on the days when her father Thomas Hendrix first arrived home from the war. There was Phillip West, tall and handsome, sitting up there on the wagon, *ready to conquer the world*, she thought. She remembered when their eyes first met and how she couldn't breathe or say anything to him from being too nervous. To her, he was a prince who came out of nowhere to rescue her from her loneliness; a stranger from South Carolina who God sent to her at just the right time in her life. But now he was gone, and she would have to find a way to make it by herself. *At least I have my children*, she thought, *and I will spend the rest of my days living for them.*

Chapter Nine

Thomas sat near the open window in his chair looking out toward the sagebrush fields, and the sound of a soft breeze blowing in across the tall pines almost relaxed him to sleep. It was the day after his father's burial, and his mind kept drifting back to the conversation he and his father had many years ago; Phillip had talked about Black River and what it was like growing up during the Civil War in Georgetown, South Carolina. The story of his father's journey to Georgia as a young man never seemed to get old to him, and even though he'd heard it time and time again, it always held his full attention. He felt restless since his father had died, and the only thing he could think about was visiting the place where Phillip was born. He'd never been there before, and as far as he knew, the old cabin was still standing. His grandfather and grandmother were supposedly buried on a hill overlooking the place, and Phillip had talked about visiting their graves on several occasions, but never found the time.

It was an unusually warm winter afternoon and a pleasurable day to be outdoors. Sarah was hanging bed sheets out on the line to dry when Thomas's attention turned toward her and how beautiful she looked in the open sunlight, her blonde hair blowing gracefully in the wind.

They'd worked hard together to repair the pine built home, and now, they were expecting their first child. She was only a couple months into her first pregnancy, and if he wanted to make the trip to Black River, he'd have to make it soon.

We'd take a train to Georgetown, he thought, *and then we'd travel by horse and wagon to the old homestead. I'll need to wire a message to Sarah's parents right away to let them know we're coming...*

After hanging the bed sheets out to dry, Sarah walked inside and sat in Thomas's lap.

She put her arms around him and gave him a kiss: "What's on your mind, Thomas?" Sarah could tell he'd been in deep thought.

"I've been thinking, Sarah, about us visiting my grandfather's place along Black River. Daddy always wanted to take me there, and it would mean a lot to see where he was born and raised."

"I would love to, Thomas. Do you think your mother would like to come along?"

"We can ask her tonight. I've invited her and the family over for supper. I don't know if she'll be up to going though...she seems so tired and wore out the last few days."

"She's stayed so strong for us all. I love her so much."

"I know you do, Sarah. Her life was wrapped up with Daddy's in so many ways, and it will take some time for her to get over his death."

"So when do you plan on going?" Sarah held Thomas's hand in hers.

"Day after tomorrow. We'll start getting things ready in the morning. I have to let the men down at the Sawmill know that I won't be in for a few days."

Thomas put his hand on Sarah's stomach: "Our first child. Do you think it'll be a boy or girl?"

"It's hard to say, but if my instincts are correct, it's going to be a girl."

Thomas smiled: "A baby girl...just as sweet and pretty as her mother."

"Or it could be a boy, just as nice and handsome as his father,"

Sarah added.

"We'll have to order one of them nice baby beds I saw displayed down at the general store the other day. And after we get back from Georgetown, I'll finish putting in that new floor in the extra room for our little girl...or boy." Thomas's eyes suddenly gazed out the window as if something had captured his attention: "I wish Daddy was here with me to go visit his parents' graves. It would've meant a lot to him if we could have gone together. After Grandma and Grandpa died, Mama said he never was the same. Now...I know how he felt."

Sarah could tell Thomas was hurting a lot inside, and although he'd tried his best not to show it, his silence at times revealed his grief. Just when it looked as if a small ray of light would spark in his eyes, it'd quickly dissipate into sadness once his thoughts drifted back toward the absence of his father. She knew the trip would mean a lot to him, and in some lasting way, help Thomas find closure.

That evening, Annie, Silas, and Mark came over to eat supper, and Sarah hoped it would help cheer Thomas's spirits. The table was filled with ham, cornbread, rice and gravy, turnips, peas and mashed potatoes.

Thomas said the blessing over the meal:

"Lord, we thank you for the food we are about to receive. Bless the hands that prepared it. Thank you for Mama and the rest of the family being here with us. We ask for your guidance as we go about our daily lives. May your presence be with Mama during this time of grief and separation from Daddy. We all miss him dearly. Amen."

"Go ahead, Thomas..." encouraged Sarah, passing the ham around. "I know you've been anxious to tell Annie all afternoon where we're going."

Silas and Mark grabbed for the rice and gravy.

"Where is that, Thomas?" asked Annie.

"To Daddy's old home place where he was born...where Grandpa and Grandma are buried."

Annie held to her napkin trying to hold back the tears. She knew Phillip had talked about visiting his parents' graves many times.

"That will be wonderful, Son. Your father would be so proud of you."

"We'd like you to go with us, Mama."

"I would love to, Son, but I'm not able. The boys need me here and I'm not feeling too well. But I'm so glad you and Sarah are going. I can still see the place in my heart and mind, and as much as I'd like to go, I want to remember it like it was when I last saw it. It holds a lot of special memories."

Tears began streaming down Annie's face.

Thomas got up from the table and walked over to his mother. He knelt down beside her and put his arms around her: "I love you, Mama. I know you miss Daddy a lot, and we'll make it through together."

"I'm sorry for crying so much. I wanted to be strong in front of everyone."

"There's nothing wrong with crying, Mama," said Thomas.

Sarah got up from the table and hugged Annie too, then Silas…then Mark.

"You all sure know how to make a mother feel loved," said Annie, wiping the tears from her eyes. "I have the most wonderful children, and daughter-in-law, in the world."

"And we have the most wonderful mother," shared everyone.

After the meal, Sarah thought it would be nice to cheer everyone up with some dessert: "Ok everybody…it's time for some blackberry cobbler!"

"My favorite!" exclaimed Silas.

"Can I have the first piece?" asked Mark.

"You sure can," replied Sarah. She passed everyone a portion.

"Mmmm. That tastes wonderful, Sarah."

"I'm glad you like it, Annie."

"How about some coffee, Mama?" suggested Thomas.

"I think I will, if Sarah will have some with me?"

"Two cups coming right up," smiled Sarah.

It didn't take long for the boys to finish their dessert.

"Can I be excused now?" Mark asked.

"I guess I need to go too," said Silas, "we've got to put the mule in the barn before it gets dark." Silas had taken charge of his younger brother the last few days, and it comforted Annie in knowing her sons looked after one another.

Sarah and Annie walked out onto the front porch to drink their coffee, the sun no longer visible in the western sky, and Thomas left with his two brothers.

Sarah and Annie sat talking...

"He reminds me of Phillip a lot...Thomas does," shared Annie, "the older he gets, the more I see his father in him."

"I'm worried for him, Annie..."

"This trip will do him a lot of good. A man has to travel off sometimes to find his way home."

Sarah admired Annie's wisdom. "When we get back, I want us to do something special together. You'll have to help me get the baby room fixed up too," smiled Sarah, rubbing her hand across her stomach.

"This will be a special time for you and Thomas. I can remember when Phillip and I had our first child. It only seems like yesterday when he rushed out the door to go get the doctor. It was in the middle of the night when little John decided to be born, and Phillip was so nervous he put his pants on backwards trying to get dressed..."

Annie and Sarah both laughed.

After they put the mule in the barn, Thomas and his two brothers sat underneath the old walnut tree talking; the stars began to appear in the night sky and the chilly air encouraged them to build a small fire.

"It won't ever be the same without Daddy around," said Silas, putting another stick on the fire. "Funny thing is, I feel like he's still right here with us somehow, at least his spirit anyways."

"Life is short and swift when you think about it. I just thought he'd be here forever." Thomas stared long into the fire.

"I watched Mama sitting in her chair this morning; she looked like she'd aged several years the last few days. I wanted to walk up to her and take all her pain away, but I couldn't. I'm going to start doing more for her," said Silas.

Mark sat silent, his mind still unwilling to accept the fact that his daddy wouldn't be around anymore to take him coon hunting at night, or early morning fishing down at the creek.

"It seemed like the last few weeks that's all he talked about, his mom and dad. It's almost like he knew he wouldn't be here much longer."

"I tried to wake him up, but he wouldn't," said Mark, his eyes watering up. "I kept calling his name…but he couldn't hear me."

Thomas looked over at his younger brothers and thought about how life would now change for them; no longer having a father around would make things more difficult.

"Life is sometimes hard to understand. It's filled with laughter one day, and sadness the next. The older you get, the more you realize how unpredictable it is. All you can do is hope for the best and accept the things you can't change," said Thomas.

"I just wish Daddy could've lived to be an old man," said Silas. "None of his grandchildren will ever know how great of a man he was."

"We'll keep his memory alive, Silas. The things he did, the things he said, will always be a part of who we are."

They sat and reminisced until the fire had burned low and their thoughts were at rest.

****

The train ride to Georgetown reminded Thomas of his trip a few years previously when he'd left to propose to Sarah. She was soundly asleep next to him, her head resting on his shoulder as he looked out across the passing landscapes…torrential rains pouring down. It was sleeting too, and the cold front moving through would bring snow along the Carolina coast. He looked at the ring on Sarah's finger, and his mind drifted back to Sampit River, the day he'd asked for her hand, when the snow fell gently in the early winter months along *The Walk*. His father had gladly approved of their marriage and it would've been nice to have seen Phillip hold his first grandchild. Thomas reflected on what Silas had said around the fire a few nights before: *none of his grandchildren will ever get to know how great of a man he was.*

The train whistle woke Sarah up, and when she looked around, she noticed the depot was completely covered with snow.

"It's so beautiful, Thomas."

"I've been watching it fall the last few miles. You've been sleeping like a rock."

"I didn't realize I was so tired. I'm glad you let me sleep. I hope my parents are here waiting for us." Sarah looked around. "There's Daddy, I can see him sitting in his wagon by the station. I wonder where Mama is…"

Thomas put Sarah's winter coat on and assisted her off the train, making sure she didn't slip on the ice that had formed on the steps. It had been a few years since Sarah had been home, and as she looked around, she noticed the historic town hadn't changed very much. Her father, William, was in bad health, but he wanted to take his daughter and son-in-law to the old homestead along Black River. His hat was pushed down low on his head, and the collar of his jacket was pulled up to his ears. The winter winds chilled William's bones, and his beard had turned completely white the last few years. He had a smile on his face as he waved through the falling snow. Sarah's mother, Margaret, was at home sick of a fever, having been bed-ridden the last few days. She'd tried her best to gain her strength before they arrived, but her temperature remained too high, and it would have been dangerous for her to get out in the cold. Thomas had only planned to stay a couple of days in Carolina, long enough to visit his grandparents' graves and put his thoughts to rest concerning his father; and Sarah had hoped she could find some time to spend with her mother.

"Hey, Daddy, it's so great to see you! Where's Mama?"

"She's at home sick with a fever. She wanted me to tell you that she loves you very much and not to worry, she'll be ok."

"Thomas, if we have time, maybe we can stop by and see Mama before we go back to Georgia."

"Your mother would like that very much," said William.

Thomas agreed.

He helped Sarah onto the wagon then put their luggage in the back, one large suitcase for her and a small one for him. Sarah had always liked to travel large, and she never lacked for the suitable attire, always making sure she had the right clothes to wear. And now that she was pregnant, her variety of apparel seemed to have extended itself.

Thomas kept his arm around her as they rode along, keeping her warm.

"Wasn't expecting this much snow this early. Sure makes things a little more difficult getting around," said William.

"I'm glad we got to see it. We hardly ever get to see any snow farther south," said Sarah.

William tapped the reigns of the horses, moving them along faster.

"The snow will be falling harder tonight. We need to get you two settled in the cabin before it gets worse."

"Is it in good shape, the cabin?" asked Thomas.

"I haven't been there in a few years. But the last time I saw it, it appeared to be holding up well." William looked over at his daughter. "So how's the baby getting along?"

"She's doing fine. I meant to say, it's doing fine, since we don't know for sure what it's going to be yet," smiled Sarah.

"What are you going to name it if it's a girl?"

"Dovie," smiled Sarah.

"And if it's a boy?"

"Oscar, after Thomas's middle name."

"I know you must be proud, Thomas."

"Yes sir. I sure am. I just wish Daddy could've been here to see it born."

"I'm sorry about Phillip. Ever since I'd heard he'd passed, I haven't been able to get my mind off the days when we were young, plowing with them stubborn mules and picking them long rows of cotton in the fields. He sure could pick a row faster than anyone I'd ever seen."

"Daddy talked about those days. Do you have any memories of my Grandpa? Daddy kept so much inside about his father."

"I sure do. John was a good man. He was wounded during the Civil War, and it left him with a limp in his leg. I know he was proud of your father. I remember John talking about him on several occasions when I was a boy. Your grandpa would come over in the evenings and talk to Daddy on the front porch until the rooster crowed, then he'd walk home alone, wounded leg and all. His last days were spent taking care of your grandmother Margaret; he only lived a week after she died. They're both buried near a grove of oaks."

"Daddy wanted to come back and visit their graves."

"I was there the afternoon they put John Willie to rest. His wife's grave still had fresh dirt on it. The two of them loved each other more than life itself. We always said that if one of them were to go, the other would follow. And that's how they went, one right after the other."

"I'm worried about Mama, Daddy. I hope she's getting better."

"Dodie is with her now making sure she's being looked after. The doctor stops by every afternoon on his way to town to make sure she's taking her medicine."

The road they were traveling on followed along the river, and the snow on the trees reminded Sarah of a pretty painting she'd seen once hanging on a wall in someone's house, but she couldn't remember where. She felt warm sitting next to Thomas, and being with her father made her feel like a little girl again. She looked at William's white beard and for the first time realized how much he was aging. She sensed the changing of the seasons in her life and in the life of her parents, the passing of time that leads from one generation to another, and it saddened her. She knew now that this trip meant as much to her as it did to Thomas. She'd forgotten just how fast life passes by, and being reminded of it inspired her to make the most of her time in Carolina.

The snow began falling harder as they passed by some large oaks towering on both sides of the road.

"What a beautiful old entry gate, Daddy."

"The long forgotten *Johnston Plantation*. They say the owner committed suicide when he lost his wealth after the war. A sad ending if there ever was one."

Thomas and Sarah looked beyond the entry gate toward the large plantation home that had now collapsed with age.

"I can feel the history in this place," said Sarah.

"This used to be a rich fertile community, but everyone that lived here either moved away or died." Sarah could tell her father enjoyed talking about the past. "And there's the old Hicks Store. That used to be the place where the men gathered on the front porch every Sunday for conversation. Mr. Hicks worked that store until he was nearly ninety."

After they passed the line of oaks along the road, Thomas could see a cabin in the distance, all alone on top of a rising hill.

"There it is…the old West place. Looks like the old cabin's still standing strong," said William.

The road leading up the hill had no wagon wheel tracks dented into the earth, no horses' hooves…no signs of anyone having visited the place in a long time.

Thomas took the view in, his mind racing back to everything his father had told him. It was as if he'd gone back in time, back to his father's childhood, back to the years that had molded and shaped his father into the man he'd come to be. He could see his dad plowing with a mule in the fields during the planting season or stacking wood near the barn for the winter months or walking down to the river with a fishing pole in his hand during the summer. He looked for the grove of oaks, the place his grandparents were buried. And there, overlooking the land as if to protect it, were two graves, alone with no other markers of stone to rest beside. The weight of his father's death seemed to subside for the moment, as if the place had brought his father back to life, back to the prime of his youth before he'd left his parents behind, back to the years before he'd traveled to Georgia to find a life of his own.

William stopped the wagon near the half fallen-down barn, close to the front gate of the cabin.

"Well…here we are. The place of your father's birth," said William, the snow flakes sticking to his beard.

Thomas helped Sarah down from the wagon.

"Look, Thomas…two old rockers on the front porch," smiled Sarah. "I bet your grandma and grandpa used to rock in those chairs."

Thomas paused for a moment, imagining his grandparents sitting there, rocking back and forth.

"You two best be getting some firewood up for the night. I imagine it's going to be getting cold in that old cabin. Those fallen down barn boards over there should warm things up nice. I need to be getting back before dark."

"Daddy, thank you so much for bringing us out here. Tell Mama I hope to see her soon."

"She'll be glad to see you, Sarah."

William reached behind his seat and held up a small sack. "Here, Thomas, some meat to cook. There's a batch of coffee in there too. I'll return in a couple of days to carry y'all back to the train station."

Thomas thanked William for the meat and coffee.

"Take care, William," said Thomas. "See you in a few."

William tightened his coat and hat and slowly road away.

Thomas walked up to the front door that'd been boarded up with two boards across the middle, one half-loose and hanging down. He pulled the loose one off first, then the other, and gently opened the door, the faint light from the outside gleaming in for the first time in years. The smell of settled dust and aged wood filled the air, and the wind softly whistled through the small openings in the shutters. Thomas pressed down on the floor with his feet as he walked in, making sure there were no rotten boards beneath that might give way or break into. He was assured everything was safe.

"Sarah…"

"I'm right behind you…"

"What do you think?"

"A little bit of cleaning and dusting, and it'll be like new."

"The fireplace appears to be in good shape. I'll go get some of those barn boards and start us a little fire. But first, let's find an oil lamp."

"Here's a candle over here, Thomas."

"I hope it burns…"

Thomas struck a match and lit the candle successfully.

"Romantic," whispered Sarah.

Thomas smiled. "A small kiss will do for now."

"I only said it was romantic. Nothing about a kiss," smiled Sarah. "There. Half now and half later, after we get settled in."

"Ok, Mrs. West. Seeing you are a woman of your word," smiled Thomas.

****

The fire slowly warmed the inside as Sarah rested in Thomas's arms. She'd worked hard at cleaning the rooms while Thomas stacked a large pile of boards from the barn near the front porch. The snow kept falling outside, and the wind howled and whipped against the framing of the cabin.

"You'll never guess what I found while cleaning the rooms."

"A box full of gold…"

"Nope. Something better."

"What could be better than a box full of gold?"

"Close your eyes…" Sarah reached in her pocket and took out a small book, placing it in Thomas's hand.

"Can I open my eyes now?"

"Yes…" smiled Sarah.

He opened his eyes, and to his surprise, he held in his hand his grandmother's diary.

"I found it in the bottom of a *hope chest* in the back bedroom."

Thomas rubbed his hand gently over the cover as if to feel the history contained within the underlying pages.

"Sarah, I can't believe you found this. Will you bring me the candle?"

Sarah placed the candle on a stand next to the chair.

Thomas opened the book and randomly turned to one of the pages, reading it to Sarah…

August 5th, 1865

This afternoon, my husband returned home safe from the terrible War Between the States. I am so glad the great conflict has finally ended. Heaven has smiled on our home again, and we are back together as a family. To hear John say the blessing over the meal at the dinner table this evening made me cry, just hearing his voice again; and knowing the children didn't have to worry about their father dying in battle gives me great comfort. The moon was full tonight and the stars shone bright over Black River as John sang to me my favorite song while holding me in his arms on the front porch. It was a perfect ending to an already perfect day. I am truly a blessed...

"Read the next page, Thomas. I want to find out what happened the following day..."

"Since you are so curious, I'll let you read it to me," smiled Phillip.

Sarah turned the page and read...

August 6th, 1865

I woke up this morning with the comfort of having my husband by my side. He slept so gently through the night for having been through so much the last few years. I love him so much. I'd planned for us to have a romantic picnic on the bank of Black River this afternoon, on a beautiful spot we used to go to when we first got married. The weather turned out to be so lovely, and the colors of the leaves, the gentle flowing of the river, and the calm setting provided John and I with such a wonderful time alone. It was good to know the romance was still there. We talked about many things, and in particular, about our son Phillip. John is concerned about his future, and wants him to travel to Georgia with Thomas Hendrix to see if he can find a life there. It was nice to meet John's friend from the war today, and I can see why he and John have a lot in common. As I write these words, my heart is heavy over the thought our son leaving home. I have tried not to think about it, but a mother's life is wrapped up in her children. He has grown up so fast, and I wonder where the years have gone. It seems like yesterday when I held him in my arms as a baby, and now, he's a grown man. Life passes so quickly. John and I are so proud of Phillip, and he'll always be our precious firstborn. It will be difficult letting him go...

Sarah put her hand to her stomach, thinking of her and Thomas's firstborn. Margaret's words seemed to echo within her and find an emotional path to her heart.

"Why are you crying, Sarah?"

"Because...I can feel what your grandmother was feeling. Your father was her firstborn, and we're about to have ours. She gave herself to raising her children, and then to see her son grow up and move away at such a young age had to be difficult. I didn't think that much about it until now, how sad my own mother must have been over me moving to Georgia. I just want to go hold Mama and tell her how much I love her. I hope she's ok, Thomas."

"Your father said she's getting stronger every day. I'm sure she'll be just fine."

"I hope so. I guess I'm worrying too much. I didn't expect to become so emotional after reading just one page, but I'm glad I did. It's reminded me of the most important things in life. I love you Thomas."

"I love you too, Sarah."

They sat and talked until the fire burned low. The wind outside calmed to a small whisper and the cabin warmed to a comfortable temperature. Sarah fell asleep in Thomas's arms, and he picked her up and carried her to bed.

The following day, Thomas woke up to a calm morning. Other than the singing of a few winter birds, it was quiet - too quiet. The life that used to be here was completely gone. It was a very peaceful place, yet sad — the mournful quietness of a generation passed. He thought about his grandmother's words that Sarah had read in her diary last night...*life passes so quickly*, and he wanted the past to come back alive. He wanted to meet his grandfather and grandmother he'd never seen before, but had always heard so much about; he imagined them sitting in their rocking chairs on the front porch watching a warm spring sunset. He wanted to see his father again, reunited with his parents, walking along the hillside on a sunny, summer day, or sitting around the kitchen table sharing memories of their life along Black River. *Just to hear their voices* he thought, *would mean more than anything.*

The day would prove to be wintry and cold — the early morning sun quickly hidden by the snow filled clouds. After breakfast in bed, courtesy of her husband, Sarah spent the rest of her day reading

Margaret's diary. Thomas kept the fire going, and Sarah's requests for fresh coffee kept coming.

"Listen to this, Thomas,"…

October 29th th, 1884

The fall leaves are so beautiful this time of the year, and the different colors always seem to cheer me up. I haven't felt too well lately, but John opened the shutter for me this afternoon to let the sunshine in my room in hopes of lifting my spirits. A light wind managed to blow a leaf through the window onto my bed. I knew what tree it came from as soon as it'd entered; it'd fallen from the old maple near the barn. I sat up as soon as I saw it, and watched it float back and forth until it rested at my feet. It seemed so small and insignificant at the time, one leaf out of a million dropping in for a surprise visit. Yet somehow it made me smile. It reminded me of the little things in life that mean so much and how often we take them for granted. I don't want to be ungrateful, and John has watched over me hand and foot since I've been ill. I know that he doesn't mind…it helps him feel needed; and he always makes me feel wanted and important as well. Maybe I'll be able to get back on my feet soon and John and I will be able to go for a short walk together…

Sarah turned the pages of the diary, hanging on to every word as she read. She felt like she'd known John and Margaret, and the cabin and the place took on a whole new meaning for her.

Thomas stood near the living room window listening to her read, looking out toward the hill to where the graves of his grandparents were, the snow covering their monuments.

Sarah continued…

January 8th, 1885

The winter winds have now come and the snow has covered the fields. John can hardly walk on his bad leg anymore, and the cold weather has kept him in his chair all day. He doesn't want to admit it, but his health is fading fast, as well as mine. His dreams at night have gotten worse too; they're always the same...his mind entrenched somewhere on the battlefields between the North and the South. He tries to be strong for the both of us, but he knows our days are few. Maybe that's why he keeps having those bad dreams, trying to do battle against the hour glass of time. Not long ago, just before winter, we both walked up to the grove of oaks on the hill. He hadn't been up there in years, especially with his bad leg and poor health. But that day, he found the strength. And even though he didn't say why we he wanted to walk up there, we both knew; it's the place where he wants to be buried. My hands can hardly write the words down on paper now, and my mind is starting to forget things. But despite my fading memory, I'll always hold to Black River, my children, and the man that I've had the pleasure of sharing my life with...

"That's the last page in her diary," said Sarah. "It looks like she wanted to write something else, but the last part is unreadable."

"Those must have been her last words," said Thomas.

"That's so sad. After reading her diary, I feel like I've known her my whole life. I can see now why your father felt so much about this place."

"Part of him never left," said Thomas. "It'll be getting dark soon. I think I'll walk up to the grove of oaks and pay my respects to my grandmother and grandfather."

"The snow is falling hard, Thomas, and it's freezing outside. Please be careful."

"I will." He kissed Sarah on her cheek.

Sarah knew the main reason for their stay was for Thomas to find closure with his father's death. She held the diary to her chest as she stood at the window and watched her husband walk up the hill in the snow toward the two graves that held and defined everything about who his father was, and in many ways, who Thomas was. He kept his head down as he walked, the cold wind hitting hard against his face. He knew that every step he took wasn't just for him, but for his father as well. The graves were fenced in with an iron gate that faced the cabin. A large limb had fallen from one of the old oaks nearby and damaged one side of the fence, nearly falling down on one of the monuments. Thomas knelt down and brushed away the snow that had covered the words on the grave. The first marker was his grandmother's:

Margaret West. Born April 29th 1810, Died January 8th, 1885.

The last page in her diary, Thomas thought, written the day she died.

Thomas read…

Here rests an angel dear to us…a beautiful autumn leaf at our feet, and her eternal memory shall fill our lonely paths till in Heaven we shall meet!

Thomas turned his thoughts to his grandmother…

"Grandma, I'm sorry I never got to meet you in this life. We have enjoyed our visit here. Sarah found your diary in an old hope chest and has been reading it; it has meant so much to the both of us. You would love her, Grandma. She's a wonderful wife and friend. Thank you for giving me such a good father. I know you missed your son very much after he left home, but now you two are back together again. Please tell Daddy I miss him…"

Thomas could no longer hold back the tears; they poured down his face like falling rain.

He brushed away the snow on his grandfather's grave:

Confederate Soldier. John Willie West. Born December 8th, 1801, Died January 15th, 1885.

Thomas thought about what Sarah's father had said the day before, that John had passed away only a week after his wife.

He read the words:

His rifle now lies beneath the earth…the Old South beside him doth rest, and his memory twill forever remain here, near the one he loved the best!

Thomas wiped the tears from his face…

"Well, Granddaddy, we traveled a good long ways to get here. Daddy wanted to come back here many times to see you and Grandma, but never had the chance. He kept a lot inside after you both passed away, and I never imagined what he was going through until now. Mama sure is hurting a lot too. We all are. Losing a parent sure is a terrible thing. Life won't be the same without Daddy, but he left us a good path to follow, just like you left him. I know you went through a lot during the war, seeing all kinds of terrible things. But you never gave up; and that's one thing Daddy taught me. We'll be leaving to go back home in the morning, Sarah and I. We sure have enjoyed our visit. Please tell Daddy I sure do miss him…"

Thomas put his hand on his grandmother's and grandfather's grave one last time before walking back down the hill, feeling as if the weight of his father's death had been lifted somehow after visiting his grandparents' place of rest.

****

The following day brought clear blue skies, and the warmth of the sun melted much of the snow that had covered the Carolina soil; only small patches of ice lingered here and there in the late shadows of the trees and wooded structures. Sarah had just finished cooking a nice warm meal on the old wood stove when she heard a knock at the front door. She looked out the living room window, and to her surprise, saw her father and mother standing on the porch together. She'd expected her father to be alone. Sarah rushed to welcome them inside, and at that moment, all of her worries that'd been weighing on her mind since she'd heard her mother was sick…subsided. Her mother wasted no time in helping Sarah set the table, and it brought back memories of when she used to help her mother in the kitchen.

After eating their meal, Sarah and her mother spent the afternoon sitting in front of the fireplace talking and catching up, a mother and daughter conversation that Sarah had longed for, the one thing she needed in order to make the trip complete.

In the meantime, William and Thomas loaded the wagon and made sure everything was boarded back up before leaving for the train station.

It was a time of healing for everyone, and Thomas and Sarah would never forget their visit to Black River and their stay at the snow-covered cabin, where the past was brought back to life through a diary Sarah had found nestled at the bottom of a hope chest.

Chapter Ten

Nearly six years had passed since Phillip was buried at Oak Grove, and Mark and Silas, now young men, were influenced more by the culture around them than they were by their mother's sincere admonitions. They'd developed a skill other than farming in which they tended to be very productive at - making moonshine. Not far from Annie's log cabin, the land sloped downward as it made its way toward Bay Gall creek, the low land, where they worked a copper still close to the fresh running water. The government revenuers were always showing up whenever moonshiners least expected them, so Mark and Silas kept spotters in the trees to let them know if any strangers were approaching while they were making their spirits. Many people from the county would come buy moonshine from them, and sometimes the West brothers would make special runs to people outside of Georgia. They made and filled the glass bottles full of shine, and the bottles filled the homes of many country and city folk alike that paid good money for it.

One day Thomas went down to the still to warn Mark and Silas of government revenuers in the area.

"Hey, Mark. Hey, Silas. How's the moonshine business?"

"Well, Thomas, we made more money these last few weeks selling moonshine than we did all last season selling cotton. When are you going to get in on the profit?" asked Mark.

"It's not worth it, boys. I don't have any interest in making or selling the spirits. I'm doing fine just like I am. One day, you're going to get caught and wish you'd never made or sold any yourselves."

Mark and Silas had a bad tendency to drink way too much shine, sometimes to the point of shooting their pistols at each other, just for the fun of it, and even worse, they'd shoot each other's hat off the other's head, the moonshine making them do crazy things they ordinarily wouldn't do. Their mother Annie was against their moonshine dealings and she let it be known that she never wanted to see any around the cabin.

"The revenuers are up near Finch's Mill. They'll be coming down the creek soon and scoping the whole area out. You need to cover up the still and make sure you both stay out of sight for a while."

"Thanks, Thomas, we owe you one," said Silas, pouring the last batch of shine into some jugs before sealing them tight.

Within a few hours, the revenuers were all over the West farm, but they never found the moonshine still that belonged to Mark and Silas, thanks to the warnings of their older brother. A couple of the revenuers came up to the front porch of Annie's log cabin where Thomas was sitting, carving on a small piece of cedar with his pocket knife.

"Good evening," said the revenuers.

Thomas, wearing a felt hat with the front pulled down just above his eyes, nodded his head and acknowledged their presence. Even though he didn't make or sell whiskey, he didn't like the idea of revenuers coming on his land like some gold diggers without a claim.

"You've probably figured out by now that we're government revenuers trying to find illegal makers and runners of moonshine. We've heard tale that some West boys have been making some in this part of the country. You don't happen to know anything about that, would you?"

"I sure don't. I don't make moonshine, neither do I sell it, but if I ever run up on any of them makers or sellers you're talking about, I'll be sure to let them know you're looking for them," Thomas said with a grin on his face. The revenuers eventually left, unable to find or prove anything against the West boys.

Married with kids, Thomas had a lot to lose if he ever got caught making whiskey, and so stayed away from the stills and the liquor that often sent his kinfolk to jail; unlike Mark and Silas, who lived the single life and saw no danger in making personal investments in the illegal trade. Thomas and Sarah lived not far from Annie's log cabin in a nice pine-built home, busy raising four children of their own: Dovie, Oscar, Phillip, and John Willie. Their marriage was centered on love and respect for each other in the best and worst of times, surrounding themselves with a warm family environment and faith in the things that made them strong. They had a lot in common with each other in their background and lifestyle. Their union didn't exist by sharing some political belief system or by being educated in the schools of higher learning, nor did it flourish by mingling with elite circles in certain regions of society or in privileged communities, but it was held together by sharing the same deep core values of faith, family and home. They were two ordinary people who fell extraordinarily in love, enjoyed life together and raised a family the best way they knew how.

One day, while Thomas was working at the nearby sawmill, Sarah decided to go and visit her mother-in-law Annie who was drawing water from the well as she approached the cabin.

"Hello, Annie. How are you doing today?"

"I'm doing fine, Sarah. I hope everything is all right."

"Oh yes, I just wanted to come and spend some time with you."

Sarah was holding little John Willie in her arms.

Mark came walking in from the cotton field as Sarah arrived, smiling and looking cheerful: "Hey Sarah, you look pretty today."

Since Mark's breakup with Carrie, he began falling in love with Sarah, his own brother's wife. He didn't mean for it to happen, but his loneliness made him more eager for companionship, even if it was *forbidden love*. He'd sought advice from Sarah the whole time he was dating Carrie, and after their breakup, his reliance on her deepened. She noticed his advances at times, but passed them off as nothing serious, knowing he was crushed and heartbroken over his failed relationship. She thought Mark looked handsome, but never did it enter into her mind to have any sort of an adulterous affair with him. She believed in being faithful to her spouse and would never want to do anything to ruin her relationship with Thomas or with her children.

"Mark," said Annie, "please take this bucket of water to the kitchen for me while I talk with Sarah."

Mark smiled at Sarah as he passed by to get the water. Sarah smiled back, trying not to be rude, but she knew she had to keep her distance, not wanting to mislead Mark in any way, sensing he'd become infatuated with her.

"Sarah, I want you to know that if you ever want to talk about anything, please feel free to tell me. I feel like something is troubling you and I want to be of some help."

"I know, Annie. I always feel comfortable coming to you. You've been such a blessing to me and Thomas, and I can never repay you for all the help you've been to the children. Isn't little John Willie so cute?"

Sarah tried to change the subject and focus the attention on the baby instead of her.

"Why, he sure is. He's got the cutest little cheeks and the funniest little laugh," said Annie.

Mark came back outside after taking the bucket of water to the kitchen. He gave his mother a warm hug, then went back to the fields to pick cotton, but not before telling Sarah goodbye and inviting her to come over more often.

Annie and Sarah took little John Willie inside to make some homemade lemonade from a basket of fresh picked lemons Annie got from the farmer's market. Sarah was thinking of Mark as she took a lemon and squeezed the juice into a jar. She couldn't get her mind away from the fact that Mark was in love with her, and she didn't know how to deal with it, or how to face it. The lemon she squeezed slipped out of her hand, and as she tried to grab hold of it, she accidentally knocked over the jar, spilling water all over the kitchen table and onto the floor.

Annie turned around and saw her hands trembling.

"Sarah, my word…why are your hands shaking like they are?"

"I don't know, Annie, I guess my nerves are worse than I thought. I better be getting back home with little John. Thomas will be home soon from the saw mill and I have to get supper ready."

Sarah grabbed little John, trying not to let her emotions show the part of her that revealed responses to things unwanted. Annie knew something was wrong but couldn't quite figure it out. When Sarah got back home, she hurried inside to wash her hands as if she'd been guilty of some great sin. *I haven't made any advancement towards Mark, why should I feel guilty,* she thought.

As she put little John down in his baby bed, she heard a knock at the door: "Thomas, is that you? Why are you knocking on the door?"

When she came into the living room she saw that it was Mark.

"Mark, what are you doing here? I thought you were in the field picking cotton."

"I was, but I got to thinking about you and I had to come over and tell you how I feel. I don't know how to explain it, but I think I'm falling in love with you, Sarah."

"Mark, you can't be. You know it's impossible for us. Thomas is about to be home from the saw mill and he wouldn't know what to think if he found you here with me alone in the house."

"Sarah, I just need for you to answer this one question and then I'll go. Do you have any feelings for me?"

"No, Mark, I don't have any feelings for you other than you being my brother-in-law. I am in love with my husband and to no other man. I know you are upset about Carrie and the way she left you, but that loneliness will be filled again by someone that is meant for you..."

Mark seemed to let her words go through one ear and out the other, unwilling to accept no for an answer, and the whisky in his system didn't help any; ever since last summer, after the breakup, he'd been drinking everyday. He asked Sarah to think about what he'd said and that he'd come back later. He heard Thomas ride up in the front yard and so slipped out the back.

Thomas walked in and saw Sarah standing there like she'd just seen a ghost.

"What's wrong, Sarah?"

"Nothing, I'm fine. How was your day?"

"It was a little rough. I'm thinking about leaving the saw mill and helping Mark and Silas on the farm."

"Are you sure you want to do that?"

"What do you mean?"

"Never mind…whatever you feel like you need to do I'm behind you one hundred percent. I just want you to know that I love you."

She walked up to Thomas and put her arms around him, hoping he hadn't noticed her concerns.

"I love you too, Sarah."

That night, after they went to sleep, Sarah had a bad dream. She dreamed she and Mark were having a love affair. Thomas had come home from work and found them together in each others arms. He told Mark to leave, but he wouldn't, and they began to fight, first with words, and then with fists. She dreamed Mark pulled a pistol out of his coat pocket and attempted to shoot Thomas who'd fallen to the ground. She kept screaming Thomas's name and it woke him up.

He rolled over in the bed and tried to calm her down: "Sarah, its ok, it's just a bad dream. It's not real. There's no need to worry. It's just a bad dream. Are you ok? What were you dreaming about?"

"Yes, I'm ok. I don't remember. I'm sorry, Thomas. I didn't mean to wake you. I guess I've had a lot on my mind lately. I'm fine now."

Thomas got up early the next morning to go work at the saw mill. Sarah had gotten up an hour before and cooked him a nice warm breakfast - her husband's favorite meal: ham, bacon, eggs and grits. After kissing him goodbye, Sarah stood on the front porch and watched Thomas ride away until he was out of sight, her hands shaking from thoughts of Mark coming over without her husband being there. As the hours went by and the days progressed, she worried whether or not Mark would drop by unexpectedly, but he never did. She hoped he'd erased the whole notion of his love for her out of his head.

****

Apart from falling in love with his brother's wife, Mark had always been a respectable young man. Even now, with thoughts of Sarah running through his mind, he still felt like he held himself to a certain code of ethics. From what he could remember about his father, it gave him a certain sense of pride and understanding of what it meant to earn an honest living, even though he was knee deep in making and selling unstamped whiskey. But that oddity could be explained away by his definition of *making ends meet by whatever means necessary*. He was a young man when his father had died; and soon after, he'd lost his enthusiasm for hunting coons, unlike his brother Silas, who never missed out on the opportunity of running dogs along Bay Gall creek. His desire in hunting gave way to an interest in girls. He was more suited to the city life, or the fast lane, as most folks called it. He would visit town more than his brothers, and the Lake View pavilion was the perfect place to meet up with his friends. Tall and slender, hair black and thick, tanned skin and a charming smile and wit that revealed a quiet intelligence, the ladies loved him. Someone who wasn't afraid to take chances, his self confidence attracted everyone around. And on one particular night, late last summer, Mark's good looks caught the attention of one of the prettiest girls at the pavilion. Lake View was a summer recreational place, with bath houses, boat ramps and diving boards extending from the dam over the swimming pool with a beach-like shore many termed "Statesboro's Tybee," always active with young people. Mrs. Bland ran a concession stand in the pavilion that overlooked the water and dances were held at night on the extended platform beneath the string of lights powered by a Delco battery system. Bands from all over the region came to perform, and the sound of the banjos, guitars and fiddles could be heard late into the long summer nights. Every once in a while, someone would come through that was gifted at playing the piano, and it was on one of those nights that Mark fell in love with a beautiful young lady from Savannah who was staying with her relatives for the summer. The scheduled piano player had played in many venues in big cities, and his knowledge of love songs and ragtime music set the dance floor moving. When Mark drove up in his brand new Model T he had purchased with his bootlegging money, Carrie couldn't help but notice the tall slender figure walk from his vehicle to the pavilion as if he owned the world. She was only staying for the summer, and the last thing she expected was to fall in love.

She looked at Rosie sitting across the table and asked, "Who is that good looking guy?"

"There are plenty of guys around, Carrie. Could you be a little more specific?"

"The one standing at the bar dressed like he owns the place."

"Oh…that's Mark West. I don't know that much about him. Just that he lives out in the country…sort of a farm boy."

"Sure doesn't look like a farm boy to me…"

Mark didn't notice Carrie at first. He was busy talking with the guys and looking for a girl to dance with, which wasn't a problem for him on most nights. He stood at the bar where they served food and drinks, and all the girls clinging to him made Carrie wonder if she'd ever be noticed.

While sipping on his bottled coke, Mark's feet danced to the music streaming from the piano.

"So what's going on tonight, Lance?"

"Busy as usual. I guess you haven't noticed that gal sitting over near the piano, have you?" Lance worked behind the bar, and he kept Mark up to date on who was who and who they were going with. "Isn't she a beauty?"

Mark turned around. As soon as his eyes caught a glimpse of Carrie, he'd made up his mind to ask her for a dance.

"Say, Lance, what's her name?"

"I don't know, but she's staying with her cousin Rosi Reynolds. She comes from a wealthy family from what I've been told."

"That doesn't make any difference. How much you want to bet I can get her to dance with me?"

"I'm not up for losing any money tonight. Knowing you, she'll be in your arms before the next song's played."

"I better get to moving then. Looks like he's finishing up on the last tune."

Mark walked over to the man behind the piano and whispered a request after placing a wad of money in his tip jar: "Can you play '*A Pretty Girl Is Like A Melody?*'"

"I sure can, mister. Is it for someone special?"

"That pretty girl sitting over there."

"You got it. Here it goes."

Mark walked over to the table where Carrie was sitting and introduced himself: "Hello, my name is Mark West, and I just paid that man a good sum of money to play a song for us. Sure would disappoint him if you didn't dance with me."

"Is that an offer?" asked Carrie.

"It is if you want it to be," smiled Mark.

Rosie whispered to Carrie: "Why not, you said he was handsome."

"Don't you say anymore, Rosie," laughed Carrie. "Ok, I'll dance with you this once. But it's only because I don't want to disappoint the piano man."

"I'll accept that," smiled Mark.

Carrie wasn't used to someone being so confident, and to find herself dancing in the arms of a country boy was a little out of her comfort zone. Her hair was pure blonde, and her green eyes and soft tan complimented her innocent smile. Her accent was not altogether southern, yet, she possessed the spirit of a Georgia girl.

"So, how did you know I'd say yes?" asked Carrie, holding Mark's hand as they walked onto the dance floor.

"I didn't. But I'm glad you did. Cause I would've lost a lot of money if you'd said no."

Carrie looked at Mark with surprise.

"Just kidding…"

"You better be," smiled Carrie.

A soft rain began to fall over the pavilion, and the piano music echoed against the drops that fell across the open-sided structure. One song turned into two, and before they realized it, they'd danced the night away in each other's arms.

When the last song ended, Carrie was out of breath, her emotions swept away; not from dancing too much, but from the way she was now feeling, or rather falling…head over heels. For a moment, she'd forgotten about who she was and the wealth she'd come from. *I can't give myself away so easy* she thought. She pretended as if it was late and she had to go, but not before letting Mark know how much she'd enjoyed it.

"It was nice meeting you, Mark. I hope to see you again…"

"What about tomorrow? They're going to have a swimming contest over at the pool, and after dark, a party on the beach. Why don't we all meet up around noon? Rosie can bring you…"

"Sounds great! We'll be here," smiled Rosie.

"But Rosie…"

"But Carrie…" Rosie's eyes convinced her.

"Ok… we'll see you tomorrow at noon," smiled Carrie.

As Rosie and Carrie left the entrance, they saw a group of cars surround Mark's model T near the entry gate. When the men got out of their vehicles, they pushed Mark up against the side of his car.

"Stop Rosie, something bad is about to happen. You have to go back."

"It's nothing, Carrie. He'll be ok." Rosie kept driving, never turning around.

"Rosie, is there something you're not telling me? You said you didn't know that much about Mark. Are you hiding something from me?"

"He's a bootlegger. That's all."

"So…that's all. He's just a bootlegger. Why on earth didn't you tell me when I first asked you?"

"Just relax, Carrie. Everybody knows it. Besides, he's handsome, remember."

"I guess you're right," giggled Carrie.

She knew Rosi saw right through her. It didn't matter to her that Mark was a bootlegger. All that she was interested in was having a good time during her summer stay.

"So…what do you think they wanted with him?" asked Carrie.

"With a bootlegger, there's no telling. It might be anything from money to selling in someone else's territory. If you really want to know, just ask him."

"I would never. Besides, it really doesn't matter…remember…"

****

Mark knew he had to keep his personal business hidden from Carrie, her lifestyle being somewhat normal and less dramatic than his. Those men showing up at the pavilion last night could never happen again, and he was determined more than ever to keep that part of his life away from her.

It was daybreak, and Silas needed Mark's model T ford to make a whiskey run to Carolina. The only transportation left for him to take to the pool to meet Carrie was the horse and buggy. But he'd had a wonderful idea and was sure to make the most of it: *he'd ask Carrie if she'd like to ride with him sightseeing through the countryside, a wonderful opportunity to spend some more time with her.*

It was a cloudless day over the pristine lake, and when Mark arrived at the pavilion, Rosi and Carrie were lying out in their *Jantzen* swimming suits on the sandy beach deepening their tan.

"Hey, Rosie. Hey, Carrie."

"Hey, Mark. Your model T doesn't quite look the same in the daylight," laughed Carrie.

"Actually, it turns into a horse and buggy after midnight," joked Mark.

"You don't seem to have any broken bones anywhere," smiled Carrie.

By her remark, he knew she'd seen the men last night.

"Oh, that was nothing, just a little misunderstanding. But it's all good now. Not to change the subject or anything, but, I was thinking, that after the contest, we might take a buggy ride in my *daylight model T* along the river road if y'all wanted to. The scenery is beautiful this time of the year."

"Sounds like fun, Carrie. I have to do a little shopping this afternoon, but you and Mark can go. We'll meet back here for the party tonight."

Carrie looked as if she wanted to stick her head in the sand and hide, but knew that was impossible. However, she trusted her cousin's intuition and decided to go, but not before having some fun on the chute to chute and enjoying a nice swim around the lake, the water cooling her off in the hot summer heat.

As she sat on the sand, Mark put a towel around her to dry off with, her body still wet from the refreshing swim. Mark couldn't help but notice how smooth her skin was and how her eyes gleamed beautifully in the open sunlight.

"Tell me, Mark, why are you so interested in me?" smiled Carrie, knowing she had his full attention.

"Well...the fact that you're one of the prettiest girls I've ever seen. And besides that, you're a great dancer too."

"I wondered whether or not I was too clumsy last night."

"If you were, I didn't notice..."

"So what did you notice?" smiled Carrie.

"Some beautiful lady who swept me off my feet," smiled Mark.

"Well, I don't know about that, but I need to change into something different if we're going to take that buggy ride."

Mark smiled. He was glad she hadn't changed her mind. As he got the horse and buggy ready, Carrie went to the women's bath house to change into something more appropriate. Mark kept thinking about how much his lifestyle would have to change if his relationship with Rosi's cousin developed into something more serious. He'd always lived on the edge, not caring about the consequences of bootlegging or fighting against the law; and for the first time wrestled with the possibility of straightening his life out. He combed through his hair the best he could while looking in the rear-view mirror and whistling the tune to the song he and Carrie had danced to the night before: *A Pretty Girl Is Like A Melody*. He brought the buggy around close to the entrance, near the ticket booth, to pick Carrie up. She'd put her hair up in a pony tail, and Mark could sense she was more relaxed than before.

As they rode along the river road, Mark shared with her the stories passed along to him from the older generations: "See over there on that high ridge. That's where old Nevils Creek church used to stand before Sherman's troops tore it down."

"It's so lovely out here."

Mark stopped the buggy at the edge of Nevils Creek. He helped Carrie down and walked her over to a large sycamore tree standing near a turn in the creek, its crown towering high above the other trees and reaching out over the water.

"This is my favorite place to come and relax," said Mark.

"Is this where you take all your girlfriends?"

"You're the first."

"I didn't know I was your girlfriend..."

"Well, I meant...you're the first girl."

"I must be special then," smiled Carrie, her eyes fixed on his.

Mark put his arms around Carrie, her body next to his. She knew she'd let her defenses down, but it didn't matter, she wanted to be vulnerable in his arms. She put her lips to his, and there, in the shades of sunlight gleaming through the cypress trees against the giant sycamore, they kissed. She didn't think it would happen so fast. She'd always been good at keeping her passions in check, but Mark was too charming, too handsome.

"I wasn't expecting that," said Mark. "But thank you."

"You're welcome," replied Carrie. She turned and paused: "The country life is so peaceful. Just being out here helps to clear my mind."

"A pretty girl like you shouldn't have any worries…"

"Oh, but I do. Life can get pretty confusing at times. But out here, in these quiet moments, problems that seemed so large become so small."

"Well if it helps you that much, I'll have to bring you out here more often."

"You just might have to do that," smiled Carrie.

Mark knelt down near the creek's edge.

"Is the water deep?"

"Deep enough to throw you in," smiled Mark.

"You wouldn't…I have my nice clothes on."

"They'll dry…"

Mark picked her up and tossed her in the water. He took his shoes and shirt off and jumped in behind her.

"Mark West, I'm going to…"

Before she could get another word out, Mark silenced her with a romantic kiss. Her heart raced with passion.

"What am I doing?" laughed Carrie. "If my parents saw me now they would fall over and die. In the middle of a creek, soaking wet, kissing a guy I barely even know…"

"What about you? How do you feel about it?"

"I think it's kind of amazing," smiled Carrie, kissing Mark again.

The light from the sun no longer reflected off the trunk of the sycamore: "We have to be heading back. It's getting late," said Mark. "The beach party will be starting soon at Lake View."

They both dried off the best they could and walked back to the buggy, hand in hand, knowing something special had formed between them.

****

When Mark and Carrie arrived, there were candles lit everywhere. The music from the pavilion filled the night air and a large crowd of people were dancing beneath the string of lights set all along the beach.

"Well if it isn't the two love birds," said Rosi.

"Very funny," said Carrie, sitting down beside Rosi on the sandy beach while Mark walked over to the concession stand at the pavilion, leaving them to talk alone.

"So, how did you enjoy your countryside tour with the country boy?"

"It was fun," smiled Carrie.

"Do you like him?"

"I just met him, Rosi. Although, I have to admit…he's a nice kisser."

"What? You didn't?" Rosi amusingly shocked.

"Yes, I did, and don't you tell anyone."

"Your secret is safe with me," laughed Rosi.

Mark came back with some drinks.

"What's all the laughter about?" asked Mark.

"Just a little girl talk," smiled Rosi. "Thanks for the soda."

"You're welcome."

Carrie put her hand in Mark's while they sat beneath the stars: "Isn't this so relaxing? Sand. Water. Soft music. Candles…"

"I can't remember the last time I've looked up and noticed the Milky Way. It sure is a pretty sight." Mark took his last swallow of coke. "So…can I have a dance with the prettiest little *Milky Way* on earth?"

"I'll have to think about it. Only if Rosi says it's ok," joked Carrie.

"I'll be waiting right here for you two," smiled Rosi.

Mark had never opened up to another girl before like he did with Carrie. And as the night wore on, they found themselves in each other's arms, slow dancing to the music in the midst of the flickering candles with the sand beneath their feet and a soft breeze blowing in across the water.

After the last song ended, they sat alone on the sand looking up at the stars.

"Tell me, Mark, what do you want out of life?"

He looked up at the Milky Way and thought about the numerous stars that seemed so close, yet so far away: "I just try and take each day as it comes. Why do you ask?"

"Oh, I don't know. I was just wondering."

"Well, I know one thing that I want for sure."

"What's that?"

"Another kiss." Mark put his lips to hers.

"Not so easy. You have to answer one more question first," laughed Carrie.

"Ask away…"

"Do you think two people, who are vastly different, can be happy together?"

Carrie put her hand in his, wondering how he would respond.

"I think as long as they love each other, they can overcome any differences between them. Now can I have my kiss?"

"Not just yet…" smiled Carrie. She felt the answer to her question was more complicated than Mark's response, but it was the answer she'd expected. "I wish life could be as simple as the 'love solves everything' mentality. However, I have to admit, it can carry two people a long ways."

Mark gently put his finger to Carrie's lips, as if to silence the current of questions concerning love and life that troubled her. She wanted to fall in love, but the underlying truth was too overwhelming…she couldn't. Not with Mark. There were too many differences in lifestyle, too many obstacles to overcome. And besides, even if she could, she knew her parents would never except a relationship based solely on love. There had to be wealth. However, for the short term, Mark's kiss seemed to clear up her confusion.

"Do you still think love can't solve everything?"

"You're a nice kisser, Mark West. But I still have my doubts," smiled Carrie.

Days passed...then weeks. They spent hours together, riding through the countryside and hanging out by the pool. But on one particular evening, when they were supposed to meet at Lake View, Carrie didn't show up.

Mark saw Rosi sitting alone at one of the tables under the pavilion and walked over to see if anything was wrong.

"Hey Rosi. Where's Carrie?"

She handed Mark a folded up letter. "Carrie wanted me to give this to you."

He walked to the edge of the platform overlooking the water and read the letter:

"Mark, I really enjoyed our summer together. Thank you for everything...the buggy rides, the dances, the talks. I'll always remember our first kiss under the sycamore tree. I know you must be wondering why I had to leave without saying goodbye. I didn't want to hurt you in any way, Mark, you have to believe me, but our lives are so different. I wanted to believe as you do, that love can keep two people together no matter their differences, but I find it too difficult. I knew you were a bootlegger as well, even though you tried your best to hide it from me. I feel it is best for the both of us if we didn't see each other anymore. I do care for you deeply and it was the hardest decision I've ever had to make. Thank you for making my summer memorable and I will always cherish our time together. Sincerely, Carrie."

Mark closed the letter, and as he dropped Carrie's note into the water below, something inside him died...never to awaken again. As time went on, he would drink more and more, and his loneliness would lead him down a path of destruction and a tragic ending.

Chapter Eleven

*I*t was a beautiful sunny day and Sarah felt like going for a late evening walk, some outdoor leisure she'd been longing for since the steady rain had kept her and the children inside. She walked alone, enjoying the scenery and fresh southern air, the smell of wild flowers being blown about by a soft warm wind. She came to the narrow wooden structure over Bay Gall creek, admiring the calm waters flowing so peacefully beneath - the sight of red-finned pikes swimming in the shallow sunlit water. Looking up, she saw Mark walking up the road with a bottle of whiskey in his hand. She wanted to run, but didn't want to over exaggerate the situation, gathering herself for whatever confrontation might take place.

"Hey, Sarah. It sure is a pretty evening, isn't it?"

Sarah smiled, but didn't feel like saying anything.

"Have you thought about what we talked about the other day?"

"What you talked about, Mark. Not me. Nothing has changed from what I told you before. I was hoping you wouldn't bring it up again."

She told him there was no chance of her ever liking him and that he was a nice looking man and there were plenty of unmarried ladies out there that he should date. But he was unable to accept the fact that she wasn't interested in him, the alcohol affecting his perception to a certain degree.

She tried to walk away, but he grabbed her arm.

"Mark, let go of me. You're hurting my arm. You're drunk!"

About that time, Thomas happened to be riding up the road on his horse. He had gotten off work a little early to go talk to Silas and Mark about helping them on the farm. When he saw Sarah trying to remove Mark's hand from her arm, he jumped off his horse and ran to where they were standing.

"Sarah, what's going on? Mark, why were you grabbing Sarah's arm?"

Mark stood there not knowing what to say. He loved his brother, but his emotions and love for Sarah had blinded his mind to what was sensible, and the whiskey had gotten to his head.

"We just had a little disagreement, that's all."

"I don't understand. What kind of an argument would you be having with my wife?"

Without thinking, Mark replied, "I'm in love with her."

Thomas stood there in shock, looking at Sarah. "Is that true, Sarah?"

Sarah thought about the dream she'd had a few nights before and wondered if it was all about to unfold. She looked at Thomas with tears in her eyes and said, "Yes. Your brother has been trying to make advancements towards me, but I've made none towards him. I want you to know that, Thomas. I have no feelings for him."

Thomas asked Sarah to go back home. "It won't take long," he said. "Don't worry. I just want to talk to Mark alone."

She asked Thomas not to stay too long and to come home as soon as possible. Somehow she felt like something bad was going to happen. She wanted to scream and make the whole madness go away, but life's corrupt nature was taking its course and she felt powerless against it.

As soon as she was out of sight, Thomas and Mark walked down to the barn, near Annie's cabin, to discuss Mark's love for Sarah - an intense conversation between two brothers who'd always been close. The sun was going down, and the light in the barn that beamed through the windows began to slowly dissipate. Thomas walked over to an oil lamp hanging on a nail and put a match to its wick, the light casting their shadows against the barn wall.

"Mark, if you will just say that you didn't mean it. That what you said outside about Sarah was just a lie and that you've had too much to drink, then I'll believe you."

Mark was silent.

"If you're not going to say anything, then I'll say it for you. Stay away from Sarah."

Mark didn't like his brother telling him what to do, though he knew he was right. Thomas tried to reason with him, but his heart was set on Sarah and nothing his brother said changed his mind.

"Mark, I don't know what has come over you. Don't you understand that Sarah is my wife?"

Mark argued with Thomas to the point where they began hollering at each other, physically fighting in the barn. Thomas was as big as Mark and both seemed to be evenly matched as they traded punches. Thomas lost his balance as he tripped over a sack of feed, causing him to fall backward against the horse stall. He hit his head hard against the gate, causing a terrible gash. Mark knelt down beside him. Thomas looked up at his brother, dazed and confused, holding his head in extreme pain. Mark took his shirt off and pressed it against the wound, trying to stop the bleeding.

"I'm sorry Thomas. I didn't mean to hurt you. You're going to be all right. Try not to move."

"It's not your fault, Mark. It's the liquor in your system. I sure am feeling light headed…"

In just a little while, Thomas was dead. Mark let go of his brother, his hands trembling with fear as he stood there in shock from what had just happened, the blood of Thomas all over his hands and clothes. He walked to the well to draw some water to wash his hands with, his mind consumed with how he was going to explain away his brother's death. *They'll never believe it was an accident,* he thought, *especially if they find out why we were arguing.* After he walked back to the barn, he sat there, trying to figure how he was going to dispose of Thomas's body. He thought about taking him off somewhere in his car, but knew someone might see him. Instead, he picked his body up and put him in back of the wagon. He could see the lantern through the barn window still burning in the cabin, but didn't see anyone awake or moving around. He hitched the mule to the wagon and rode down to the lowland near the creek to look for a place to bury his brother. After finding a secluded spot, he lit a lantern, then dug a shallow grave near the water's edge. The shadow of Mark digging into the earth displayed itself against the hard oaks, brought to life by the light of the lantern, and his darkened form, that would haunt him for the rest of his days, now larger than life, flickered back and forth against the branches where only the wild animals could see it in its frantic movement. He took the body from off the wagon and dragged it to the freshly dug grave. He looked at his brother one last time before placing him in the dampened earth, saying a few words over his lifeless body…

'I'm sorry, Thomas. I didn't mean for this to happen. I had too much to drink and couldn't control myself. You know I loved you and would have done anything in the world to keep from hurting you. I won't be able to tell anybody what happened, so no one will be visiting your grave but me. It would kill Mama if she ever found out the truth. I know your children are going to miss you, and Sarah. I'll tell them you had to go away and that you love them very much.'

Mark covered the body of his brother with dirt, then went back to the log cabin as if nothing bad had happened. But his conscience bothered him, and it kept him awake all night drinking whiskey.

Sarah knew something was wrong, for it had been hours and still Thomas hadn't returned. All the children had been put to bed while she sat up waiting on the front porch, hoping to see her husband come riding up the road any minute, sitting tall and handsome on his horse. She fell asleep in her rocking chair, unable to keep her eyes open after the minutes turned into hours.

****

The early morning sound of the birds chirping and the roosters crowing woke Sarah up from her shallow sleep, and for a moment, she'd forgotten why she was sitting on the porch. The sun had made its way above the tree line and a light fog hovered low in the surrounding fields as she looked around and realized Thomas hadn't come home. Her worst fear came to pass when she saw his horse standing in the front yard, his saddle still attached and his gun in its pouch. She ran inside to tell Dovie to watch after the children while she left to find out where Thomas was. In her mind, she hoped he'd stayed up late working things out with Mark and somehow fallen asleep at his mother's cabin. She ran all the way to Annie's house, holding her dress up to one side, calling out Thomas's name, hoping he would answer, yet feeling a foreboding darkness and dreadful awareness that something terrible had happened. Once there, she looked everywhere around the farm but didn't see Thomas anywhere. *Where could he be*, she thought. She knocked on the front door of the cabin in panic, somewhat paralyzed by her own sense of danger, hoping Thomas would answer and cause her worst fears to subside. Annie came to the door and asked if anything was wrong. She told her that Thomas hadn't been home all night and that his horse was standing loose in the front yard.

Annie called Silas and Mark to the door.

"Boys, have either of you seen Thomas?"

"The last time I saw him was last night when he left on his horse to go back home. We'd stayed up late talking in the barn," replied Mark.

"What about you, Silas?"

Silas stood there trying to think of where Thomas might've gone. "I've been busy around the farm. I haven't seen him for days."

Sarah looked at Mark to see if she could detect anything unusual about him, anything out of the ordinary that would convince her of any wrongdoing on his part. She noticed he couldn't look her in the eyes, and the smell of alcohol had clung to his clothes. *Something bad has happened*, she thought, but she was too afraid to confront him, not knowing how he would react if she questioned him.

Annie told her not to worry; that Thomas had probably gone off somewhere and would be back soon. "Come inside and let me fix you some coffee, Sarah."

Annie didn't know what had been going on behind the scenes Sarah thought, because if she did, *she'd be worrying too.*

"I would love to, Annie. But the children need me, and I want to be home in case Thomas shows up. I'll let you know as soon as he comes home."

Annie gave Sarah a warm hug.

Sarah left to find a quiet place to think things through, to find some sort of way to put the missing pieces together. *Am I worrying too much or causing any unnecessary panic?* When she made it back home, she searched through Thomas's saddlebag for any clues...any signs that might lead to where he might be. Nothing. She had to get a hold of herself. Her thoughts raced back and forth through the previous evening, punishing herself for not staying behind with Thomas. But he'd asked her to leave so he could talk with Mark alone. *Where could he have gone afterwards? He wasn't going anywhere else but home.*

For days, Annie kept the children for Sarah while she went looking for her missing husband. Silas asked Mark about the conversation he and Thomas had had in the barn the night before he went missing. Mark told him it was a private matter between him and Thomas. Silas began to detect something wasn't right with Mark and asked him to go help find Thomas, but he refused and said there was no need in looking for him, that he'd left for good. Silas asked him the reason why he would say such a thing. *Thomas had no reason to leave for good*, he thought. *He was a happily married man with four wonderful children.* Everything was going well for him, and it just didn't make sense to Silas why he would leave without any plans of coming back.

Silas walked out to the barn to look for any clues or signs of where Thomas might've gone. As he looked around the barn, he noticed a patch of dry blood on some hay in the horse stall. When he knelt down on the ground, he found Thomas's pocket watch and wondered, *why would Thomas's pocket watch be lying on the ground in the horse stall?* He believed Mark was the only person that knew the answer concerning the blood and the pocket watch: "Mark, would you come here for a minute. I've found something."

Mark was standing near the well with a liquor bottle in his hand when Silas called for him to come to the barn. The alcohol he'd drank all night plagued his mind with visions of his brother coming back from the dead.

"Mark, do you know anything about how this blood got here and whose blood this is? Now, before you say anything, I just want to ask you about this watch. Do you know who this watch belongs to? I can tell you, Mark. This pocket watch belongs to Thomas because I bought it for him."

Silas opened the pocket watch and showed Mark the picture of Sarah that Thomas kept in it.

"Now you have to be honest with me. What happened here and where is Thomas?"

Mark put his hands over his face and began to weep. He wanted to tell Silas everything and free himself of the guilt he was carrying, but he couldn't get the words out of his mouth. He couldn't bring himself to tell Silas that he had accidentally killed their brother and had buried him down near Bay Gall creek. He couldn't find it in himself to tell him the real reason why he and Thomas were talking and that their conversation was over his love for Sarah.

Silas walked up to Mark and asked, "Did you kill him, Mark? Is that the reason for the blood on the hay? For God's sake, tell me what happened!"

Mark went running out of the barn, down the winding road to Sarah's house. He had to talk with her about what had happened to Thomas and explain to her that he didn't mean to hurt anyone. When he approached Sarah's house, he began to weep when he saw her standing on the front porch alone. He looked at her and paused, trying to find the right words to say to her, his voice trembling, his hands shaking.

"Sarah, I'm sorry. Thomas and I had a little argument last night. It all happened so fast. You know I had too much to drink and I wasn't thinking clearly. Sarah, I can't help the way I feel about you. When Thomas told me I had to stay away from you, I lost it."

"Mark, what are you saying? Did you kill Thomas? You have to be honest with me."

"All I can say is that he's never coming back. He's gone, Sarah, and he's never coming back."

Sarah felt in her heart that Mark had killed Thomas, but she didn't realize it was an accident. To her, there was no need in trying to get any more information out of him. Mark took Sarah's hand and asked her if she could ever forgive him. She looked at him for a minute, somewhat sad, yet, at the same time, filled with anger, gently removing his hand from hers. She couldn't find it in herself to say anything. She had to face the reality that she was alone now, that her husband had been killed by his own brother. She thought about her children. *How can I provide for all of them now that Thomas is gone?*

As far as calling the law, she'd ruled that out. She didn't want Annie to suffer any kind of investigation or trial involving two of her sons. Her struggle was more with herself and how to move forward with her life. *If Mark killed Thomas, then he's never coming back, and I must reconcile myself to that sad reality.*

Silas continued looking for Thomas on the West farm, but Mark did a good job of concealing the place where he'd buried him. Days went by, then weeks, and still no sign. Annie knew something bad had happened to her son, but didn't say much or talk to anyone about it. She didn't want to think about what could have happened to him, and there were his children and wife to think about. Dovie, Oscar, Phillip, and little John Willie, all needed emotional support, and Annie took up time with them as often as she could. Sarah would never go to Annie's house again unless she knew Mark wouldn't be there. She didn't want to see his face anymore.

Chapter *T*welve

*T*he rain had been falling for days and finally subsided to a light mist over the West farm, the sky still thick with clouds blocking the light of the early morning sun. Fall weather had arrived and the leaves were floating in the air like wind driven snow flakes, finding their place of rest on the lowlands of Bay Gall creek, creating a fresh layer of foliage. It appeared as if life was normal again, but deep down inside, Sarah still felt an overwhelming weight of grief. She tried to be strong for her family, but she found it more difficult as the days passed and it became more obvious that her husband wasn't coming back. She'd held on to a small ray of hope that maybe Mark hadn't done the unspeakable, that Thomas would somehow find his way home. But now, reality had set in. She knew he was gone, forever. Her heart ached for a return to normalcy, to the way things were before Thomas's disappearance, and she often thought of her children and how their lives had forever changed.

It was early morning, and Phillip and Oscar were in the back yard chopping some oak near the smokehouse, building calluses on their youthful hands as they swung the ax back and forth, stocking a pile of wood for the stove. Dovie helped her mother with some things in the house, a fall cleaning they called it, as little John Willie played on the living room floor with some hand-carved wooden toys. As Sarah and Dovie were hanging a fresh washed curtain over the living room window, Sarah saw Mark walking up the road toward their house, his movements somewhat controlled by a certain degree of whiskey in his system. He hadn't attempted to visit her since the last conversation they'd had a few weeks before, and now that Thomas was gone, her resolve to reject his every offer had only grew stronger. Her hands began to shake with fear as she dropped the curtain to the floor. *Whatever he is coming to see me about can't be good,* she thought. *Why would he even think I'd be interested in him after what happened to Thomas, unless he believes I don't think he killed him?* She tried to keep her composure. She told Dovie to go out to the backyard and get the clothes off the line. "Take little John with you," she said.

Dovie never saw Mark walking through the front gate.

Sarah met him on the front porch.

"Hello, Sarah."

"Hey, Mark. What brings you this way?"

"It's been weeks now since we've talked. Don't you think you should give me a chance? Sarah, you need a man around the house and someone to help you look after the kids. I know what you're thinking, but I didn't murder Thomas. It was an accident."

"An accident? What do you mean by an accident? An accident that Thomas is gone and he's never coming back? That doesn't make any sense, Mark."

"That is all I can tell you, Sarah. It's best you don't know the whole story."

"Best I don't know the whole story? By that, do you mean, it's best I remain in the dark about where my missing husband is? Best that my children are now without a father?" cried Sarah, the tears streaming down her face.

"I'm trying to be as truthful and honest with you as possible, Sarah. I know you and the children are hurting."

"If you're trying to be honest, then why are you covering it up and not telling me what really happened?"

"I want to, but there is only so much I can tell you…"

"Mark, please stop talking. I don't want to hear anymore."

"You're right. I'm sorry. It's probably best not to talk about it anymore. At least let me look after you and the children."

"We've made it these last few weeks without a man around the house and we can make it from here without one. Your mother Annie has helped us and I couldn't ask anything more than that."

"I've never stopped loving you, Sarah. Please give me just one chance," pleaded Mark, walking closer.

He tried to hold her hand, but she yelled for him to let go. The children heard their mother's scream in the backyard and ran into the house to see what was wrong.

Before they made it to her, Mark disappeared out of sight, afraid that someone might've heard the commotion.

"Mama, what's wrong? What's wrong, Mama?"

"Nothing, Oscar. Nothing at all. It was just a big spider crawling on my shoulder and I panicked. I managed to get it off and now everything's ok."

I have to get away, she thought, *even if Thomas's death was an accident. I don't feel comfortable living near Mark anymore.* To her, there was only one route of recourse, and that was to leave, to get out of Bulloch County and go back to South Carolina to her family. She knew Mark would keep trying to see her while she lived so close to the West farm. *Leaving will be for the good of everyone involved, even if it goes against everything I believe in, or everything I want for myself or for my children.* She didn't want to leave them behind, but there was no way she could take them with her and find the means to support them. Annie helped to provide a lot of the emotional and physical support she needed the next few weeks, but Sarah needed much more. She needed Annie to take sole custody of her children and raise them as her own. Sarah tried to find some way to talk to her, to let her know her thoughts and intentions, but she didn't want to go to Annie's house now that Mark seemed so desperate. She happened to remember that Annie always went to church on Sundays at Oak Grove, and that is where she would talk to her.

Sunday came, and Sarah, anxious and afraid Annie wouldn't be there, had all of the children dressed early and ready for church. When they arrived at Oak Grove, she saw her mother-in-law sitting in the same pew where she always sat, looking so graceful. A smile came over her face and she felt like everything was going to be ok somehow. *If it wasn't for Annie*, she thought, *I wouldn't know what to do or who to turn to.* She was the stronghold of the West family through the years, and to Sarah, she was an angel. Annie's faith and endurance gave Sarah the strength to make it through the tragedy of losing Thomas, the strength to face the obstacles that life had suddenly put in her pathway. She walked over to where Annie was sitting and sat down next to her, putting her arms around her, trying to hold back the tears she felt so deep inside.

After church, she asked Annie if she could talk to her alone. The children played in the church yard while they walked over to the cemetery. Annie had wanted to put some flowers on Phillip's grave.

"Annie, I have something I need to ask you. It concerns the children. Something has come up and I have to go back to South Carolina. I wish I could tell you the reason why I have to go. I can't afford to take the children with me...I don't plan on coming back to Georgia."

"You don't have to say anymore, Sarah. I don't understand all that's going on, but I know that if you didn't have to leave, you wouldn't. You've been the best daughter-in-law I could ever ask for and have given me four wonderful grandchildren. You loved Thomas more than any woman ever could have and I have nothing to blame you for. I would be honored to look after your children, and in a way, by having them around, I feel like I still have Thomas with me."

Sarah began crying, unable to hold back the tears any longer. She was overcome with emotion hearing the compassion and understanding in Annie's voice. She wrapped her arms around her and told her how much she loved her and how great a mother-in-law she'd been to her. She wanted to tell Annie everything, but she couldn't tell her that Mark was the real reason for her leaving.

Sarah took the children back home. After her conversation with Annie, she couldn't help but think of what their future might hold. *How can I leave them when they need me most? They no longer have a father, and now, they'd be without a mother.* But she trusted Annie, and if anyone could provide a mother's love, it would be their grandmother. She wanted to spend some time with them before leaving for Carolina. The hardest part would be telling them they couldn't go with her.

While they sat together at the kitchen table, she explained to them that she had to go away for a while and that they were going to have to stay with their grandmother Annie.

"Dovie...you'll need to help your grandmother watch over little John Willie. He'll need a lot of attention and care. Oscar...Phillip...I need you two to be strong for your mother. It's tearing me apart to have to leave you here. But I know your grandmother loves you very much and she'll do all she can to make sure you live a normal life. Words can't express how much sorrow I feel. You've had to suffer the loss of your father, and if that wasn't enough, now your mother has to go away for a while. I wish I could tell you all the reasons why I have to leave, but when the time is right, you'll understand."

At first, they didn't want to listen to what their mother had to say, but Dovie, the oldest child, helped them to accept the fact that it was in their best interest to stay with their grandmother. It was a sad and tragic time for Sarah and her children when she had to tell them goodbye. The tears flowed down their faces as they watched their mother ride off in the distance down the long and winding road, never knowing if they'd ever see her again.

Sarah stepped onto the train knowing she wouldn't see her family for a long time. As the train made its way to Savannah, she sat in her seat quietly looking out the window thinking about her children. She knew they had to accept some hard things the past few weeks.

There was a light rain falling and water droplets formed on the window.

Sarah thought to herself...

I hope Oscar takes after Thomas and doesn't fall into the footsteps of Mark or Silas. He's got such a big heart and wants to do what's right. Hopefully Phillip and little John Willie will do the same. I know Dovie is a strong person and I will miss our talks together. I couldn't have asked for a better daughter. I hope they all know that I love them and I hope they will one day understand why I had to leave. I will speak their names daily until I take my last breath.'

Sarah wore a locket around her neck that contained a picture of Thomas. She opened the locket and looked at Thomas with tears running down her cheeks...

'I'm sorry Thomas. I knew I shouldn't have left you by yourself that night. I wish I could turn back time, but I can't. I didn't know what to do with the kids, having no way to support them, so I entrusted them to your mother ...I know they'll be in good hands with her. I don't know what will become of me without you and the children in my life. The pain seems more than I can bear. I'll never forget what we had and I'll always cherish your memory...'

A black lady helped keep Sarah hid for weeks in order to keep Mark from knowing her whereabouts, and as time passed, she would change her name to Billie, move to Myrtle Beach, South Carolina, and never return to Georgia.

Now that Sarah was gone, Mark would have to face his passions alone, and his hopes of ever having her as his wife forever faded out of sight.

He made many attempts in trying to figure out where she went to, but with no success. "Silas, do you know where Sarah might've gone or why she left?"

"I don't have a clue, Mark. Maybe she went to look for Thomas."

Silas didn't believe Sarah had gone to look for Thomas, but he was at a loss as much as Mark was in trying to find out where she went.

I can't figure out why she would leave all her children behind. It just doesn't make any sense, thought Silas.

Annie kept quiet about Sarah's whereabouts. She'd made a promise to her to keep the whole situation confidential. The West farm wouldn't be the same without Thomas or Sarah around. Life, or the tragedy of it, had taken them away, breaking the family circle and leaving an empty void that would never be filled again. Annie would sit in her rocking chair, evening after evening, picturing Thomas, Sarah, and the children, living in their pine home down the road, coming and going, laughing and spending time together, stopping by for a visit. Now, the pine-built home was empty, like an old abandoned building having no soul or life in it. At least she still had a part of Thomas and Sarah with her through her grandchildren, keeping their memories alive.

Chapter Thirteen

One sunny afternoon, while Mark was sitting on the front porch of the West log cabin, he noticed a man walking up the road in a cautious manner, as if looking for something or someone. When he made it to the front gate of the cabin, one could easily tell he was a stranger in this place, for not many souls wandered along the West's land without fear of trespassing.

The man struck up a conversation with Mark: "Good morning. I'm kind of lost. I went hunting this morning with some friends of mine and got crossed up. You don't happen to know where I am do you?"

"Well…you're dab smack in the middle of the West Farm. I'm Mark West. You have to be new in these parts to get mixed up out here."

"It's my first time hunting in the Bay Gall. I sure would be obliged, Mr. West, if you could tell me how to get back out near Rocky Ford road."

Mark gave the man directions, pointing him south through the cattle gap, then past the tobacco barns in the open fields toward the main road.

"Don't stray too far off the path though, or you'll end up right back where you started from," said Mark, with a hint of laughter.

"I think you gave me easy enough directions to follow. I really do appreciate it. Say, you don't happen to know where I could get a good taste of moonshine do you?"

Mark looked cautiously at the man, then said, "I sure do. Follow me and I'll give you a taste of moonshine you won't ever forget."

He took him down through the field to the moonshine still near the creek. It was unusual for him to show a stranger his still, but Mark had a 'born sense of danger' and the man seemed to pose no threat. However, when they made it to the still, the stranger seemed to act more nervous than usual, and it made Mark suspicious. He didn't have his gun with him, and Silas wasn't there to watch his back.

The newly made shine was kept underneath a small shelter near the creek bank, and when Mark reached down to get a jar, the stranger took his gun out and pointed it at him. "Hold it right there, Mr. West. You're under arrest for making unstamped liquor. I'm an agent for the government."

Mark let go of the bottle, unsure if the stranger was telling the truth or just trying to steal his shine.

He saw the uncertainty on Mark's face.

"Here's proof if you need it," said the man, showing Mark his badge.

I should've never trusted a stranger, he thought. "Who would've figured?"

"That's right. Now turn around and put your hands behind your back."

The revenuer arrested Mark and took him to the county jail.

As soon as Silas heard what happened, he drove to the jailhouse to see his brother. The jailor took him back to Mark's cell.

"Well, you've really gone and done it this time? How could you have been so careless? You know them revenuers have been after us for years now," said Silas, feeling somewhat sorry for Mark. "Never mind what's happened. I feel bad and somewhat responsible. Do you need anything?"

"Yeah…a jug of shine."

"You know the answer to that one."

Mark went from a joking to a more serious tone. "I didn't see it coming, Silas. He lied right through his teeth."

"You can't trust anyone, Mark." Silas held his head down and thought for a moment. "It doesn't matter now. We just need to get you out of here."

Not long after, Mark appeared in court.

'The State versus Mark West' was announced in the court room.

"The defendant waives copy of indictment and list of witnesses. Also, the defendant waives being formally arraigned and pleads guilty to be punished as for a misdemeanor," spoke Mark's defense attorney R. Lee Moore to the Judge. Judge H.B. Strange then handed down the sentence.

"Whereupon, it is considered, ordered and adjudged by the Court that you, Mark West, serve twelve months on the chain-gang of Bulloch County, or on the public works of such other county, or on such other public works as the proper authorities may direct. Said defendant may be discharged at any time before the completion of this sentence upon the payment of a fine of two hundred dollars, including costs of officers of Court."

The judgment was signed in open court the 31st of July, 1925. After the court session ended, Silas paid the amount necessary to have Mark released from jail and thus fulfill his responsibilities to the State. He was glad Silas was there to get him out of trouble, but it wouldn't be the last time he'd see behind the bars of a jail cell. Silas told him they'd have to be careful until things calmed down.

"Well, Silas, I can tell you right now, that I'll never give another stranger a drop of our home brew."

"I don't expect we'll be making any moonshine for a while, Mark. We've got to lay low until we know it's safe. Neither one of us can afford to get caught again."

When Silas and Mark made it back home, they walked in the front door of the cabin and saw their mother Annie sitting in the rocking chair looking out the window, holding a picture of their daddy in her hands. They could tell she'd been crying as she quickly wiped away the tears from her eyes.

Mark walked up to his mother and gave her a warm embrace. "Hey, Mama, I've always loved that picture of Daddy."

"There's not a day that goes by that I don't think about him. Sometimes it seems I can hear his voice calling my name, but when I look around, he's not there." Annie paused. "I'm glad you're home, Son."

Annie's hair was turning gray, and her hands that had labored so long for her family were now worn with age. Her heart ached for her sons and for their well-being, and she often thought back to the time when Phillip was alive. Mark was just a young teenager when his father passed away, and he didn't know how to deal with the sudden loss. Annie knew that without Phillip, there would be an empty void left in her sons' lives, and sometimes she attributed Silas's and Mark's wild side to his absence. She tried to do her best for them, and they knew she loved them unconditionally; even when they broke the law, she loved and prayed and never stopped being there for them. She didn't say anything to Mark about being arrested for his whiskey dealings, and her silence instructed him more than any words of criticism ever could. She slowly got up from her rocking chair and put the picture of Phillip back on the fireplace mantle, next to the portrait of Thomas. She was still grieving over his absence, even though some years had passed since her son's disappearance. She picked up his picture and wiped the dust from off the glass and the frame, and Mark could see the tears streaming down her face. It was almost more than he could bear. He knew his past actions were the cause of deep grief his mother was now feeling. He wanted to walk up to her and tell her everything about that night, about the fatal accident, but he knew it would only break her heart even more. Annie gently placed the portrait of Thomas back on the fireplace mantle next to Phillip's, as if to tell them goodnight. She sat back down in her rocker and talked with her sons until the sun set low over Bay Gall creek.

"The time will come when I won't be around anymore. I'm getting up in age and I'm beginning to think more and more about the day when I won't have enough strength to get out of bed. If anything were to happen to me, I need to know you will all stay together and love each other as a family. No matter what happens to me or how feeble I get, always know that I love you and that I tried to do the best I could for my family."

Silas and Mark didn't know what to say. They'd never heard their mother talk about getting old or dying before and it was an emotional moment for them as they reflected on her words and what she was trying to tell them. They'd taken her love for granted and never really considered all of the sacrifices she'd made for them through the years. They promised her that they'd do everything in their power to keep the family together, and assured her, that no matter how feeble she might become in this life, they'd always take care of her.

Annie needed this moment with her sons and they cherished these times with their mother.

Chapter Fourteen

It was the mid 1920s, when John decided to move back home near the West farm from Emmanuel County, an area he'd been residing in for almost a decade, working in the timber trade. While there, he'd married a pretty girl named Rachel Greenway at Bishop's chapel, and they'd had one son together, John Robert. John Robert was fourteen when his father moved back to the Lockhart District, into a house across the road from Wash Beasley's place, not far from *Nevils Creek*. John was the oldest of Annie's children, and after the disappearance of his brother Thomas, his thoughts turned back to the Bay Gall and to the open fields of home. It was John who'd cared for the farm years ago when his father Phillip was away during the weekdays traveling, and a part of him had always remained there.

There was lightning to the north when John and his family rode along the winding road to the old log cabin, the place of his upbringing. He stopped the horses at the top of a little knoll overlooking the farm, taking in the familiar scenic view. He put his arms around his wife Rachel sitting next to him, giving her a kiss, as their son slept soundly in back of the wagon. *Home*, he thought, as he looked out across the open fields, feeling a slight drizzle of rain tapping him on his hat and coat. Sacred thoughts rushed through his mind as he remembered back to the time of his childhood. He recalled the afternoon that his father had passed away and it brought him a sudden sadness. The closeness of home reminded him of many things he'd long forgotten, so many kind recollections…so many fond memories.

"It's all there, Rachel, nestled in the middle of those open fields, the place where my mother and father raised me. I can never forget my father's labor, his hands rough and calloused from the plow, and my mother's care, watching over us like a mother hen."

They could see the smoke in the distance from the wood burning stove hurling upward from the kitchen into the cloudy sky, and John knew his mother was cooking supper. He passed by the tobacco barns and through the cattle gap, coming to a stop underneath the old walnut tree.

The kitchen door slowly swung open, and the shadow of John stretched out across the splintered floor to where his mother was standing.

"Mama…"

Annie turned around.

"John! I can't believe it's you! Welcome home, son!"

John and his mother embraced, while Rachel and John Robert stood close by, smiling. Annie looked over John's shoulder and saw his family near the open door.

"Rachel, as lovely as ever," said Annie. "And, John Robert, give your grandmother a great big hug. Y'all come in and sit down at the table. I'm just about finished cooking supper. Mark and Silas will be in shortly from the fields. John Robert, your cousins would love to see you…they're all inside the cabin. Will you go tell them supper is ready?"

It had been a while since John Robert had seen Dovie, Oscar, Phillip, and little John Willie. He ran out the kitchen into the cabin from the back porch, almost tripping over a piece of wood that had fallen from the stack piled neatly near the door.

John looked out the kitchen window and saw Mark and Silas walking in from the barn, both looking tired and worn out from the long day's work.

He yelled out to them: "Well, if it ain't the two most wanted moonshine runners south of the Appalachian Mountains."

They looked up and saw their brother John, his head stuck out of the kitchen window, smiling from ear to ear.

"John, our long lost brother," yelled Silas.

Mark walked up to the side of the cabin near the chimney bricks and reached underneath the house, pulling out a jug of moonshine. He motioned to John, still looking out the window, to come outside. Annie didn't approve of having any whiskey around the house and for good reasons. So John snuck out without giving it away, and all three took a few swigs as a welcome home celebration for John's return. *"It's good to have you back home, brother,"* said Mark, feeling the strong drink hit his chest. Annie looked out the kitchen window and called them all inside for supper, her eyes failing to see the jug of whiskey Silas quickly hid behind his back.

Everyone sat around the long wooden table in the kitchen, the oil lamp lighting the room after the sun had gone down. Annie asked John to say the blessing over the meal…

"Dear Lord, it sure is good to be home again. I sure have missed this place. My precious mother…the cattle gap…the old walnut tree…all bring back cherished memories. I ask you to bless the kind hands that prepared this meal. Keep us all safe from harm. Amen."

"Dovie, pass me the biscuits please," asked Oscar, sitting across the table.

"Fried chicken. My favorite food," said John.

"He's talked about your cooking ever since we've been married, Annie," said Rachel. "He's been dying to eat one of your home-cooked meals."

"Tell me, John, how long will y'all be staying?" asked Silas.

"Well, we're not going back to Summertown. We've decided to put our stakes down here. There's a nice little homestead not far from Nevils Creek, next to the GP Miller farm."

"It's a good place," said Mark.

"That's great news to a mother's ears," said Annie. "It will be like old times again with everyone back home."

John looked up and saw a picture of his father Phillip hanging on the wall: "I sure do miss Daddy a lot. It doesn't seem that long ago when we were all sitting here, at this same table, talking about planting cotton, going fishing…hunting coons down near Bay Gall creek. I sure have lost track of time. But I want to make up for it now."

"Son, you've done well for yourself. Look at the pretty wife you've married and the strong son you have. We're just glad to have you back."

"That's right, John," said Silas. "We're a family. And no matter what comes our way, we'll see it through together."

****

While John helped out on the West place, he also worked on the GP Miller farm, near Nevils Creek, where he and his family lived.

One sunny afternoon, Mark and Silas saw John at the blacksmith's shop with Adolphus Parker, working on a broken plow-blade he'd needed fixing. Adolphus, or Dolphus, as his friends called him, was the local blacksmith and his place bordered the West farm near Annie's.

"Good afternoon, Mr. Dolphus. Sure is a pretty blue sky today."

"Sure is, Silas. I think I'll take my wife Willie Emma and my daughter Eleanor to the river this afternoon and do some fishing as soon as we fix this blade."

"Sounds like the perfect place to be on a day like this. Say, John, you want to go fishing with me and Silas down at Nevils Creek?" asked Mark taking his hat off, wiping the sweat from his forehead with a handkerchief.

"Well, I reckon I can. But first, let me go get my rubber boots. The water is a little higher than normal at the bridge and I want to get to the good fishing holes without getting my feet wet."

Nevils Creek bridge wasn't far from the GP Miller farm where John worked, and he often loved to fish there, the last main fishing place before the creek run into the Ogeechee River. It was a beautiful run, a creek where the cypress trees joined its flow of water through the untouched land and where those who settled near its banks felt its quiet presence.

"Hey, Mark, be sure to bring us a good jug of whiskey. If we don't have any luck catching fish, we'll at least have a good jug of shine to drink," smiled Silas.

Silas had forgiven Mark of any wrongdoing he might've had in the disappearance of Thomas. He missed his brother more than life itself, but couldn't prove anything against Mark, who never talked about that mysterious night. To Silas, if Mark killed his own brother, he would have to face his Maker for it, either in this life or in the next, and suffer the consequences of covering up his sins. Once, John asked Silas what happened to Thomas, and he told John what Mark told him, that *Thomas was gone and was never coming back.*

It was like old times again for the West brothers as they walked along the old Savannah Rd to the creek bridge. Mark and John had rubber boots on, but Silas went barefoot, his pants legs rolled up to this knees. Only Thomas wasn't there, and as long as he was missing, there seemed to be a dark cloud that rested over their time together.

After catching a mess of fish, they turned the jug upside down.

They sat by the creek for a good long while, lost in the spirits, without a care in the world. Long after the jug had gone dry Silas took the string of fish out of the water and cooked them over an open fire. By then, the stars shone bright in the night sky.

Mark was passed out from drinking too much.

After John and Silas ate some fish, they rested on the ground next to the fire, looking up at the stars.

"Say, Silas…"

"Yeah, John…"

"I sure do miss Daddy. There are so many questions I'd like to ask him about life. Questions about his upbringing in South Carolina and what his father and mother were like. I was so busy doing my own thing that I never took the time to talk with him about his past."

"I know what you mean. It's ironic how time puts things in perspective, but we can't turn back the time. We've got to accept things as they are."

"He sure lived life to the fullest. Out of all the things he taught me, there's one thing that stands out in my mind the most."

"What's that?"

"Never quit. Whenever bad things happened to him, he kept on going, never letting the hardships of life take him down. There's not a day that goes by that I don't think about him. I never got to say goodbye. He was here one minute and gone the next."

Mark finally woke up, a little disoriented at first, looking over at John and Silas sitting by the fire before realizing where he was.

"I sure am hungry," said Mark.

"I think there's one more fried fish in the pan," said Silas.

Mark turned up the jug lying next to him, but it was empty.

"Say, who drank all the moonshine?"

"Well, if you'll go home and look in the mirror, you'll have a pretty good idea."

John and Silas laughed.

After Mark ate the last fish, they kicked some dirt over the hot burning coals and walked back to the log cabin in the dark, accidentally leaving one of their rubber boots near the water's edge.

****

A few weeks passed since the day they'd gone fishing at the creek, the farm work keeping them busy in the fields, leaving little time for leisure. One ill-fated evening, after John finished his work on the GP Miller farm, he was confronted by Arthur Clayton, a co-worker of his.

"Hey, John…did any of you West boys lose a rubber boot?"

"Sure did, Arthur, a few weeks ago."

"Well, one of my boys found a rubber boot the other day walking down by Nevils creek."

"Good. Do you have it with you?"

"Well, not exactly. I figured that boot should be worth some kind of reward."

"A reward? Are you serious?"

"I'm not giving you the rubber boot unless you pay some kind of reward money to get it back."

"Well, Arthur, you can wait until every well in the county runs dry before you get any kind of reward money out of me for my own rubber boot."

Tension rose high between the two as they left the GP Miller Farm.

A few days after the boot incident, Arthur Clayton left the GP farm with his wife and son in a horse drawn wagon, while John left on a saddled horse. They'd both gotten off work and were on their way home, the sun going down behind the western horizon. As Arthur was riding by the West place, he heard a pistol shot come from John's house. John had fired a shot off in the air to let his family know that he was home from work, something that he did quite often. But Arthur didn't like it, especially in light of the argument that he and John had had just a few days before concerning the rubber boot. Arthur thought John was shooting at him, or at least trying to scare him, so he stopped the wagon and told his wife he was going over to John's to ask him why he fired the pistol. His wife begged him not to go, but to no success. When Arthur stepped into the yard at John's house, they began arguing and fighting, the confrontation turning fatal when John pulled his pistol out and shot Arthur Clayton dead.

Arthur's wife knew something tragic had happened when the noise of the fighting ended after the shot was fired, no longer hearing any arguing in the distance. She jumped out of the wagon with her son and ran over to where John was standing. There was her husband, lying on the ground in his own blood, lifeless, shot right through the chest. She knelt down and grabbed him screaming, "*I told you not to do it. Why did you have to do it?*"

John tried to console her, but she was in too much grief, holding tight to her dead husband. He helped load the body into the Clayton wagon and watched them slowly ride away.

The next day, the sheriff came out to arrest John. He drove up with a few of his deputies as John sat in his rocker on the front porch, his pistol still on his side. He'd been there all night, his thoughts going back and forth between Clayton and the shot that had ended his life. He'd done the right thing he was sure of, *but would others see it the same way.* He'd never wanted to kill anyone in cold blood, and if Clayton hadn't threatened his life, he'd still be alive. *Surely the law would have to see it for what it was…self-defense.* He wondered if he'd made the right decision in coming back home to the Lockhart District. *This never would've happened if I'd stayed in Summertown.*

"Hello, sheriff. I guess you're here about Clayton."

"That's right, John. Miss Clayton came by my office this morning and explained everything that happened."

"Well then, you know I was only defending myself from being killed."

"We're going to have to let the jury decide that for us. Until then, I'm going to have to take you in."

John went inside and told his wife Rachel not to worry, that he would be cleared of all charges once the truth was known.

As soon as Silas and Mark heard what had happened, they rushed over to John's house, the dust flying high in the air as they made their way across the Bay Gall. Rachel had sent John Robert over to Annie's cabin to let them know about John shooting Clayton.

When Mark and Silas got there, the sheriff was handcuffing John, his wife standing on the front porch crying.

"Now hold on sheriff," said Silas. "There's no need in taking him in so soon. Don't you think you should learn the facts before you charge a man with murder?"

"I know how you feel Silas. And I hate to be the one to have to do this. But you know the routine. He'll have to be tried in the court of law to prove his innocence."

The sheriff put John in the car.

"Don't worry, John. We'll drive into town as soon as we talk to Rachel," said, Silas.

After listening to Rachel tell the story of how it all unfolded, Silas was convinced that John would be set free. "Don't worry Rachel, he'll be justified when it's all said and done. It's obvious that he was only defending himself."

Mark and Silas drove to town in Mark's model-t ford to see John at the jailhouse.

"Hello, sheriff. I guess you know why we're here."

"I'll get the keys and take you back to see your brother. But don't try anything foolish." The sheriff paused. "You still making moonshine Mark?"

"You know I don't make moonshine anymore. I've cleaned up and walking the straight and narrow."

The sheriff walked them back to John's cell.

"Ok, boys, you don't have much time. Say what you have to say and then you'll have to go."

Mark and Silas walked into the small cell their brother was now confined to. John was lying on his cot, the blood of Clayton still on his shirt.

"You all right, John?" asked Silas.

"I guess so, under the circumstances."

"Now, John, we know this is a clear cut case of self defense. Your wife told us that Clayton was drinking and out of control when he came into the yard. You were afraid for your life and had to defend yourself. The jury will have to see it for what it is."

"I hope so, Silas. I hate for my family to see this happening. Will you tell Mama that I'm sorry for any unnecessary worry I've put her through and that I'm all right."

"I sure will. Now don't worry yourself. You'll be out of here in no time."

The Bulloch County Times published an article stating: "*West is bound over for killing Clayton.*" A portion of the article read: "It was disclosed that ill-feeling had existed between the men previously over the loss of a rubber boot by one of the West brothers. The boot was found by a lad living with Clayton. West's plea was self-defense. It was made to appear by witnesses that Clayton bore a reputation for violence."

Another article from the Bulloch County times stated: "*West on trial for killing of Clayton.*" A portion of the article read: "John W West, age 50, is on trial for his life in superior court here charged with the murder of Arthur Clayton, age 30, whom he shot to death at his home in the Lockhart district on May the 8th. The jury trying the case was given the consideration of it at eleven o'clock this morning, following the delivery of the charge by Judge Knight, presiding."

Annie didn't attend the trial of her son. She didn't like to see him in danger of being convicted for murder, as any mother wouldn't. She'd always taught her children to be neighborly and treat every stranger with kindness. Seeing all of this culminating to murder charges was heartbreaking for her, but she supported her son and sent word to him quite often during the process.

Mark, Silas, and Lizzie were present when the verdict and sentence were handed down. The following named jurors were empanelled to hear the above stated case: Homer Holland, T.Y. Akins, Eli P. Kennedy, Josh T. Nessmith, G. Emmit Hodges, W.A. Holloway, C.W. Anderson, Willie E. Brannen, B.M. Everett, and Morgan O. Anderson. The jurors returned the following verdict: "We, the jury, find the defendant, John W. West, guilty of voluntary manslaughter, this 29th day of July, 1926. We fix the penalty at not less than two years and not more than five years in the penitentiary."

Judge Knight handed down the following sentence:

"Whereupon it is the judgment of the Court that you, John W West, be taken hence from the Court House to the common jail of Bulloch County and be kept in safe custody till demanded by a guard from the Penitentiary, and be taken hence by said guard to the State Farm at Milledgeville, or such other place as the Governor shall direct. And be there confined at hard labor for the space of not less than two and more than five years, and be then discharged."

John held his head down after hearing the guilty sentence, his face filled with regret over the whole incident. It was difficult for him accepting the jury's decision with manslaughter; he just knew he'd be set free on grounds of self-defense.

Silas and Mark tried to console him, but to no success, knowing he'd have to serve time behind bars.

Annie sent her son a letter the day after he was sentenced to prison…

Dear son,

I'm thankful you're still alive. You have so much to live for. I wish you didn't have to go to prison, but my prayers will be with you until you come home again. I love you son…

His mother's words consoled him more than anything, and it gave him the strength to face the coming days. As time passed, he fulfilled his minimum sentence of two years in prison. He was glad to finally be released and couldn't wait to see his family again. Silas met him at the prison gate to take him home.

On their way back to the Bay Gall, Silas asked John, "Well, what's the first thing you're going to do when you get back?"

"I'm going to sit down with my wife and son and tell them how much I love them. I don't want to ever leave them again." With a tear in his eye, he asked, "How's Mama?"

"She's doing well. She's excited about you coming home and plans on fixing you a nice home cooked meal."

"I can taste it now, Silas. There's nothing like Mama's cooking."

It had been a long two years for John, and he returned to the Bay Gall much older in spirit than before. Prison life had changed him, but more than that, the events that had brought him there. The healing process would now begin, and the closeness of family and the familiar surroundings of home were the things that he held to the most.

Chapter Fifteen

Oscar West, the son of Thomas, was given the responsibility of farming a portion of the West farmland when John had been away in prison. He was tall and strong like his father. At fourteen, he worked the land planting crops, chopping cotton, picking tobacco, pushing the plow as hard and productive as any grown man. His education was limited during his early years, the fields and the farm being scaled more important than the books and the blackboard. Not far from the West log cabin was a one-room country school, Olliff Bay, situated near Bay Gall Creek and Nevils Creek Church. Nevils Creek Church, at one time, had been positioned on a high bluff near Nevils Creek, formally known as Bonnell Creek, on lands belonging to James Young. But years after Sherman's March to the Sea, not long after the turn of the century, Nevils Creek Church was moved to the banks of Bay Gall Creek. Most children Oscar's age, who lived in the area, attended Olliff Bay School; but his days in the classroom would be few and far between.

He and his siblings grew used to living with their grandmother Annie, although it took some time to adjust. She protected them from the dangers around and treated them as if they were her own, giving them the same motherly love and care. They'd all been without a father the last few years, and there was still no word from Sarah. The last time

Oscar remembered seeing his father alive was early one morning at the cattle gap, a place between his house and his grandmother's. And then, one dismal day, his mother Sarah left him waving goodbye near the cabin as her image faded forever into the sad horizon. Both of his parents…gone.

It was getting close to noon and Annie, Rachel (wife of John West), Dovie, and Bertie Rea (daughter of Rachel Greenway before she married John West), rode down to the creek in a wagon where Oscar and his brothers, including his cousins, John Robert and Clyde, were swimming. Annie and Rachel had made them some peanut butter and jelly sandwiches and lemonade. It was times like this that Annie cherished. Her younger sons were growing up fast, and there were days when she wished time would just stand still, that none of her children or grandchildren would ever grow older. She knew Oscar and his siblings had to grow up way too fast, without a father and mother, and it was on days like this that she looked for the simple laughter in their faces.

When they made it to the creek, the boys were resting on a wide sandbar.

"Come on, boys. We thought we'd have a nice little picnic," said Annie.

She spread a white sheet in the back of the wagon and placed the sandwiches and lemonade on top. The boys had worked up a good appetite swimming and were excited to hear their grandmother's call to eat: "Thanks, Grandma. Hey, Aunt Rachel!" the boys all shouted.

"Slow down and take your time eating," smiled Annie.

While the boys crowded around the wagon, Dovie and Bertie Rea walked over near the creek and put their feet in the water.

"Dovie, do you ever wonder where your father is?"

"I think about him all the time. Whatever happened to him caused Mama to leave as well. I'll find out some day…" said Dovie, with a tone of uncertainty.

"I imagine you miss your mama a lot."

Dovie didn't want to talk about it. She loved her mother very much and felt an emptiness inside ever since she'd left.

"It's been hard, but Grandma has been like a mother to us. She spends a lot of time with me like Mama used to."

"Grandma, can John Robert and Clyde spend the night with us? We want to camp out in the yard tonight if it's ok with you," asked Oscar.

"You know we've got church tomorrow. If they're going to stay, they'll have to bring some church clothes."

"Thanks, Grandma." Oscar walked up to his grandmother and gave her a warm hug, kissing her on the forehead. She was the one true source of normalcy for him and his siblings.

They all loaded up in the wagon and rode back to the cabin. Once there, the boys jumped out and walked to Clyde Neely's house to get his Sunday clothes, then to John Roberts.

"John Robert, did you order those shoes I gave you the money for?"

"I sure did, Phillip. I've been keeping them for you under my bed in a box."

"Good. I want to wear them to church tomorrow."

Later that evening, the boys worked hard near the tobacco barn putting up a tent to camp out under. It was more like a covering instead of a tent. They'd tied one side of a bed sheet to the back of the wagon and the other to some wood poles stuck in the ground.

"Oscar, tell us a scary story," said little John.

The night sky was lit up by a full moon that seemed to be as large as the sun creeping above the tree line. There was an owl hooting in the distance and the cry of a panther sent chills up and down their spines. They all sat close to each other while Oscar told a story…

"Once upon a time, long years ago, there was a Bay Gall creature that roamed these woods. No one had ever seen it, but from the footprints found, it was huge. On one particular night, when the moon was shining bright, the Bay Gall creature went on the rampage. It started killing livestock and eating them clean to the bone. The men of the community got their dogs and guns and went after the beast. Whatever it was, it made a weird noise and sound that could be heard for miles…"

As he continued the story, Dovie and Bertie Rea covered themselves with white sheets and snuck around the cabin. Just as Oscar was about to finish, Dovie and Bertie Rea came running out screaming with the whites sheets over their heads. All the boys got scared and ran into the cabin, leaving little John Willie all by himself. He sat there crying until Dovie and Bertie took the sheets off and let him know they weren't real ghosts.

The next day arrived and it was time to get ready for church. Phillip got his new shoes out and put them on to wear with his Sunday best. When he walked into the living room, Dovie began laughing. Phillip had had John Robert to mail order him some white dress shoes.

"Phillip, where on earth did you get those white shoes from? They make you look like you're walking on clouds."

"That's better than walking on dirt," said Phillip, with a slight frown on his face.

When the others saw Phillip's white shoes, they started laughing too. He ran into the kitchen where Annie was and told her about the others making fun of his shoes.

Annie looked down and smiled: "Phillip. I don't see anything funny about your shoes. They look good on you. They don't mean any harm by laughing at you. It's just that they haven't ever seen white dress shoes before. You have nothing to be ashamed of. Now straighten up your collar and be proud of your white shoes."

There were many more Sundays like this to remember, and life around the West log cabin brought a sense of belonging to the West children. These were the younger years of a new generation, and although there were tragic events that touched their paths, they were still surrounded by the unending love of family. If anything, the past brought them closer together, and the unexplained circumstances that had left them without a father and a mother made them look to each other for strength and guidance.

Chapter Sixteen

Many years passed along Bay Gall creek and some of the grandchildren of Annie had grown up and had families of their own. Dovie, the oldest of Thomas's children, married Freddie Finch, and lived not far away on old Finch Road. Oscar married Lillie Mae Woodcock, and stayed on Nevils Creek Church Road across the creek from Annie's log cabin. Several seasons had come and gone, and Annie's hands had grown tired with age. In her latter years, she began to lose her eyesight, and Silas hired a lady from Atlanta to look after her and help her around the cabin. She never lost her spirit, but on one cold winter day in January of 1940, her spirit left her body. Silas had risen up early one morning to make her breakfast, but when he walked into her bedroom to wake her up, he realized she wasn't breathing.

He dropped to his knees and wept like a child…

"Oh, Mama, I'm sorry that I wasn't here to tell you goodbye. Oh, Mama, why did you have to leave us? I need you so much. I'm going to miss you, Mama. You were the best mother in the whole world."

Silas got up from his knees beside his mother's bed and kissed her one last time. He quickly sent word to John, Mark, and Lizzie that their mother had passed away from this life into the next. The winding road that led to Annie's log cabin would never be the same, losing the one person who'd given it such meaning and purpose. Her passing was the ending of a generation that could never be replaced, and her memory would forever be a part of her children and grandchildren. Her warm spirit that had filled her home with such unconditional love for so long was now suddenly gone. She and Phillip West had made a wonderful life together, beginning many years before when her father had returned home from the war. It was love at first sight, and their lives were joined for better or for worse. Although to her, there were no bad days with Phillip. They'd met with tragedy with the death of their two young sons, but they'd made it through together. They always did, make it through together. She'd loved Phillip more than life, and the day he passed was a loss she never could get over, although she'd tried her best to be strong for her family. She was the one to outlive the other, and to have to say goodbye to the love of her life was the hardest thing to do. But now, she would be laid to rest next to his grave. Their passing was the closing of a meaningful chapter, but the pages that were written by Phillip and Annie would forever be a part of the winding road along Bay Gall Creek.

The funeral took place at Oak Grove Baptist, and everyone showed their love and respect for Annie Hendrix West. She'd been a faithful member her whole life, and it was said by those who knew her that she'd sell her hens to have enough money to give her tithes to the church.

During the funeral service, Annie's sister got up and sang a song in her memory, followed by many in the community that testified of the numerous ways Annie had been such a blessing to them and to their families. Afterwards, the minister spoke a few words…

"We are gathered here today to mourn the death and celebrate the life of Annie Hendrix West. Many people never hear a sermon behind the pulpit. For most, the only sermon they will ever hear is the life that someone lives in front of them. And so it was with Annie. Her life was a sermon that helped encourage all who came in contact with her. She never spoke an unkind word to anyone. I never heard her complain of any thing she might have been going through or question God for any evils that might have befallen her. She will be missed and the world is worse off without her. I hope her sons and daughter know how much she loved them and how she always asked the church to keep them in their prayers. Mark, Silas, John, and Lizzie... I am truly sorry for the loss and pain you are feeling today. But the one thing that your mother wanted more than anything else in the whole world was for you to walk in the paths of righteousness. She will not have lived her life in vain if you were to walk in those paths and turn from the things that cause you harm. She often spoke of her son Thomas, and how much she missed him."

Mark began to weep uncontrollably when the minister mentioned Thomas's name and how much his mother had missed him. He'd tormented himself ever since that dreadful night.

The minister continued...

"Now as we go and lay our dear sister in the ground, let us remember that her spirit is with God who gave it but her memory remains here with us. Let us not forget her life and the things she stood for. And may we always remember Annie Hendrix West."

It was a sad walk from the church to the cemetery. Once they got to the place where Annie was to be buried, the people sang the hymn *"Shall We Gather at the River."*

After they lowered Annie into the ground, Mark walked back to the little country church where his mother had spent most of her life praying, finding the inner strength she'd always seemed to possess.

He went into the sanctuary alone and knelt down at the altar...

"O Lord, forgive me for the wrongs I've committed against my family, and in particular, against my brother Thomas. I loved my brother and miss him more and more every day. If you can tell him something for me, please tell him that I've seen my transgressions and the error of my ways. Tell him I never meant to hurt him or cause Sarah to go away and leave her children behind. Lord, one of your most humble servants has now entered into your kingdom, my dear mother. I know she'll be welcomed by your angels who've watched over her steps for so many years. Please let her know we love her and that her sons and daughter miss her very much...please tell her that our lives will never be the same without her down here beside us."

John, Silas, Mark, and Lizzie stayed beside their mother's grave a long while talking until the sun set low and the last rays of light touched her place of rest. They'd lost their father many years before, and now, the one who'd kept them all together, was no longer there to kiss them goodnight.

*C*hapter *S*eventeen

*P*hillip sat listening to his favorite radio program in the living room...

"We interrupt this program to bring you a special report. The Japanese have attacked Pearl Harbor, Hawaii. President Roosevelt has just announced."

"John Willie, come in here. Quick! Listen to what they're saying on the radio."

"The attack also was made on all naval and military activities on the principal island of Oahu. The White House is now giving out a statement. The attack apparently was made on all naval and military activities on the principal island of Oahu. A Japanese attack upon Pearl Harbor would naturally mean war."'

The radio transmission lost signal and only static noise could be heard. Silas tried to get the station to come in clearer but to no success.

"Just turn it off," said John Willie. "The reception will be better this evening and we'll try it again."

"You know what this means, don't you?"

"Looks like we're going to war. I can't believe we've just been attacked."

"I've got to go tell Oscar. Where is he?"

"I think he went to the store to get some flour and a block of ice. At least that's where he said he was going when I left his house about an hour ago."

Silas ran across the creek to Oscar's house, not far from Bennie Hendrix's place. He could see them coming down the road in the wagon…Oscar, Lillie Mae, and the children. They were just getting back from Tom Lane's store.

"Oscar. Pearl Harbor has just been attacked by the Japanese. Looks like we might be going to war with Japan. They just announced it on the radio. John Willie wants to know if you all want to come over to Uncle Silas's tomorrow and listen to the broadcasts."

"I reckon we will, Phillip. We'll all have supper together."

"Sounds good. See y'all later."

That night, Lillie had trouble sleeping. She stayed up most of the night thinking about the US going to war and what it meant for Oscar and his brothers.

"What's wrong Lillie? Is it about what Phillip heard on the radio? About going to war?"

"Yes. I'm scared you might have to go away overseas. And if you do, you may get killed or badly wounded. Or worse yet, you might get captured and taken prisoner. You know how they torture people. And the children won't have a father and I'll be left without a husband."

"Don't worry yourself, Lillie. You know all of that is in God's hands. Now try and get some rest and we'll talk about it tomorrow."

The next day, around 12:30 in the afternoon, everyone gathered at the old log cabin to listen to the radio. President Roosevelt was going to deliver a national address to Congress. John Willie turned it to a clear station and everyone sat quietly listening to the broadcast, hanging on to every word the President of the United States had to say:

"Mr. Vice President, Mr. Speaker, members of the Senate and of the House of Representatives, yesterday, December 7th, 1941, a date which will live in infamy, the

United States of America was suddenly and deliberately attacked by naval and air forces of the Empire of Japan...the attack yesterday on the Hawaiian Islands has caused severe damage to American naval and military forces. I regret to tell you that very many American lives have been lost...No matter how long it may take us, to overcome this premeditated invasion, the American people in their righteous might will win through to absolute victory...With confidence in our armed forces, with the unbounding determination of our people, we will gain the inevitable triumph, so help us God...I ask that Congress declare that since the unprovoked and dastardly attack by Japan on Sunday, December 7th, 1941, a state of war has existed between the United States and the Japanese Empire."

For a minute or two, no one said a word. Then Phillip walked over to the radio and turned it off: "I can't believe it. We're going to war with Japan."

"I'm sure we'll aim our tanks toward Hitler as well. He's an evil man," said John Willie. "He's the cause of this *World War.*"

The rest of the evening would be spent around the dinner table discussing the bombings at Pearl Harbor and the possibility of a draft. Conscription was instituted once again in 1940 through the Selective Training and Service Act.

The next two weeks passed with much anxiety, but Christmas time was near, and Oscar and his siblings planned for a family Christmas dinner together. There was a light snow falling outside, and the wind made it feel colder than it really was. The women put up a Christmas tree, and the spirit of St Nicholas was in the air as the men sat near the fireplace talking about the war.

"Oscar, me and John Willie's been thinking about joining the war efforts. We're not married and don't have any children of our own, but you have a family to look after. We want you to stay here and take care of the farm."

"Phillip, you don't..."

"It's settled, Oscar," said John Willie.

A few months after Congress declared war, John Willie joined the army February 5th, at Fort Sill, Oklahoma, and Phillip joined May the 6th, at Fort McPherson, Atlanta.

****

Oscar had seen both of his brothers off to war, and although he hadn't spoken to John Willie and Phillip in person in a while, he'd receive postcards from them through the mail. He'd hear from his sister Dovie from time to time as well. She'd moved to Charleston, SC in 39', and Oscar thought back to the day when she'd decided to leave Georgia. He remembered standing in the yard drawing water when she came walking up the dusty dirt road, her hair unfixed and somewhat out of order, her facial expressions revealing a slight despondency. She didn't have any means of transportation and whenever she'd needed to go somewhere she'd walk to his house. He didn't have a car, but he had a wagon, and he used Mr. Bennie's mule to take him wherever he needed to go.

"Hey, Dovie. What brings you by this time of the day?" asked Oscar, sitting a bucket of water on the front porch.

Dovie walked through the front gate trying to hide her troubled emotions, smiling the best she could.

"I just wanted to come by and see how my younger brother was doing."

"I'm doing well, Dovie. Lillie and I've been putting up vegetables all day."

Oscar knew something was bothering his sister. He could see the look of concern on her face, had seen it before when she and Freddie weren't getting along too good. She and Oscar sat on the front porch and talked a while.

"Oscar, do you ever wonder where Mama is? I often think about where she might be or what she might look like. It's been almost eighteen years now since she left. I wonder if she's even alive."

"I don't know, Dovie," said Oscar, remembering the day when his mother left them. He was only fourteen years old when she told them goodbye, disappearing out of sight. There were so many questions he wanted to ask, but no one around to answer them.

"Oscar, there's a reason why I came over this evening. I wanted to see if you would let me borrow five dollars."

"Five dollars…What on earth do you need five dollars for?"

"I need the money to take a train to Charleston. Freddy and I need some time apart and I thought I would take a vacation to Carolina. We've got some cousins there and I've already let them know I'm coming to visit."

"Are you sure this is what you want to do?"

"I'm really not sure of anything right now but I feel like it's the first step I need to take."

"How does Freddy feel about all of this?"

"He knows we need some time alone. I love Freddy and we've had many good years together. But if I don't get away and think things through, I'll fall to pieces."

He'd given Dovie the five dollars she'd needed and had taken her to the train station in Rocky Ford. She'd stayed longer in Charleston than she'd planned on, and the longer she stayed, the more at peace she had with herself in making it her home. A few years had passed since she'd first moved there, and the *World War* still raged in Europe and the Pacific.

One afternoon as Dovie was walking down the streets of Charleston window shopping, she came across a woman that looked very familiar to her sitting on a bench in front of a ladies department store. She walked up closer, trying not to be too noticeable. The woman turned around and she recognized who she was right away. It had been years since she'd last seen her, but there was no mistaken identity. *It has to be her.* The lady had the same demeanor and facial expressions from what she'd remembered about her, but now, only aged.

Dovie walked up behind the lady and said… "Sarah."

The lady turned around and looked at Dovie.

Dovie looked at her with tears running down her face. She could hardly breathe.

"Hello, Mama."

"Dovie...is that you?"

"Yes, Mama."

Sarah fought to keep back the tears, so many emotions rekindled, so many past memories flooding through her mind. Dovie sat down beside her on the bench, feeling somewhat uncomfortable at first, not knowing how her mother felt about seeing her, or whether she even wanted to talk to her. Sarah reached out her arms to her daughter and the two embraced.

Dovie wept uncontrollably.

"Oh, Mama... I've missed you so much. I can't believe it's really you."

"I've missed you too. If you only knew how much. My precious Dovie."

The two of them sat there for what seemed to be hours, talking, laughing, mostly crying. It was a wonderful reunion between a mother and daughter, and the years of emotional suppression, which kept them in bondage for so long, were now released.

"How did you ever find me?" asked Sarah.

"It was by accident. I didn't know you were here in Charleston. I'd visited a few years ago and ended up moving here for good. I woke up this morning and something told me it would be a good day to go shopping. I've walked by this store a thousand times since I've lived here."

"I'm glad you walked by it one more time. It's hard to believe we've been living in the same town and never crossed paths until now."

"I guess the timing wasn't right. God must have had this moment in mind since the first day I moved here," said Dovie.

"Well, I think I've talked up an appetite. How about you? Are you hungry?"

"I sure am."

"How would you like to get some dinner?"

"I would love to!"

The two of them walked together to a nice restaurant around the corner. Dovie couldn't believe how much she and her mother were alike: the style of clothes they wore, the way they fixed their hair, the manner in which they walked. For the first time since her mother had left Bulloch County she felt alive again, like each breath she took was now worth breathing. She didn't realize until now how much she'd been holding back and keeping inside. Seeing her mother again released all of the emotions that had been suppressed for years. She had so many questions she wanted to ask her, but didn't want to dampen their reunion or spoil their evening in any way. She knew her mother would have to be the one to ask the questions and give the answers.

After they were seated in the restaurant, the waitress walked up to their table and asked them what they would like to drink. They both answered at the same time: "Iced tea with lemon in it."

Sarah and Dovie laughed.

"I'll give you two a few minutes to decide what you want to eat before I come back and take your orders," said the waitress.

The restaurant was filled with people, but to Dovie, it seemed like it was just the two of them, mother and daughter.

"Tell me, Dovie, how is everyone doing back in Statesboro?" asked Sarah, looking through the menu.

"They're all doing well. Grandma Annie passed away a few years ago."

Dovie could see a few tears trickle down her mother's face.

"I'm sorry to hear about that, Dovie. Annie meant a lot to me. She was there for me when I needed her the most."

The waitress came back to the table to take their orders. After she walked away, Dovie wanted to continue the conversation.

"I didn't know she meant so much to you."

"There are so many things I want to share with you, Dovie. I know you have a lot of questions about the past," said Sarah, wiping the tears from her eyes. "How are the boys doing?"

"John Willie and Phillip are in the military. Oscar married a girl named Lillie Mae Woodcock."

"I miss them so much. I never did want to leave you all behind. It was a decision I had to make at a time when life was very confusing for me. I can't tell you everything, but Annie was like an angel to me during those times."

"Mama, I know John Willie and Phillip are away in the military, but Oscar is still home and I know he would love to see you."

"Has he asked about me? I didn't know if any of my children ever cared to see me again. I thought that maybe you would all be angry with me for leaving."

"Oh, Mama, I could never be angry with you. I know how much you loved us and I knew there had to be some reason for you leaving. I can remember that day like it was yesterday. I can still see the hurt in your eyes when you had to tell us goodbye."

"I can't go back to Georgia, Dovie. I don't know if Oscar would be willing to come here and visit with me or not."

"What about writing a letter and letting him know how you feel? Let him know that you would like to see him. I have his mailing address."

"What if he doesn't respond? I'm afraid he wouldn't want to see me."

"I know how Oscar feels. He has a good heart and he talks about you all the time."

"It's good to know that he still thinks about me. I guess I could write a letter to him and see what happens."

That evening Sarah went home and worked on writing a letter to Oscar. She sat at the table with paper and pen in hand and wondered how she should begin after so many years. So many broken emotions, so many scattered thoughts that needed to be put back together again. *Would a few lines be enough?* She wondered if anything she wrote down could even convey her sincerest desire to heal the wounds of the past and reunite with her children. She wouldn't try to explain away her absence or silence as a mother. A letter wouldn't be the place to discuss the tragic past. It was tragic, and she knew that no amount of written words could heal the wounds or erase everything that had happened. It would take time. But she'd start the process somehow. *Her unexpected reunion with her daughter couldn't have just been happenstance.* And this thought inspired her more than anything. She sat quietly at the table, unable to write anything down for a while, her thoughts lost somewhere in translation.

Her letter would be short and simple...

Dear Oscar,

I know it's been almost twenty years now since I've made any contact with you. I hear you are doing well and have married a sweet girl named Lillie. I met Dovie in front of a ladies department store here in Charleston, South Carolina the other day. There are so many things I want to talk to you about but would like to discuss them in person. I can't come to Statesboro for certain reasons, but I would love for you to come to Charleston to visit me. I will understand it if you decide not to come, but I would love to see you again more than anything else in the world. I love you son.

Sincerely, Your mother, Sarah West.

Oscar sat on the front porch at Harvey Newton's place resting his feet one hot afternoon. He'd stopped sharecropping for Bennie Hendrix and was now farming for Harvey. The house that he lived in was still close to Bennie Hendrix's farm and Mr. Bennie still let him use his mule whenever he needed to. As he sat relaxing on the open porch the mailman drove up to his front yard, the dust flying high in the air as he came to a sudden stop. He got out of his vehicle whistling a new Ernest Tubb song as he sorted through the envelopes: "How's it going, Oscar?"

"I'm doing all right. Just resting my feet a little while before I head back into the fields."

"Well it sure is a hot one. Don't have a sun stroke out there." After handing Oscar his mail, he got back in his car whistling the same tune as before.

After he drove away, Oscar went through the mail and came to a letter from his mother. He had to look at it a few times to make sure he wasn't misreading it. He called for Lillie Mae.

"Lillie, I think I have a letter from my mother."

"Are you sure, Oscar?"

Oscar handed Lillie the envelope. She opened the letter and read it out loud. After all these years he didn't think his mother would ever want to see him or talk to him again. He knew she loved him but didn't understand why she'd left so suddenly, without word. Now she was asking him to come to Charleston to see her. It took a while for it all to sink in. Lillie handed him back the letter and he held it in his hands for hours, trying to reason things out in his mind.

After a few days passed, Dovie took a trip down to Statesboro from Charleston. She wanted Oscar to go over to Freddy's house and get some of her furniture and personal belongings. She told her oldest brother everything she and her mother had talked about and how much Sarah wanted to see him.

"Tell me, Dovie, is she anything like you expected her to be?"

"In many ways she is. I didn't think she and I would be so much alike or have so much in common. It was kind of amazing seeing so much of me in her, or should I say, her in me."

"Oh no... don't tell me she resembles you. Now I know it'll be a depressing trip having two of you around."

"Very funny. But I take that to mean you are going to see Mama?"

"I can't wait to see her, Dovie. It's a moment I've been waiting for all these years."

"I have to leave for Charleston the day after tomorrow. I know Mama will be glad to hear you are coming next week. Where are you going to store all of my things from Freddy's house?"

"I talked to Bennie Hendrix and he said we can store them in the old house, if that's ok with you."

"That will be great. I owe you one, Oscar."

"No, you owe me five."

"What do you mean?"

"You still owe me five dollars from when I purchased your train ticket the day you left for Charleston. Remember?"

"You're right. I have to make myself a note to pay you back," smiled Dovie.

"Just kidding," smiled Oscar. "I didn't mind helping you out when you needed it. In many ways, I owe you more than that. You found Mama again and that is all the payment I need."

****

The day after Dovie left for Charleston, Oscar hitched up Mr. Bennie's mule to his wagon and rode over to Freddy's house across the branch to load up Dovie's things. Freddy was sitting on the front porch playing his guitar when Oscar pulled up. He was a wonderful guitar picker and Oscar sat down for a while and listened to him play a few songs. Plato once said *'music gives a soul to the universe, wings to the mind, flight to the imagination…and life to everything,'* and it was the sound of music that gave life to everything for many people in the Bay Gall. After Freddy finished playing, he leaned his guitar against the corner of the porch and talked with Oscar about Dovie.

"I'm sorry about everything, Oscar. I loved Dovie the first day I met her and I still do. I didn't want things to turn out the way they did between us."

"I know, Freddy. I've always liked you and you'll always be part of this family."

"You've always been there for us, Oscar. We sure had some good times together through the years."

Oscar paused for a moment: "Dovie still loves you, Freddy. She just needed to get away for a while…"

"I can't blame her. I've had a lot to think about being here all by myself."

"Don't be too hard on yourself. Everything will work itself out in due time."

Oscar thought about his words to Freddy, and couldn't help but think about his own mother: *Everything will work itself out in due time.*

He worked all evening going back and forth with the mule and wagon, unloading Dovie's things in Mr. Bennie's old house. At one point, he decided to take a short break and stop by JB Daughtry's store.

JB's grandmother ,Delina Jo, and Oscar's great grandfather, Thomas Hendrix, were brother and sister. The Daughtry house was a popular country store at a road crossing not far from the Ogeechee River.

Oscar walked inside and saw JB standing behind the counter: "Hello, JB."

"Hey, Oscar. You look like you've been sweatin' up a storm."

"I've been moving things for Dovie all afternoon. I thought I'd stop by and get a soda and some crackers."

"I tell you what, Oscar, you pick out what you want and it's on me."

"I sure appreciate it, JB."

"Well…it's the least I can do for one of the hardest working men of our community. Have you heard from your brothers?"

"They send a postcard home from time to time."

"We're proud of Phillip and John Willie's service, Oscar. Hitler will soon meet his end. Those bombings on Berlin should have him shaking in his boots."

"I hope so, JB. He's an evil man." Oscar paused for a quick drink of soda. "How's Maxine doing?"

"She just got back from a trip up north with her friends. She's upstairs resting."

Oscar talked with JB for a little while longer, then started back to moving Dovie's things. As the sun went down, he finished unloading the last piece of furniture, his back worn out from all the lifting. By the time he walked the mule back to Mr. Bennie's barn, the night sky appeared and a full moon lit up the fields around him. He looked up at the stars and thought about the next day when he would go to Charleston to see his mother. As he stood by the edge of the barn, he heard an ambulance going down Old River Rd at a high rate of speed. In the bright moonlight, he could see the vehicle as it drove by in the distance, leaving behind a trail of dust that swept across the fields. He wondered what could have happened or who might've been in the ambulance.

Lillie had prepared Oscar a nice supper, and as they sat eating, she could tell he had a lot on his mind. She knew he was somewhat uncomfortable about going to see his mother again after so many years. She walked over to him and gently rubbed his back.

"Oscar, I know you're a little nervous about going to see your mother. I just want you to know that I love you and that everything will work out between you and her."

"Thanks, Lillie. I need all the reassurance I can get. I don't know how I'm going to react or what I'm going to say."

"I can't imagine what you're feeling inside. But you'll know what to say when it's time."

Oscar put his hands on Lillie's. She'd always been there for him whenever he had needed her.

"Did you hear the ambulance just after dark?"

"No, I didn't hear a thing. Where was it at?"

"It was on Old River Rd going toward town. I hope nothing bad has happened."

The next day Oscar took a bus ride from Statesboro to Savannah, then to Charleston. To him it seemed like it took forever. He thought about what he would say to his mother and how he would say it. He looked down at his hands and noticed they were shaking. As he looked out the bus window, he began to think back to the time when he was a boy…

"'Mama, why do you have to go away? I don't want you to leave,' pleaded Oscar.

'I know, son, but you'll be in good hands with your grandma Annie. I'm going to miss you so much, but when the time is right, we'll see each other again.'

Sarah reached down and put her arms around him. She handed him a small picture of him and her together and told Oscar that one day they would be together again just like in the photo: 'Now you keep this, Oscar, and always remember what I told you.'"

A loud passing truck brought Oscar back from the past. He reached in his pocket and took out the photo that his mother had given him, remembering his mother's words...w*hen the time is right we'll see each other again.*

The bus pulled up near the street where his mother lived, and as he stepped off, he noticed how clear the sky had become. *No clouds.* He considered it a good sign. He walked along the sidewalk looking for the number to the house. As he approached the residence, he could see a woman sitting on the front porch in a rocking chair. He didn't see Dovie anywhere. She was supposed to meet him there to help make things a little more comfortable. As he walked up the walkway toward the steps, the lady spoke his name: "Oscar."

"Mama..."

Sarah stood up as he walked onto the porch, her eyes fixed on his. Oscar took the picture out of his pocket she'd given him many years ago and handed it to her. The tears flowed down her face as she recalled the young child he was then compared to the grown man he was now. He began to weep when his mother embraced him. He remembered how she used to hold him when he was a boy and to feel his mother's love again seemed to heal every emotional scar from the past.

"Son, I'm so glad you came. I can't believe how much you've grown. You're tall just like your father was. I can see a lot of him in you."

"It doesn't seem real, Mama. If I'm dreaming please don't wake me up. I never thought I would ever get to see you again."

"I know, son. I've been hoping this day would come for a long time. Come on inside. Dovie is in the kitchen cooking a nice dinner for us."

Sarah and Oscar walked into the kitchen. Dovie was busy putting a meal together, looking like she needed some assistance.

"Hello, Oscar, you're just in time. Hand me those peeled potatoes."

Sarah smiled, enjoying Oscar and Dovie working together. Oscar ended up doing more work in the kitchen than Dovie.

"It never ceases to amaze me how Dovie can begin cooking something in the kitchen and I always end up finishing whatever it is she started," said Oscar smiling.

"That's because you're so much more a better cook than I am," smiled Dovie.

"Thank you for recognizing that."

After lunch, they went into the living room to look at old pictures. Dovie had brought a few with her and Sarah had kept a box of them from many years ago. Oscar had brought some more with him from Statesboro to show their mother what the rest of her children looked like now that they were grown.

"Just look at Phillip and John, both of them in their military uniforms. I can't believe how the years have passed and how old they are now."

"Oscar, do you remember when little John Willie was a baby? You used to hold him in your arms and rock him to sleep."

"I remember."

"I sure hope John Willie and Phillip are ok. War is a terrible thing. But I'm so proud of them for serving our country."

Hearing Sarah's concern for John and Phillip made Oscar and Dovie realize that their mother had never stopped caring for them. She'd always kept a mother's heart. They realized now more than ever the pain and suffering and loneliness she must have gone through all by herself all these years. No one to console her.

Dovie reached over and gave her mother a hug: "I love you, Mama."

The tears flowed again.

Sarah wanted to tell them everything. The past came back to her as if it had all happened yesterday, as if time had reversed itself and her wounds were as fresh as the morning sun. She wanted to deal with it, the emotional storm. She welcomed it. This was what she'd wanted all these years, to be reunited with her children. After all, it wasn't because of anything they'd done wrong that had brought her to South Carolina. They deserved her love and she realized it now more than ever.

After spending hours looking at old photos and catching up on lost time, they hadn't noticed it was past midnight. It was an unforgettable reunion between a mother and her children...an inseparable bond restored after so many years of separation.

After Dovie went to bed, Oscar and his mother sat on the porch talking, the stars shining bright in the night sky.

"Mama, I know you've suffered the most out of all of us. We had each other and Grandma during all this time, but you had to go through this all by yourself all of these years. I just want you to know that I've missed you and I love you very much."

"I've missed you too, son. I've spent hours thinking of you all and wanting to come visit my children more than I'd wanted to take my next breath. I hope we can have many more days like this. I would love to meet your wife and children."

"I will plan a trip in the near future for them to come to Charleston and meet you."

"That would be great, Oscar."

Oscar left for Statesboro early the next morning. When he arrived in Savannah, he had to change buses and get on one going to Statesboro. As he sat waiting, there was a man sitting next to him reading the newspaper.

"Anything interesting in there, mister?" asked Oscar.

"Well, the front page says, 'JB Daughtry shot to death in his home in Statesboro, Georgia.'"

"Who did you say?" asked Oscar in shock.

"JB Daughtry. Do you know the man?"

"I sure do. He was my neighbor."

Oscar thought back to the night when he was standing beneath the moonlight near Bennie Hendrix's barn, when the ambulance sped down Old River road. He knew now it was JB Daughtry in the ambulance. It was hard for him to think about JB being dead. *I can't believe it,* he thought. *I just talked to him the other day.* Other than hearing about JB getting killed, the last few days for Oscar had been like a dream. Reuniting with his mother had changed everything, and he'd plan for more trips to Carolina to visit her.

Chapter Eighteen

Mark and Silas hired one of their nephews to help them on the farm, mainly to tend to the horses. This meant making sure there was an abundance of roughage stored away and a consistent time schedule for feeding. Allen was good at that, always on time, and he kept watch over the horses as if they were his own children. He knew their weight and took great pride in providing them their necessary portions, putting the hay to the scales. He worked long hours in the stalls, and on clear days, he'd take the horses for runs along the countryside.

On one particular spring day, he'd fallen asleep on his front porch, and the late evening hours caught him by surprise. *The horses*, he thought, *it's past their feeding time.*

"Lottie, I've got to go over to the West farm and feed the horses before it gets dark," hollered Allen, putting on his hat as he rushed off the porch. He was married to Lottie Mae, the daughter of Lizzie West, sister to Mark and Silas.

"Ok. Just make sure you don't stay out too late. Remember, in the morning we've got to get up early and go to Statesboro to the doctor to get my heart medicine," reminded Lottie Mae, feeling a slight pain in her chest.

Lottie knew that if Mark and Silas were drinking, her husband might decide to join them. There wasn't a day that went by that the West brothers weren't drinking or giving someone else something to drink, and this worried her.

Allen didn't make it to the West farm until the sun went down, the stars appearing in the night sky as he walked into the stable to feed the horses.

"How are you doing, ole boys? I've got your favorite food," said Allen, going from stall to stall, whispering to each horse.

Silas looked out of his cabin window and saw a lantern lit up in the barn. He thought *it might be a thief trying to steal one of his horses, or worse yet, some of his moonshine in the barn loft.* He grabbed his pistol and walked out to the stable, looking around to see if there were any others hiding in the shadows. He eased open the barn door, the sound of the rusted hinges making a creeping noise. When Allen turned, Silas fired the pistol, shooting him in the chest.

"Silas…," moaned Allen.

Silas recognized his voice. He ran over and sat Allen up against the stall.

"Allen, I'm sorry, I didn't know it was you. What were you doing in the barn this time of the night?"

Allen was groaning in pain. He didn't have much breath left in him: "I should've told you I was late in feeding the horses. Don't blame yourself, Silas. Tell Lottie Mae I love her and that…"

Allen breathed his last breath before he could finish his last words.

Silas closed Allen's eyes with his hand.

Instead of going to the law, Silas left Allen in the barn for the night, his body resting against the stall. After covering him with a blanket, Silas climbed up the ladder into the loft to get a jug of whiskey, hoping the spirits might ease his thoughts. He sat on a straw bed all night drinking, talking to himself more than anything, the tragic event playing out over and over in his mind. *Could I've done anything different? Why didn't he let me know what he was doing?* By early morning the jug was empty but his nerves were still on edge.

Before going to the law, he stopped by the doctor's office to get some medicine, needing something to calm his nerves down with.

"Come in and sit down, Silas. What can I do for you?" the doctor asked.

"Well doc, my nerves are kind of shot this morning. Do you have any kind of potion for extreme nervousness?"

"What do you think it is that's causing this extreme nervousness, Silas?"

"It's kind of complicated, but, I shot a man last night."

The doctor inquired more into the story and told Silas he better go tell Sheriff Mallard right away.

After leaving the doctor's office, Silas visited the sheriff and told him about the incident.

"Tell me, Silas, do you think you killed Allen?"

"He's dead, sheriff. I didn't know what to do. It all happened so fast and it was dark."

"Well, we better ride on out and take a look. Silas, I hate to tell you this, but you're going to have to ride with me in the car. If Allen is indeed dead, I'm going to have to arrest you. So please don't try anything foolish, ok?"

"You don't have to worry about me, sheriff. I just want to get it over with. I don't know how I'm going to tell his wife about it. She's going to go to pieces."

The sheriff and Silas rode out to the West farm. When they entered the stable, the sheriff walked over to Allen's body and confirmed that he was dead. He asked Silas how the whole thing unfolded and where was he standing when he fired the pistol.

"I was standing over here, sheriff. It all happened so fast, and when Allen turned around..." Silas held his head down, his mind coming to grips with the fact that he'd taken Allen's life.

"I'm sorry, Silas, but I'm going to have to take you in."

"I understand, Sheriff."

Now it was John and Mark's turn to visit Silas in jail.

John found himself speaking the very same words to Silas that Silas had spoken to him some twenty years previously: "Don't worry, Silas. You'll stand clear of the charges. Allen was in your barn at night without you knowing about it, and as tragic as it was, you were just trying to protect what was yours."

Mark didn't say much. He just stared down at the floor, his mind in deep thought. Silas had been like a father to him through the years and he hated to see his brother fall into this kind of misfortune.

"Well, boys, it looks like it might be up to you two to run the farm now. I may have to serve some time for this one. I'm really worried about Lottie Mae though. She hasn't been doing well physically and this may be too much for her to handle. She and Allen were as close as a husband and wife could be."

"I'll go over and check on her this evening, Silas. Don't worry about a thing. It's all going to work out," said John.

****

A couple of days had passed since the death of Allen Bolton, and Silas was still in jail waiting on his murder trial. In the meantime, Lottie Mae, Allen's wife, was having chest pains, having never gone to the doctor to get her medicine after the tragic incident with her husband. She told her mother that her chest was hurting her quite severely. Her mother gave her a simple dose of medicine to help relieve the pain.

"Mama, I have to go outside and get a breath of fresh air. I can hardly breathe."

"Ok, Lottie, but don't stay outside too long. You need to lie down and get some rest. You've been through a lot the last few days."

"I know, Mama. Thank you so much for being here with me during this time. You don't know how much that means to me."

She then walked outside into the front yard and stood by the well for a moment, taking in deep breaths, trying to get air into her lungs. After a few minutes, she collapsed to the ground.

Lizzie noticed her daughter had been outside a long while. She looked out the front door to check on her.

"Lottie! Lottie!" Lizzie called.

Lottie didn't answer. Her mother walked outside and discovered that her daughter had fainted to the ground. When she knelt down and tried to wake her up, she realized Lottie was dead. Lizzie screamed. She tried to call for help, but it was too late.

Upon hearing of the death of Lottie Mae, Sheriff Mallard went immediately to the Bolton home. He made inquiry as to the circumstances of her death, wanting to make sure that there was no link to the death of her husband.

The sheriff drove back into town to tell Silas.

He walked up to Silas's cell.

"Silas, I have some bad news."

"Don't tell me that I've already been found guilty without a trial, sheriff."

"No, Silas, something worse than that."

Silas got up from his cot and walked up to the iron bars that separated him from Sheriff Mallard.

"What can be worse than being found guilty of murder charges?"

"It's your niece, Lottie Mae. Her mother found her dead in the front yard by the well. Your sister was with her right before she died and said she'd been complaining of chest pains the last few days."

Silas was overcome with emotion. His shoulders slumped down and his strength seemed to leave his body. He walked back to his cot, wondering, *how can so many bad things be happening all at once?* The sheriff knew he was in a lot of grief and asked if there was anything he could do. Silas thanked the sheriff but said he just wanted to be left alone for a while.

The Bulloch Times read: "*Wife follows husband to grave.*"

A short portion of the article stated: "Funeral services for Mrs. Allen Bolton, age thirty, were held Wednesday morning at Oak Grove Church, in the Lockhart District, four days following the interment of her husband in an adjoining grave. The husband was Allen Bolton, age thirty-three, who was found dead in a horse stable on the premises of

Silas West his landlord. West is now being held in jail awaiting further action in the premises."

To Silas it all seemed like a bad nightmare. But he didn't have much time to grieve the death of his niece before his trial began on April 26th, 1944.

'*The State versus Silas West*' was announced in the Bulloch County court house. The following named jurors were empanelled to try the above stated case: Wiley T. Akins, Sam L. Brannen, J.C. Denmark, Z.L. Jenkins, J. Colon Akins, Fred S. Smith, A. L. Roughton, T. Jesse Mikell, J.W. Hagan, J.C. Lanier, C.H. Stokes, and Clate Mikell. After hearing the testimony of the witnesses including that of the sheriff and Silas West, the jury handed down the following verdict...

"We, the jury, find the defendant not guilty."

Silas was relieved to hear the words *not guilty*. Mark and John were present at the trial, and they looked at each other with a sigh of relief as well, knowing Silas wouldn't have to go to prison; however, they still mourned the loss of Allen and Lottie Mae.

The first thing Silas wanted to do once he was released from jail was to visit his sister Lizzie. She'd lost her daughter and son-in-law in a matter of days, and he knew she'd suffered the most.

It was raining when he pulled up in the front yard of the home where his sister was staying. She was on the front porch sitting in a rocking chair, all alone. She looked so sad and frail, and Silas knew he'd played a major role in her grieving. When she saw Silas, she began crying, the sight of her brother bringing back everything that had happened the last few days: the death of Allen in the barn, the death of her daughter by the well – both losses so sudden and so tragic.

Silas got out of the car and stood in the rain for a moment, waiting for some kind of response from Lizzie. He didn't know if she even wanted to see him or talk to him. *Forgive me Lizzie.*

He slowly walked up to her and put his arms around her.

"Lizzie, I'm sorry. If I could turn back the time, I would. So much has went wrong these last few days that didn't need to. I know there's nothing I can say or do to bring Allen or Lottie back, but I just want you to know that I'm sorry."

"It's not your fault, Silas. It was just one big accident with Allen. And you know Lottie's heart was already weak and having problems. I'm sure the stress of losing her husband didn't help her condition any, but you can't blame yourself for that."

Silas needed to hear his sister say those words: *It's not your fault, Silas.* He'd blamed himself for everything that had happened to Allen and Lottie, and to know that she didn't hold any ill feelings toward him made Silas feel better.

After spending some time with Lizzie, he drove back home to the Bay Gall, back down the winding road to the old log cabin. Mark and John had been waiting for him there; they wanted to make sure Silas was all right. The three of them sat and talked a while underneath the old walnut tree, reminiscing on the past…forgetting the present. The rain had subsided to a light mist. That night, they didn't drink any whiskey, only water from the well.

Chapter Nineteen

*M*oonshine and murder was the deadly mixture for Silas and Mark in the 1940s. The farm was doing well, but the West brothers' profit came from making whiskey. Many would think they would've straightened their lives out after all the things they'd been through. However, Mark and Silas only got worse. *World War II* was about to come to an end in Europe, but for the West brothers, a war of their own was just beginning. Silas had recently been cleared of murder charges for the death of Allen Bolton, but there would be more shots fired and bloodshed on the West place. No one could condemn the brothers for defending themselves on their own property, and to underestimate their resolve to pull the trigger when necessary would be a fatal mistake. But to wet the steel barrel of a gun with stray drops of moonshine only created an atmosphere for disaster.

John West had signed the family temperance pledge in the West family bible in the early 1900s: *We the undersigned solemnly promise by the help of God to abstain from the use of all intoxicating drinks as a beverage.* But no where did you see the names of Silas or Mark on that page. They were bent on producing, selling, and consuming the spirits, and no one would get in their way. Their skills and stills dated back before the years of prohibition, before the *Volstead Act*, on through the great depression, and well into the 40s. They'd had their past run-ins with revenuers and federal agents, and they knew how to avoid the law when necessary. No taxes would ever be paid to the government on their brew and no licensing applied for. They'd made that decision when the first vapor of alcohol turned into a liquid, and no amount of legislation would influence them otherwise.

Fall weather was in the air, and the leaves fell from the trees and landed at the foot of the stills near Bay Gall creek as the West brothers turned their mash into wash.

"Hey, Mark, we've got a long list of clients who want to buy a large share of our moonshine. We better put in the extra hours if we're going to meet the demand."

The West brothers were known to be the best at making the spirits, and this made their home brew a popular commodity.

"I know, Silas. It sure has been a profitable year. We've got more orders from Carolina than we do from Georgia."

Their list of clients ranged from neighbors to relatives to the law, and they treated everyone the same when delivering the goods. It was pure shine. Not watered down. And they knew trust and a good product went a long ways. But not every sell goes well. One afternoon, Leland Hendrix went over to visit Silas and Mark on the West farm, some say to buy moonshine. On his way to the West farm, Leland walked by Emmit Hendrix's place, Mrs. Curtis and Tump being in the front yard at the time. He spoke a few words to them and then walked on to the West farm. The winding road going to the West log cabin went near the West's well, just a few feet from the front porch. Mark was about to go to the fields to pick cotton when Leland walked up to the well to get a drink of water. Then something went terribly wrong. Leland and Mark got into a heated argument from what seemed to have been a simple misunderstanding, and after a few words the fatal gun shot was fired. It appeared to Mark that Leland was reaching into his pocket for a knife. Afraid for his life, Mark backed up to the doorway of the cabin, reached under the bed to get his gun, then shot Leland with a double barrel clear back to the well...a single birdshot from the left-side barrel striking him in his chest. Leland went backwards, grabbed the well posts, then fell down...dead.

Silas was in the barn loft storing moonshine away when he heard the shot: *Who in the world would be shooting this time of the day, and at what? Might be revenuers*, he thought. He climbed down the ladder after putting the last bottle of shine up, cautiously walking out the barn door. As he looked around, he saw Leland in the distance lying on the ground near the well and Mark kneeling down beside him with the double barrel shotgun still in his hand. Leland was their cousin and they'd always gotten along well. Silas couldn't think of any reason that could've triggered the shooting but one: *whiskey*. Through the years, he'd seen a lot of men shot to death when filled with the spirits.

He walked over and knelt down beside Leland who'd taken a good bit of shot to the chest. Silas asked Mark what happened, but Mark just held tight to his shotgun, mumbling a few words that didn't make any sense. Silas carefully took the gun out of his hands, placing it on the ground behind him.

'Mark, you've got to get a hold of yourself. We have to tell the sheriff. They'll sure enough come looking our way if Leland doesn't return home."

"I thought he was getting a knife out, Silas. He threatened to cut my throat. He was reaching into his front pocket..."

"It's too late to reason it out now, Mark. We can't bring him back. We'll just tell them Leland tried to cut you with a knife and you had to defend yourself. I know it didn't work out too well for John claiming self-defense, but at least you'll have a fighting chance."

Silas went over to Sam Wright's house about a mile up the road and asked Sam to let the sheriff know that Leland Hendrix had just been killed.

When the sheriff arrived at the West place, Mark and Silas were standing over Leland's body by the well.

"What happened here, boys?"

"Things got a little out of hand, sheriff, and I had to shoot Leland in fear for my own life," said Mark.

"Is that true, Silas?"

"Just like Mark said, Sheriff."

The sheriff knelt down beside Leland's body and could see that he'd taken a good bit of shot from his waist up.

"Well, we'll have to take his body into town for examining. In the meantime, don't you two go anywhere…I need to ask some more questions."

After learning more about the shooting, the sheriff arrested Mark and put him in the county jail to await trial. He was assigned defense attorney W.G. Neville to defend him in court. A.M. Deal also assisted the defense team.

The Solicitor General was Fred T. Lanier.

The first trial began on October 25th, 1945.

The State versus Mark West was announced in court. The following named jurors were empanelled to try the above stated case: Arnold Parrish, Charles Nessmith, W.C. Denmark, Louis Stephens, Joe S Brannen, P.B. Brannen, Willie Allen, W.J.Akerman, J.C. Martin, E.R. Harnock, I.A. Brannen, and H.M.Royal.

"The State elicited the following evidence from the witness on direct examination: 'As to whether or not since the defendant had been in jail he had made any statement as to who did the shooting, well, yes sir, he has. He said he did the shooting. He said he was standing in the door to the house at the time he shot. He said that if Hendrix had taken one more step he would have been on the porch. As to whether or not he stated this was the gun he used, well, he said the double barrel gun that was lying under the bed with the empty shell in was the gun he used.'

On cross-examination, the witness Deal, testified:

'As to whether or not at the time I had the conversation with the defendant in the jail he also told me why he shot Mr. Hendrix. Well, yes sir, he told me why. As to whether or not that was in the same conversation in which he told me about having shot him, well, I would not swear that it was exactly the same time I was talking to him then, or whether it was another time when I was talking to him about some people, but he has told me why he did it.'

On redirect examination, the witness answered: 'as to whether or not at the time he told me he had shot Mr. Hendrix, anything was said about why he shot him, well, no sir, I don't think so.'

On re-cross examination, he testified: 'As to whether or not I can tell you when he did tell me why he shot him, well...'

Mr. Lanier, Solicitor General: made the following objection: 'If your Honor please I object to any statement that he might have made in his own behalf, after this homicide had taken place, because it would be a self-serving declaration and not admissible.'

The Court: 'That's true.'

Mr. Neville, of counsel for the defendant, stated to the Court: 'If your Honor please. I'm asking for the whole conversation and I am trying to refresh his memory as to what did take place. I'm asking him if at the same time the defendant told him about shooting Mr. Hendrix, if he also told him at the same time why he shot him.'

The Court: 'If he did that he can state it.'

The witness: 'After I went back up there that night...'

Mr. Lanier, Solicitor General: 'If your Honor please that is a different time from the time he made the statement about shooting him, and any statement he might have made that night to Mr. Deal in his own behalf would be self-serving declarations and would not be admissible. The Courts have held that where a man fired a gun and then went away for a half a minute one hundred yards that it is not admissible. The two statements were made altogether at different times and it is not admissible.'

The Court: 'When was the first statement made?'

The witness answering the Court: 'The first time he told me why he did it was at his house while sitting on the porch.'

Mr. Lanier, Solicitor General: 'I have not gone into that statement, but I asked him about the statement he made down here and he did not say anything about why he did it.'

The Court (Addressing Mr. Lanier): 'All you did was to bring out.'

Mr. Lanier: 'Yes sir.'

Mr. Neville, counsel for the defendant, continues with the witness: 'As to whether or not I did have a conversation with the defendant on the night of the killing and he told me why he did it. Well, yes sir. That was at the scene of the offense and before I brought him to town and put him in jail. As to why he said he shot him, well…'

Mr. Lanier: 'I want to renew my objections and if there is any doubt on your Honor's mind about the admissibility of this testimony I'll be glad to show your Honor some authorities. The Court had held time and again you can't do that.'

Mr. Neville: 'Yes, and the State has no right to bring in part of a conversation and leave out the rest of it. We are asking for the whole conversation and the truth of the case. He has a conversation with the Sheriff down here in the jail in which he told him he shot Mr. Hendrix and we are contending that at the same time he told the Sheriff why he shot him.'

Mr. Lanier: 'I am objecting to the conversation.'

The Witness: 'At the time he told me where he was standing when he shot Mr. Hendrix in that conversation he did not tell me why he did it. The other time he did tell me.'

The Court: 'I rule that question out.'"

Further examination was made concerning ballistic testing…

"The witness, Stothard Deal, Sheriff, sworn for the State, testified: 'I asked the defendant whether he shot Mr. Hendrix with buckshot or birdshot and he said birdshot, high-powered shell. And I asked him if it was six and one-half or seven shot and he said yes. As an officer I have had quite a lot of experience with guns and shells, yes sir. I was present and did the shooting myself when one of these was shot into the card board that you have in your hand there, yes sir…'

At this time, Mr. Neville, as one Counsel for the defendant, interposed the following objection: 'If your Honor please, I presume that he is getting to display these things to the jury and I want to object to it before he does, on the grounds that the witness has not qualified as expert sufficiently to testify that a gun fired over and over again in the same manner and form and with the same type of shell will make the identical pattern and shot. They charge this man with having shot Mr. Hendrix, and then they go out here after that and take some other shells and fire at different targets. And if your Honor please, that is wholly irrelevant and inadmissible and is not part of the res gestae and it is based on mere conclusions. There is no way to tell whether two identical shells would make the same pattern of shot even if they are identical shells and shot from the same gun. And we object to them going into that.'

The Court: 'Are the shells of the same type and shot from the same gun that the defendant used?'

Mr. Lanier: 'Yes sir, your Honor.'

The Court: 'I'll let him testify.'"

The jury listened to all the evidence presented against Mark and returned the following verdict…

"We, the jury, find the defendant, Mark West, guilty of murder this 25th day of October, 1945. We, the jury, recommend to the court, mercy."

The sentence of Judge JL Renfroe was handed down as follows…

"Whereupon it is the judgment of the court, that you, Mark West, be taken from the Court, and taken to the common jail of Bulloch County to be kept in safe custody till demanded by a guard from the Penitentiary, and be taken hence by said guard to the Penitentiary in Atlanta, or to some other place as the Governor shall direct and be there confined at hard labor for the space of your life."

On hearing the sentence, Mark sank down in his seat. The defense team was disappointed that such a *verdict* and *sentence* had been given against their client. They felt the trial had been mishandled.

The guards took Mark in handcuffs back to the county jail.

"Don't worry, Mark. We're going to ask for a new trial," declared his defense team.

John and Silas left the courthouse in disbelief, shocked that Mark had been sentenced to life in prison.

The next day Silas went to speak to Mark's lawyers to see if there was any way to overturn the sentence.

"Silas, we're going to call for a new hearing. Don't worry. We'll file the request in a couple of days once we get all our reasons for a new trial put together. We're confident we'll get the sentence overturned."

After talking with Mark's lawyers, Silas drove to the county jail to see his brother.

"Mark, you have a visitor," informed the jail guard.

Silas stood in front of Mark's cell and tried to bring some ray of hope.

"I'm sorry, Mark. I know it looks bad now, but I just left from speaking to your lawyers. They believe a new trial will overturn your life sentence. From the information they gave me, it looks like you stand a good chance."

Mark was silent for a moment: "There's not a day that goes by that I don't regret what happened to Thomas. Sometimes I feel like all of this is the judgment of God on me for what happened to him."

Silas didn't know what to say. Mark had never brought up the matter about Thomas since the day of his disappearance. He began to think back to the time when Thomas went missing: the blood, the pocket watch…the questionable words of Mark: *He's gone and he's never coming back*. Silas didn't want to condemn his brother for anything at this point in his life, especially when facing a life sentence, but he couldn't help but wonder about the meaning behind the statement that Mark had just made.

"Mark, I want you to know that we're not going stop here. We're going to keep fighting until we get you out of jail."

As Silas was leaving the jail house, he was approached by two deputies: "Silas West, you are under arrest for the unlawful sale of unstamped liquor," informed the deputy.

Now, Silas found himself sitting in the same jail just minutes after visiting his brother there. John was the only brother that wasn't arrested in the incident. He seemed to have learned his lesson after serving time in prison some twenty years earlier. Until now, neither Mark nor Silas had ever served any prison time. But John knew what it was like, and he didn't want to do anything that would send him back behind bars; after all, he had a family to look after.

The motion for a new trial for Mark was filed on October 31st and again on December 10th, 1945. Information contained in the motion for a new trial included Mark West's own defense testimony of why he shot Leland Hendrix…

"…he (meaning Hendrix) walked around the house on the well side and he stopped a few feet from the well and I walked around there to get my sack to go back to the field as I was picking cotton, and when I was coming around the house I stepped on one of the dogs on the ear. I told the dog to get out of my way, and he asked me if I was talking to him and I said no, I was talking to the dog. He said you are a ___ ___ liar and a son of a ___. He made a move for me and said I'll cut your ___ ___ head off and before he got to me and he was about four feet from the porch he ran his hand in his pocket like he was getting his knife and I backed all the way to the door and reached in there and got my gun. I never had the time to get the gun up to my shoulder, but got it up about that high (defendant indicating with hands). And he said 'I'm going to kill you' and kept coming on me and I pulled the trigger and he did not fall there but he wheeled around and went back and caught hold of the posts on the well and threw his arm around the post. And when he fell he did not fall right there by the post but he fell out in front of the well."

After other arguments were formulated by Mark's defense team, the motion for a new trial was sent to the Supreme Court of Georgia to determine whether or not the lower Court of Bulloch County erred in refusing a new trial based on the evidence provided in the motion.

Three months later, the Supreme Court of Georgia made a ruling on April 2nd, 1946, rendering the following judgment…

"This case came before this court upon a writ of error from the Superior Court of Bulloch County. And after argument had, it is considered and adjudged that the

judgment of the court below be reversed because the court erred in refusing a new trial. All the Justices concur."

When the West family was informed of the Supreme Court's decision, it was like a chance at life again for Mark. He'd get another opportunity to convince the jury that he was innocent and that he was only trying to defend himself before Leland killed him.

"Mark, I know the jury will eventually find you innocent of all charges. They now realize they have to rely solely on the facts and the facts say you are not guilty."

"I hope so, John. I've been sitting here in this cell wondering how long I'll be incarcerated. I didn't realize how much it really meant to go and come as you please until now. I've spent hours closing my eyes, walking along the winding road to the old log cabin. I sometimes hear Mama calling my name, saying, *'supper's ready.'* Sometimes I imagine running through the cotton fields, touching the cool waters of Bay Gall creek."

John sat there, quiet, letting Mark talk. He knew Mark needed to open up and share his thoughts with someone he could trust.

"Just keep a positive outlook, Mark. The new trial will start soon and we'll give it everything we've got."

On April 24th, the second trial for Mark took place and the court was packed to capacity. After each side presented their case before the Court, the jury returned the following verdict...

"We, the jury, find the defendant, Mark West, guilty of Voluntary Manslaughter, this the Twenty-Forth day of April, Nineteen Hundred and Forty-Six. And fix a penalty at not less than eight years or not more than twelve years."

The following sentence was handed down from Judge Renfroe...

"Whereupon, it is the judgment of the Court that you, Mark West, be taken from the Court House to the common jail of Bulloch County and be kept in custody till demanded by a guard from the Penitentiary, and be taken hence by said guard to the Penitentiary in Atlanta or such other place as the Governor shall direct and be

there confined at hard labor for the space of not less than eight years nor more than twelve years, and be then discharged."

The defense team for Mark would file another motion for a third trial. The center point of discussion in this motion for a third trial contained more statements from Mark West and some from Leland Hendrix's wife that were left out of the previous motions. Mark West gave further testimony on what occurred the day he shot Leland Hendrix...

"Mr. Hendrix come up, spoke, and I asked him where he was going, all cleaned up, and he said he had come to Statesboro the day before and got drunk and went on back home that day with Bruce, his nephew; and then went up to Brinson Thigpens and got some liquor. He said that day he got up and drank it and him and his folks had a row and he slipped off and ran away from them and was on his way to hunt some more liquor."

Mrs. Leland Hendrix gave the following testimony...

"I was in Statesboro with him (Leland Hendrix) on the afternoon before he was killed. As to whether or not he was intoxicated or drinking or anything of the kind, he drank a little something or other. I don't know what it was, whether it was whiskey or beer, not enough to get out of the way though. He wasn't in anyway intoxicated. Anybody else wouldn't have told it on him but I could. I went back home with him, we went back home together. There was not any fuss between him and any other member of the family that night or the next morning before he went to Mark West's. At the time of the killing he did not own a pocket knife. I was with him on the afternoon before he was killed when he went to the store of Mr. Emit Akins and tried to buy a knife. He had spoken to Mr. Akins about a knife. He did not get a knife cause Emit didn't have them."

The Court of Appeals for the State of Georgia rendered the following judgment as to whether or not Mark West deserved a third trial:

"This case came before this court upon a writ of error from the Superior Court of Bulloch County; and, after argument had, it is considered and adjudged that the judgment of the court below be affirmed."

The rendering of the Court of Appeals ended the trial period for Mark West. He would now have to serve at least eight years in the State Penitentiary.

David Leland Hendrix was buried in the Hendrix cemetery on Old River Rd, leaving behind a wife and eight children, the youngest being thirteen years of age. It was a tragic ending, a sudden loss, and a sad goodbye for his family and friends - the ones who loved him most - and his absence left them with many unanswered questions. Even though Leland's death was vindicated through Mark's conviction, his children were left without a father and his wife…a widow.

Leland Hendrix and Mark West were 4th cousins.

Chapter Twenty

Silas had his day in court on January 30ᵗʰ, 1946, for selling moonshine.

"The State versus Silas West," announced the court. The following named jurors were empanelled to try the above stated case: Wyley Fordham, B.D. Nessmith, Emit C. Deal, John L Akins, W.W. Mann, J.M. Pope, Hamp Youngblood, Lovin Smith, J.W. Hagan, Monnie Gay, J.M. Smith, and G. H. Clark. After the evidence was given, the following verdict was given:

"We, the jury, find the defendant guilty, this January 30ᵗʰ, 1946."

The following sentence was handed down by Judge Renfroe:

"Whereupon, it is considered, sentenced and adjudged by the court that you Silas West, the defendant in the above stated case, do pay a fine of two hundred dollars for the cost of this prosecution, and in addition thereto do work in the public work camp, or in one of the public works, or at the State Prison Farm for and during the full term of twelve months. Provided however, upon the payment of said fine, the defendant may be permitted to serve said term outside of the confines of said Public Work Camp, on the public works, or at State Prison Farm, so long as he conducts himself in an orderly and law-abiding manner and violates no laws of this

State, and obey all orders and directions of this court and to report to his probation officer, on the first Saturday of each month during the period of twelve months, and until the further order of the Court."

After this incident, Silas would never again get in trouble with the law.

Mark was sent to *Reidsville Prison* to serve his time. Some say he wrote a book behind bars concerning the events that had happened on the West place…

The falling of the leaves brings back numerous memories from the past, for it was in the time of autumn when my life began to crumble, and the warm air of my youth gave way to the winter winds. My bones ache to return to Bay Gall creek and my heart longs to see the old log cabin nestled in the midst of the open fields.

In 1949, some three years after being sentenced, the Bulloch County Sheriff escorted an inmate to the state penitentiary in Reidsville where Mark was being held. The sheriff knew Mark, a distant relative of his through the Hendrix family, and he wanted to talk with him alone.

After the sheriff's visit, someone killed Mark that same day, leaving a hole in his head, the *undisputable* evidence that clearly revealed a murder had taken place; yet, his death certificate falsely showed he'd died of a heart attack.

No charges or conviction.

No legal investigation or official inquiry.

No jury or trial.

A cold case never filed.

The sheriff said he believed *someone in prison* must've thought Mark was giving some kind of inside information away during his brief visit that would've incriminated them.

It was also said by a notable judge of Bulloch County that drugs had been involved. One relative said Mark had a bunch of cash on him when they found him dead. Another said he was killed by a prison guard.

Others believed he was avenged for the death of Leland Hendrix.

Whatever the reason, it was a sad ending for a man whose conscience tormented itself ever since that dreadful day when his brother was tragically killed. Mark would never live to see his release date from prison; instead, his freedom came at the hands of an unknown murderer.

When Silas heard of Mark's death, he walked to Emmit Hendrix's place, saying to Mr. Emmit, "They've killed him. He's dead. They've killed my brother."

Mark's body was sent back home to the old log cabin in the Bay Gall, where the wound on his head revealed his fatal ending. Silas knew his brother had been murdered, but what could he do. He couldn't fight the prison system or whatever *powers to be* covered up the truth about his brother's death.

After lying in a casket for a few days in the cabin, Mark's body was taken to Oak Grove Baptist church and buried next to his father, Phillip Admiral West. There was a light rain falling, and the misty air sent a cold chill through the crowd that had gathered. Silas leaned over his brother's grave at the end of the funeral sermon and asked Mark to forgive him…

'I'm sorry, Mark. I didn't think they would ever charge you for murder or manslaughter and send you to prison. I feel like I'm at fault somehow for your death. If only I'd been more of an example to you instead of running whiskey and being somewhat of an outlaw. I'm sorry you had to die alone in that cold forsaken cell. At least you are here now beneath the earth next to Mama and Daddy. I know you and Thomas are now at rest and your conscious is free from guilt. Tell Mama and Papa I love them and I hope to see you all again someday.'

Silas paused for a moment then looked over at his father's grave, and the words engraved on his marker reminded him that there is still good that exists in the world: *Kind Father Thou Art Gone to Rest*. He then looked at his mother's grave, and it was all he could do to keep from weeping; he missed his mother more than anything in the world. Phillip West had planted a fertile ground in the Bay Gall for his family, and the dark shadows that stretched over it from time to time never dissipated the kind harvest that had grown there…he had brought it with him from Black River.

John West died in 1960 at seventy-five years of age. Not long after John passed, Lizzie, their sister, died. Silas was the last one left living of the children of Phillip and Annie West.

He spent a lot of his time in his last years reflecting and thinking about the past. In his younger days, he carried a pistol with him wherever he went and bore the reputation of being an outlaw; many people were afraid of him. In his latter years, he repented of his past deeds, reformed his ways, and tried to make up for all the wrongs he'd done. The sheriff of Bulloch County said between Mark and Silas, Silas was the toughest; but the sheriff added…in his aging years, Silas changed for the good.

****

One afternoon, while Silas was chopping wood, Oscar West and Clyde Neely walked over to the cabin to pay their uncle a visit.

"Hey, Uncle Silas."

Silas turned around and saw Oscar and Clyde. He put the ax down next to the wood pile and walked over to the gate where they were standing.

"Hey, Oscar. Hey, Clyde. It sure is good to see you two."

Silas noticed Clyde had a dog standing next to him.

"What kind of dog do you have there?"

"It's a redbone," said Clyde, rubbing the dog's ears. "His name is Tony."

Silas smiled as he remembered the puppy Mark had gotten for Christmas many years ago when they were just boys. He walked up and knelt down beside the dog, putting his hand on his head: "Hello, Tony. I knew a redbone with the same name many years ago."

Silas's smile quickly turned into a tear as he thought about the past and how everyone was gone.

He stood back up and asked, "How are Lillie Mae and Bertie Lee doing?"

Oscar and Clyde told Silas they were doing well and invited him to eat supper with them; they were all getting together at Oscar's house.

"It's good to know you all are thinking of me, but I have to get this firewood inside and do a few things around the cabin before it gets dark."

That night, Silas sat alone by the fireplace thinking about his mother and father, about his brothers and his sister…all gone. He could hear their voices all through the cabin, days of yesteryear echoing throughout his memory, sentimental memories of the past before death had separated them from one another.

As he sat in his rocker, his mother's voice filled his thoughts: "Son, remember to always say your prayers before you go to bed and never let the sun go down on your wrath."

"Ok, Mama." He could see her standing near the fireplace.

She walked up to him and gave him a kiss on his forehead: "Good night, Son."

He suddenly woke up and realized he was dreaming.

He took down the small picture of his mother from the fireplace mantle and kissed her goodnight, something he did quite often since the day she'd passed. He then walked over to his bed and pulled back the covers to rest for the night…falling asleep never to awake again.

Silas died in the old West log cabin in 1965.

In his only surviving written letter, he wrote to his brother John…

"And think what a mother we had. How she prayed for us and tried to teach us. We would not heed her teaching then, but thank God, it isn't too late. I hate we have wasted so long a time in sin and caused her so many heartaches and tears. The least we can do is to try to meet her on that golden shore."

No one lives on the West place now, but the old log cabin still stands. Thomas's bones still lay somewhere, long dissolved beneath the earth, quietly resting near Bay Gall creek. Many years have come and gone since Phillip, Annie, John, Thomas, Lizzie, Phillip Jr., Paul, Silas, and Mark were alive, but their memories, especially the good and cherished ones, will always remain along *The Winding Road*.

The End

Thoughts by the author…

In the first few prints of the novel, the book had *Based on a True Story* on the front cover. After much thought and consideration, I decided to change it to *Based on many True Events* for concerns I had that some might think that everything written in the novel actually took place. *Based on a true story* does not mean the same as *a true story*. These two phrases are similar but not identical. It has been said that "*a true story* is the reenactment of an actual event or events, while *based on a true story* refers to the recreation of a story with changes to the storyline to suit the audience's understanding and expectations…but the basic storyline can be verified with an actual story." Such is the case with *The Winding Road*, it is close akin to *based on a true story*, but for sake of clarity and accuracy, I have changed it to *based on many true events*. This should clear up any misunderstandings for those who may not be familiar with these particular phrases and just what they mean in the world of literature. I have attempted to provide in these back pages all the facts and actual events in the documentary portion of this book to help the reader separate fact from fiction. This novel contains and covers many true events throughout, things that actually happened within the West family, but many events are fictional in order to create the overall storyline.

We must all be guardians of our families' pasts, and in writing down our history, we preserve who we are and where we came from. Many seek to preserve their past by sharing stories with loved ones without ever writing anything down. But after they pass away, or when memory fails, all knowledge is lost, never to be shared or told again. It is up to us, the living, to piece together and preserve what stories remain, what memories recall, and in cherishing the past, we preserve the future…

—TS Beasley

Family Photos and Documentary information

Thomas B. Hendrix
Civil War Soldier
Father of Annie Hendrix West

Elizabeth Dickson (Dixon) Hendrix
Wife of Thomas B. Hendrix
Mother of Annie Hendrix West

Historic memorial service held

Soldier honored during Confederate Heritage Month

Special to the Herald

A Confederate Memorial Service was held last week for Private Thomas B. Hendrix, who fought for the South during the Civil War.

The service took place at Oak Grove Church Cemetery, which is located between Rocky Ford and Portal, in rural Bulloch County. April is Confederate History and Heritage Month in Georgia, and the ceremony was held to pay homage to a native son of Bulloch County.

Private Hendrix enlisted in Savannah on July 4, 1862, and initially served in Capt.

See **SERVICE**, Page 3

Robert Miller's Company of Partisan Rangers. Until early 1864, the hussars of Miller's Rangers were responsible for guarding the South Carolina coastline between Charleston and Georgetown.

During the spring of 1864, Miller's Rangers (officially known as Company C of The 21st Battalion of Georgia Cavalry) became Company B of The Seventh Georgia Cavalry.

In June 1864, Hendrix was captured at Trevilian Station, Virginia, and was incarcerated at Point Lookout, a Union prison in Maryland, for the remainder of the war.

Although he managed to outlive the end of the war by 20 years, the circumstances of his death are unclear – he died in 1885 from a shotgun blast of undetermined origin near his Bulloch County home.

More than 100 people attended Saturday's memorial service, which was organized and con-

Special

Frank Hendrix, left, is the grandson of Private Thomas B. Hendrix. Thomas Hendrix was a Bulloch County native who fought in the Civil War. Standing with Frank Hendrix is Ted Lewis, a historian with Metter Sons of Confederate Veterans Camp.

ducted by the Metter and Statesboro Camps of The Sons of Confederate Veterans.

Information below taken from an article written about Thomas B. Hendrix by Hu Daughtry...

"Thomas B. Hendrix may have commenced his somewhat-abbreviated journey in life during the second month of 1829. The venue of his birth was Bulloch County, Georgia –not so very far from The Ogeechee River and The Screven County line. At the time of The 1860 Federal Census Enumeration of Bulloch County, Tom B. Hendrix possessed a wife, a trio of young sons, and land valued at approximately two thousand dollars; hence, in the vernacular of The Ante-Bellum Pine Barrens, he was a considered to be "A Yeoman Farmer" – who worked his own land without the assistance of slave labor. There is little doubt that he and his sons were well acquainted with the phrase "hard work!"

On January 19th, 1861, The Great State of Georgia elected to sever its ties with Mister Lincoln's Union of American States; thus, for several weeks, until it officially joined The Confederate States of America, Georgia was a sovereign and independent republic. It is interesting to note that the delegates from the counties of Bulloch and Screven ardently supported the successful ordinance of secession; therefore, during the earliest days of 1861, Tom Hendrix and his kindred became denizens of The Confederate States of America.

Ironically, by Independence Day of 1862, Thomas B. Hendrix had journeyed to Savannah and enrolled in a local partisan ranger unit known as Miller's Rangers; history tells us that Savannah was Georgia's largest and most populous city at the onset of that War for Southern Independence. The majority of the men who belonged to Miller's Rangers hailed from the counties of Bulloch and Screven; the fighting equestrians who composed Miller's Rangers were officially designated by The Confederate War Department as Company C of the 21st Battalion of Georgia Cavalry. From their inception (during the summer of 1862), until early 1864, the hussars of Miller's Rangers primarily patrolled The South Carolina Coastline – between the crucial and strategic seaport cities of Charleston and Georgetown. During The Spring of 1864, the mounted paladins of Miller's Rangers became an integral part of Robert E. Lee's Famed Army of Northern Virginia; so, during the final annum of The War, Company C of the 21st Battalion of Georgia Cavalry became Company B of The Seventh Georgia Cavalry. Lamentably, in June of 1864, Private Thomas B. Hendrix (along with many others from Bulloch and Screven) became a casualty of war. He was captured by Yankee Horse Soldiers at a place known as Trevilian Station, Virginia. Many scholars and students of American History believe that this sanguinary encounter at Trevilian Station may have been one the largest and most significant cavalry engagements of The American Civil War.

In any event, following his capture by the enemy, Private Tom Hendrix was detained in a Federal Prisoner-of-War Camp – for the remainder of that Colossal Conflict which pitted North against South. Somehow, with the aid of Divine Providence, he managed to survive nearly a year in That Draconian Den of Torture and Perdition known as Point Lookout, Maryland. While incarcerated at Point Lookout, this native son of Old Bulloch was compelled to combat not only starvation, disease, and The Hostile Elements of Nature, he was also forced to deal with sadistic and barbaric prison guards -- who often delighted in firing among The Defenseless Southern Prisoners for both sport and pecuniary gain. Finally, in mid-June of 1865, Tom Hendrix was released from Point Lookout Prison; needless to say, as soon as humanly possible, the grizzled old veteran began the arduous and grueling journey home to Bulloch County. It was time to begin The Post-Bellum portion of his Earthly Pilgrimage. Approximately a score of years after The Fall of The Southern Confederacy, The Grim Reaper came for Tom Hendrix; he was believed to have been in his 57th year of existence. Both oral and written accounts indicate that his cause of death was a gunshot wound to his stomach / abdominal region. Some believe that the shooting of Thomas B. Hendrix was accidental and self-inflicted. One version of his untimely death specifies that during some unnamed month in 1885, Tom was on a fishing excursion on The Old Hiram Rigdon Place – which was located across Mill Creek from his residence. As the story goes, whenever Tom went fishing, he always carried an old musket with him – for snakes and other undesirable varieties of wild varmints which he might encounter. While pulling the musket from his cart (by its barrel), it accidentally discharged and shot him "in the gut." He bled to death before he could seek any medical attention. Another version (which is far more credible) is such that Tom Hendrix was robbed and murdered while on a fishing trip on The Hiram Rigdon Place. Family lore tells us that Old Tom was known to carry large sums of money on his person; many believe that one of his neighbors, who was familiar with his habits and idiosyncrasies, purloined his money and assassinated him. However, the authorities ruled his death as accidental and self-inflicted; in essence, the assassin was never brought to justice – at least during the remaining years of his natural life.

Tom's relict, Elizabeth Dixon Hendrix, outlived him by at least 31 years; available records indicate that she passed into a state of eternal somnolence at some unspecified point between 1916 and 1920. Born in 1832, she became the bride of Tom Hendrix in May of 1850; during their 35 years as husband and wife, they procreated ten known offspring. At the time of her death, Lizzie Dixon Hendrix was a deserving recipient of a Confederate Widow's Pension. Quite succinctly, even in death, her Old Gray Warrior remained a paragon of virtue; as a result of his loyal and gallant service to The Old Confederacy, even in a posthumous state, he was still able to provide for his nearly-blind and disabled widow."

(Written by Hu Daughtry)

'From Day to Day'

The winter chill filled the air o'er Sherman's wagons
heavy load,
Welcomed by sweet magnolias frosted white along the
river road!
Where farmers' hands labored hard to gather the
harvested yield,
Of mothers tired and children born, they too didst
work the field!
The Yanks in blue marched down old Savannah road
they say,
Stealin' all the stored up food - the smokehouses
wasted lay!
By old Beasley farm they came, near Nevils Creek's
banks to camp,
Burnin' wood from the old sacred church - the fireside
outshone the lamp!
To the sea they didst march, their blue footprints long
faded away,
And the memory of their passing here fades too
from day to day...

Tony S. Beasley

Sherman's March to the Sea

Sherman's troops under Oliver Otis Howard, Union Major General with the 15th Corps, around December 2nd or 3rd, 1864, with Divisions 1[st (C.R. Woods)] and 4[th (J.M. Corse)], marched by the Enoch Beasley Sr. farm along the old Savannah Rd (now called Old River Rd North). General Howard was over Sherman's right wing, the Army of the Tennessee. It consisted of the 15th Corps and 17th Corps. The 17th Corps remained on the north side of the Ogeechee, while the 15th marched down the south side of the river when passing through this area of Bulloch County, by the Beasley farm. Only the 1st and 4th Divisions of the 15th Corps marched down the Old Savannah Rd (Old River Rd), while the 3rd and 4th Divisions of the 15th marched much lower, near Statesboro.

A passed down family story . . .

Sherman's troops stopped at the Beasley homestead located alongside old Savannah. They took the meat from the smokehouse and the chickens in the yard. At one point, a Yankee soldier asked young Enoch Beasley Jr. (approx. 12 years old) to retrieve all the sweet potatoes from the storage bed. After the Yankees left, young Enoch Jr. said, "We got them Yankees!" Another Beasley said, "What do you mean? They cleaned us out." Enoch Jr. replied with a laugh, "I only gave them the small potatoes, not the good-sized ones."

This story was shared with T.S. Beasley by Albert Parker, a grandson of Enoch Beasley Jr.

[Enoch Beasley's homestead was adjacent to, southeast of, the Beasley Family Cemetery, beside the Old Savannah Rd (now Old River Rd).]

John W West...Confederate Civil War Soldier

Tony,

West was paroled or furloughed from Jackson Hospital along with J. Harleston Read Jr. in July 1864 (Read's father was appointed major of the 21st in May 1864) and presumably the two men returned to SC--or tried to. It appears Read returned to Charleston which suggests West was with him? The elder Read died there in 1866 and was interred there. It may be possible, but I am speculating, that John W. West died in Charleston sometime at or near the end of the war. You may want to check with Magnolia Cemetery in that city.

Good luck,
 C.L. Ferguson
Author of Hollywood Cemetery: Her Forgotten Soldiers: Confederate Field Officers at Rest

Confederate Abstract Information: from South Carolina State Archives

First Name: John W.   Last Name: West
Rank: Private
Company: A

Unit/Regiment: 21st South Carolina Infantry
Enlisted at: Georgetown, SC, December 20, 1861 at age 35

Wounded: July 10th, 1863

On last Roll: September/October, 1864 (absent, sick at Jackson Hospital, Richmond Va.)

Remarks: Admitted to Episcopal Church Hospital, Williamsburg, Va. August 19, 1863, with anasarca. Furloughed for thirty days on September 4th, 1864.

The Winding Road is based on many true events and facts:

1. <u>Phillip Admiral West coming to Statesboro, Georgia and his relationship with Annie Hendrix</u>:

The timing of Phillip Admiral West moving to Statesboro, Georgia from Georgetown, SC and Phillip's and Annie's age are altered to coincide with the timing in the novel. His marriage to Annie E Hendrix actually occurred on May 11th, 1884. It is not known the exact year Phillip came to Statesboro, or what age he might have been at the time. Also, it is not known if Phillip's father, John West, ever knew Thomas Hendrix while serving in the Civil War in South Carolina. It is believed John West made it back home to Georgetown after the war; however, there is no known record of his death. The storyline in the opening chapters of the novel, as it relates to the friendship between John West and Thomas Hendrix, is based solely on the close proximity in which they both served, between Charleston and Georgetown, and also on the fact that John West's son, Phillip, came all the way from Georgetown sometime after the war to the Bay Gall, eventually marrying Thomas's daughter Annie. As to whether or not Phillip came with Thomas Hendrix from South Carolina to Georgia is uncertain. There is conflicting information as to the year Phillip West was born, his grave monument showing it to be 1852. However, an 1860 census shows him to be twelve years old. This would make his birth year 1848. Later census records, such as the 1910, have him born around 1860. Also, the age of Annie is not exact. There is no grave marker listing her birth date. She died in 1940. Some accounts have her being born in 1863, such as the 1900 census record. This would make her too young to have gotten married shortly after the *Civil War*, only being a child. As stated earlier, we know according to probate records, that they were married in 1884. If she was born in 1863, she would have been twenty-one at the time of her marriage. Just how long Phillip knew Annie before 1884, or just how long Phillip lived in Bulloch County before marrying her is unknown.

2. The accidental death of Thomas B. Hendrix:

Below is an explanation concerning the death of Thomas B Hendrix, Annie's father, found in a Hendrix family Book entitled, "Descendants of Daniel Hendricks, Sr" compiled by Patty M Mulnix.

"Tom Hendrix was accidentally killed at the old Hiram Rigdon place just across Mill Creek. Tom started to pull his old musket out of the back of the horse cart, pulling it by its barrel. It discharged accidentally, the load of shot striking him in his stomach, killing him instantly. (Rigdon Family, Iris Hendrix Brannen)"

3. The disappearance and death of Thomas O. West:

The death of Thomas West by his brother Mark West and Mark's love for Sarah are based solely on circumstantial evidence: stories that were told to me by neighbors & close family members, etc., throughout the years. The exact cause of Thomas's death was never filed; it was never made known to the public, and therefore, remains an unsolved mystery. It is said by some that Mark West wrote a book while in prison covering the events that occurred on the West place. No one has ever been able to locate a surviving copy. There are a few alternate/varying accounts of how Thomas may have died, and where Thomas may have been buried. One account says Thomas was buried next to Bay Gall creek. This account says Mark showed their father one day while he was drunk, where he had buried Thomas. Another account, given in the song "The Violent Years" by Felton Bevill, nephew of Allen Bolton, seems to give the place of Thomas's grave next to the barn in the yard near the West log cabin. Another account says that Mark was standing with his mother, Annie, in front of the cabin one day, and she asked Mark if he knew where his brother Thomas might be. The account said Mark pointed in a certain direction from the cabin and said he was out there, meaning, his body was not far from the house. The account said Annie was never quite the same after Mark told her. There are also varying accounts as to how Mark may have killed Thomas. One source said Mark told Sarah, "If I can't have you, no one else will." They said she was afraid for her life and a black family helped her stay hidden until she was able to leave on a wagon.

Alternate versions of my gr-grandfather Thomas West's death in earlier editions of this novel:

In earlier editions of *The Winding Road*, I had Thomas West being killed by his own brother with a knife. But after much thought and consideration, I decided to change the way Thomas was killed by Mark. As a gr-gr nephew to Mark, and having only circumstantial evidence to prove my gr-grandfather was actually killed by him, I had to give Mark the benefit of the doubt. I altered the reading to say Thomas's death was an accident…that Mark didn't mean to kill his own brother. Instead of being stabbed with a knife, Thomas accidentally falls and hits his head against the stall. Whatever happened, and in whatever manner Thomas was killed, it was a definite tragedy for the West family, and it would forever change their lives. It forced Sarah to change her name to Billie and move to South Carolina, leave her children to be raised by their grandmother Annie, and never return to Georgia again.

4. Bootlegging by the West brothers:

Records show the West brothers were involved in making whiskey during the Prohibition era and afterwards. Court records show Mark was arrested in 1925 for making whiskey. Court records show Silas was arrested in 1945 for selling unstamped liquor. In the song "The Violent Years," Felton Bevill says, concerning the West brothers, "bootlegging was the business." Many contemporaries of the West brothers in the Bay Gall have shared stories of the West's moonshine making. It was also said that one of the sheriffs of Bulloch County during those years would obtain moonshine from the West brothers; he would also warn some of the moonshiners in the Bay Gall when revenuers were in the area so they could avoid being detected.

5. <u>The shootings of Leland Hendrix, Arthur Clayton, and Allen Bolton and sudden death of Lottie Mae (Neely) Bolton</u>:
I have included in this book images from microfilm, some newspaper, some court records, of the shootings of Leland, Arthur, and Allen. The information concerning Allen Bolton also reveals the sudden death of Lottie Mae Neely Bolton, daughter of Lizzie West, granddaughter of Phillip and Annie West. All of these events were true tragedies that occurred on or near the West place.

6. <u>There was a coon dog named Tony in the Bay Gall on the old West place</u>...[the coon hunting contest in the novel is fictional].

It is true that Silas West hunted with a coon dog named Tony.

I took this picture in 2016 of the tree that Tony the coon dog would always run up to when coming back from hunting in the Bay Gall. Tump Hendrix pointed it out to me while driving me around on his mule and sharing the history of the area with me. The tree has a bend halfway up the trunk...

7. <u>The killing/murder of Mark West in Reidsville Prison</u>:

It was a fact that Mark West was murdered in Prison in December of 1949. Sheriff Harold Howell visited Mark in prison the day he was killed. Howell shared with me and others that someone had killed Mark, but he didn't know for certain as to the reason why. One person said Mark had a lot of cash on him at the time. Another individual stated that a prison guard killed Mark. Judge Joe Neville said he thinks drugs were involved. However, all of these testimonies are off record because no one was ever brought to trial for Mark's death. Some family members remember seeing the hole that was put in Mark's head, the heavy blow or shot that took his life. His death certificate states he died of a heart attack. But as to the conditions which led to his heart attack, the line says "none." Someone definitely got away with murdering Mark West in Reidsville prison. Did Mark know something that would have revealed corruption in the prison system? Did they kill Mark because they thought he shared incriminating information with Sheriff Howell that day? Why wasn't his murder ever investigated or officially verified?

Glen Dora West (daughter of John Robert West) recalled seeing the casket of Mark West. She said his body was put in a casket and brought back to the West Log Cabin in Bulloch County in the Bay Gall. She remembers her and Shelby Jean Beasley looking at Mark in the casket. The year would have been 1949. Glen Dora would've been around 8 or 9 years old at the time.

"O grant to me now my humble request,
Thou Maker of men of dust,
And reveal Mark West's cold deadly fate,
His untimely death unearth!
Alone and forsaken behind cold bars,
Of prison's sure murderous plots,
The blood of his body still doth cry,
From the beds of Reidsville's cots!"

——*TS Beasley*

8. <u>Sarah West flees to South Carolina and reunited with her children years later:</u>

I have an audio recording of my grandfather talking about his mother's letter and her request to see him again after so many years. He talked about his sister Dovie on the tape as well and her move to Charleston (1939). He also mentioned the events surrounding JB Daughtry's death (1944) at the time of receiving his mother's letter (1944). There are certain elements of the reunion between Oscar and his mother Sarah that are created, such as Oscar having a picture of himself when he was a boy and showing it to his mother when they first meet after so many years. This and other elements of the reunion were added for creative dialogue purposes. Oscar describes on the recording the reunion with his mother after so many years, and says his sister Dovie was there that day too. I have included a 1920s written letter mentioning Sarah West, the only existing letter covering those years of tension on the West place during the 1920s. In the novel, Sarah flees shortly after John Willie West is born. But in actual history, John Willie is a young boy by the time Sarah leaves for South Carolina. Oscar states on the tape he was about 14 years old when his mother left them behind. That would place the date of Sarah leaving for Carolina about 1926 or 27, some 6 or 7 years after the death of Thomas West. There is some uncertainty as to the actual facts surrounding the reasons why Sarah West left Georgia. Was her relationship with Mark mutual? Did Sarah actually have feelings for Mark? Did Sarah and Mark have an affair? Or was it, as the novel suggests, an unwanted relationship, one that never happened? Was Sarah devoted to Thomas and her marriage? There seems to exist, in this only surviving letter of those times, an element of tension between Sarah and some of the members of the West family…

1920s original letter from Lizzie West (daughter of PA and Annie West) to Silas West, her brother…6 pages long… shown on the following pages…

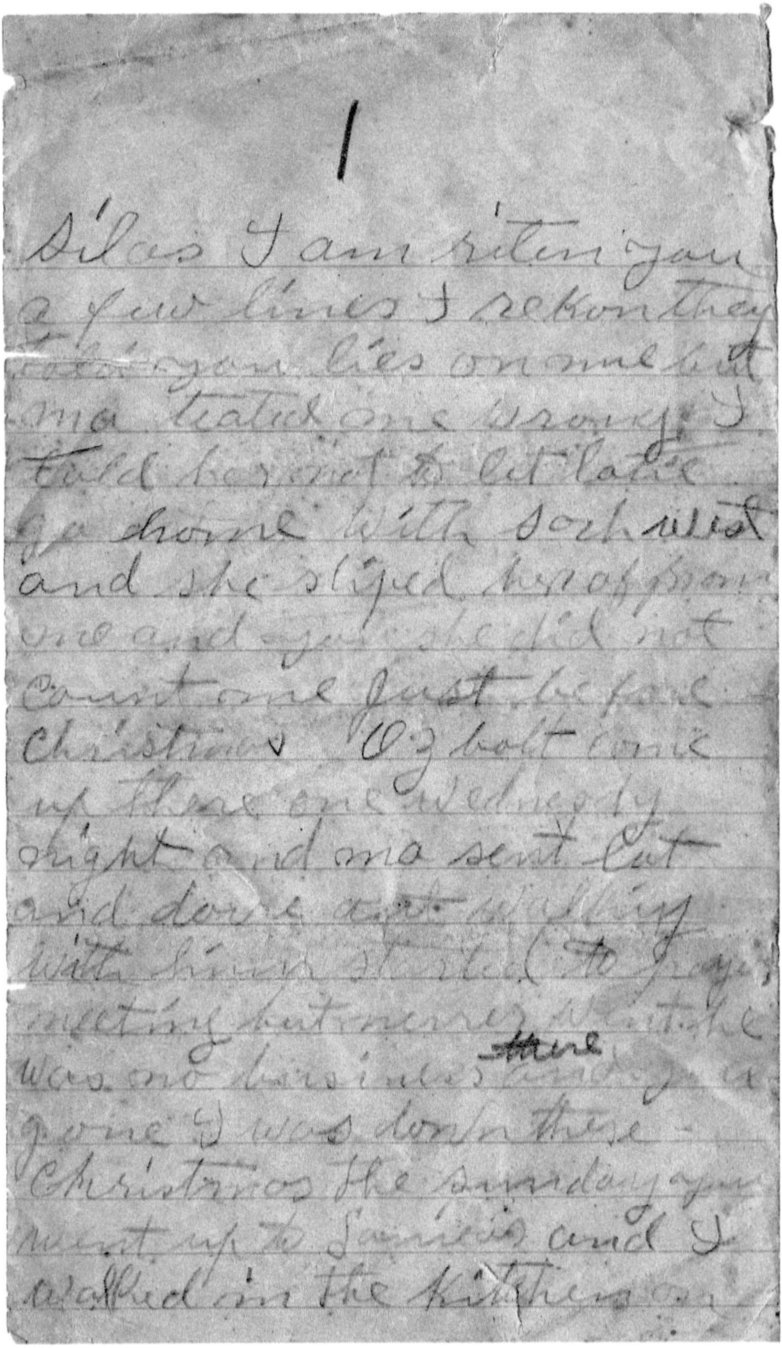

1

Silas I am ritin you
a few lines I rekon they
told you lies on me but
ma teated me wrong I
told her not to let Patie
go home with soch west
and she sliped her off from
me and you she did not
count me Just before
Christmas O.J holt come
up there one wednesday
night and ma sent out
and done art walking
with him stild to Joy
meeting but never was it he
was no boisindes there a
gone I was down there
Christmas the sunday you
went up to Smitts and I
walked in the kithen on

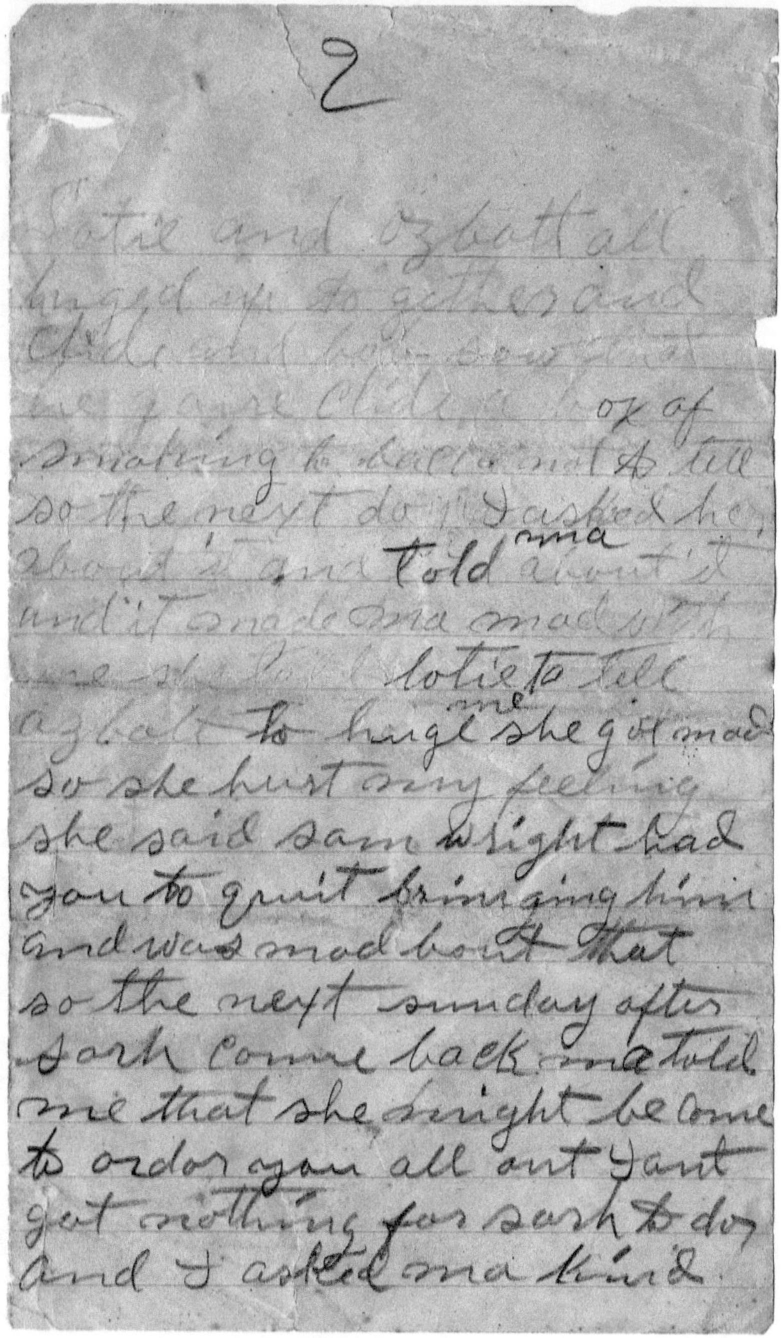

2

lotie and ozbett all
huged up to gether and
Clide and bob now that
me your clide a box of
smoking tobaccornot to tell
so the next day I asked her
about it and told ma about it
and it made ma mad with
me she told lotie to tell
ozbet to hug me she got mad
so she hurt my feeling
she said sam wright had
you to quit bringing him
and was mad bout that
so the next sunday after
sark come back ma told
me that she might be come
to order you all out yant
get nothing for sark to do
and I asked ma kind

3

not to let lotie go to
her home she let her go
she wont let her stay with
me just one night I think
you ought to whip her for
going I went there last
monday morning to see
her she tried to keep it
hid from me I asked her
in reason to go get or send
and get her and she bless
me aut I hated to talke
to her like I did but I
hate to see any body do
like ma by sarh cun
come there any time of
the week and take lot and
dorie off from there and
and there is nothing bad about
that but I cant say nothing

4

what time such aint
there oscar or philip rt there
ma starte all this by
letting lot go to her house
I aint rite I said I was
rite and and said I ma
done rong bring him to
my face ma cuse me
and John wrong John
and rachel had a falling
aut about choping cotton
or milus and he come up
here in a aught and he shot
his pistol off at the boy
hole and said come
up here and stay here
a while and he told
John I was rite he said
ma done wrong he begged
me and John to go down

5

there and gun sash
of but we would not go
and he told ma we war
going to shoot her house
a black lie so the next
night ma sent for me
and John to go down
there and we went and
she cused me and John
both bulldozing her
and we could not tell
her nothing she Blessed
us aut god knows I was
at home when John the
said if she had a gun
she would shoot of shot
us and me at my house
she told us both nerver
to foot there again sash
west caused off this

6

Ma cursed me and
John of thing that was not.
so she throwed up the
land to us we had not
said nothing about land
John told her he did not.
want a foot of that she
just was mad about
miss sarh she said if
you did like it you
could leave there to if
you dont what she does
Lottie need a boss you
take her in your charge
and rule her as whip her
I suffered for lot ma did
not. if soah rules done
I mean for you to take
lottie in charge as send
send her to me

Lizzie West's 1920s letter to her brother Silas West
transcribed by TS Beasley…

Silas I am writing you a few lines. I reckon they told you lies on me but Ma treated me wrong. I told her not (to) let Lottie go home with Sarah West and she slipped her off from me and you. She did not count me. Just before Christmas, Ozbolt come up there one Wednesday night and Ma sent Lot and Dovie out walking with him. Started to prayer meeting but never went. He has no business there and you gone. I was down there Christmas the Sunday you went to _____(?) and I walked in the kitchen on Lottie and Ozbolt all hugged up together and Clyde and Bob saw that. He gave Clyde a box of smoking tobacco not to tell. So the next day I asked her about it and told Ma about it and it made Ma mad with me. She told Lottie to tell Ozbolt to hug(?) me. She got mad so she hurt my feelings. She said Sam Wright had you to quit bringing him and was mad about that. So the next Sunday after Sarah come back Ma told me that she might be com(ing) to order you all out. I ain't got nothing for Sarah to do and I asked Ma kind(ly) not to let Lottie go to her house. She let her go. She won't let her stay with me just one night. I think you ought to whip her for going. I went there last Monday morning to see her. She tried to keep it hid from me. I asked her in reason to go get or send and get her and she bless(ed) me out. I hated to talk to her like I did but I hate to see anybody do like Ma by(but?) Sarah can come there any time of the week and take Lot and Dovie off from there and then nothing is said about that but I can't say nothing. What time Sarah ain't there Oscar or Phillip it (is? or ain't?) there. Ma started all this by letting Lot go to her house. Sam Wright said I was right and said Ma done wrong bring(ing) him to my face. Ma cuss me and John wrong. John and Rachel had a falling out about chapping cotton for Miller and he come up here to stay a night and he shot his pistol off at the boy. _____ (?) and Sam come up here and stay here a while and he told John I was right. He said Ma done wrong. He begged me and John to go down there and scare(?) Sarah off but we would not go and he told Ma we was going to shoot her house. A black lie. So the next night Ma sent for me and John to go down there and we went and she cussed me and John both (for) bulldozing her and we could not tell her nothing. She blessed us out. God knows I was at home when John come. She said if she had a gun she [*probably referring to Sarah*] would shoot at us, shot us, and me at my house. She told us both never to foot there again. Sarah West caused all this. Ma cussed me and John of thing that was not. So she throwed up the land to us. We had not said nothing about land. John told her he did not want a foot of that. She just was mad about Miss Sarah. She said if you did not like it, you could leave there too if you don't like what she does. Lottie need(s) a boss. You take her in your charge and rule her or whip her. I suffered for Lot, Ma did not, if Sarah rules Dovie. I mean for you to take Lottie in charge or send her to me.

{End of letter}

<u>Examination of Lizzie's letter to Silas:</u>

I don't know if any additional pages existed in this letter, but the six pages that have survived provide us a significant glimpse into the social atmosphere on the West place and among the West family during the 1920s in the Bay Gall. The reference of John West firing his pistol, coupled with the mentioning of Miller (a reference to the GP Miller farm), could very well place the writing of this letter in the year 1926, when John West shot Arthur Clayton. Lizzie West had married Walter Neely, who fought in WWI. They had one daughter named Lottie Mae, and two sons, Bob and Clyde. Walter was murdered a few years after the war, and during the 20s, Lottie lived with her grandmother Annie. Lottie is the center subject of Lizzie's letter to Silas. The persons referenced by name in the letter are Silas West, John West, Rachel Greenway West, Sarah West (wife of Thomas West), Annie Hendrix West (referred to as Ma), Peter Ozbolt (referred to as Ozbolt), Lottie Mae Neely, Bob and Clyde Neely, Oscar West, Dovie West, G P Miller (referred to as Miller), Sam Wright. All of these people were good people. Notice the absence of Thomas West and Mark West. Lizzie takes the time to involve everyone else but Thomas and Mark. By this time, it appears Thomas is dead. There is a lot of tension felt by Lizzie toward Sarah, and it appears that other West family members shared her sentiments. Again, I am only speculating. I do not know the root cause of the tension. The issue with Lottie Mae going to Sarah's house seems to be only surfaced. I think there is a deeper cause of Lizzie's dislike of Sarah, and it could be related to Thomas's disappearance and the circumstances surrounding his death. Did Lizzie and other members of the West family blame Sarah for the tragic circumstances on the West place? Did Sarah flee to South Carolina for fear of Mark or for fear of other members of the West family? Why didn't Lizzie mention Mark's name? He was living on the West farm at the time and was very much involved in all that was happening. Was she afraid of her own brother and what Mark might do if he was implicated in any manner in this family feud? So many questions unanswered. The last generation left little clues. But what they did leave behind, leaves us to believe that whatever happened was tragic and sad, and this tragedy and sadness kept them from revealing the whole story. I took the stance in the novel that Sarah loved her husband Thomas, and that she didn't wish to have an affair with Mark. I felt she later fled to South Carolina out of fear toward Mark, and was afraid to remain in Georgia not knowing how he would treat her. This is my interpretation; however, I do not know all of the details of what happened. I have revealed only what I am able to, and this knowledge is linked together with only faint circumstantial evidence and speculation. According to family, Silas West briefly visited Sarah in South Carolina in their later years. They supposedly talked about the past and ended the visit on good terms. In Lizzie's letter, she says her mother Annie cussed her. She later used the word blessed. Cuss and blessed are used interchangeably and I do not feel Annie used actual cuss words. More than likely, she blessed Lizzie out in the sense that she was upset and displeased and not in agreement with her. We are not able to hear Annie's side of the story in this letter, only her daughter Lizzie's. I am sure Annie was doing all she could to keep the family together, trying to help raise Sarah's children and Lizzie's daughter Lottie Mae. One can only feel compassion for Annie in her aging years, having to deal with so much tension and strife on the West place.

Newspaper, Court, and Church records of the West Brothers as they relate to the stories in the novel...

List of Official Records...

1. Thomas O. West : Disappearance : 1920 : Oak Grove Church Records
2. Mark West : Making Whiskey : Prohibition Era : 1925 : Court Records
3. John W. West : Murder Trial : 1926 : Newspaper Microfilm : Court Records
4. Silas West : Murder Trial : 1944 : Newspaper Microfilm : Court records : Newspaper Microfilm
5. Mark West : Murder Trial : 1945 : Court records
6. Silas West : Bootlegging : 1945 : Court records
7. Felton Lee Bevill : "The Violent Years" Delmar recording : song written/recorded by Felton, personal/public chronological account/testimony of events on West place

After many hours of research, I was able to unearth a few official records of the West brothers as they surfaced in public knowledge. I have listed them in chronological order to give the reader or researcher a basic timeline of events as they occurred. These records in no full measure reveal the true character or image of the West brothers, but provide us a small gateway into their lives as it relates to the awful tragedy and misfortune that confronted them. The prohibition era and great depression certainly affected the lives of the West brothers in some negative way, but in other causes, the tragic events that followed them were created by other complex circumstances.

Record 1: An official church record of Thomas O West's disappearance : Oak Grove Baptist Church

As far back as I can remember, I grew up hearing stories of my great-grandfather disappearing or being murdered. My grandfather Oscar shared with family that he was about 7 or 8 years old the last time he saw his father, and it was at the cattle gap near their house. He said he remembered his father telling him he couldn't go with him that day. Growing up, I never did ask my grandfather any specifics about his father's disappearance. He kept a lot of his past inside, and I didn't want to ask anything that might have been too personal. Granddaddy passed away in 1992. It seemed only by chance that I came across this record at Oak Grove Baptist Church. I took a picture of this membership page not thinking much about it at the time, just baptismal dates, etc. But when I got home, I enlarged the record image, and to my amazement, discovered the entry next to my gr-grandfather's name: disappeared June 1920. I couldn't believe it. After all these years of research. After countless hours of going through local newspaper microfilm and court records, I finally had an official record of my gr-grandfather's disappearance. It is one thing for family history and facts to be passed down by oral tradition. But to find an official record dispels all suspicions. Not only did I now know the exact year, I also now knew the exact month.

It is interesting to note that in the same month Thomas West went missing, Mark West took control/ownership of the land on the West homestead...

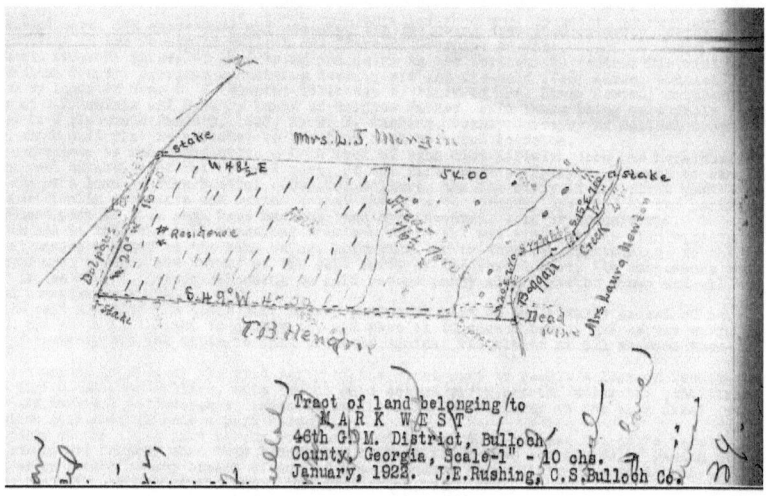

The place marked *residence* is where the log cabin stood. The Mongin, Hendrix, Newton, and Parker families were their neighbors during this time...

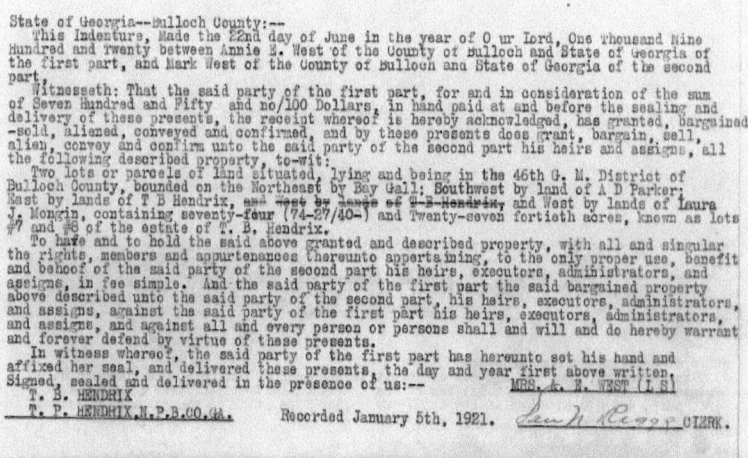

Record 2: Newspaper: Mark West making whiskey during Prohibition
Era: 1925

This is the first official record of any of the West brothers making
moonshine whiskey. There are records of other West relatives making
moonshine back in Georgetown, SC, but this is the first in Bulloch
County, GA. According to a neighbor-relative near the West place, a
contemporary of the West brothers, the type of moonshine the West
brothers made was mainly corn liquor, although they tried other types.
They made their shine near Bay Gall creek. Another contemporary-
relative (Mongin) described to me how Mark West was caught for
making shine. He said a revenuer came up to the cabin, pretending to be
lost while hunting. After talking with Mark a little while, he asked Mark
if he had any liquor to drink. It was then that Mark took him to his still,
by that time trusting the stranger. Little did Mark know it was a
government agent...

```
=o=o=o=o=o=o=o=o=o=o=o=o=o=o=o=o=o=o=o=o=o=o=o=o=o=o=o=o=o=o=o=o=o=o=o=o=o=o=o=o

The State
   -vs-                      Making whiskey.
Mark West
     Defendant waives copy of indictment and list of witnesses; also waives being formally
arraigned and pleads guilty. to be punished as for a misdemeanor.

                              John C.Hollingsworth, Sol.Gen.
                              R.Lee Moore Deft. Attorney.

              -------Sentence----------
     Whereupon , it is considered, or-dered and adjudged by the Court that you Mark West serve
Twelve months on the chaingang of Bulloch County, or on the public works of such other county,
or on such other public works as the proper authorities may direct; said defendant may be
discharged at any time before the completion  this sentence upon the payment of a fine of Two
hundredDollars, including costs of officers of Court.
     Judgment signed in open court, this 31st day of July,1925.
John C.Hollingsworth, Sol.Gen.
                              H.B.Strange,Judge S.C.C.C.

=o=o=o=o=o=o=o=o=o=o=o=o=o=o=o=o=o=o=o=o=o=o=o=o=o=o=o=o=o=o=o=o=o=o=o=o=o=o=o
```

JP Mongin remembered when his father Willie Mongin, John Wright,
and Willie's brother-in-law, Mitchell Woods, visited the West farm one
day. He said Mitchell wanted to get some whiskey from Mark. Mark
gave Mitchell two jugs of moonshine. Willie didn't like drinking and did
not like Mitchell having the jugs of shine in the car. Mitchell was holding
a jug in each of his hands and would not let them go. As they were
pulling off from the West farm, Willie noticed a car coming at a high

rate of speed down the road to the West place. He got scared thinking it was revenuers. He drove off the road and out of sight as the car speeded by. Willie noticed the people in the car and said, "Oh that's so and so. They are coming to buy some whiskey from the Wests."

One day, the Beasley Brothers, John G., Ernest, and Earl, went to get some moonshine from the West Brothers. When they arrived at the West place, they parked their truck at the gate. The West brothers were in the back yard when one of the Beasley brothers volunteered to go get the moonshine. The other two brothers remained in the truck. They noticed that when their brother made it to where the West brothers were, he put his hands up above his head. They said, "Oh no, they made him put his hands up in the air." Turned out, their brother was in no danger at all. He was just resting his hands on an overhead frame board just to talk with the West brothers…

Mark and Silas not only were good at making shine, they enjoyed drinking it. One day, they were drinking until they completely gave out. It was said that they sent young Oscar out to get some more shine. Mr. Emmit let Oscar use his car, but they forgot to tell him the brakes didn't work. On his way out, a cow was standing in the road. When Oscar tried to stop, he quickly discovered the brakes didn't work like they supposed to. He ran straight into the cow…

A funny story was shared with me by Darrell Mixon, concerning Mark West. Darrell stated that his father was going to visit Silas West one day because they were good friends. Darrell's father was riding his horse to the West place down a road that led from the Mixon land to the West land. He said as his father was riding down the path on his horse, Mark West stepped out into the road from behind a tree unexpectedly, and scared young Mixon half to death. Darrell's father said that Mark had straggly hair and a beard at the time. Mr. Mixon said he was already afraid of Mark and the surprise encounter added to his fright…

It was said that the West brothers would have spotters in the trees while they made their shine, keeping lookout for revenuers…

Record 3: Newspaper & Court records: John West shoots Arthur Clayton in 1926.

WEST IS BOUND OVER FOR KILLING CLAYTON

John W. West was remanded to jail Tuesday, following a hearing before Justices E. D. Holland and Farley Donaldson, for trial in superior court on the charge of murdering Arthur Clayton.

The killing occurred in the Lockhart district on May 8th, near Rocky Ford. According to testimony adduced at the hearing Tuesday, both men were drinking. They were farming on the property known as the Laura Blitch place. Clayton was returning to his home about 10 o'clock at night and was passing near the house occupied by West. While he was some distance away a pistol was fired in front of West's house. Clayton resented the firing of the pistol and, accepting it as a challenge, with much profanity declared his intention to ascertain the cause of the firing. His wife and small boy were with him. His wife sought to dissuade him from trouble with West, but they engaged in hand-to-hand combat. While thus engaged West shot and killed Clayton. West's plea was self-defense. It was made to appear by witnesses that Clayton bore a reputation for violence.

I was disclosed that ill-feeling had existed between the men previously over the loss of a rubber boot by one of West's brothers. The boot was found by a lad living with Clayton. West declined to pay a reward for the finding of the boot and Clayton refused to permit its return without reward.

Both men were married.

WEST ON TRIAL FOR KILLING OF CLAYTON

John W. West, aged about 60 years, is on trial for his life in superior court here charged with the murder of Arthur Clayton, aged 30, whom he shot to death at his home in the Lockhart district on May 8th. The jury trying the case was given the consideration of it at 11 o'clock this morning, following the delivery of the charge by Judge Knight, presiding.

West and Clayton were both employed on the farm of G. P. Miller in the Lockhart district. According to the evidence, Clayton was drinking. In going to his home at night he passed near the home of West. On this occasion, West is said to have fired off his pistol as a signal to his family that he had returned home. Clayton heard the shot and was enraged at it, regarding it as a threat. With oaths he approached the West house and, after a fight, was slain. The defense claims that the killing was in self defense.

-o-o-o-o-o-o-o-o-o-o-o-o-o- o- -o-o-o-o-o-o- >o-">o- - - >-o-o-o- -o-o-o-o-o-o-o-o-o-o-o-o- -

```
The State
   -vs-                    Murder.
John W.West
The following named jurrors were empanelled to try the above stated case.
            1 Homer Holland        6 W.A.Holloway
            2 T.Y.Akins            7 C.W.Anderson
            3 Eli P.Kennedy        8 Willie E.Brannen
            4 Josh T.Nessmith      9 B.M.Everett
            5 G.Emmitt Hodges     10 Morgan O.Anderson
who returned the following verdict;- We the Jury find the defendant John W.West Guilty,
of Voluntary Manslaughter,
    This the 29th day of July 1926.

                                   C.W.Anderson, Foreman.

    We fix the penalty at not less than 2 and not more than 5 years in penitentiary,

                                   C.W.Anderson, Foreman.

                    ...........Sentence...............
Georgia..Bulloch County.
The State
   -vs-
John W.West
    Verdict of guilty, at the July Term, 1926, of the Superior Court of said County.
    Whereupon it is the judgment of the Court that you John W.West be taken hence from
the Court House to the common jail of Bulloch County and be kept in safe custody till
demanded by a guard from the Penitentiary, and be taken hence by said guard to the State
Farm, at Millidgeville, or such other place as the Governor shall direct, and be there
confined at hard labor for the space of not less than two and more than five years,
and be then discharged.
This 29 day of July 1926.
John C.Hollingsworth, Sol.        Jon.P.Knight,
                                  Judge Alapaha Circuit Presiding.
```

-o-o-o-o-o- o-o- o-o-o -o-o-o o o-o-o-o-o-o-o-o-o-o-o-o-o-o-o -o-o-o-o-o-o-o-o-o-o-o-o-o-o-o-o-

WIFE FOLLOWS HUSBAND TO GRAVE

Young Mrs. Bolton Dies From Heart Attack Shortly After Her Husband's Death

Funeral services for Mrs. Allen Bolton, age 36, were held Wednesday morning at Oak Grove church, in the Lockhart district, four days following the interment of her husband in an adjoining grave.

The husband was Allen Bolton, age 33, who was found dead in a horse stable on the premises of Silas West, his landlord, about noon Thursday. Mrs. Bolton said her husband left home late Wednesday evening to attend to the feeding of some livestock in the stables at West's farm. Faced with the charge of having fired the shots which ended Bolton's life, West admitted that he had shot him in the belief that he was an intruder late Wednesday evening, but that he was not aware that the shot had been fatal. He said he went immediately to a neighbor's house, and that the next day he came to Statesboro. Sheriff Mallard says West visited a physician Thursday morning and asked for a potion for extreme nervousness and told the physician that he had shot a man. After the discovery of Bolton's body, accompanied the sheriff back to his home and described the position from which he had fired the fatal shot. West is now being held in jail awaiting further action in the premises.

Because of the conditions above outlined, Sheriff Mallard went immediately to the Bolton home Monday evening upon hearing of the death of Mrs. Bolton, and made inquiry as to the circumstances of her death. Mrs. Bolton's mother stated that the daughter had returned home from Statesboro and made complaint of pain in her chest; that she took some simple dose; that a few minutes later she fell in the yard and died immediately. The mother said her daughter was known to suffer from heart trouble.

-0-0-0-0-0-0-0-0-0-0-0-0-0-0-0-0-0-0-0-0-0-0-0-0-0-0-0-0-0-0-0-0-0-0-0-0-0-0-0-0-0-0-

```
THE STATE         :   No. 462
VS.               :   In Bulloch Superior Court, April Term, 1944
SILAS WEST        :   Murder

      The following named jurors were empanelled to try the above stated case:
           1.  Wiley W. Akins          7.  A. L. Roughton
           2.  Sam L. Brannen          8.  T. Jesse Mikell
           3.  J. C. Denmark           9.  J. W. Hagan
           4.  Z. L. Jenkins          10.  J. C. Lanier
           5.  J. Colon Akins         11.  C. H. Stokes
           6.  Fred S. Smith          12.  Clate Mikell
who returned the following verdict:
      We, the jury, find the defendant not guilty. This the 26th day of April, 1944.

                                         ___Clate Mikell___
                                              Foreman
```

-0-0-0-0-0-0-0-0-0-0-0-0-0-0-0-0-0-0-0-0-0-0-0-0-0-0-0-0-0-0-0-0-0-0-0-0-0-0-0-0-0-0-

Jury Acquits West Of Bolton Murder

In superior court last evening a verdict of not guilty was rendered by the jury trying the case against Silas West, charged with the murder of Allen Bolton. This incident occurred about five weeks ago in the Lockhart district. Bolton, it is understood, was a tenant on the West farm. He was found dead in the stable on the West premises. West, in Statesboro about the time of the discovery of the body, had told a physician that he had killed a man the night before

Record 5: Court Records. Mark West shoots Leland Hendrix. 1945

```
THE STATE     :     No. 548
vs.           :     In Bulloch Superior Court, October Term, 1945
MARK WEST     :     Murder

The following named jurors were empanelled to try the above stated case:
          1.  Arnold Parrish          7.  Willie Allen
          2.  Charles Nessmith        8.  W. J. Akerman
          3.  W. C. Denmark           9.  J. C. Martin
          4.  Louis Stephens         10.  E. R. Warnock
          5.  Joe S. Brannen         11.  I. A. Brannen
          6.  P. B. Brannen          12.  H. M. Royal
and returned the following verdict:
    We, the jury, find the Defendant, Mark West, guilty of Murder. This the 25 day of Oct.

                              I. A. Brannen
                                   Foreman

    We, the jury, recommend to the court, mercy. Oct. 25th, 1945.

                              I. A. Brannen.

                            SENTENCE
    Thereupon, it is the judgment of the Court that you, Mark West, be taken from the Court
to the common jail of Bulloch County and be kept in safe custody till demanded by a
guard from the Penitentiary, and be taken hence by said guard to the Penitentiary in Atlanta,
or such other place as the Governor shall direct and be there confined at hard labor for the
term of your Life.
    This 25 day of Oct. 1945.

W. T. Lanier                              J. L. Renfroe
Solicitor General                 Judge Superior Court, Ogeechee Circuit

(MOTION FOR NEW TRIAL FILED OCTOBER 31, 1945.)
```

```
This December 10th, 1945.

                    A. M. Deal

                    W. G. Neville
                  Attorneys for Movant

    The recital of fact contained in the foregoing amendment to and of the original motion
for new trial is hereby approved as true and correct; and all of the grounds of the amendment
are approved and the amendment is hereby allowed and ordered filed.
    This December 10th, 1945.

                    J. L. Renfroe
          Judge Superior Court Bulloch Co., Ga.
```

Record 6: Court Records. Silas West arrested for bootlegging. 1945

The following Bills were handed into open Court by the Grand Jury Bailiff, C. C. Ak—

THE STATE
VS.   Unlawful Sale of Unstamped Whiskey   True Bill
SILAS WEST

- - - - - - - -

-o-o-o-o-o-o-o- - - -o-o-o-o-o-o-o-o-o-o-o-o-o-o-o-o-o-o-o-o-o-o-o-o-o-o-o-o-o-o-o-o-o-

THE STATE   :   No. 547
    VS.   :   In Bulloch Superior Court, October Term, 1945
SILAS WEST   :   Unlawful Sale of Unstamped Liquor

The following named jurors were empanelled to try the above stated case:
1. Wyley Fordham   7. Hamp Youngblood
2. B. D. Nessmith   8. Jovin Smith
3. Emit C. Deal   9. J. W. Hagan
4. John L. Akins   10. Ronnie Gay
5. W.W. Mann   11. J. M. Smith
6. C. J. M. Pope   12. G. W. Clark
who returned the following verdict:
                    VERDICT
    We, the Jury, find the defendant guilty, this Jan. 30, 1946.

                                        J. M. Smith
                                          Foreman
                    SENTENCE
    Whereupon, it is considered, sentenced and adjudged by the court that you Silas
the defendant in the above stated case, do pay a fine of $200 - - - - Dollars, to
the cost of this prosecution, and in addition thereto do work in the Public Work Camp,
the public works, or at the State Prison Farm for and during the full term of 12 month
    Provided however, upon the payment of said fine the defendant may be permitted t
said term outside of the confines of said Public Work Camp, on the public works, or at
State Prison Farm, so long as he conducts himself in an orderly and law-abiding manner
violates no laws of this State, and obeys all orders and directions of this court, an
to - - - - - - - - - - - - - - - - - as probation officer, on the first Saturday
month during the period of 12 months, and until the further order of the Court. Upon
ure of the defendant to comply with these conditions upon which this sentence is prob
shall be committed to serve the sentence as declared inthe first paragraph above of th
ment of the court.
    The defendant has 10 days in which to pay fine.
    This 31 day of Jan. 1946.

Fred T. Lanier   J. L. Renfroe
Solicitor General   Judge Superior Court of Bulloch

-o-o-o-o-o-o-o-o-o-o-o-o-o-o-o-o-o-o-o-o-o-o-o-o-o-o-o-o-o-o-o-o-o-o-o-o-o-o-o-o-o-o-o-

Record 7: Delmar Records: "The Violent Years". Atlanta, GA

Recorded at Delmar Records; Atlanta, GA ; written and recorded by
Felton Lee Bevill (nephew of Allen Bolton)
The Violent Years : a chronological account of the events that
transpired on the West Place 1944-45 : recorded on a 45 vinyl. Felton
replaced the real names with fictitious names in the song. For instance,
fictitious names Jud and John are Mark and Silas West respectively.
Uncle Amos is Allen Bolton. The Petyon brothers are the West
brothers. It appears that Felton only referenced two real names, little
Johnny (John Willie West b. 1920) and Oak Grove church. Felton more
than likely wrote and recorded this song sometime after the death of
Silas West in 1965. Felton died in 2003. At some instances, it's hard to
make out the words to the lyrics. I did my best to listen and transcribe
the words to paper. There may be others with a better ear to transcribe
more accurately.

Felton Lee Bevill was the nephew of Allen Bolton, the man that Silas
West shot and killed in 1944.

Lyrics to "The Violent Years"…

"In the violent years of the Peyton brothers [West brothers] is (a) how
my story goes,
Never escaping (?)from the lawless life of the men at the end of the
road.
Bootlegging was the business, and the farm was a <u>cover up</u> (?),
The good folks round all knew the truth, but nobody said a word.
I remember one day when we was kids and playing down near the barn,
Little Johnny [*John Willie West b. 1920*] fell over somebody's grave buried
in the <u>hitch</u> (?) of the yard. And old Jud [*Mark West*] he come to the
door yelling like a man insane,
Said you better get the devil out of here right now, said you're walking
on my brother's grave [*could be a reference to Thomas West*].
Well time passed on and we soon forgot about what old Jud [*Mark West*]
had said,
For everybody down that county knew he was a little bit touched in the
head.
And then one day we got the news that my Uncle Amos [*Allen Bolton*]
was dead,

Shot him in the back in the barn one night, so the only witness said.
Well we buried his body at Oak Grove Church on a rainy Saturday,
And old friends come from miles away just to pay their last respects.
Only witness lived to stand was his darling wife [*Lottie Mae Neely*], but
she passed away that Monday morning, and we put her by his side.
Well the murderous case never come to trial, and not that I recall.
So time passed on and the years rolled by and all the talk was gone.
Then one day a nearby farmer stopped in so they tell, and it cost his life
as the story's told, for a cool drink from the well.
Well no one else was quite sure just which one fired the gun,
Cause brother Jud [*Mark West*] blamed it on John [*Silas West*], and John
[*Silas West*] said it was Jud [*Mark West*].
But they sent old Jud [*Mark West*] to prison [*Reidsville Prison*] and there
they say he died [Mark was murdered in prison in 1949],
as _____ (?) law and justice _____ (?) the folks had paid the
price.
Well the old gay house still stands today, much like in the days of old,
And they say no one goes there anymore but the snakes and the ghosts.
And the wind and the rain beat in through the walls,
And _____ (?) secret of the Peyton brothers [*West brothers*] at the
end of the road."

End of song

Although this personal account from Felton Bevill, through his written
song and Delmar recording, is not an official document/record, it does
provide us some important chronological details about all that he
recalled concerning the events that occurred on the West place. I was
unable to discover this recording before Mr. Felton passed away, and so
lost much background information for his song. This song, *The Violent
Years*, can be interpreted as his public testimony/witness as to what he
recalled and heard and witnessed concerning the West brothers, or as he
fictitiously named, the Peyton brothers. Felton more than likely wrote
and recorded this song sometime after the death of Silas West in 1965.

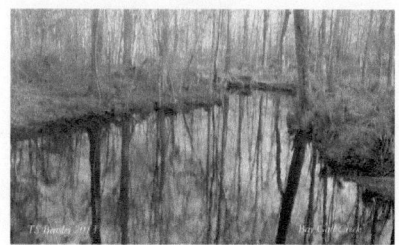

Bay Gall Creek on Nevil's Creek Church Rd...

"Bay Gall Creek"

The past quietly flows in the mist of Bay Gall creek, beneath the
pines it reflects the passing of time,
The trees and sky touch its surfaced sun's light, as nature pauses to
capture its stillness of rhyme.
Its banks have long felt each winter's felt flow, the cold passing
winds pass o'er its shallow hold,
Passing the flooding of memories long forgotten, the telling of
remembered stories now told.
Shades of night darken its long darkened path, the light of the
Moon gives it life,
Till the sun shines on its banks in the morning, and ends all the
darkened long strife.

————*TS Beasley*

Bay Gall creek on EC Hendrix dirt road...

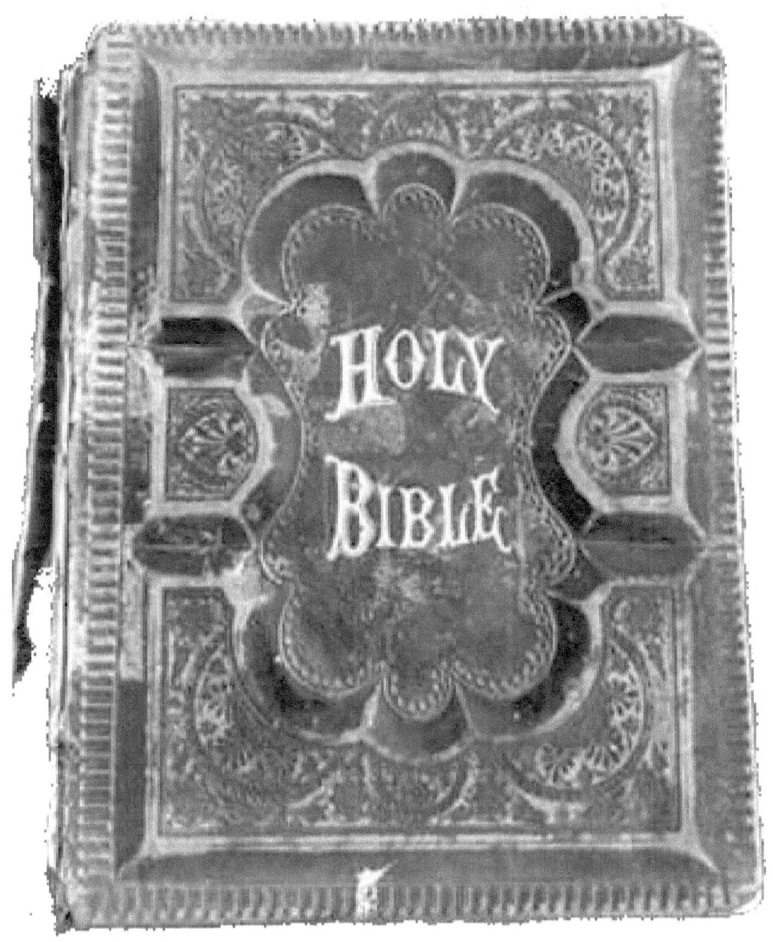

This is a picture of the old West family bible...

It last belonged to old man John Willie West, son of PA West and Annie Hendrix West...but preserved to the present day by the Hendrix family.

...old man John W. West died in 1960 in the old West log cabin

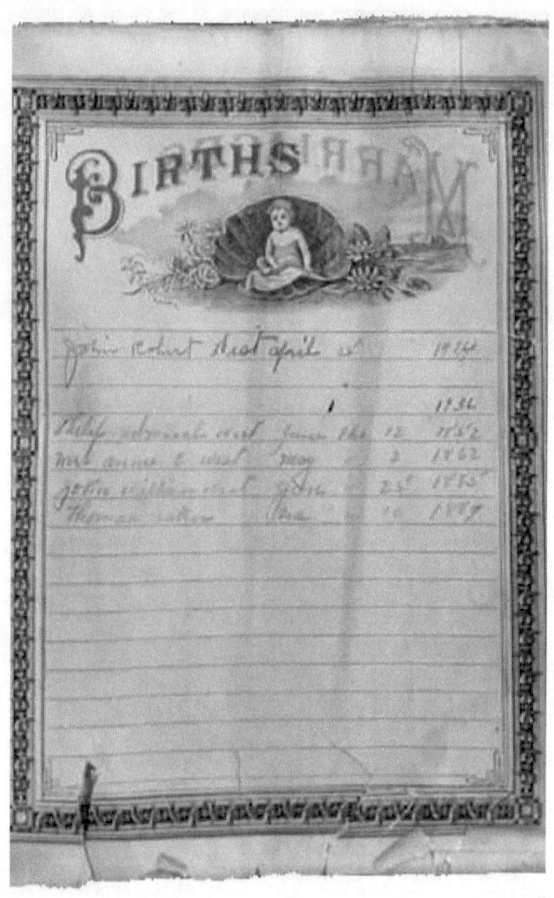

An inner page in the middle of the old West family bible that lists some of the names
of the original Wests and their births...

Notice...P A West's full name is Phillip Admiral West. This is an original entry
that dates back to the early 1900s. He married Annie Elizabeth Hendrix shown
here as being born in 1862. Their son Thomas West's middle name is verified here
as being Oscar. John Robert West was the son of old man John Willie West and
Rachel Greenway. It shows here that he was born in 1914 and his father John
Willie West was born in 1885, the first born child of P.A and Annie Hendrix
West. P.A and Annie would give all their children bible names...

Annie Elizabeth Hendrix West [the wife of Phillip West from Georgetown
SC]
& grandson Oscar West

"*A Tribute to Annie E. Hendrix West*"

Annie West's old log cabin, O rest in ageless peace!
Let us find in your falling timber our humble release!
The fields that were sown on your harvested soil,
The blood and the sweat of your hard work and toil!

The cotton that was grown and picked by your hand,
The quilts that were made, the broom sage brushed sand!

The water from the old well, though shallow to draw,
The horses and the mules, the barns filled with straw.
The precious family Bible and your old rocking chair,
The past and the present are all gathered there.

Your bowed humble head, and prayers that you prayed,
Your pleadings of love for your sons who had strayed!
O rest in ageless peace on Heaven's most peaceful shore,
Your work has long since ceased…Toil on earth ne'er more!

——*TS Beasley*

Annie E. Hendrix West holding her gr-granddaughter Annie Mary Dean West (daughter of Oscar West) or her gr-grandson Archie T. West...

The young girl to left is thought to be Mary Dean Hendrix, daughter of Emmitt Claude and Curtis Mallard Hendrix, or some other Hendrix girl...

Annie Mary Dean West was named after her gr-grandma Annie. After her cousin Mary Dean Hendrix said "I think Mary Dean is a pretty name," Oscar and Lillie Mae added Mary Dean to their daughters name...

...the old West cabin and kitchen in background

Annie Mary Dean West
…old West place…1935/36
…notice, this child favors the child that Annie Hendrix West is holding…

Waldo Finch (younger boy on left, son of Freddie Finch and Dovie West) and John Willie West (older boy on right, son of Thomas and Sarah West) on old West place...

Photo taken on Old West Place...
(Waldo Finch, son of Freddie Finch and Dovie West)

Photo taken on Old West Place...unidentified West or Hendrix boy...

William Oscar West

Photo of unidentified West or Hendrix boy…possibly Phillip West

Silas and Mark West: year 1911
@ Thomas and Sarah West's Wedding
The swastika Mark is wearing was a symbol of good will in 1911.
The Nazi Party didn't adopt the symbol until 1920.

Dodie West, sister of Sarah West
Picture taken on wedding day of
Thomas & Sarah West
January 8th, 1911

Sarah West on her wedding day to Thomas West
January 8ᵗʰ, 1911

...there is some evidence to suggest that the lady in this picture is actually Lizzie West, daughter of P.A and Annie Hendrix West. It had been assumed that the young lady was Sarah West, especially since her sister Dodie West from South Carolina was taking pictures with them the same day in Bulloch County on the West place...as seen in the previous photo on Sarah's wedding day to Thomas...

Probably Tom's wedding day, January 8, 1911, in Bulloch County, GA.   *Courtesy of Great-grandson, Tony Beasley*

Thomas West on his wedding day
to Sarah West
January 8th, 1911

The swastika Thomas is wearing was a symbol of good will in 1911.
The Nazi Party didn't adopt the symbol until 1920.

"*Poem Dedicated to Thomas West*"

Just neath the earth…in the cold soil of night,
The bones of thy body doth decay,
In shallow hidden ground, thy form tis no more,
Thy memory forever doth stay!
Neath the whispering pines, down near the creek,
In the Bay Gall where water floweth still,
Is the resting place of young Thomas O West,
A soul that someone didst kill!
Where the owls do howl, in the darkness of night,
Where the bobcats hunt down their prey,
From the old log cabin, down through the field,
Young Thomas O West doth lay!
How didst it then happen, or happen to thee,
That cold hand that took thy life,
Twas it thine own kin or brother by blood,
Tis with a gun or with a knife?
We mourn thy breath quickly stolen from thee
Thy gift from God above,
We weep for the hands that shed thy blood,
Whose hands didst not love.
O come dear Father, in Heaven on earth,
And shine your light on his place,
Where Thomas O West doth solemnly rest,
On earth in Heavenly grace!

——*TS Beasley*

Thomas Oscar West
son of
Phillip & Annie West

This photo of Thomas O West is a close-up of the full body photo, reversed. Notice his eyes in this picture are looking straight in front of him. In the full body photo, his eyes aren't looking straight ahead. Notice the backdrop is the same as the full body photo, but reversed.

Prince George Parish / Post Office:
Georgetown South Carolina 1860 Census

The father of Thomas West was Phillip West...listed as being 12
The father of Sarah West was William Capers West...listed as being 10

Thomas and Sarah were actually first cousins who fell in love with each other and got married...[something not uncommon in the old days]

Latter years of Sarah "Billie" West...

Sarah used the name "Billie" when she moved from Bulloch County, GA to Charleston, Georgetown, and Myrtle Beach, SC in the 1920s. She would later marry Noah Lawton. They lived in Myrtle Beach, SC near the international airport, just off of Old Socastee Hwy. Sarah died in 1963 from cancer, in the home of her niece in Georgetown, SC. The story of Oscar West seeing his mother again for the first time since he was fourteen years old is factual. In 1944, he got a letter in the mail from his mother, asking him to come see her in Charleston, SC. This account given by Oscar a few months before his death was recorded on audio tape. From then on he would take trips to see his mother through the years, up until the time of her death. Sarah was buried at Gourdines Chapel, in Andrews, SC...the place of her birth.

Sarah "Billie" West Lawton and Noah Lawton
South Carolina

Sarah "Billie" West, Dec 23, 1895 - Apr 11, 1963,
Daughter of William Capers West, 1850 - 1915, and
Theodosia Moyd West, c. 1865 - 1934.
Married: 1. Thomas O. West, c. 1886 - c. 1920;
2. Noah Lawton, 1905 - 1971.

Mary Lucy Smith West, Sarah "Billie" West Lawton, Nora Smith Stout

Mary and Nora were sisters…

Brenda Stout, Nancy Stout, Sarah "Billie" West Lawton

Sarah "Billie" West Lawton

Dovie Elaine West

Birthday Party for Elaine at her grandma Sarah "Billie" West's house in
Myrtle Beach, SC

1950s

Mary (Sarah's friend) getting ready for the party, front yard at Sarah's house.

Friends at the party…

Sarah's friend, Mary, with Mary Lucy Smith West

Sarah "Billie" West Lawton

Sarah "Billie" West

John Willie West Jr. with his grandmother Sarah "Billie" West

This is a rare picture of Sarah with one of her grandchildren, taken either in Virginia or Myrtle Beach, SC.

Richmond, Virginia was where her youngest son, John Willie West, lived after the 2nd World War…

[Photo: circa 2010]

This is the house that Sarah "Billie" West spent her final days in before passing away in 1963. This house is in Georgetown, SC. It was the residence of Sarah's niece, Mrs. Delton Belton Kennedy (Ila Jane West Kennedy), daughter of Sarah's oldest brother, John West. Several loved ones were gathered around her bedside at the time of her death. Her son Oscar and granddaughter Barbara were able to visit her during this time. She never made it back to Georgia during her lifetime, but kept in touch with her children through the years. At the time of her passing, one of her sons, Phillip West, resided in Myrtle Beach, SC in the same neighborhood as his mother. John Willie and Dovie visited her often as well and she knew she was loved. Some said she tried to say something at the end, but her words were too faint to understand. The burdens of life she had carried for so long had finally been put to rest. She loved her children and family dearly, and her reunion with Thomas West in Heaven became a reality the moment she closed her eyes on this earth…

Mrs. N. J. Lawton Of Georgetown Died Thursday

Mrs. Sarah Lawton of Myrtle Beach and Georgetown died at the home of her niece, Mrs. D. B. Kennedy at an early hour Thursday morning. She had been in ill health for several years and seriously ill for the past six months.

Funeral services were held Friday in the Mayer Funeral Home Chapel. Officiating was the Rev. W. P. Queen of the Sampit Charge Methodist Church. Burial was in the churchyard of Gourdines Chapel Methodist Church.

Mrs. Lawton, a daughter of the late William Capers West and the late Mrs. Doshia Moyd West, was born in the Suttons section of Williamsburg County on Dec. 23, 1895. Mrs. West had spent most of her life in Williamsburg and Georgetown counties but had passed the last few years at Myrtle Beach.

Surviving are: her husband, Noah John Lawton of Myrtle Beach; three sons, John W. West of Richmond, Phillip A. West of Myrtle Beach and Oscar West of Statesboro, Ga.; a daughter, Mrs. Dovie Michel of Charleston, 11 grandchildren; one great grandchild; a brother, Herbert West of Georgetown; two sisters, Mrs. Dodie Ward of Andrews and Mrs. Eva Ward of Georgetown, and several nephews and nieces.

Gourdines Chapel in Andrews, SC

The resting place of Sarah "Billie" West Lawton. Her grave marker reads Sarah Lawton. Several of her loved ones are buried here, including Sarah's two sisters, Dodie and Eva, and one of her brothers, William Capers West. Noah Lawton is also buried here near Sarah…

Silas W. West
(son of Phillip Admiral West and Annie E. Hendrix West)

Facing Picture L to R:
John Willie West, Oscar West, Silas West

Mary Lou Smith West, Silas West, Lillie Mae Woodcock West

Facing Picture L to R:
Back Row: Phillip West with hat on and Rubbert Hendrix
Front Row: Oscar West and Silas West

1930s

Oscar West on left, Silas West on right
Rubbert Hendrix (holding shotgun) & Phillip West with hat on

1930s

Rubbert Hendrix holding gun, Silas West holding end of barrel, Phillip West
holding pistol, Oscar West standing on porch

Picture taken in 1930s on West Place

Silas West (wearing hat) and Freddy Finch (husband of Dovie)

Silas W. West

Virginia Beach…early 1960s

John Willie West Jr. and Silas West
Richmond, Virginia
September 1964…the year before Silas passed away…

Silas West, son of Phillip & Annie West

"A Day with Silas West"

The year was 1959, and Silas was ready to take his hogs to market
to the Stockyard in Statesboro. He asked Tump to go with him.
They arrived in Statesboro that morning to drop the hogs off, but
it wouldn't be until around two o'clock before Silas would get a
check. In the meantime, they went and got something to eat in
town. When they got back to the Stockyard, and got paid for the
hogs, Silas asked Tump if he would take him to Portal, to Phil
Aaron's store, to get something to drink. The next day, Silas was
going to take Tony, his coon dog, hunting, and the weather was
cold. It was winter time. Tump had just gotten back from Florida
on his honeymoon, and it was the day after he got back that he
drove Silas to Statesboro, then to Portal. Silas said he needed
something to drink since he would be hunting in the cold weather,
and it would help with his congestion. When they got to Phil
Aaron's store, Phil addressed Silas as Mr. West, out of respect, and
informed him that he had gotten in some new bourbon and
wanted him to try them out. Silas agreed. He poured Silas a shot
of each type to see what he thought of them. Silas drank them and
made his choice of which type of bourbon he wanted. After
leaving Phil Aaron's store, Silas asked Tump to take him by Punk
Stewart's store to buy some mullet. Once they left Stewart's in
Portal, they went back to the Bay Gall to Silas' cabin. It was
getting late in the day, and Silas wanted Tump to stay and eat
some mullet with him. Needless to say, it was late at night before
Tump finally made it back home to his new bride…

Silas W. West

<u>The Last Letter From Silas W. West</u>   (Original reading/spelling kept)

Every body is harping on when the end of time will be what difference does it make
If it tomorrow are a thousand years the question is we be ready to meet it if death should
Call every pearson when he dies that is the end of time for him we cant get ready after death and we are told it
will come in a twinkling of an eye want that be a sad time if we are not ready he has give us all a chance read
your bible start the new testament read it through you want understand it...
Page 2....good the first time you read it over but when you lay down at night pray to God to take care of you and
to give you knowledge to understand his word ask him to for give you for your wrongs and mean and keep on
praying and if you mean it he will hear when you when you wake up every morning thank him for spairing you
through the night and ask him to take care of you through the day and show you the right way and help you to
follow it...
Page 3...if you are in earnest he want turn you down you will see how much better you get along and how better
peace of mind you will have don't read it like you wood a news paper read slow and study closely he will help
you understand it you want to ask some body else what it means and if you hear people talking about the bible
you will know where and what they are saying is in the bible are in the bible or not don't depend...
Page 4...on the preacher or any body to read the bible for you study it your self and you will know read one
chapter right behind the other one to get the meaning of it you will understand it better every time you read it
over and you will get more interested in it every time you read it for instance take from the 8th chapter of
Hebrews on will kill the catholice it tells you after the coming of Christ that did away with the priests and...
Page 5...burnt offerings that Christ was offered up and died for our sins he is the only meditator between us and
God he intercedes to God for us if we beleave on him and do his will and not the hard shells doctorine fore
ordained and preedestentld sure God predestinated his son Jesus and ordained him in the beginning to be
crucified for our sins he knew some would beleave and some would not and them that beleaves is his
Page 6...elect and chosen ones that is plain he tell us them that beleave shall not be damed but them that beleave
not is damed all ready he says temptation and offence will come but woe to the man by whom they come sin
against the wholly ghost is blasphemy against God meaning on not beleaving on christ and speaking against
Christ and the spirit if you read the wholly ghost did not come until Christ ascended to heaven read where he
told his deppiles he would send them...
Page 7...the comfort witch is the wholly ghost the 14th chaper of saint john could explain to you right on but
read search the scripture diletently and pray to God for guidance read the too bible verces the more you read
the bible the more you want to read it you will fine comfort in it then any thing in the world and think what a
mother we had how she prayed for us and tried to teach us we would not heed her teaching then but thank God
it ant to late not all I hate...
Page 8...is we have wasted so long a time in sin cause her so many heart ackes and tears and the least we can do
is to try to meet her on that golden shore life is short we don't know what moment we will be snatched into
eternity a man that study the bible and see your mistake before it is to late one sin is as bad as another the God
that said don not kill that same God said do not kill that same God said do not steal do not commit adultery,
Page 9...also the God that said don't kill the same God says do not lie do not bear false witness if you commit
one you are guilty of all read second james second chaper the bible says not to keep company unbeleavers to pull
your self out from among them you cant go along with the sinners and server God they ant a man in that
community that is fit to associate with john ought to read he will have to change his way of living if he want to
Page 10...go to heaven it is in the new testament a dozen times about living in adultery it cant be denied Christ
said devorces was not in tended from the beginning tell the old fellow he is getting close to the end he better
repent and beleave while he can there aint a night passes I don't pray for you all I have read the whole bible
through one time and the new testament 6 times and learn some thing new every time I read it thank God I
don't have to ask no one to explain the bible to me no more...
Page 11...as to devorces read the 19th chaper of matthew we cant dispute Christ on words I am not bemeaning
john he may get mad with me but I still love him I love his soul and want to see it save and now is the accepted
time if we don't beleave Christ we don't beleave God and we make him out a lier heaven and earth shall pass
away but not one of his words will pass away start at matthew read on through revelation one chaper right after
the other read some every day if you stop reading you will...
Page 12...wean off from him take the parples and miracles and study them good I trust to God you will stop and
think if we live in sin and die in sin what can we for read first petter 4th chaper 18th verce and if the righteous
scarcely be save where the undgodly and sinner appear the wages of sin is death study the book of romas good
when you get to it will tell you about predestination.

<u>Uncle Silas was born 1891</u>

"O Silas, thy repentance doth bring God's gracious peace,
And in God's mercy, His forgiveness and release!
And think what a Mother! Thy thoughts didst recall,
Her prayers and tears for thee, on thee didst fall!
Her teachings didst bring you to Heavens blissful door,
When thou didst meet her again on that golden shore!"

———*T S Beasley*

"Silas West's funeral [Oak Grove Church Cemetery] 1965"

Silas West's Funeral

From left to right...

John Willie West Jr, John Willie West Sr, Mary Lucy Smith West, Freddy Finch

Oak Grove Baptist Church

Bulloch County, GA

1965

Oak Grove Baptist Church

The congregation originally met in a corn crib structure. Sometime later, they built this church on the same location, near a grove of oaks on a sandy ridge. It is believed this building was built around 1909 and torn down around 1948. Thomas B Hendrix's family attended Nevils Creek Primitive Baptist Church before the Civil War, as his name is on the Nevils Creek Church membership. Just before the war, in 1856, Oak Grove Church was established. The land on which the corn crib resided belonged to Thomas B Hendrix, whose grave is the oldest dated in the church cemetery. After the war, many of the children of Thomas are listed on the Oak Grove Church membership, such as Thomas P. and Annie and G. W. Hendrix. Annie would marry P. A. West from Georgetown, SC, and both of them were very active in the church. All of their children were given bible names, and church records show they were all baptized. P. A. West is listed as being part of the building committee when the church planned to rebuild. Thomas P. Hendrix would deed the land over to the church in the 1920s… for a place of worship and a cemetery.

John West son of Phillip & Annie West

Rachel Greenway wife of John West

*John Robert West (left) first driver of the Bookmobile for the Library in
Statesboro, GA. John Robert is son of John and Rachel Greenway West*

*Oak Grove Church
John Robert West was church treasurer
He is on far right with envelope in his shirt pocket*

Ruth Bland West…wife of John Robert West
[daughter of Frank Bland and Annie Wright Bland]

Glen Dora West, daughter of John Robert and Ruth Bland West

John Robert West's tractor on old West place...

John Robert used a mule and push plow when he first bought the West farm in 1945. He would later purchase his first tractor. The couple in the photo is Pete Peeples and wife Mary Bland Peeples. Mary is the sister of Ruth Bland West. Before Mary passed away, she shared with the author her memories of the Wests, including stories her mother had shared with her. Mary was born in 1927 and passed away in 2015. Her grandmother, Mary Jane Hendrix Wright, was the sister of Annie Hendrix West...

John Robert West and wife Ruth Bland West

Lottie Mae Neely

(daughter of Walter and Lizzie West Neely) and (wife of Allen Bolton)

Bob and Clyde Neely (sons of Walter and Lizzie West Neely)

Clyde Neely (son of Walter and Lizzie West Neely)

Clyde Neely and wife Bertie Lee Woodcock Neely

Clyde Neely (son of Walter and Lizzie West Neely)

*Dottie Mae 'Dutchie' Bolton (daughter of Allen Bolton and Lottie Mae Neely
Bolton) and Monty Neely (son of Clyde Neely)*

"A recollection by nephew [Mr. Still] of Allen Bolton"

The February 1944 when Allen was killed, I was about eight years old. We lived in a big house outside of Rockyford, GA. When anything bad would happen, our family and relatives would come to our house. The night before Allen's funeral, Aunt Lottie was there with the family. I remember she had a small baby girl. There was a bad storm at the time. The wind and lightning and thundering would rattle the windows, and she acted like she was very scared. The baby was crying a lot. I remember how upset she (Lottie) would get when someone would say anything about Uncle Allen. I only got to see the baby (Dottie) that one time. After Lottie died, her daughter was raised by Lottie's family. I did get to see her at the hospital when mom was sick. She came to see her. When she was there she fainted. Someone said she could have been pregnant. It was in the early seventies. She would have been about twenty-six at the time. I never got to see her again…

Dottie Mae "Dutchie" Bolton

Lizzie West Neely (daughter of Phillip and Annie)

With grandchildren Monty and Joyce Neely

Phillip A. West,
Son of Sarah West, Dec 23, 1895 - Apr 11, 1963
Grandson of William Capers West, Sep 25, 1850 - Sep 1, 1915, and
Theodosia Moyd West, c. 1860 - Feb 20, 1934.

Phillip West appears to be in his teens in the above picture. Notice he is wearing his white shoes.

Phillip A. West,
Son of Sarah West, Dec 23, 1895 - Apr 11, 1963
Grandson of William Capers West, Sep 25, 1850 - Sep 1, 1915, and
Theodosia Moyd West, c. 1860 - Feb 20, 1934.

Phillip West son of Thomas and Sarah West

Phillip A. West top right during WWII

R: *Phillip Admiral West, Dec 22, 1915 - June 7, 1985,*
Son of Thomas O. West, b. abt. 1886, and
Sarah "Billy" West West Lawton, Dec 23, 1895 - Apr 11, 1963.
L: Beatrice S. Taylor West Devine, b. 1929~1933,
Daughter of William Herbert Taylor, 1901 - 1977, and Lizzie Mills Taylor, 1901 - 1987.

Phillip Admiral West and wife Elizabeth Beatrice Taylor West

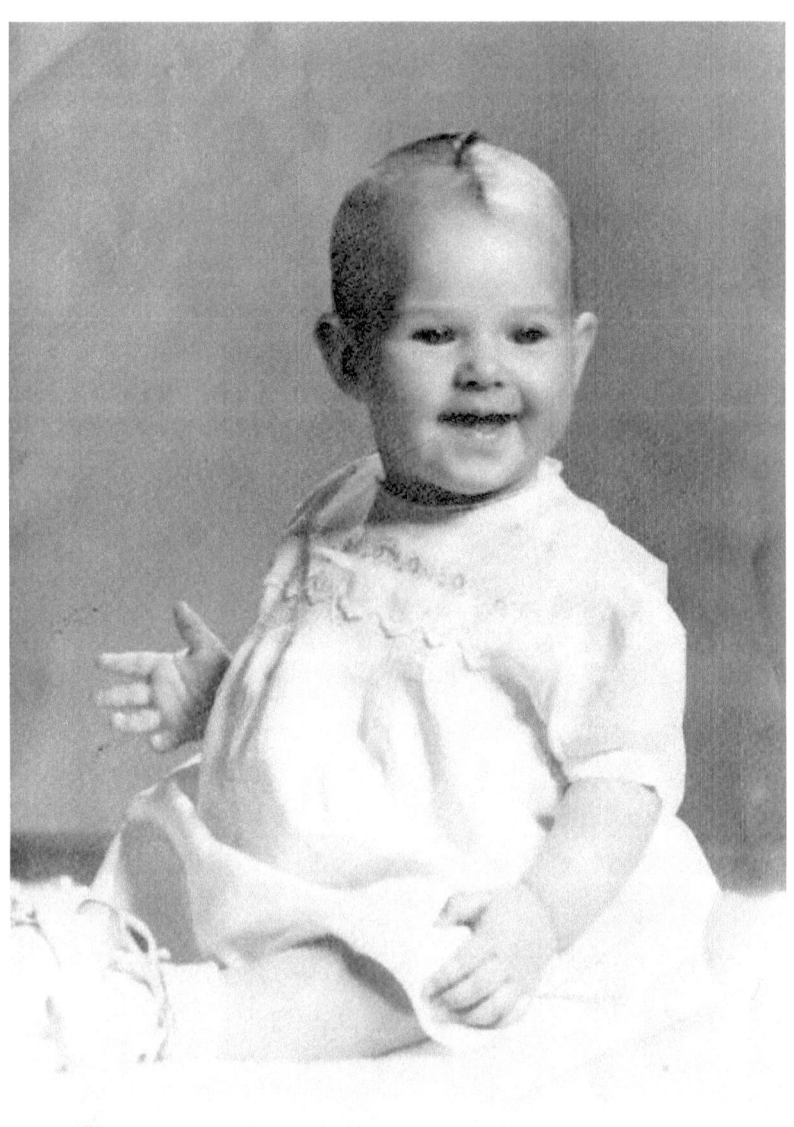

Dovie Elaine West

Beatrice Taylor West holding daughter Elaine...
South Carolina

Dovie Elaine West

Beatrice Taylor West with two of her daughters…Elaine and Jo Ann

1950s

Elaine and Jo Ann West... 5 & 3 yrs. old...Georgetown SC

L to R: unknown boy, Elaine West, unknown boy (possibly Timmy West),
unknown girl, Jo Ann West, unknown girl...
August 1958...Myrtle Beach, South Carolina...a West Residence...

L to R: unknown boy, unknown girl, Elaine West, Jo Ann West in front of her,
unknown boy...South Carolina

Dovie Elaine West, Jo Ann West, Sarah Jane West, Phillip Timothy West

Children of Phillip Admiral West and Beatrice Taylor West...

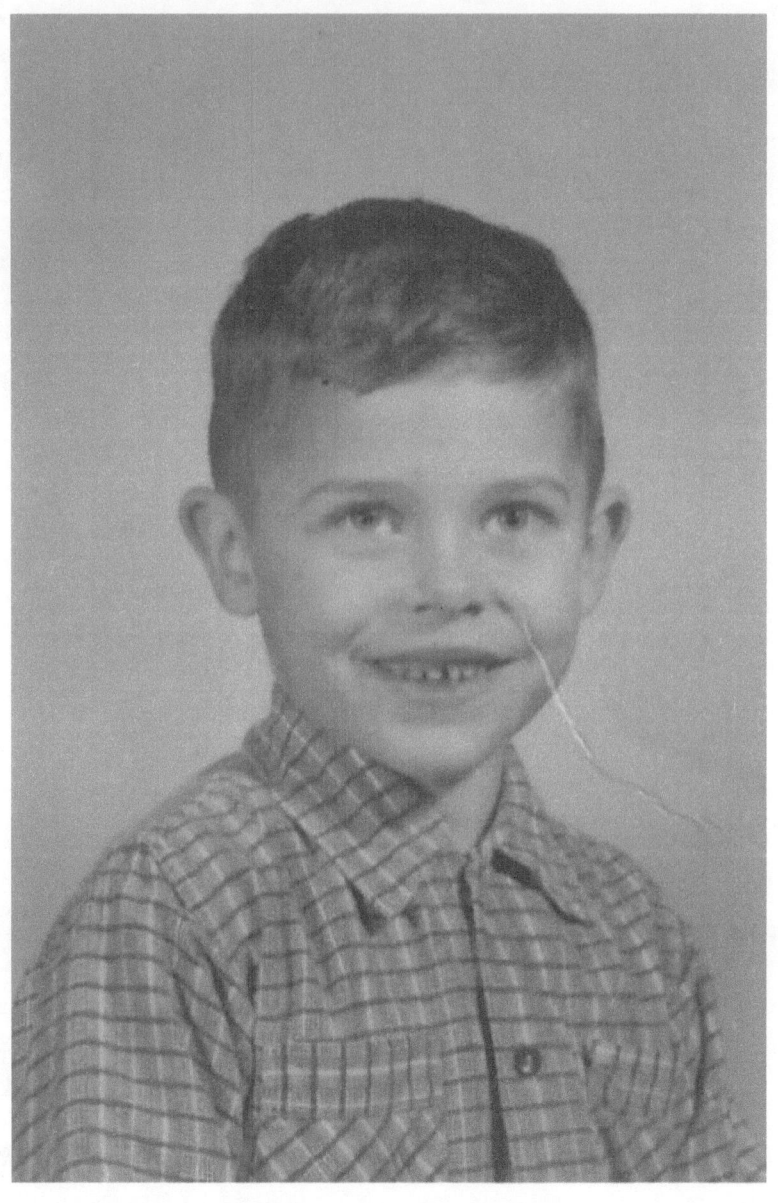

Phillip Timothy "Timmy" West

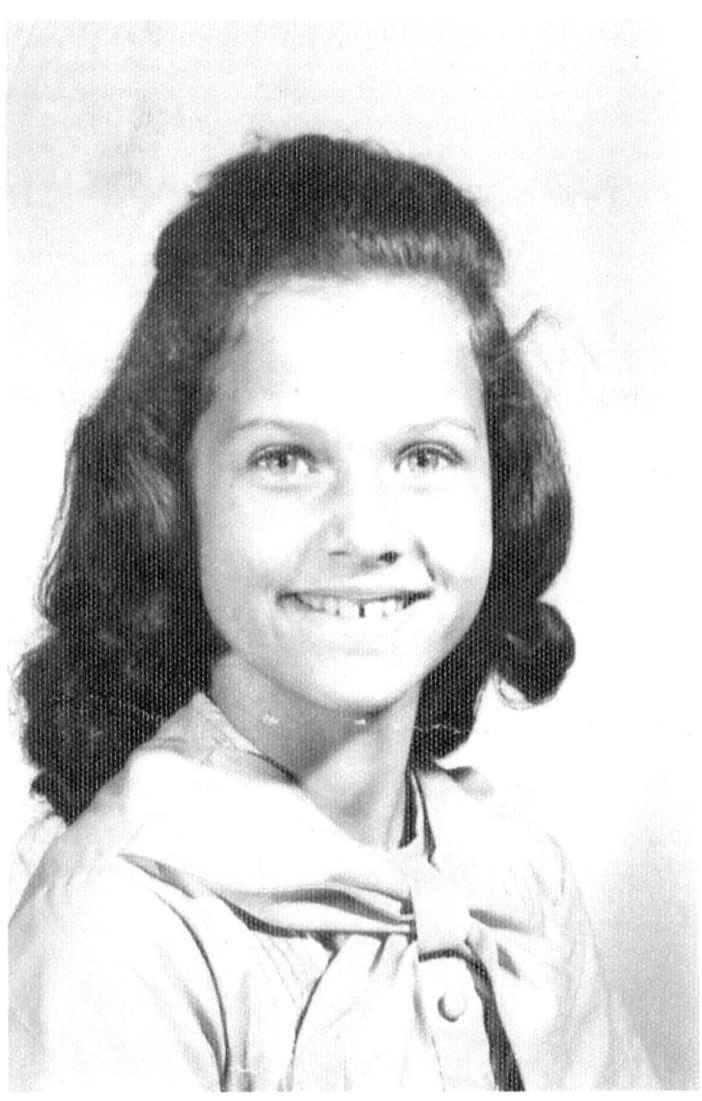

Dovie Elaine West

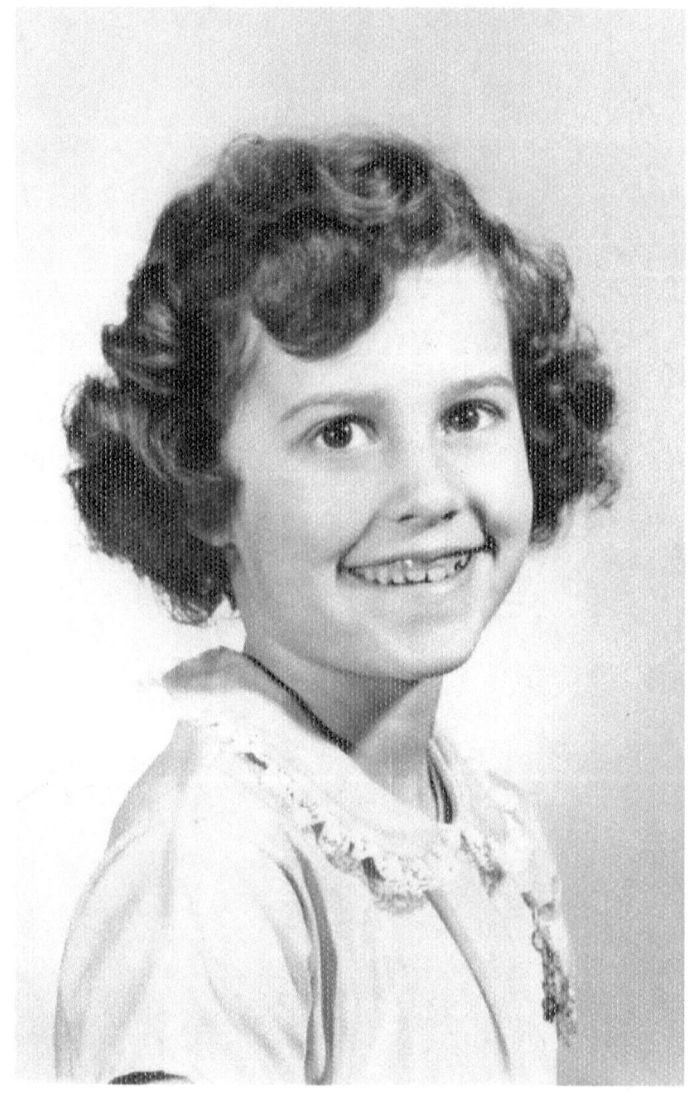

Jo Ann West

Dovie West Finch Michel, Jo Ann West, Doug Grady, Elaine West

John Willie West Jr. and Timmy West

Elaine West, John Willie West Jr., Jo Ann West

Elaine West...June of 1961

Sarah West, Timmy West, Jo Ann West

*May 1969 DOVIE WEST MICHEL'S HOUSE IN CHARLESTON
ASHLEY AVENUE ACROSS FROM MUSC*

Beatrice with two of her daughters…Sarah Jane and Jo Ann West

Sue Ann Finch, Phillip A. West, Dovie West Finch Michel, Margaret, Beatrice
Taylor West Divine, Sarah Jane West…South Carolina

Timmy West, Sue Ann Finch, Mae Finch, Elaine West

Timmy West

Sarah West

Sarah Jane West

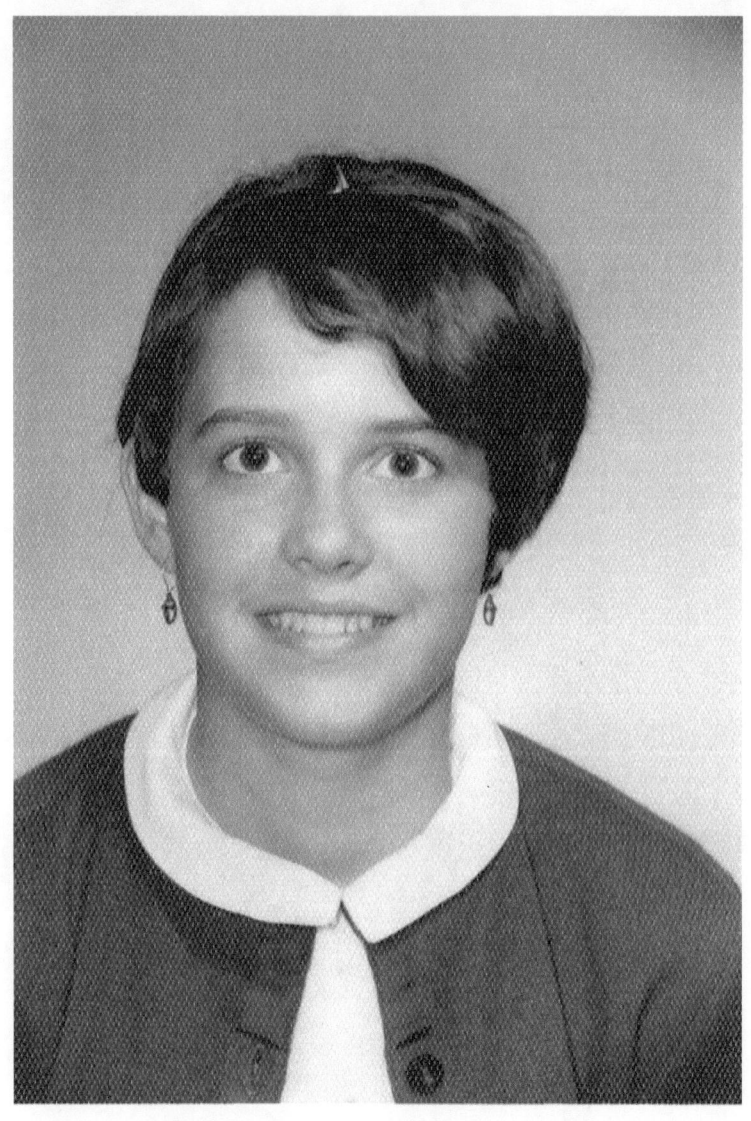

Jo Ann West

Elaine West

Mary Lucy Smith West and Beatrice Taylor West

John Willie West and wife Mary Lucy Smith West

John Willie West son of Thomas and Sarah West
Military Photo WWII

Phillip West, unknown man, John Willie West during WWII

John Willie West and Mary Lucy Smith West
Walmsley Blvd, Richmond, VA

John Willie West, Mary Lucy West, John Willie West Jr.
Walmsley Blvd, Richmond, VA 1956

John Willie West Jr.
Walmsley Blvd
Richmond, VA

John Willie West and son, John Willie West Jr.
Richmond, Virginia

Mary Lucy Smith West and son...John Willie West Jr.

John Willie West Sr. and son...John Willie West Jr.

William Oscar West, John Willie West Jr., Sue Ann Finch, Teresa Beasley, and Carolyn Beasley…

April 1967 at Oscar West's place on Ben Hendrix farm…

John Willie West Jr., Teresa Beasley, Carolyn Beasley

Oscar West place on Nevils Creek Church Rd

April 1967

Barbara Ann West Beasley, Mary Lucy Smith West, Shirley Beasley

Oscar West place on Nevils Creek Church Rd

April 1967

John Willie West, Bobby Knight, Wanda Knight
Oscar West place on Nevils Creek Church Rd…April 1967
Mr. Bennie Hendrix's white house in the left background and Ed
Thompson's house is in the right-center background in the distance…

Bobby Knight, John Willie West Jr., Linda Knight, Pam Knight, Teresa Beasley, Carolyn Beasley, Wanda Knight

Oscar West place on Nevils Creek Church Rd

April 1967

William Oscar West, Mary Lucy West, Clint West, John Willie West Jr.

Rocky Ford, GA July 1969

John Willie West Jr. drinking from the downtown well...

William Oscar West, Clint West, Mary Lucy West, John Willie West Jr.

Rocky Ford, GA downtown well...

July 1969

Dovie West and John Willie West Jr.

Rocky Ford, GA downtown well…

July 1971

John Willie West Jr. at the Beasleys
Bulloch County, GA…April 1969

Beasley House in background…

John Willie West Sr. and John Willie West Jr. at the Beasleys
Bulloch County, GA...April 1969

Beasley House in background...

Visiting with the Beasley Family…May 1969

Sitting down at the table in the kitchen for breakfast…

*John Willie West Jr., Mary Lucy Smith West, Barbara Ann West Beasley,
Shirley Beasley, Teresa Beasley, Carolyn Beasley*

John Willie West and wife Mary Lucy Smith West

William Oscar West…studio picture

William Oscar West
Grandfather of TS Beasley

Dovie West, Apr 3, 1912 - Jan 1985,
Daughter of Sarah West, Dec 23, 1895 - Apr 11, 1963;
Granddaughter of William Capers West and Theodosia Moyd West.
Married: _____ Michel

Freddie Finch and wife Dovie West Finch
1930s

Dovie West

Dovie West

Dovie West and Barbara Ann West

Lillie Mae Woodcock West and Dovie West

Oscar West's place on Nevils Creek Church Rd

Bulloch County, Statesboro, GA

Dovie West and Mary West
Charleston, SC

Dovie West Michel and Charlie Michel
Charleston, SC

Waldo Finch, Sarah "Billie" West, Mary Lucy West

Waldo Finch, son of Freddie Finch and Dovie West Finch…

Noah Lawton, Charlie Michel, Phillip West

South Carolina

Phillip A. West, Emmitt C. Hendrix, Vernon Hendrix
Taken in the Bay Gall...

John Willie West and Phillip Admiral West

Facing Picture
L: William Oscar West
R: John Willie West
[brothers]

...well at Oscar's house on Nevils Creek Church Rd

John Willie West and his sister Dovie West Finch...

Oscar West and his sister Dovie West Finch…

Oscar's house…

William Oscar West,
Son of Tom O. West and Sarah "Billie" West West,
wife, Lillie Mae Woodcock West,
Boys, l to r: Johnny D.; Archie Thomas; William Richard "Billy.
Girls: Barbara, in arms; Mary, standing.

Picture above, Mr. Benjamin "Bennie" Hendrix and his wife Pearl visiting with the West family during Christmas. Oscar West lived just down the road from Mr. Bennie on Nevils Creek Church Rd and farmed as a sharecropper for him for several years. The house that the Oscar West family lived in no longer stands there, but Mr. Bennie's house still remains. Oscar's house was bought and moved to a location along Rocky Ford Road, where the owner remodeled and bricked it in. So much history surrounds the place where Oscar and Lillie Mae West raised five children, but the old days are quickly being forgotten...

Oscar and Lillie Mae West...

Picture of Mr. Bennie Hendrix's barn where Oscar kept his mules, Pete and Mollie. When Oscar plowed in the fields, Mollie would keep Pete in line, even though he was a lot bigger than she was. Pete was the male and Mollie the female. Oscar's son Johnny remembers as a boy when Pete and Mollie would run around the block after he tossed corn cobs at them, finally returning to the barn behind the fence after they made it full circle. Oscar could be heard singing songs in the distance such as "In The Pines" while plowing with the mules in the field, something he did from dawn to dusk. The two large live oaks near the barn are very old, possibly dating back to the time of James David Hendrix, the father of Thomas B. Hendrix. It was near this barn that Oscar saw the ambulance leaving a path of dust behind on Old River Rd one full moon night after JB Daughtry was shot and killed...
[Photo of barn taken by TS Beasley: circa 2015]

Mary Lou Smith West, Lillie Mae West holding Barbara Ann West, Mary West, Billy West, Johnny West...standing by well at Oscar's house

Billy West, John Willie West, Johnny West

Standing in front of the well at Oscar's house…

Bulloch County, GA 1940s

Mary Lucy Smith West

Mary grew up in Schuyler, VA, and her family were neighbors with Earl Hamner (who wrote The Waltons and whose life was represented by "John Boy"). Her father and Earl's father worked together at the old Soapstone Mill in Schuyler. They call it Walton's mountain, but the real name is Spencer's Mountain...

Sisters...

Mary West and Barbara West

*Annie Mary Dean West and Ralph Hendrix...first cousins
...at Oscars house*

Mary West and Johnny West
Children of Oscar West
@ Oscar's house

Johnny West and Barbara West
Children of Oscar West

Front: *Eugene Clinton 'Tump' Hendrix, unknown, Archie West, Dirlie Sue Hendrix,*
Back Row: *unknown, Annie Mary Dean West, Mary Dean Hendrix,*

Tump, Sue, and Mary Dean Hendrix are children of Emmit Hendrix.
Archie and Mary Dean West are children of Oscar West...

Photo taken at Emmitt Hendrix's homeplace in the Bay Gall...

Betty Vickery, Mary West, Bonnie Vickery, Ralph Hendrix, Neatha Woodcock, Billy West, Neely girl, Archie West...

Oscar West married Lillie Mae Woodcock, daughter of Roan C. and Lizzie Mae Marsh Woodcock. The Woodcocks had nine children, and Sunday dinners and family gatherings occurred often at the Woodcock homeplace in the country. As you can see in this picture in the early 1940s, this was an era of horses and wagons and motor vehicles all sharing the same roads in Bulloch County, GA...

Oscar Vickery, Ruby Woodcock Vickery, and children Betty, Bonnie, and Jimmy...

...siblings

Emory C. and Mary Lorine Woodcock

Unidentified lady, Ruby W. Vickery her son Jimmy, Manthie W. Hendrix, Bertie Lee W. Neely, Lizzie Mae Marsh Woodcock, Margie Rooks Woodcock, Lillie Mae W. West holding her son Johnny West...1940s.

JC Woodcock, Emory Woodcock, Lonnie Hendrix, Roan C Woodcock, William Oscar West, Oscar Vickery ...1940s.

Coy Woodcock and wife Margie R. Woodcock holding child...

...old Woodcock homeplace

Roan C. Woodcock, Lizzie Mae Woodcock holding Annie Mary Dean West (her granddaughter) and Neatha Woodcock (her daughter), Lillie Mae Woodcock West holding her son Archie Thomas West...1930s.

A lot of courting was going on back in those days at the Woodcock homeplace, with Roan and Lizzie Mae having so many children...

Roy Knight married Neatha Woodcock in the 1950s...

They can be seen here standing underneath the giant Sycamore tree that stood in the front yard at the Woodcock place...

Here's another young couple on the Woodcock homestead...

JC Woodcock and Runette Rooks Woodcock...

Wedding Day…

Emory C. and Alleene E. Woodcock…

Sitting on the Woodcock front porch...wedding bells are ringing.

John "Johnny" West and Tibby Bunch West...

Roan C. Woodcock and Lizzie Mae Woodcock standing at the corner of
the house. Ralph Hendrix holding bat, Neatha Woodcock sitting on
brick column, Lonnie Hendrix and Manthie Woodcock Hendrix…

The Woodcock House…

The Woodcock cousins often gathered together for fun and fellowship
at the Woodcock home. Similar in many ways to the TV series *The
Waltons,* the Woodcock children grew up during the great depression
and before WWII. Just across the branch and creek from the
Woodcocks lived the George Clifton family. Mr. Clifton married
couples in the community during those days, and it was in his house
where Oscar West and Lillie Mae Woodcock said their wedding vows.
Oscar said, "If I would have tried to kiss her before we got married, she
would have slapped my jaws." The stories and memories are numerous
and invaluable, and it would be a great source of entertainment to write
a book on the Woodcock homeplace…

Lillie Mae Woodcock West with her mother Lizzie Mae Marsh Woodcock cooking in the kitchen at Lizzie Mae's house. Lillie's mother cooked some of the best chicken and dumplings and everyone loved cooking in her kitchen. Notice the old wood stove in the background…

Oscar West, Lillie Mae W. West, Lizzie Mae Woodcock, Neatha W. Knight, Mary Lucy Smith West, Margie R. Woodcock, Connie Knight...

Oscar West and Lizzie Mae Marsh Woodcock...in Lizzie's kitchen...

*Margie Woodcock, Lizzie Mae Woodcock, Lillie Mae W. West, Mary West…
Bobbie Ann Woodcock holding child…*

Ruby Woodcock and Archie T. West…at the Woodcocks…

First row: Bobbie Ann Woodcock, Joe Woodcock, Jimmy Vickery, Johnny West…
Second Row: Barbara West (sitting on brick column), James Vickery, Betty
Vickery, Margie R. Woodcock, unidentified lady…
Third Row: Lizzie Mae Marsh Woodcock, unidentified lady, Lillie Mae Woodcock
West…
Fourth Row: unidentified girl, Ralph Hendrix, Manthie Woodcock Hendrix,
Archie West…
Fifth row: unidentified girl, Billy West

Front porch at the Woodcocks where Roan C and Lizzie Mae Woodcock lived…

Late 1940s

Johnny, Archie, Billy West
Sons of Oscar West
1940s

Oscar West's homeplace...

Johnny, Archie, and Billy West
Barn in field used to store Irish potatoes, corn, etc., and shelter for a milk cow...
Nevils Creek Church Rd. Oscar's house on opposite side of dirt road...

Billy and Johnny West...

Lillie Mae Woodcock West with all three of her sons...Archie, Johnny, and Billy.

Archie West, Mary West holding Elaine, Beatrice Taylor West, Lillie Mae West and Barbara Ann West…Nevils Creek Church Rd…early 1950s.

Archie West, Barbara West, Billy West...

Barbara West standing on gate, Stout girl on right…
Nevils Creek Church Rd…1940s.

Johnny West, James Vickery, Joe Woodcock...

Barbara Ann West, Hilda Thompson, Edmund Thompson, Robert Gay
...at Mr. Bennie Hendrix's house

Barbara West holding cousin John Willie West Jr.
Nevils Creek Church Rd...1957

Lillie Mae West, John Willie West, Barbara Ann West
Nevils Creek Church Rd…

William Oscar West, Lillie Mae West, Gene Stout, Waldo Finch, Barbara West

Oscar West, Lillie Mae West holding John Willie West Jr, Barbara A. West

Barbara Ann West

Barbara Ann West

Barbara Ann West

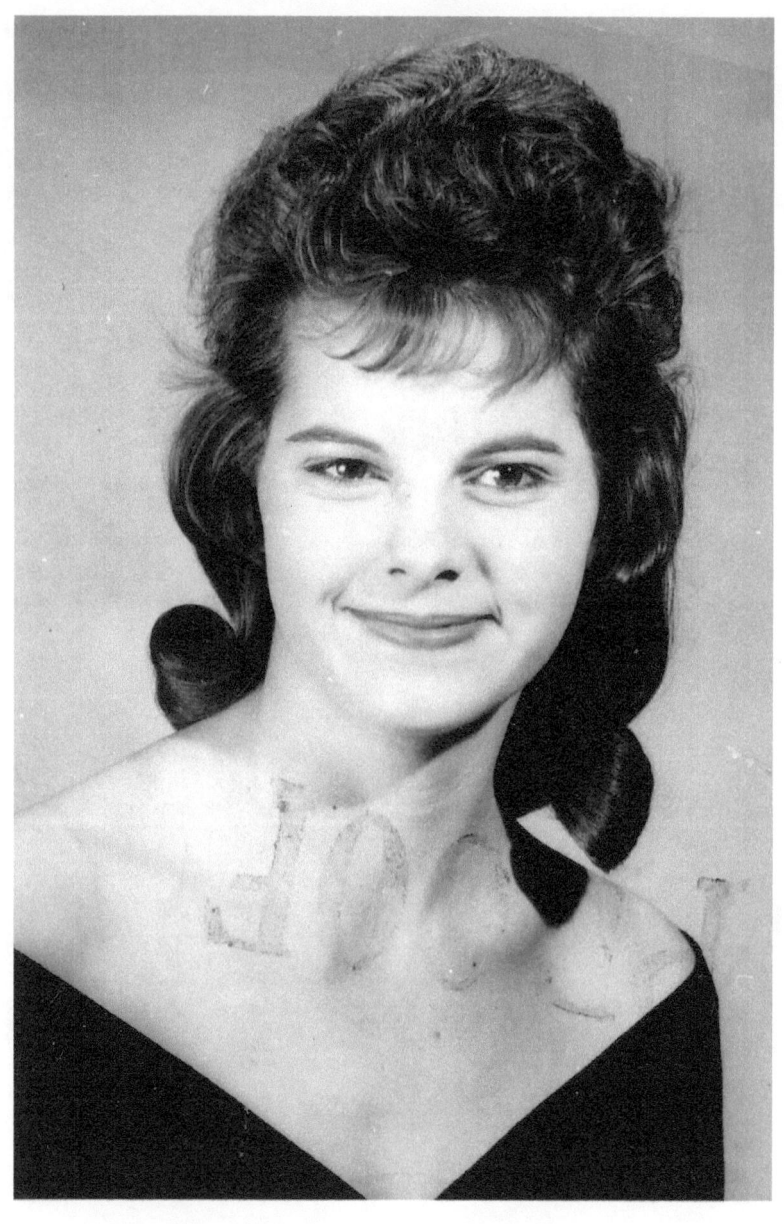

Barbara Ann West Beasley

Barbara Ann West

Portal Prom…10th grade.

Barbara Ann West

Barbara Ann West in beauty pageant at Portal High School
Barbara is contestant #12

Left Side: #1 Sylvia Allen, #2 unidentified, #3 Linda Vickery, #11 Janice Ellis, #4 Christine Daughtry…
Right side: #10 Kay Carter, Emma Small, #9 Jennifer Hunnicutt, Jean Bragg, #8 Ann Hendrix, Carolyn Blackburn…

Christine and her sister Bennie Daughtry took Barbara around all day to try and find a dress for the beauty contest, but couldn't find one. So Barbara's sister Mary took Barbara to Statesboro and bought the dress she is wearing in this picture from Tilly's or Henry's…

Barbara was in the 10th grade during this pageant…

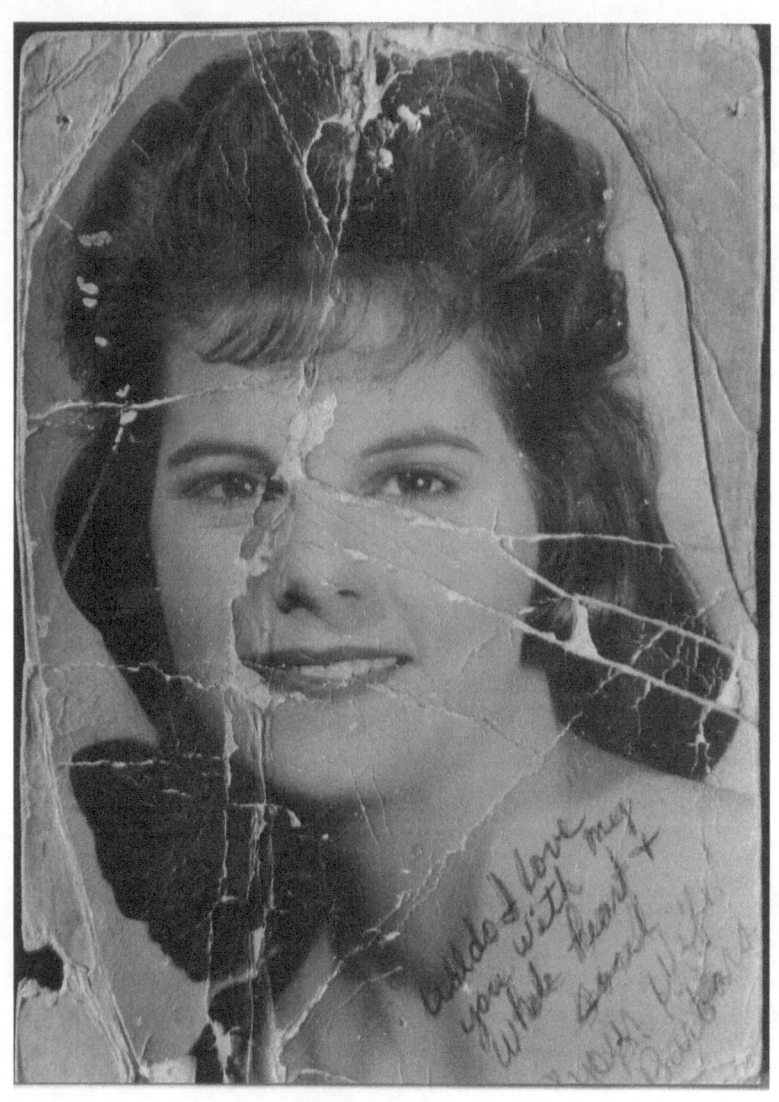

Barbara Ann West Beasley

Waldo Beasley and Barbara West Beasley

Wedding night…December of 1962. Photo taken in Garden City, GA

Waldo Beasley and Barbara West Beasley holding daughter Carolyn...1964/65.

Barbara West holding two of her daughters Teresa and Carolyn...1964/65

Barbara West Beasley, Mary Lucy Smith West, Lillie Mae Woodcock West,
Waldo Beasley, Carolyn Beasley, Teresa Beasley...

Nevils Creek Church Rd

Oscar West place on Mr. Bennie's farm...

Teresa Ann Beasley   Carolyn Beasley

Barbara Ann West   Waldo Beasley,
Beasley, b. Sep 11, 1945   b. Aug 29, 1939

Barbara West and John Willie West.
Oscar West place on Nevils Creek Church Rd

Barbara West, Mildred Beasley West holding son Mike, Ricky West…

The Beasley house in the country…

Barbara West holding daughter Shirley…1960s.

Waldo and Barbara West Beasley with Teresa, Carolyn, Shirley…
…swimming in Cobbtown, GA…late 1960s

Barbara West Beasley holding daughter Shirley...

Beasley house in the country...

Waldo and Barbara...

5 Pictures of Barbara's Baby Shower for her son Tony S. Beasley...1971
Given by Verdell Finch...

Picture #1

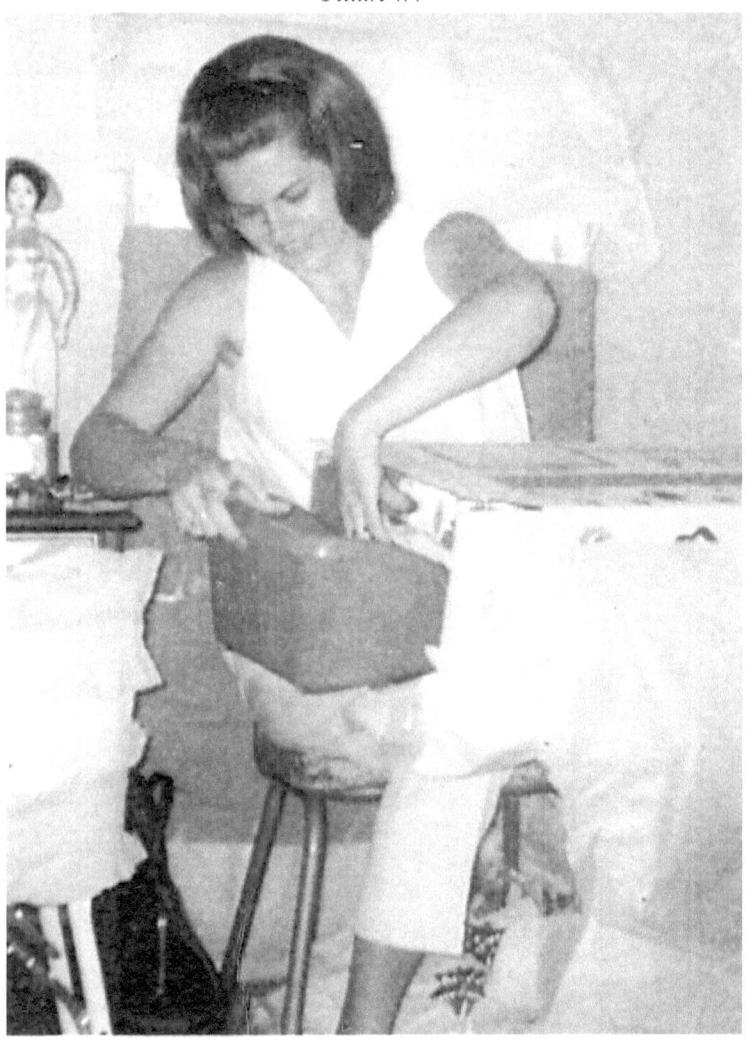

Barbara West Beasley

Pictures #2 and #3

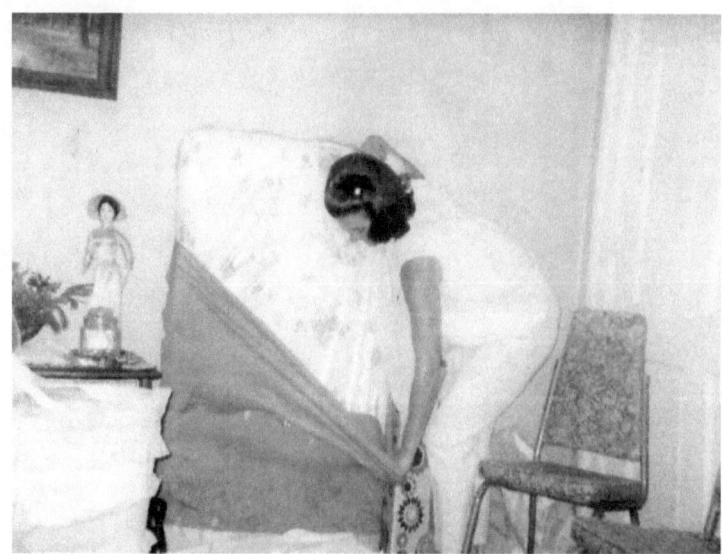

Barbara opening more gifts…

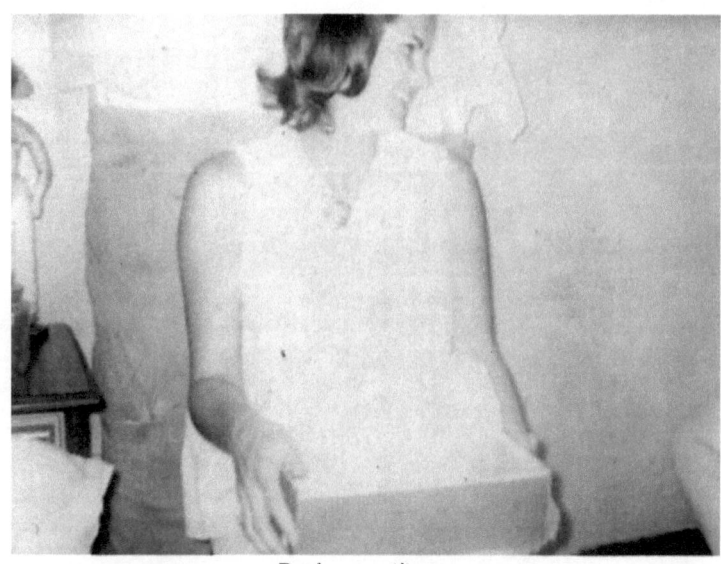

Barbara smiling…

Pictures #4 and #5

Time for fun and games…Barbara blindfolded / Tibby Bunch West on couch…

Mrs. Finch, Tibby West, Mildred West, unidentified lady, Mary West Knight
In front…Mrs. Saunders, unidentified lady, Barbara West, Lillie Mae West

Waldo Beasley with his two sons...Tony and Travis Beasley.

The Beasley homeplace...

1970s

Tony S. Beasley and Travis W. Beasley

Photo taken on steps at Marion and Geraldine Stewart's home in the country near Oak Grove Baptist Church…1970s

Brothers…
Travis W. Beasley and Tony S. Beasley
Photo taken in Beasley house in the country…1970s

Barbara Ann West Beasley holding son Tony Beasley

William Oscar West and Lillie Mae Woodcock West taking a
picture with their grandson Tony Scott Beasley…not long after he
was born.

Statesboro, GA
1971

My precious mother holding the guitar...(A Mother's Day tribute)

"Dear Mama, your whole life has been a wonderful song, tender lyrics
written by the pen of your loving heart. Your melody of kindness and
care have taught me through the years, and it will carry me throughout
the rest of my life. I've never heard you play out of tune, always playing
every chord with unconditional love, from beginning to end, with hands
that have never strayed from being a loving mother. Your song will
never end Mama, no matter how feeble or tired in body you may grow,
but will remain in my heart forever..."

With love, your son...Tony Beasley.

[Written for my mother May 24th, 2015}

The place of my mother's birth…

This old pine built house belonged to Coot Hendrix; my grandfather Oscar West sharecropped for him during the mid-1940s for a short while. My mother and I took this picture several years ago…the house is no longer standing. It was located in the Bay Gall on Mallard Pond Rd. The world of high society and wealth wouldn't think much worth existed here, or no person of importance could be born here, but they would be tragically mistaken. For that little framed house represents a place that sheltered one of the most precious women ever born on God's green earth, my precious mother. This rustic small dwelling represents the spirit of humbleness that has rested on my mother throughout her whole life, and there is no richer abode in this whole world that I'd rather claim or inherit than the place of my mother's birth…

———*TS Beasley*

My precious mother…

She was born a sharecroppers daughter, the last of five children, and I am eternally grateful to God above for letting her be my earthly mother. I would hate to imagine what my life would've been like without her…or if my mother would've never been born…or if I'd had a different mother on this earth? I would be forever lost, a wandering soul without any sense of direction. She has been my guardian angel, and she has never once let me down. Her wings have carried me over deep wide valleys and through fierce raging storms and in long dark nights…protecting me from the coldness of this world, an angel whose halo has only been filled with the warmth of her unconditional love. In her, I see God, for God is love, and her faith in God has given me light. And although my angel feels more aches and pains, she is still my strongest protector, my greatest guide, and my surest hand. And I plead with my Heavenly Father above to watch over my precious mother…to comfort her in her aging years…to remember her labor of love and unselfish life…and to strengthen her body so that she may be with us for many more years to come…

I love you with all my heart Mama, and to me, you are the best mother in the whole world!!!

Your son, TS Beasley

My father and mother walking together behind the house
beside the Ogeechee River...

As I watch my parents grow older and become more feeble, my spirit
slowly dies within me. I ask the Lord to lengthen their days and grant
them good health so that I can spend more precious time with them, but
the years are passing so quickly. My mother and father give me a reason
to live, a purpose that carries me into each and every unknown
tomorrow. Without them, I know my days on earth will be few and my
spirit will grieve itself into that eternal city where we'll never grow old
and we'll never have to say goodbye again...

——TS Beasley

My West family genealogy...
{Collage: Top left: Barbara West Beasley, Top right: William Oscar West, Bottom left: Thomas Oscar West, Bottom right: Tony Scott Beasley}

Genetics plays an important role in our lives, who we are, and where we come from. Growing up, I always loved to hear the "*older ones*" talk about the old West place, of the many stories my grandfather Oscar West shared from his past. He had a great memory, and it was filled with a deep love for his grandma Annie Hendrix West who raised him after his father was killed and his mother moved to Charleston, SC. My father's side of the family, the Beasleys, is well documented, but I didn't know much about my mother's side, the Wests. I had so many questions. Where did they come from? How did they get to Bulloch County? I only knew bits and pieces and no one in our family had ever researched in detail our West history. One day, sometime around 2010, I decided to find out the answers to the many questions I and many others had in our West family. It was during this time that it came to my mind to write a one page dialog between two West family members to try and make my research more creative and interesting, not knowing it would go beyond one page and later develop into *The Winding Road*...

The Author's West family ancestry:

Benjamin West b. ca 1736 d. ca 1810
Moved from New Bern, NC to Sumter District, SC around 1767
...first settled on Lynches Creek in St Marks Parish
Joseph West b. ca 1755 d. 1849
Came with his father on horseback from New Bern, NC
Revolutionary War Soldier who fought with Francis Marion
Pension records reveal his service record...
Benjamin Powell West b. ca 1780 d. ca 1820/30
Owned/operated a saw mill, plantation was located in modern day
Manning, SC / owned several hundreds acres of land
West place shown on 1825 Mills Atlas/Surveyed by SH Boykin 1821
According to a Manning historian, the West residence on the map was
located on what would later become downtown Manning on the corner
of Church St and Boyce St. / Manning wasn't chartered until 1855
Admiral West b. ca 1799 d. ca. 1860
Land located on Black River in Williamsburg County, SC
John Willie West b. ca 1820/25 d. unknown
Land located on Black River in Georgetown, SC
Civil War soldier for Confederacy
Phillip Admiral West b. ca 1852 d. 1914
Phillip moved from Georgetown SC to Bulloch County, GA
Land located on Bay Gall creek in Bulloch County
His grave marker reads "Kind Father, Thou Art Gone To Rest"
Thomas Oscar West b. 1886/87 d. June 1820
Land located on Bay Gall creek in Bulloch County
Disappeared in June 1920
William Oscar West b. 1913 d. 1992
Lived near Bay Gall creek...
Barbara Ann West m. Waldo Beasley
...mother of TS Beasley, Author of *The Winding Road*...

My grandfather on the Beasley side…

Charles "Charlie" Beasley, Claudine Finch Beasley, Waldo Beasley

The model A ford that Charlie is driving belonged to his father James "Jim" Lafayette Beasley…Early 1940s

My grandfather Charlie died at the age of 56 in 1974, when I was 3 years old. I only have a few faint memories of him. He and Grandma Claudine had two children, Waldo and Mildred, and lived mainly on the old Beasley homestead in Bulloch County on the Ogeechee River. Granddaddy Charlie did move his family to Savannah during the 1940s, and it was at that time my father used to sell peanuts in the parks, on Bay Street, and along the waterfront to have enough money to go to the movie theaters to watch westerns. My father attended Massie St and other Savannah area schools during this time, and in the early 50s, Granddaddy Charlie moved his family back to Bulloch County.

——TS Beasley

Charlie Beasley holding his daughter Mildred, Claudine Finch Beasley, and Waldo Beasley standing next to his father facing his mother...

Charlie and Claudine Beasley with their two children…Waldo and
Mildred…standing near the park on Barnard and Harris St, the first
place they lived at when Charlie moved to Savannah…

James "Jim" Lafayette Beasley...Gr-Grandfather of TS Beasley

It was said that Jim liked to ride his horse and buggy to church at Nevils Creek Primitive Baptist near Bay Gall Creek. His cousin Geraldine Mixon was in the garden on one such occasion when Jim was passing by in his buggy. He asked her if she had heard the song "Don't Sell Daddy Anymore Whiskey." This song was released around 1951. Jim died not long after in 1953 in his home at 81 years of age...

Photo taken by TS Beasley, September of 2014…
Nevils Creek Primitive Baptist Church…

Across the road from Nevils Creek Church was the old Olliff Bay
Schoolhouse. Many children in the Bay Gall and along the River Rd
attended Olliff Bay. Bay Gall Creek is just behind the church. It is the
oldest Primitive Baptist Church in the state of Georgia. Its original
location was on a bluff near Nevils Creek on the Old River Rd, what
used to be called *Old Savannah Rd*. After General Sherman's troops
destroyed a good portion of the structure, it was moved up to Finch's
Old Mill on Ponderosa Rd on Bay Gall Creek. Then, around 1915, the
church building was moved back down creek to where it sits today.
Herman Beasley was about 16 years old at the time, and he was very
instrumental in helping move the timber from Finch's Mill using a team
of horses or mules. Many names on the roll in the Beasley family date
back as far as 1810, one being Pheriby Beazley (Beasley), wife of
Revolutionary Soldier Thomas Beasley who settled along the Ogeechee
River only a mile or so away from the present church location. Jim
Beasley and his wife Maude, were on the role as members. Other
Beasley names on the roll: Enoch and Emily Beasley, Steven Beasley
(Brother of Enoch Jr.), Neomy Beasley, Jane Beasley, Emmaline
Beasley, Adeline Beasley, Jennie Beasley, B. T. Beasley, Claude Beasley
and Bertie Rea Beasley, Joe Beasley, Eula Beasley, Pat Beasley, and
Herman Beasley…

James "Jim" Lafayette Beasley, Joseph Beasley (brother of Enoch
Beasley Jr.), John Beasley (brother of "Jim")
[It was thought at one time the man in the middle was Enoch Beasley
Jr., father of John and Jim. But an additional discovered copy of this
photo stated on the back it was Joseph Beasley]

[Photo obtained from Enoch and Emily's granddaughter]
Photo: believed to be Enoch Beasley Jr. and his wife Emily Burch
Beasley. Enoch owned land along the Ogeechee River and was a planter.
During shad season, he would have the fish delivered to his family
members along the Old River Rd. He kept his own honey bees as well,
and it was said he loved to drink lemonade…

Deeds-Mortgages : 1891 Indenture : Beasley Grist Mill
Two of Enoch's brothers, Joseph and Wash (short for Washington),
along with Enoch Jr., owned/operated a grist mill and gin. The land for
the grist mill and gin was granted by their mother Emeline Beasley, wife
of Enoch Sr.

Enoch Sr. and Emeline lived next to where the Enoch Beasley Cemetery
is today. According to Eleanor Parker Akins, Emeline was a very pretty
lady, and to keep her gray hairs from being seen as she got older, she
would put black smut from the fireplace in her hair. Part of General
Sherman's troops marched along the Old River Rd right by the Enoch
Beasley Sr. homeplace during his famous *March to the Sea*, but no stories
survived or were recorded as to how Enoch's family was treated or how
they were affected. His wife Emeline was 22 years younger, and together
they had 9 children. Emeline was also the sister of Elizabeth D.
Hendrix, mother of Annie E. Hendrix West…

[Photo taken by TS Beasley : 2016]
Enoch Beasley Jr. House...

This is the house of Enoch Beasley Jr. situated along the Ogeechee
River in northern Bulloch County. No one knows exactly when it was
built, but it dates back to the late 1800s/early 1900s. The last family to
live in this house was my father, his sister Mildred, and their parents,
Charlie and Claudine Finch Beasley. This was the house Granddaddy
Charlie and Grandma Claudine lived in when my precious father, Waldo
Beasley, was born. Gr-Grandma Maude Dixon Beasley, wife of Gr-
Granddaddy Jim, died in this house after spending the night here. Jim
had already passed away during this time. It was said she woke up in the
middle of the night after having a dream of Jim coming to her bedside
and kissing her on the cheek. The next morning, she passed away...

The old Beasley house is silent and its frame falling down,
It now sits quietly in the pines,
And ne'er again will it feel the warmth of the sun,
Only the shadows of long ago,
If only time could go back to the warm days gone by,
Where it now sits quietly in the pines,
Then the old house could feel the warming of the sun,
And its past we then would know...

———— TS Beasley

<u>Beasley Family Line of TS Beasley</u>

According to family tradition, 3 brothers came over to NC, where they went their separate ways. One was a circuit rider, one settled near Aiken, SC, and Tom wound up in Bulloch Co. GA near the Ogeechee River.

From Huxford's "Pioneers of Wiregrass GA" Vol. 6, p. 9: "Thomas Beasley, R<evolutionary> S<oldier> ... emigrated to Bulloch Co. GA in the 1790s, with his family, some of the children, including Elijah, being about grown at the time; and died in Bulloch Co. between 1825 and 1830."

Thomas Beasley: Planter b. abt. 1748 Onslow County, North Carolina d. abt. 1829 Bulloch County, GA: said to have been from Onslow, NC, owning land along Beasley Creek. Revolutionary Soldier. In the late 1700s, he moved to what would become Bulloch County, GA, eventually purchasing 800 acres of land along the Ogeechee River.

William Thomas Beasley: Planter b. abt. 1775 Onslow County, North Carolina d. abt 1852 Bulloch County, GA: according to DAR, William and his wife are buried in Enoch Beasley Cemetery.

Enoch Beasley Sr.: Planter b. 1804 Bulloch County, GA. d. 1875 Bulloch County, GA: buried in Enoch Beasley Cemetery. His grave epitaph reads: "Remember me as you pass by, as you are now so once was I, as I am now so you must be, prepare for death and follow me."

Enoch Beasley Jr.: Planter b. 1852 Bulloch County, GA. d. 1926 Bulloch County, GA: buried in Enoch Beasley Cemetery.

James "Jim" Lafayette Beasley: Planter b. 1873 Bulloch County, GA. d. 1953 Bulloch County, GA: buried in Enoch Beasley Cemetery.

Charles "Charlie" Beasley: b. 1918 Bulloch County, GA d. 1974 Bulloch County, GA. Buried in Oak Grove Baptist Church Cemetery.

Waldo Beasley: b. 1939 Bulloch County, GA d. 2014 Bulloch County, GA: buried in Enoch Beasley Cemetery. Father of TS Beasley, Author of *The Winding Road.*

<u>West Family Photos Continued...</u>

Billy West

William "Billy" Richard West

Billy West and Max Carter

Fort Bliss Texas...1959

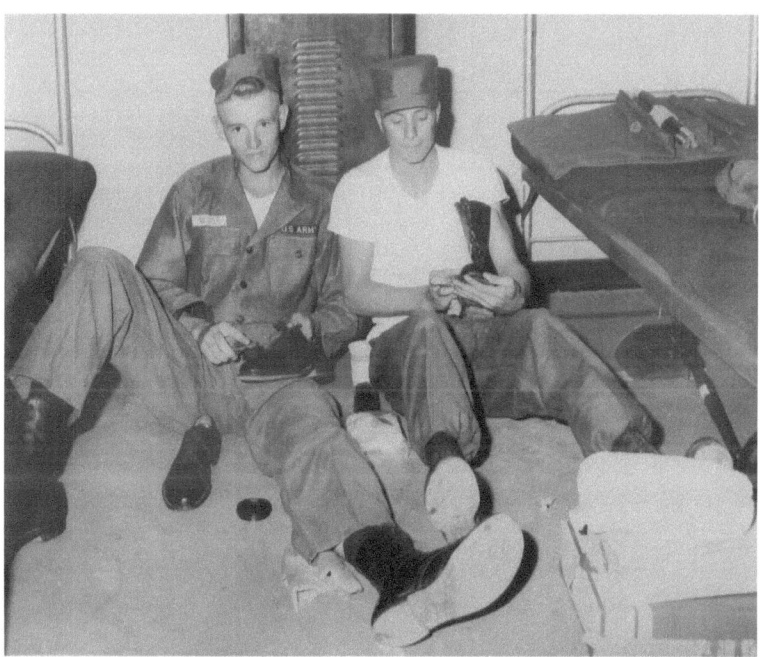

Billy West and Max Carter…Fort Bliss, Texas 1959

Standing next to Billy is Max Carter from Portal…Max said Billy walked across the Rio Grande into Mexico and purchased the guitar he is holding in this picture…

Courtesy of Nephew, Tony Reasley

**William Richard "Billy" West, Aug 22, 1941 - Jan 4, 2005,
Son of William Oscar West, Nov 8, 1913 - Oct 30, 1992, and
Lillie Mae Woodcock West, Nov 15, 1918 - Feb 7, 2001.**

Billy West and Mildred Beasley West

Waldo and Barbara's house in the country...

Billy West and Mildred Beasley West

Waldo Beasley's house in the country...

Billy West, Oscar West, Waldo Finch

Lillie Mae West, Oscar West, Billy West, Dovie West Finch

Picture taken at Oscar West's house on the Bennie Hendrix farm on Nevil's Creek Church Rd. Notice Billy West's guitar sitting on front porch...1960s.

Faye Marsh and Teresa Beasley sitting in left rocker. Linda Knight and Angie West sitting in right rocker. Ricky West and Carolyn Beasley sitting down on porch in front of rockers...

Johnny West, Rocky West, Yancey West, Billy West sitting on car...

...Ricky West and Clint West standing in front of car...

...Waldo Beasley's house in the country

...Charlie Beasley's house and pickup truck can be seen in the background

Charles "Charlie" Beasley holding grandson Travis W. Beasley

Waldo Beasley holding son Tony S. Beasley

Billy West holding son Yancey West

Charlie was Waldo's father and Billy's father-in-law

Waldo's convertible car / Waldo and Barbara's house

William Richard "Billy" West, Mildred Beasley West and children...
Angie, Yancey, Ricky, Mike, Rocky...

Family Photo taken at Bible Baptist Church in Statesboro, GA

Billy West, Doy Knight, Waldo Beasley

Billy West and Waldo Beasley

William Oscar West, William "Billy" Richard West, and West child...

Nevils Creek Church Rd near Mr. Bennie's pond...

John D. West

John D West

John D. West

Johnny and Tibby West

Courtesy of Nephew, Tony Beasley

John Darvey "Johnny" West, b. July 12, 1943,
Son of William Oscar West, Nov 8, 1913 - Oct 30, 1992, and
Lillie Mae Woodcock West, Nov 15, 1918 - Feb 7, 2001.

Johnny and Tibby West

Johnny West and Tibby West

Johnny West and Archie West

Brothers...

John D West, Tibby West, Clint West
Nevils Creek Church Rd...Oscar's house on Bennie Hendrix farm...1960s

Johnny, Tibby, Clint, and Wendy West

Lillie Mae Woodcock West and granddaughter Autumn West
...Autumn is the daughter of Johnny and Tibby West

Archie Thomas West

The Oscar West homeplace…

Seen here in this picture is Archie Thomas West, firstborn son of William Oscar West. Archie's middle name Thomas was given to him after his grandfather Thomas Oscar West. He is standing in the yard with his uncle John Willie West who was living in Richmond, Virginia during this time and would come down to Georgia once a year to visit his family, usually during peanut harvesting. In the distance to the left, you can see Mr. Benjamin "Bennie" Hendrix's white house which sits at a dirt road intersection on Nevils Creek Church Rd; Mr. Bennie is who Oscar sharecropped for when they lived on his farm. This is the place where my mother and her siblings mainly grew up, and the history here is rich and detailed. To the right in the picture, you can see Mr. Ed Thompson's house just up the dirt road in the distance that belonged to Ernest Beasley. This picture was taken in the 1940s, and amazingly, the two houses seen here are still standing. It was here where Oscar plowed with a mule from sun up to sun down in the open fields while singing "The Fields Are Turning Brown," where Oscar later got his first tractor and tried to stop it one day by yelling "whoa" like it was a mule before running it into the branch, where all his smokehouse meat went bad one year and brought him to tears sitting at the table, where he got a letter in the mail one day from his mother from Charleston after so many years, where he grew sugarcane and boiled it in the syrup boiler, where he helped Mr. Bennie Hendrix during hog killing time and where my mother loved to eat the cracklings, where the West boys learned how to sing and play the guitars and where they loved to fish in Mr. Bennie's pond, where Oscar and Lillie and all the children picked cotton, stacked peanuts, graded tobacco, where Silas West walked across Bay Gall creek from the old West log cabin to visit his nephew Oscar from time to time, where he and Lillie Mae spent their golden years together until his health began to fade after working hard for so many years in the fields…finally moving to town to retire for the remaining part of their lives…

Girl Unidentified   Courtesy of Nephew, Tony Beasley

Archie Thomas West, b. Sep 6, 1937,
Son of William Oscar West, Nov 8, 1913 - Oct 30, 1992, and
Lillie Mae Woodcock West, Nov 15, 1918 - Feb 7, 2001.

At the time this photo was edited, the girl was unidentified. She has since been identified as Nancy Stout from Virginia...

Doy Knight, Wanda Knight, Archie West

Archie Thomas West

Archie Thomas West and Margie Lowery West

Archie West and Margie West

Ridgeland, SC

Wedding Day…

Archie T. West

Archie West, Margie holding Todd, Debbie, Tanya, Christie...

Archie West and his son Todd...

Karen West

Floy "Ouida" Hendrix holding Annie Mary Dean West...mid 1930s

...Ouida married Edward "Buck" Mallard in 1942

Mary West Knight

Courtesy of Nephew, Tony Beasley

Annie Mary Dean West, b. Nov 13, 1935,
Son of William Oscar West, Nov 8, 1913 - Oct 30, 1992, and
Lillie Mae Woodcock West, Nov 15, 1918 - Feb 7, 2001.

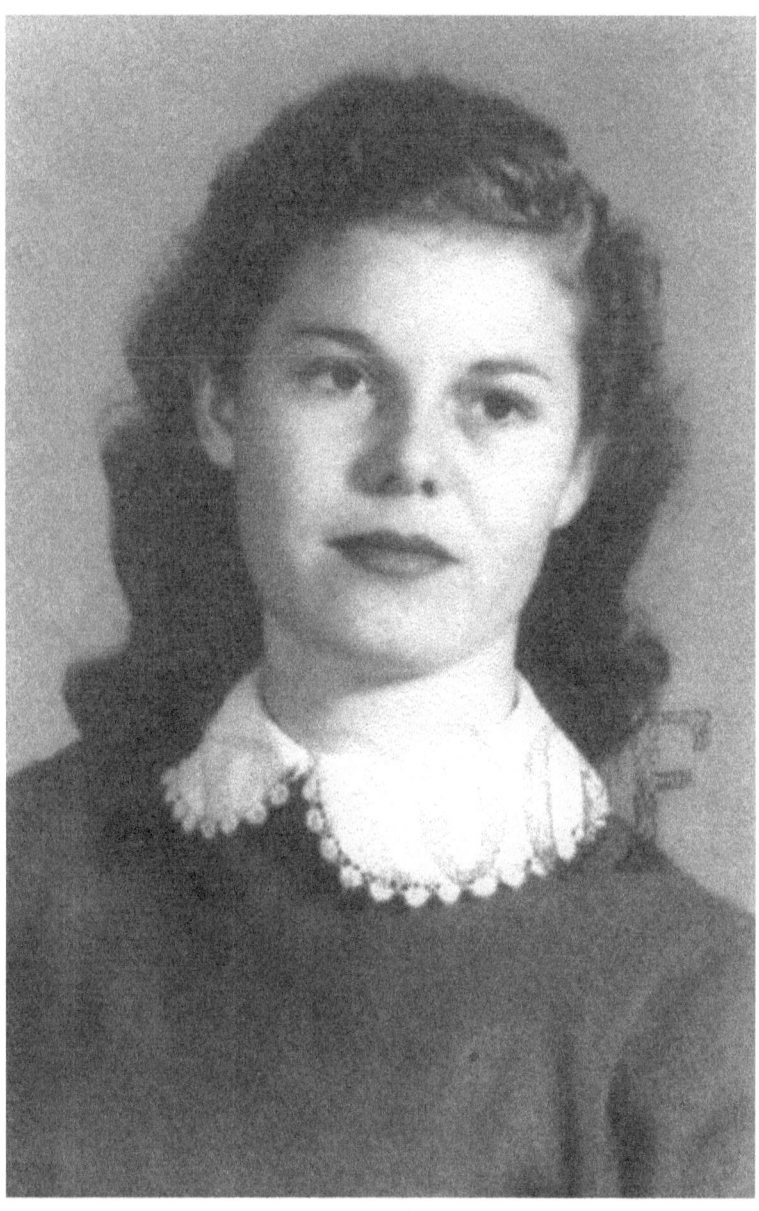

Mary West Knight

Doy Knight, Mary West Knight, Wanda Knight

Germany…

Mary West Knight and Bobby Knight

Nevils Creek Church Rd

Oscar's house on Bennie Hendrix farm...

Mary West Knight holding Bobby Knight and John Willie West Jr.
Wanda Knight is standing in front of her mother…
Feb. 1959

Doy Knight, Mary West Knight, Bobby Knight, Wanda Knight

Doy Knight, Lillie Mae West, Mary West Knight

Doy Knight family…

Doy Knight, Mary West Knight, Wanda holding Stacie…
Pam and Linda…

Claude Beasley (son of James Lafayette Beasley), wife Bertie Rea Walker Beasley (half-sister of John Robert West), Frank Bland Sr. (father of Ruth Bland, the wife of John Robert West), Dock Wright (Uncle of Ruth Bland West)

'The Old West Log Cabin'

[One of only two surviving pictures of the old West log cabin with the kitchen showing. Photo taken in the early days when the old kitchen, separate from the cabin, was still standing.] The log cabin is on the right, and the old kitchen on the left. The date of this photo is late 1940s, a few years after Annie Hendrix West's death in 1940.

The old kitchen was torn down by John Robert West in June of 1949, at which time the structure fell on him, breaking his left leg, and crushing it. Glen Dora remembers seeing the kitchen frame structure leaning, and sensed that it was going to fall on him. His daughter Linda said, "*He almost died. Mother would take me and my sisters to Bulloch County Hospital to see Daddy. He finally got on crutches and went back to West place farm. Some friends of his heard about his accident and come to the West place farm and brought him a set of airplane manuals to study and promised him a job at Warner Robbins Air Force Base as an airplane mechanic. He prayed and finally got off the crutches and could walk with a limp. He set out the West place farm with pine trees and kept that going for over 20 years before he died July 14th, 1971. The Macon GA Continental Nursery provided a government contract for 20 to 30 years program. He and Uncle Silas and Mother would put down pine seedlings 14,000 to 22,000 at a time using the tractor. The trees grew 20 to 30 years, so the crop come in about 1978-79.*"

John Robert West, son of John West, grandson of PA West, had purchased the West place in 1945. There was a wood stove in the old kitchen for cooking and a long

wood table for eating on, with benches on each side. I can picture Annie Hendrix West cooking a lot of good home-cooked meals in that old kitchen, with PA West and all the children sitting around the table, eating together as a family. Glen Dora West, daughter of John Robert West, remembers her mother cooking cakes in the old kitchen and sitting them on the kitchen windowsill in the open air.

Picture to left is Ruth Bland West, wife of John Robert West, holding daughter, Linda West, in front of Old West Log Cabin [late 1940s]. This picture view was taken in the front yard, while the picture (on the previous page), showing the old kitchen, was taken in the back yard. The shallow well was in the front yard, as well as the syrup boiler, and the barn.

Linda West Jung said, "*Daddy had the old Willis car and took Mother to the Bulloch County Hospital to have me (she stayed 3 days). They took me home to the cabin (log house) and we all lived together: Daddy, Mother, Dory, Brenda, and Me. Silas had the side room. Mother kept chickens and Daddy and Silas kept Becky and Buttercup (2 cows). They plowed with the mule until Daddy got the John Deere tractor. They made syrup in the syrup house and the mule turned the grinder.*"

There was a tobacco barn on the south side of the cabin, opposite the creek side, toward Adolphus Parker's home-place. Adolphus Parker was the local blacksmith, and was the one who built the brick chimney at the West Log cabin. Adolphus was married to Willie Emma Beasley (daughter of Enoch and Emeline Dickson Beasley). The only structure left standing on the West Place now is the old log cabin. However, it is starting to deteriorate beyond repair...a sad sight to see the old cabin falling down.

One of only two surviving pictures of old West log cabin showing old kitchen (separate building): taken in 1940s
Front: Annie Pearl Wright Bland, wife of Frank Bland Sr.
Back: daughters Annie Pearl, Myrtle, and Mary Jane

'A picture of the Old West Log Cabin'

John Willie West, son of Thomas O. West, is standing on the front porch with a shotgun in his hand; he is wearing his military uniform, which dates picture around 1945/46, just after WWII.

His wife Mary Lucy Smith is standing near the well.

It appears that John Willie, and his wife, Mary L., positioned themselves where Mark West and David Leland Hendrix would have been standing at the time Mark shot Leland at the well...

William Oscar West, John Willie West Jr., Clint West
Old West log cabin...July 1969

Old West Log Cabin

1960s...　John Willie West Jr and Granddaddy Oscar West

William Oscar West and John Willie West Jr. at West log cabin...
July 1969

Sitting by the old well...

Diagram of Old West Place

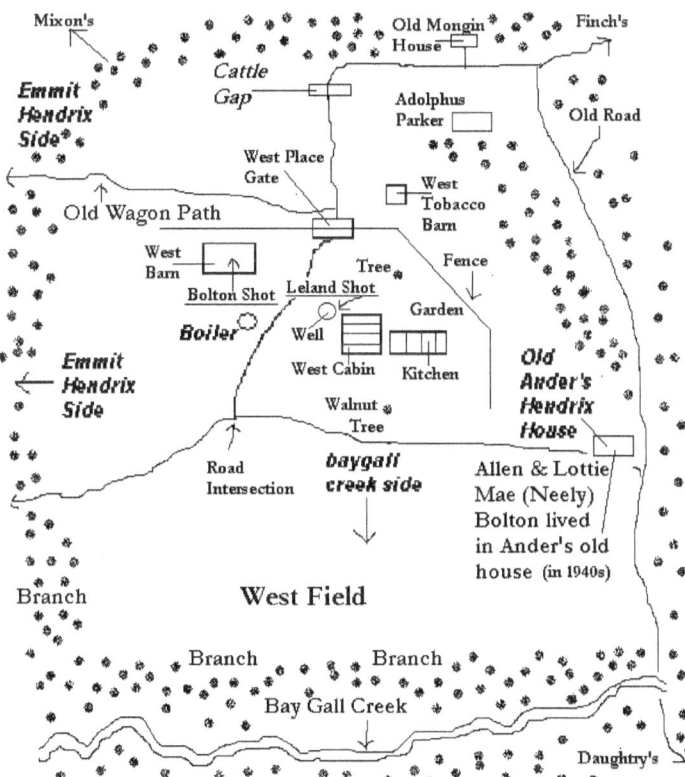

The Old Mongin house (possibly Will Mongin's place, son of William and Laura Mongin) is said to be the place where Thomas West was living at the time of his death. The Old Ander's (Andrew) house is said to be the place where Allen Bolton was living at time of his death. The Ander's house may have been the old Laura (Hendrix) Mongin place, and later, Ander's. The Mongins moved from the area in 1920. The Cattle Gap is the last place that young Oscar West saw his father alive before Thomas disappeared. Adolphus Parker was the local blacksmith and was neighbor to the Wests; he built the chimney at the West log cabin. There was a grave marker near the Tobacco barn on the branch side, but the exact location is now unknown.

Lillie Mae Woodcock West and grandson TS Beasley

1990s

Our trip to the West log cabin in the 1990s: Waldo and Tony Beasley, and Billy West...

TS Beasley with his uncle Billy West standing in the cotton field next to the West Log Cabin...

Waldo Beasley and Billy West...West log cabin...1990s

TS Beasley and Billy West...West log cabin...1990s

Waldo Beasley & Billy West at West Log Cabin...1990s

Waldo Beasley...cotton field next to West log cabin...1990s

William Richard "Billy" West at West Log Cabin…1990s

Waldo Beasley & son TS Beasley standing inside West Log Cabin...1990s

TS Beasley looking out front door of West log cabin…1990s

TS Beasley…West Log Cabin…1990s

A DAY AT THE WEST LOG CABIN...Spring of 2015
...the old West log cabin is beginning to fall down...

Johnny West and Archie West...

Barbara West Beasley, Tibby and Johnny West, Margie West...

Archie West, Tibby West, Johnny West...

Barbara West Beasley and Mary West Knight...

Tibby West, Archie West, Johnny West...
Margie West, Mary West Knight, Barbara West Beasley...

Barbara Ann West Beasley...

Archie and Johnny West…

Back: Floye "Tibby" Bunch West, John Darvie West, Barbara Ann West Beasley, and Archie Thomas West…
Front: Annie Mary Dean West Knight and Margie Lowery West…

Archie West, Johnny West, Mary West Knight, Barbara West Beasley

Barbara Conner and Barbara West Beasley...

*Tump and Jo Ann Woodcock Hendrix, Johnny West, Mary West Knight,
Tibby West and Archie West…*

Tump and Jo Ann Hendrix…

Archie West and Margie West, Mary West Knight, Barbara West Beasley, Johnny and Tibby West…

EC "Tump" Hendrix, Archie T. West, John D. West, Tony S. Beasley

"Local Historian Delma Presley visits the Beasley home…"

Much thanks to Delma Presley and his kind wife Beverly for assisting me in editorial work for this novel. They both spent several hours proofreading and their input was invaluable. Mom and I and my sister Teresa enjoyed their visit to the house in the country very much, and we were able to take a few pictures together. I would like to thank Delma once again for writing such a wonderful foreword to "The Winding Road." I count it an honor that he gave his time and energy toward helping me. He is a true and well respected southern gentleman, and someone who truly values the local history of Bulloch County…

These photos were taken in June of 2016…

Beverly Presley, Delma Presley, Barbara West Beasley at the Beasley house…

Beverly Presley, Delma Presley, Tony S. Beasley at the Beasley house…

Delma Presley visiting the graves of PA and Annie Hendrix West
at Oak Grove Baptist Church…Beverly and Barbara can be seen in the background
looking at other West family graves…

Barbara and her son Tony stop by and visit Tump Hendrix and his wife Jo Ann…2016

Thanks to Tump for taking me around on his mule and sharing with me the history of the old Hendrix place and West place. He is very knowledgeable and one of the last old-timers in the Bay Gall area. Annie Hendrix West's father, Thomas B. Hendrix, and Tump's gr-grandfather, David Hendrix, were brothers. David never made it back home alive from the Civil War, but is buried in Hollywood Cemetery in Virginia. I was able to get David Hendrix a CSA Veteran headstone put up in Hollywood Cemetery in 2020. Tump showed me where David Hendrix's house used to stand when Sherman's troops came through on their way to Savannah…

Jo Ann Woodcock Hendrix, Barbara West Beasley, Tump Hendrix

Jo Ann Woodcock Hendrix, Tony S. Beasley, EC "Tump" Hendrix

Barbara West Beasley and her son Tony visit the old West log cabin in the Bay Gall…2017

Barbara West Beasley standing inside the old West log cabin…2017

You can see the sunlight beaming through the window against the old iron bed rails. Mama is standing at the back door in the living room. This door previously led out to the old kitchen that was separate from the cabin. The old kitchen was torn down by John Robert West in the late 1940s. Mama is looking toward where the fireplace would be, rebuilt by Adolphus Parker in the early 1900s; Adolphus was the local blacksmith that lived next to the Wests. Most of the walls are giving way, and the timber has decayed beyond restoration. The old West log cabin will not be standing much longer, and when it falls, it will be the end of the last standing reminder of the West family that once lived there along Bay Gall creek many years ago…

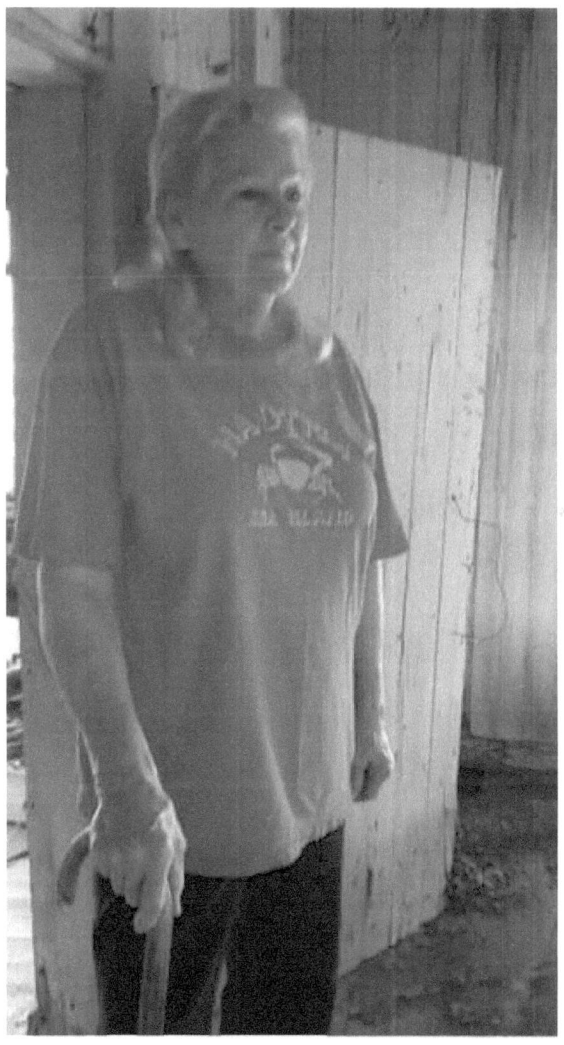

Remembering the past...

Barbara West Beasley standing at the back door in the living room of
the old West log cabin...

Barbara West Beasley and son TS Beasley

...standing inside the West log cabin

Barbara West Beasley standing in the kitchen area of the West log cabin that John Robert West built after he tore down the old kitchen...

"A West Family Poem"

The marks in the sand have long since faded,
the path now forgotten to the old West log cabin,
where the road no longer turns the unrested earth
to the place of familial haven.
Only shadows of forsaken past quietly appear,
the open fields unturned by mule and plow,
the pines softly whisper the sadness of their times,
long now torn from acquainted brow.
Winds of age have taken what once aged stood strong,
only memories of old barns remain,
and the cabin where PA and Annie long aged lived,
now lets through the sky filled rain.
Bay Gall creek still flows through the woods below,
where Mark and Silas made their brew,
where the moonshine-still cooked its brewing shine,
in a place revenuers ne'er knew.
The last letter of Silas to his oldest brother John,
the words he wrote many years ago,
"Remember our precious mother," he recalled with pen,
"...the pain we caused her below."
The old West family bible long aged since been kept,
the faith Granny Annie left us behind,
the Scriptures she read to my grandfather Oscar,
in my precious mother...I now find!
May the long winding road now long been forgotten,
remind us of things that truly matter,
like the old West log cabin and aged family bible,
and the love our memories oft gather...

——TS Beasley

TS Beasley – West Log Cabin – 1990s – Author of "The Winding Road"